THE FIRST
KOTHAR THE BARBARIAN
MEGAPACK®

This volume collects the first 3 books of the
Kothar sword & sorcery series. Included are:

Kothar: Barbarian Swordsman
Kothar of the Magic Sword
Kothar and the Demon Queen

THE FIRST
KOTHAR THE BARBARIAN MEGAPACK®

GARDNER F. FOX

WILDSIDE PRESS

CONTENTS

KOTHAR: BARBARIAN SWORDSMAN

INTRODUCTION

More than a century ago Albert Kremnitz, a German philosopher no longer widely read, wrote that "the Industrial Revolution, The Age of Materialism, will almost certainly drive people back to mysticism rather than away from it. In the beginning, of course, popular taste will seem to move in quite the opposite direction, toward the mundane and the banal, toward the frenetic pursuit of possessions, toward a contempt for all that is lyrical in man. The first stage will see no attempt to justify this distaste for the mystic and the unexplained. Although this stage will be prolonged for many years, and how many years no one can even hazard a guess, it will gradually give way to another stage in which the course of mankind will find itself troubled by what it has cast aside.

"During this stage there will be many explanations as to why the mystic nature of man no longer has any value in an ever changing world, yet none of these 'explanations' will remove the sense of unease, the nagging realization, the painful awareness that man, for all his material progress, remains bound to all that is barbaric in his past. The fourth stage will see a great reversal of the first stage, and as never before man will plunge with enthusiasm into an attempt to understand, and to participate in, the 'dark' energies of his nature.

"If compelled to predict the time when this fourth stage would come about I would set the date at midpoint in the twentieth century, at which time the Industrial Revolution will itself be undergoing the transition to which all revolutions, indeed all things, are subject."

Kremnitz goes on to describe this "new Age of Heroes." He states that since the modern hero will have been dwarfed by his environment, the popular demand for larger-than-life heroes will have to be satisfied by the recreation of mythological supermen, or, as he predicted with amazing insight, the invention of heroes so magnificent, so fantastically endowed with super-powers, that they exist only in the fantasy projections of man. Such a superhero is Kothar—Barbarian Swordsman.

From the world beyond, or past, recorded time Kothar comes. From out of the deepest, most violent recesses of mankind's dark, collective memory, Kothar the gigantic barbarian strides, the enchanted sword Frostfire glittering in his mighty hand. Lusty, hot-blooded, masterful, unafraid of things real or unreal, Kothar dominates the misty, bloody world created for him, and for us, by the distinguished American writer Gardner F. Fox, and though Kothar's world existed in another age, another dimension, it comes vividly to life. Mapped, charted, chronicled, with history, language, literature, and conventions of its own, the world of the godlike barbarian mercenary becomes as real, and in some strange way perhaps more real than the world we live in. So skilled a writer is Gardner Fox, so cunningly does he spin this epic tale, that we come to accept the world of Kothar almost without realizing that we have done so.

Because Kothar is so real his age becomes real. Having accepted Kothar himself, we find it no effort to accept the other fantastic persons and creatures which inhabit his world. Everything falls into place, so well has Gardner Fox succeeded in convincing us that in order to participate in Kothar's adventures we must suspend disbelief. And after reading the first few pages of this savage tale that is what we do, and gladly. We come to know the sorcerers, dragons, eloquent wraiths, witches—all the strange beings who move through the pages of Kothar: Barbarian Swordsman. Because we have suspended disbelief, have postponed judgment, we are untroubled by logic; indeed the story itself has its own peculiar logic which seems to explain any misgivings we might have. Yes, we tell ourselves, why should Kothar, his friends or his enemies, behave in any other fashion?

Why should we be inclined to disbelieve when there is even a detailed map of Kothar's world to help us to completely understand it? When we are informed that as a boy Kothar was cast up on the shores of Grondel Bay we have simply to look for it on the map, and we find it. Of course, we exclaim, there is it on the map! And there, too, are all the kingdoms and territories, all the sinister and forbidden places, all the sources of danger and delight. As moderns grown tired of introspective heroes we find it refreshing to "identify" with the unthinking responses of the barbarian swordsman. Using his simple intelligence as an uncomplicated guide to action, Kothar follows his emotions wherever they lead him, confident of his ability to deal with any threat which may come his way.

Kothar is in the line of all mankind's heroes. He is kin to the knights of Camelot and the famous marshals of our own Wild West. He is the loner, the soldier of fortune, the paid but heroic mercenary—but with an important difference. Kothar is not only larger than life; he is not bound by the logic of life. Kothar exists in mankind's dreams and, therefore, he transcends reality. As Albert Kremnitz so correctly pointed out, we in the mid-twentieth century have need of heroes so different from ourselves that we cannot return to even the mightiest heroes of the past; we must invent heroes so all-powerful that they can have no connection with mankind as we know it because in our history there was never a hero so marvelous that he was not inevitably brought to ruin by sickness, betrayal or death.

As Albert Kremnitz has stated on another occasion, "Ordinary men must, whether aware of it or not, seek to destroy their heroes, no matter how much they admire them, since the very existence of heroes is an affront to their own mode of life. The man of the future, since he will have a greater need of heroes, may realize that his heroes must live in order that he, himself, may survive."

Kothar—Barbarian Swordsman is an epic hero for any age, but it would appear that our age needs him more than any other.

—Donald MacIvers, Ph. D.

PROLOGUE

The Universe is old. Old!

For ten billion years the stars of this, our galaxy, hurtled outward across the gulfs of space. For another billion years they hung suspended at the apex of their expansion.

During the past three billion years, now that the universe is contracting instead of expanding, those stars, dim and faint with age, have been collapsing in upon themselves, rushing headlong back to their beginnings and their ultimate destruction.

In time, there will be no Time.

Ages ago, as the legends say, the race of Man knew those stars and all their planets, named and visited them, and left on those planetary surfaces vast cities, great monuments to mankind's own greatness. Once, uncounted millennia before, an empire of Man was spread throughout the universe. This empire died more than a billion years ago, after which man himself sank into a state of barbarism.

Here and there on a planet man has occupied can be seen a bit of stone-work which he left behind him as a reminder of past glory, or a few rocks of what had been a mighty megopolis, even some chunks of marble as a memento of forgotten art masterpieces. The rust and erosion of eon upon eon has bitten deep into mankind's creations.

Today, wherever man can be found on the planets of the dying star-suns, the very shapes of the continents on which he lives bear little resemblance to those he knew two billion years before. The oceans cover his cities, the desert sands his tombs and temples, while the fierce north wind ruffles vegetation that earlier man had never seen.

Today, man is a barbarian in a barbaric world. Man has reverted back to the childhood of his earliest years. He has forgotten his heritage, he has made new gods to replace the old. Man has outlived his glory.

And yet—to some men and women who live in the sunset years of the race has been given a power unknown to those men of an earlier age, yet a power famed and feared in the legendry of his people. For there are wizards and warlocks, sorcerers and witches in these days, and their spells and incantations are known to work malignant miracles.

There are also warriors, fighting men whose swords earn them fame and fortune, men inured to hardship and a way of life totally alien to the men of an earlier day. One such warrior was Kothar, cast up by the sea in the northlands of his world, a sellsword and a mercenary, a wencher after the women of his day, a freebooter and a thief, at times, whose sword Frostfire was a magic sword.

This is his saga…

From a fragment of—
THE LORD HISTORIES OF
SATORAM MANDAMOR

THE SWORD OF THE SORCERER

CHAPTER 1

The blood lay red upon his dented mail shirt and spotted his yellow hair in ghastly fashion. It ran wetly, redly, from the worn sleeve of his leather hacqueton to drop upon his big hand and ooze across the pommel of his shattered sword. It stained his fur kilt and riding boots and dripped steadily with every step he took.

Kothar staggered from the field of battle where men lay staring sightlessly up at the darkening sky, rigid now in death, and where other men were gasping out their lives. He alone of the loyal Foreign Guard was still alive, he alone still held a sword in his hand, though it was a broken one. And behind him, men were coming fast to finish off the youthful guards commander.

He was a big, brawny youth. His shock of yellow hair framed a face burned brown by desert suns and polar winds. Under his smooth hide giant muscles rippled, and normally he walked with the springy gait of a man whose body was in perfect fighting trim. A broad leather belt fitted his lean waist, from which hung an empty scabbard. Now that belt was red with blood.

Kothar was a barbarian out of the northern world of Cumberia. He was a sellsword, a mercenary whose life was given over to the god of war, that he might have food for his belly and a pillow at times for his head. There was no fear in him as he jogged along, he was afraid of no living man—or woman, for that matter—though he did admit to a kind of queasiness when magic, witches and warlocks were involved.

And a witch had given Lord Markoth the victory this day.

Rage was a rumble in his thickly thewed throat. Red Lori, the witch! Aie, she was lovely, with her long red hair and slanted green eyes, her body all white flesh and perfumed skin. Kothar had never seen a woman who made him know he was a man as Red Lori did, with her slim white legs and swinging hips.

But she was a witch!

Gossip said she would be queen in Commoral when Elfa died. Her sorceries had given Markoth the victory this day and as a reward she would ascend the throne.

He toyed with the idea of walking into the royal palace in some sort of disguise and throwing Red Lori over a broad shoulder and making off with her. His large white teeth showed themselves as his lips drew back in an amused grin. Hai, but that would put a bee in her thick red hair!

Suddenly he staggered, recovering his balance with an effort. His wounds had become an agony, of a sudden.

In his eyes, sky reeled dizzily with ground, and death swooped low above the corpses cluttering the wide Plain of Dead Trees, reaching out invisible talons to sink them in his flesh. His throat was dry—gods of Thuum!—what he would give for one lone sip of water!—and the pain of his wounds made him shudder, every now and again.

He was angling his feeble steps toward a corner of the forest, the great dark weald that stretched from Phalkarr as far as distant Abathor, for in between those boles and beneath those low hanging branches was his only hope of hiding. The mercenaries of Lord Markoth should have spotted him by this time, they should have raised the howl of pursuit. No doubt they were running for hounds to follow the trail of his riding boots. He tried to stop the flow of blood, for the drops were arrows beckoning all to follow, but the task was too great for his reddened hands and fingers.

He leaned against a tree, breathing deeply.

I must run like the wounded deer from the hunters, or else I too shall be stretched out flat upon the ground, my wrists and ankles fettered, and I shall be flayed, as is the custom of the Lord Markoth with his enemies.

The thought was a goad in his ribs, urging him forward. A red hand-print, the spill of bloody drops, were the signposts which would show the way. Ah, well, it could not be helped. He was wounded. He had fought hard and long this day to bring victory to the cause of Queen Elfa, and where men fought so desperately, men knew the bite of steel.

The agony of his flesh, the uneasiness in him at the thought of torture, drove him staggering through the underbrush, ducking to avoid a leafy branch, reeling aside from a thick tree trunk directly in his path. In the distance he heard a voice cry out halloo. They had found his red blood trail!

They were coming fast, fresh with renewed vigor, unwounded and ea-ger to win the silver deniers Lord Markoth would pay for his body so his skinners could flay the skin from it. He could imagine their hard faces and their bulging muscles as they loped along the trail of blood-drops from his body.

Kothar ran on and on.

Above his yellow poll the trees made a green canopy that hid every-thing from his eyes but a patch of white cloud and a bit of blue sky. Would that the leaves might also hide his tracks! He blundered on, head down and gasping, blind to everything but the pain and the voices growing louder and more confident behind him.

He ran for a long time; there was still strength left in his big, muscular body with the broken sword gripped in his fingers. He would sell his life as dearly as possible; these men of the southlands would never forget his dying battle. Aie! He would make the name of Kothar long remembered in this kingdom of Commoral.

Finally he slid to a halt and leaned a bloody hand against a tree bole. He shook his head like an animal brought to bay. His glaring eyes peered around him in the dense forest at a spray of red and white flowers hanging from a gigantic rock like a colored waterfall.

Kothar blinked in disbelief.

Was he delirious with loss of blood and the pain of his wounds—or was that an iron door behind those vine-flowers? He licked his lips with a swollen tongue, aware that hope was surging up into his huge chest. An iron door in solid rock? It could not be. It was a mere trick of his failing senses, of his blurring eyes with the blood dripping into them from a scalp wound.

And yet—

Kothar straightened his body slowly, daring to hope. There was a door there, rusted and disused for centuries, perhaps—but still a door. The youthful giant pushed away from the tree. Yes, the fading sunlight made it dimly visible; it was almost unseeable behind its vine and flower curtain, but it was there.

"Thanks to Dwallka," he gasped, and ran.

His arm in its leather hacqueton and mailed sleeve brushed the flower vines away. He could see the ancient metal door more clearly now and could read the forgotten sigils on its rusted surface. He could not understand them; they were written in a language dead for more than a hundred centuries, but his barbarian senses were aware of awesome magic in their twistings.

Kothar shook his wide shoulders. He did not care for magic, but he cared even less for the baying hounds and the huntsmen loping along his bloody backtrail. He lurched forward, a quivering hand stretched out to touch the rusted metal and seek across it for a ring or handle to open that ancient adit. The vines and flowers closed in behind him, leaving him in a cool, faintly hushed sanctuary.

What was this door? Where did it lead?

No matter what! No matter where!

Anywhere was better than out here with the mercenaries and their yapping dogs following his footprints. His huge brown hand caught hold of an iron bolt, slid it back with a wrench of muscles so painful as to make him groan. It had been long years since anyone had walked this way. Unused metal screeched in protest to his tug, but the bolt yielded and the door swung inward onto blackness.

Kothar stumbled into that welcoming dark.

The sole of his war-boot touched a hard dirt floor. It was cool in the gloom, and his eyes could see nothing at all. He stood swaying like a giant tree about to topple, his fingers loosing their grip on his broken sword.

Slowly the darkness died away before a pallid green radiance that seemed to fill the chamber. The light came from nowhere and everywhere. It did not ease the chill bite of the air, it was like the coldness of the grave, that air. It made Kothar shiver, accustomed as he was to the snow-cold of the northern wastes.

An angry growl rose into his throat.

He found himself staring at a flat slab of stone that rested on marble amphoras. It was a crypt, this place in hollow rock. And that dead thing wrapped in funereal garments, brown with age, was what lay buried in it. He had blundered into a tomb.

His lips twisted in a grin. Let the dead shelter him who sought life in this sanctuary. He was about to turn and close the iron door when the hairs on the back of his neck stood up.

The withered brown body on the slab—he could make out bits of whitened bone and grisly fragments of flesh and hair protruding from the rotted cloth—was moving. It sighed, as if it breathed immeasurable distances away. Its chest lifted and fell in a slow pulsing.

Dwallka of the War Hammer! What was this thing?

The corpse turned its head so that it could look at Kothar out of its empty eye-sockets. The barbarian felt the touch of eyes, even though there were no eyes to see or be seen. He stiffened, his flesh crawled, his long fingers took a firmer grip on his sword-haft.

Even as he stared, the lich sat up.

"You came at last, Kothar. I had almost given up hope for you."

The young giant opened his mouth to speak, and could not. The cadaver swung what was left of its legs over the side of the stone slab and stepped down onto the hard dirt floor. A peculiar sound rose upward from the bones of its throat.

A lassitude came upon Kothar. He began to sway back and forth, as if tired in every muscle. Hai! He was weak, too. So weak he could not stand up. The lich was doing this to him in some hellish manner he did not understand.

It was too much to stand up. He could not do it. He fell forward slowly, his legs did not bend, he simply toppled downward like a tree cut off at its roots.

Kothar lay frozen motionless on the dirt. He was alive and possessed of all his senses but that of movement. He could not so much as flick a finger. His cheek was pressed to the ground, he could feel a pebble pressing into his temple. He could hear the savage thumping of his heart, and he was aware that the corpse was moving.

This was worse than anything the Lord Markoth might do to him! Flaying knives he could understand. He had lost to the king of Commoral, and he was paying the penalty for failure. This made sense to his barbarian mind.

But this was foul. Unclean! The tomb had opened for him who was alive, and now it sought to drag him down into the coldness, into the utter absence of all life.

Kothar fought, as much as he could fight. His spirit, his savage soul, writhed and tugged to force his huge muscles to obey the dictates of his brain. They would not. He must lie here and—what?

The dead thing was approaching him with a dry rustle of brown winding-sheets. It walked as if its weight were that of the fabled Jugnoth, with heavy thumpings of the ground. It breathed with a harsh wheezing and a vast rush of air like the huge bellows which had hung before the forge at Grondel when Kothar had been a boy.

The giant lay waiting for the eldritch being to clasp him and drag his limp body toward the slab. If he was going to die here in this tomb, he wanted to bellow out his defiance, but he could make no more than a croaking noise.

Behind him, metal rasped and the iron door swung inward again. Kothar felt the fresh forest air drift past his body.

There was a silence.

The dead thing stared at the mercenaries crowding the doorway, and the soldiers of the Lord Markoth, after one horrified glance at the inert Kothar, stared back at the standing mummy.

"Great Eldrak," a man breathed.

A hollow voice murmured, "Call not on Eldrak of the Seven Hells. He listens not to carrion such as you. He is my friend, as are all the ancient gods." There was an illusion of vast distance behind the voice of the cadaver that stood on rotting feet and showing the whiteness of bones protruding through its burial garments.

A mercenary screamed and would have run except that the dead thing held him as he held the giant Kothar flat upon the ground. Terrifying laughter lifted into its throat as it began to glow with inner green fire.

The eerie radiance became brighter, and as it pulsed throughout the ancient grave, Kothar felt energy flow into his body. His wounds closed over, his blood caked and hardened, and anger rose into his brain like a madness. He stirred, he moved his hand, he rose upward.

On his feet he looked at the dead thing without fear, though with revulsion. It gleamed with verdant brightness, illuming the death chamber and the mercenaries in their mail shirts and metal helmets, with swords naked in their hands.

"Slay them," said the lich, and Kothar leaped.

His broken sword was still sharp. It could cleave through flesh and mail and leather, it could slay. The mercenaries tried to fight, but it was as if they moved in sleep, slowly and without a sense of danger. Their faces showed green from the pulsing dead thing, and their eyes bulged with the horror in their brains.

The shattered steel drove deep, again and again.

When he was finished, seven men lay dead between the iron door and the forest. Kothar stood panting over them, staring down at his red blade.

The forest was quiet; not even a jay chattered from its leafy deeps. The Cumberian drew a deep breath. It was as if the green pulsations had reached out and touched all life within the wood, and as it had touched, it had slain.

"Let drop the sword, Kothar," said the hollow voice.

He did as it commanded, without thought. He turned and stared back into the dark tomb and saw the dead thing standing in the darkness, rotted and ugly in its cerements. The green brilliance was fading slowly. It was just a corpse, a corpse that walked and spoke and seemed to be alive.

"Who are you?" Kothar growled.

"My name was Afgorkon, long and long ago."

Kothar scowled. Afgorkon? Surely he had heard Queen Elfa speak of Afgorkon who had been a mighty magician fifty thousand years ago. He tried to think, but could not, being held in thrall by the black, empty eyeholes of the dead thing standing before him, bent and brown and old.

If it could have smiled, the lich might have quirked its lips.

"In the days when this land was known as Yarth, I was a sorcerer renowned from frozen Thuum in the north to tropical Azynyssa at the equator. My spells could level a city or raise up a tempest on the sea. Even now, after five hundred centuries of sleep, I still come to the call of witch and warlock, to teach the ancient mysteries or to help a suppliant in trouble. Such a suppliant is the Lady Elfa."

"The queen?"

"Queen or witch-woman, what's the difference? Yes, it is Elfa whose call I heard, whose call roused up this rottedness which is all that is left of the man I once was. She has need of a champion, has queen Elfa—and you are the only man of the Foreign Guard left alive. You must go to her, there is a way to reverse what has happened, to snatch victory from defeat. I have shown her the way."

Kothar grumbled, "What is that way?"

"Only the sword Frostfire can do what must be done."

"Frostfire?"

"Frostfire was forged in the primal ooze by the devils summoned up by me five hundred centuries before. It was wrought of a metal fallen from the skies, it was dipped in the molten middle of the world, it was cooled in the snows on a mountain so high nothing but a sylph—a winged spirit of the air—could take it there. It can pierce any armor, any helm. It can be carried only by a man who has no other wealth."

Kothar scowled. "I'm a mercenary. I sell my sword for gold and silver. Someday I shall be rich. What then?"

The lich chuckled. "For the past five years you have been selling yourself as a soldier. Are you rich?"

"I own nothing but the mail I wear, this broken sword, and my boots. But somewhere I shall find a treasure…"

"Nothing man can own is like the sword Frostfire. Alone, it makes a man a giant among other men. But enough of this! Will you accept the sword and the task its ownership imposes—to help queen Elfa?"

Kothar grinned wryly, "And after I have helped queen Elfa, what of the sword?"

"It shall be your fee."

The young barbarian nodded, "It shall be my fee."

The lich turned and moved with those strangely thumping footsteps across the tomb. Its rotted hands moved and its withered tongue clacked, and sounds issued from the throat that was little more than bones. The words it spoke reverberated throughout the cairn, they brought down tiny showers of dirt from the root-pierced ceiling, they made the death-slab shake.

Yet they also opened an invisible door and caused a pallid glimmer by which Kothar could see, past the burial garments which still encased Afgorkon, an opening door and a chamber where lay a sword in a scabbard chained to a great leather belt on top of two chests heavy with jewels and golden coins of a kind no man had looked upon for half a million years.

"Stand," growled Afgorkon, and Kothar went rigid. The lich stepped into that dim light and lifted up the scabbard and the sword Frostfire with its thick leather belt and carried them on the bones and dried flesh of its hands out into the dimmer light of the tomb, and placed them in the out-stretched palms of the Cumberian.

The sword made a solid weight in his hands; its length was of bluish steel, and it had a golden cross-hilt. Witch-blade it might be, yet it had weight and substance, and its hilt made of silvery gold contained an angry red jewel set in its pommel. His big hand went around the haft and drew the shining blade partially from the scabbard. There were rune words there, words in a language so old no man could know their meaning. The edges looked biting sharp, honed to the keenness of a razor.

His hand clanged the blade back into its scabbard. Afgorkon watched him with empty eye sockets. "The words say, 'I was made before the world was born, for the mage Afgorkon.' Aie, the sword was mine, for I was a warrior as well as a magician in that long-ago time. Though it was made by magic, there is no magic in it, or at least I do not think so, though magic can enter it and be retained by it, as no ordinary steel will do."

The barbarian asked, "How can you part with it?"

A dry chuckle resounded in the crypt. "I have other weapons now that I am dead to this world. Where I exist, the blade Frostfire cannot, and so—I give it to you who are without wealth. See it slays those who need slaying, boy of the sea."

Kothar froze, still with his hand on the swordhilt. "What know you of the sea that flung me as a babe on the shore at Grondel bay?"

"I know what the dead know."

"My real family? Where was I born?"

"It is not for me to tell. You must live your life as the gods have decreed. That which you will do, your deeds and misdeeds, are written in the scrolls of the gods in the imperishable script of Rath. No living man can read them. Only the gods whom men worship, and the dead, can scan those lines."

"You are dead," Kothar pointed out.

"True. But were I to sin in this regard, the gods might give me life and I who have been dead fifty thousand of your years do not desire to live again, other than as now—fleetingly, for moments out of Time." The dry chuckle was soft with distance. "I am content in the place where I am. Very content, Kothar the sellsword. But now, go. The queen is waiting."

A rotted hand lifted, pointing. The iron door gaped.

Kothar moved out into the air that was fragrant with the vine-flowers. Yet the voice of Afgorkon followed him.

"Go to the hut of the witch Fristhia. There shall you find the queen."

The iron door slammed shut behind him.

The rusted bolt clicked into place.

CHAPTER 2

A grey wolf sat on its haunches, tongue lolling.

Kothar half drew his sword, but the gaunt animal at the edge of the weald did not move and when Kothar put the sword back in its scabbard and buckled the great belt at his lean middle, the wolf rose to its feet and trotted off along a narrow forest trail. It halted and turned its head and its glowing feral eyes seemed to call to the big barbarian.

The wolf would be his guide to the queen.

He walked through the stillness of the forest, pausing only once to glance back at the dead mercenaries piled here and there outside the iron door. Men would come and carry them off, but no one but himself would ever explain how they had come to find death here in this ancient weald.

They went for more than two hours through the woods, until the wolf came to a forest glade where stood a little hut roofed with sod, a single window open to the room inside. The wolf sat back and howled once, piercingly, then slunk away into the underbrush, leaving Kothar alone.

The young mercenary walked to the door of the hut and lifted his knuckles to knock, but another hand was before his; the door swung open and an old hag stood staring up at him. Her ugly face was hairy, and her nose was long and pointed, but the blue eyes in her ancient face were bright and gleeful as they searched his height and his youthful strength, and they lingered long upon the sword he carried at his side.

"Kothar," she said softly, and stepped back.

He walked into the hut, finding it clean and neat and oddly fragrant because of the dried herbs that swung from little cordings at the ceiling beams. A fire burned on a round stone in its middle as a thin grey smoke rose up to pass through a hole in the sod roof.

He swayed with weariness and the witch looked at him and smiled and gestured toward a pile of fur robes which formed a bed along one wall. She said softly, "You are tired, exhausted from the fighting and your wounds which Afgorkon healed. But now Afgorkon can do no more and you must sleep."

He did not dispute with her. He was so weary he had seemed to stumble after the wolf in a walking slumber, so that he thought at times he was dreaming all that had happened to him. The furs beckoned him; they were soft and would warm his body, and when he closed his eyelids as he lay upon them he would dream.

Kothar fell on his back across the robes and his eyelids seemed so heavy it was painful to hold them open. Yet he must remain awake for just a little while.

"Elfa?" he asked. "What of Elfa the queen?"

The hag laughed brightly. "She shall come, young man. Sleep now, sleep." Her blue eyes flirted with him, making him think of Elfa who was queen in Commoral, for Elfa had witch-eyes such as this, that flirted with him from time to time, and in his own way, Kothar understood that he had been half in love with her.

He closed his eyes and slept.

He dreamed, as he knew he would. He dreamed of the single room of this witch-hut with the sod roof and of the fire on the round stone and of the smoke and of the hag who went and breathed in the smoke and waved at it with her hands until the smoke clung to her like a grey garment made of spider webs, hiding her shape and the shapeless garments which she wore. As the grey smoke touched her garments they fell away, and the hag was no longer the hag but queen Elfa herself, naked in the grey smoke that hid her fair white flesh.

She turned and saw him staring, in his dream, and she smiled with her red, red lips and she lifted up her arms and turned, letting him see how fair was her body through the veil of smoke. All the while she sang a strange little song the like of which the barbarian had never heard.

And now—The hag was gone. It was Elfa who stepped from the grey smoke, Elfa in a scarlet kyrtle trimmed in miniver fur and thick with golden threadings. There were tiny red slippers on her feet and great ruby rings on her white fingers. Her heavy golden hair was done up in a caul of red garnets on a golden chain. This was the queen of Commoral.

She came and stood beside him where he dreamed. He looked up at her, and she bent and kissed his lips with her red, red mouth, and there was a perfume and a fragrance about her which was very pleasant to young Kothar. She slipped onto the fur robes with him and took him in her soft arms and let him pillow his head so that he forgot she was Queen Elfa, she was just a beautiful woman with golden hair. His heavily muscled arm hooked her middle, yanked her down on top of him in his dream and he held her banded to his body.

Delighted laughter woke him.

His dream had become reality. He held Elfa in his arms, and he was kissing her and she struggled against his strength, laughing softly, for a woman likes to be thought desirable, even a queen. For an instant longer he held her, relishing the feel of her soft body before he reluctantly let her go.

"You're a brute," she smiled, sliding away from him.

His giant chest lifted and fell, but he did not speak. Her wise green eyes studied his huge body as she replaced a few tresses in her disarranged hair with white, ringed fingers.

"Afgorkon must have put a fire in your blood," she murmured, glancing at him sideways. Her red lips quivered with laughter. "He has told me you can save my throne for me. He did not tell me you would all but rape me at the same time."

His barbaric blood was in a ferment. Elfa was a tease-body, as was Red Lori. Were all women? Kothar was a simple person, essentially. If a woman pleased him, he took her to bed with him. If she did not, he ignored her.

"What do you want with me?" he grumbled.

Her thin eyebrows lifted. "Oh, you're angry. I didn't mean to make you angry. I imagine you're full of life, since you escaped from the plain of Dead Trees. I'll have to excuse you, I suppose."

"Afgorkon said I was to help you."

"And you want to know how."

He swung his legs off the cot. "The sooner the better," he muttered. He walked like a stalking cat across the room, lifted the sword Frostfire and buckled its broad belt about his lean middle. In the eyes of the woman still sitting on the cot, he was a pagan soldier, a mercenary who took her gold. And yet, there was something more in this youthful giant, Elfa thought, head cocked sideways to study him.

If she were younger—She shook herself. It did no good to dream.

"You must free my wizard, Kazazael," she said suddenly, rising to pace back and forth in the little hut.

Kothar snorted, "Little good he did you! Him and his magic spells that didn't work! Where's he now?"

Her laughter tinkled out. Her fate was in the hands of a barbarian youth, a boy only lately come to manhood. Afgorkon had said this was so, and she believed the lich. Yet there was a bitterness in her mirth that rang loudly in the hut. So much at stake, so much to rest on the sword hand of one young man!

"You must go to Windmere Wood, where Kazazael hangs suspended in the air between earth and sky—flayed of his skin by orders of King Markoth. His screams of agony—for Kazazael cannot know the mercy of death—can be heard for miles around. You must free him, restore his health to him."

Kothar stared. "Dwallka! It's no easy task you set me."

Elfa smiled up at him. "You can name your own reward, if you succeed. Would you like to be a duke in Commoral? A prince?"

The Cumberian scowled. It was a heady bribe she offered, if bribe were needed to win his sword arm.

"I shall make you a prince," she said softly.

"If I succeed," he growled.

Her golden head nodded gently. "If you win back for me my queenship. A princedom as a reward. Isn't it enough?"

He grinned, "It's too much."

"And yet—perhaps not enough. There are grave dangers in Commoral, these days. Red Lori is no sorceress to hang a necromancer in the sky without safeguards against his freedom. Should you fail, you yourself may be flayed and hung there with Kazazael for all eternity. Markoth has a strong ally in Red Lori. Her enchantments put Kazazael where he is this day, after the flaying knives were done with him. She will have put up barriers past which no ordinary man could step."

He was no ordinary man, but she would not tell him that. As captain of her Foreign Guard, he had been brusque, caring nothing that one or two men under his command could boast of royal blood in their veins. With a heavy hand, he had transformed her mercenaries into a real fighting force. For a while this day, it had been nip and tuck between herself and Lord Markoth, thanks to the Foreign Guard and to the zeal of its muscular young commander.

With his fists, he had trained his men. With his skill at weapon-play, he had taught them to fight almost as well as himself. No other man could do that; this young barbarian was a born fighting man. He went straight for his objective, swinging his sword; the man who got in his way, died.

She hoped he could do the same for Kazazael.

His hard blue eyes were studying her. He rasped, "How do I find Kazazael? I've never heard of this Windmere Wood! And if Red Lori has put up safeguards against anyone helping him—surely she'll make it next to impossible to locate him?"

"There is a horse knows the way," she said softly and turning, went to a little door set in the wall of the hut and pushed open that door with her hand. By bending, Kothar could see into a small stable attached to the hut.

A big grey warhorse with red velvet reins and red velvet fittings on the high-peaked saddle on its back, stood patiently, waiting for a rider. There was silver on its ring-bits and the nails which fastened the leather saddle were of silver also, so that Kothar thought he had never seen so handsome an animal, nor such horse trappings.

"I bought him for my husband, the king," the queen was saying as the barbarian stared, "but now he shall belong to him who is my champion." Elfa smiled and the witch-lights danced in her blue eyes. "I had him from the wizard Kazazael. There may be magic in his hide."

Kothar grunted. He stepped past the queen and into the stable, lifting the red velvet reins, slipping a black leather boot into the wooden stirrup and lifting upward into the kak. He had to bend a little, for the stable roof was not very high.

"Give him his head, Kothar," the queen called from the hut doorway, as he paced the beast out into the morning sunlight where the sparrows and the jays were already chittering. He dropped the reins so they lay limp over the saddle pommel and he made no more effort to guide Greyling but sat with the small of his back to the high cantle and let the animal go where it would.

If he were a horse with any magic in him, he would find the wizard. The big grey was trotting now toward a break in the woods around the hut, and when Kothar looked closely he could make out a path between the trees that led away to the southward.

He turned to see Queen Elfa standing before the open stable door, regal in her red gown, her golden hair piled high on her head and hung with garnets. She lifted a ringed hand, waved it. Her smile was radiant with promise.

It was cool in the forest, and a little cold wind was sighing here and there through the leaves and over the rocks that peeped out from the gnarled tree-roots where they broke the ground. Sunlight came but seldom into this forest world where everything was green or brown, but when it did, it came in golden sheets with tiny dust motes dancing in its radiance.

After a time, Kothar grew hungry. He looked behind him but there was no sack or purse tied to the saddle which might hold cheese and bread, not any shield either, he noticed, and he told himself glumly that being champion to a queen might not be all he thought it. The hours went by and he grew more hungry so that he began shifting in the saddle with his annoyance like a black cloud on his face.

It was then that he heard the screaming.

CHAPTER 3

He hung high in the sky, a red thing that screamed and screamed in his agony, legs and arms moving wildly as if he swam there between the clouds. Kothar felt the golden hairs at the base of his neck stand up in horror. The chilling winds that swept the treetops here in Windmere Wood must be like salt poured over the skinless body of the wizard Kazazael.

Twice the barbarian tried to call up to him but his tongue clove to the dry roof of his mouth and he had to swallow three times before he could make his voice work. His eyes were fastened on the thing which had been a man that was like a puppet now, pulled this way and that by the winds, hung there in the sky by the magic of his enemy, Red Lori. He could not pull away his gaze, and sweat ran from his forehead down his cheeks.

A cramp came into his middle out of sympathy for the red thing that howled in pain up above. Kothar made a fist of his right hand and hammered the saddle pommel with it.

"Kazazael!" he shouted at last. "Can you hear me?"

The wizard was screaming so loudly, the wind was blowing so strongly, that no ears could have heard his words. Cupping his hands to his lips, the thickly thewed mercenary bellowed again and again, until his ears rang with the sound of his own voice.

"Kazazael! Kazazael! Kazazael!" he roared.

The screaming stopped. A hoarse throat cried back at him. "Who calls the name of Kazazael the accursed?"

"Kothar of Cumberia, the sellsword. I've come to help you."

"No man can help me now!"

Kazazael began screaming once more.

Kothar scratched his golden head. He must find some way to help the man, Queen Elfa had commanded him to do so, saying that she could never defeat Lord Markoth unless Kazazael were free to help her with his necromancies. Yet if Kazazael did not know the way to his own release, how was he to accomplish it? He bit his lower lip with his strong white teeth, thinking hard.

"Kazazael—will anything stop the pain?" he cried, unable to listen further to that awful screaming.

"Only one thing."

"And what will that thing be?"

"The cloak of the sea serpent Iormungar."

"How do I find the cloak?"

The red thing which had been Kazazael shouted down at him, but there was hopelessness in his tones, and a resignation to defeat which Kothar did not like. A man must make a fight of it, he thought, even though there is nothing left to him but black despair. Still, he listened to the instructions Kazazael gave to him, and he put them deep in his mind so he would not forget.

Then he turned Greyling on the forest path and sent him galloping away from the screaming until it faded out. Still he held the grey horse to its mad pace, as if the pounding of its hoofbeats would blot from his memory the sight of the thing in the sky.

He was still hungry, though he felt a touch of guilt about it. Kazazael was suffering far worse than hunger pangs. He tightened his belt two notches and reflected that the sword Frostfire and the warhorse Greyling were all very well, and he was proud of them, being a soldier, but if he might have a bowl of seafood stew or a thick slash of deer meat, he could appreciate the tools of his trade more properly.

The sky was darkening; night was coming on. He had fought hard, he had been through experiences which would test the nerves of any warlock who dealt with daemons, and tiredness was in his bones. Greyling was tiring too, he had run a long way, so Kothar reined him in and let him walk and blow.

The stars in the night sky were close together and very thick in the blackness. The big barbarian blinked at them in his weariness.

He wanted to slip from the saddle and remove his blanket, wrap himself in its length as well as he could, and sleep. Yet the thought of the red thing screaming in the sky drove him onward, with Greyling stumbling now in his own weariness. The forest world was long since behind them, they were moving across a great meadow-land, and faintly from afar his nostrils caught the scent of salt air.

Salt air would mean the sea and the craggy rocks where the waves rolled in and broke apart in a spray of spume and water. Kothar straightened in the saddle. He had always loved the sea—he was spawn of the ocean, having come to Cumberia long ago in a boat as a lost, lonely child—and the smell of its fragrance was a stimulant to him. He reached down and with a big hand, patted the muscular neck of the grey warhorse.

"A little further only, Greyling."

Then they would rest. His body must have sleep to dare the sea beast Iormungar in its lair and take from it the white wool cloak that had been woven by enchanted mermaids long ago, deep in some blue ocean grotto. Ah, but first let his eyes drink their fill of the restless sea lifting up its swells to batter at the coastline rocks as it had done since the beginnings of Time.

The horse came to a little headland and Kothar reined him up on the rim of the black sea rocks so that he and the horse stood silhouetted against the stars. There was soft loam and grass underhoof, for the meadow grew right up to the edge of the sea stones, and he could make out gorse and heather swaying in the wind.

Standing in the saddle, the mercenary searched the headland for some place of shelter where he might make a fire and warm his body. He saw only a fallen tree a hundred yards away and he sighed. He would make do with what he had, like any other warrior in the field.

Within moments after he lay on his side with his spine to the fallen tree trunk, with his head resting on a mattock of soft grass, he was asleep. Greyling, freed of bridle and reins and saddle, browsed on the sweet grasses, and from time to time lifted his great head and stared out over the dark waters of the ocean.

In the light of early morning, Kothar woke to the pains of an empty belly. He lay a while with his eyes closed, dreaming of the dishes he had eaten in the past until the pounding of the sea waves roused him to a realization that food, for a man who knew the shoreline, lay not far away.

With the tip of his sword he dug up clams from the shingle and caught half a dozen crabs. With flint and the steel of Frostfire he made a flame of driftwood breakings and cooked his crabs while he wolfed down the raw clams. In a little while he was rid of his hunger and he stretched in the sunlight and watched the black rocks appear on the ocean floor as the tide ran out away from the land. His hand loosed Frostfire in its scabbard. Beyond the line of black rocks, according to the wizard Kazazael, was the lair of the sea serpent Iormungar.

He waited patiently as the tide ebbed away. Then he set his feet along the coarse detritus of the shore and outward toward the rocks. His leather boots slipped a little on the rocks, they were still wet and hung with seaweeds, but he was used to the sea and he ran lightly across a line of spray-wet rocks until he stood on the very last rock of all and stared downward into a large hole where the water foamed and gurgled as it came and went.

He must go down into that hole, if he was to find the cloak. Kothar grimaced, being without appetite for a swim in these cold waters. Even as he wondered how he was going to get back up out of the hole, he stepped off the rock and plunged into the freezing waters like a stone.

Coldness caught at him, ate through his boots and mail shirt and leather hacqueton under it, stabbed his legs and arms and middle. He went down slowly through the black waters, for the to-and-fro rush of the sea buoyed him up even as he fell, so that he landed on a stone ledge that formed the outer lip of a vast sea cavern that stretched away behind him into darkness. A radiance came from the rocks and gave off a bluish light.

There was fresh air here, and no water except a few drops that had come into this place with him as he had ridden the submerged waterfall to the cavern edge. He wondered who had found this waterfall—it was invisible from the shore and had it not been for Kazazael, he would have passed it by without a glance. From the falling waters he turned his gaze to the smooth stone walls and floor of the bluish cavern.

This place was like no sea cavern he had ever seen. He saw now that the blue light came from glistening streakings on the wet walls of the cavern, as if some playful giant had dipped his fingers in blue fire and drawn their tips across those stone barriers.

Kothar began walking forward lightly, treading as might a panther on the prowl, pulling his swordbelt around in front of him so the golden hilt of Frostfire was in finger reach. His massive shoulders moved in a shrugging motion; the air of the cavern was foul and fetid; a rank stench seemed to move with the wind currents. Kothar liked the free, clean air of beach and forest; not for him this dank noxiousness.

He was annoyed, too, by an odd sound as he moved lightly across the great submarine den. At first he thought the sucking sound might be the sea itself, filling and emptying some stone cavity or other. But this he was inclined to discount, now.

The noise was too steady, and it was growing louder.

He walked on hard gravel that ground underfoot like pebbles. He glanced down, seeing a white scattering of thousands of tiny shells. No, these were not shells. They were—bones! Human bones!

Kothar shook himself, anger at his confrontation with the unknown rumbling in his thick throat. He did not like the unknown, it made him uneasy. Give him a foe with a face to battle and a weapon to match, and Kothar was at ease with the world. These powdered bones were no part of any foe he could discover.

The bones cracked underfoot as he walked on into the next cavern, a great dark chamber filled with that same blue radiance. Squinting into the blackness, he made out big oaken chests bound with iron. Kothar grinned, showing even white teeth.

What was it Afgorkon had said? He who carries Frostfire must own nothing else? By Dwallka! These wooden boxes had the look of treasure chests.

He moved toward them, peered through the dim blue light at them. No doubt about it. He lifted a dagger from his belt, pried at a rusted lock. A bulge of forearm muscles, a bending steel blade and—*spaaang!* The lock to the first chest came loose.

Kothar gripped the chest lid and heaved.

"By Elwys' golden breasts!" he panted.

He stared at jewels as big as hen's eggs—diamonds, rubies, sapphires, emeralds—at ropes of golden links—at pearls the size of small clams—at the loot of uncounted centuries. His eyes grew big. His huge hands reached out—There it was again—that noise!

Kothar turned his head.

"Gods of Thuum!"

A huge worm—white as a bleached sea shell, huge as Gargantos, as noisome as a marsh at low tide—slithered down the far wall. Its head reared up, questing, and Kothar saw its pink nostrils flare as it smelled him out. Its other end was lost in the shadows high atop the cavern ceiling, but what the barbarian saw was enough to make his heart thud in dismay.

As the slug moved, it left glowing blue slime behind it. This then, was what kept the cavern eternally lighted for any rash human who might choose to come wandering here. Kothar nodded grimly and drew his blade.

He advanced cautiously. The memory of those human bones was in his brain; he knew the worm was no mean antagonist. Other men had died within sight of that great treasure. Kothar resolved he would live to carry it away.

The worm was close now, towering above his head, and Kothar was a tall man. Its maw was opening and closing as if it tasted the human flesh awaiting its appetite. Its maw was dripping slime in great drops onto the floor as the slug undulated closer.

Kothar leaped, sword high to slash.

In mid-leap a drop of that slime from the slug's mouth splashed on his left shoulder. Agony burned through the big barbarian. A lesser man would have screamed and staggered back, to fall victim to the gaping maw. Not Kothar. He leaped forward, dodging another glob of slime.

Frostfire flashed in the blue light.

The great steel blade sank deep into blubbery white hide. With a savage curse on his lips, Kothar pulled it free, struck again. A gaping wound showed in the writhing, twisting worm. The head was moving to left and right, the maw was opening and closing, the giant slug was making a mewling sound. It was hurt, badly hurt. Faster it moved, as if to overwhelm this rash enemy with its sheer bulk.

Kothar never ceased to strike, slashing again and again at that great hulk, widening the slit in its side. The blue length of Frostfire was slimed now with ichor, it stank as the worm stank, and made the young giant snort his disgust. Yet always that blade moved, and as it moved, it cut deep into and through the worm-meat.

With a soft plop the rest of the great worm fell from the wall. Instantly it began to twist and flop about, seeking to catch this rash intruder in its domain and slay him. Twice the huge length of the creature brushed Kothar, twice it almost ran over him, nearly pinning him beneath that soft weight from which there would be no escape, not even for his mighty muscles.

Once the barbarian had to put a hand on that blubbery mass and vault over it to land catlike on his booted feet, whirling and slashing again and again with Frostfire, always at that same gaping wound.

Now the blade had cut the worm almost in half. The rear length of the creature was barely moving. The head was lower, now, inches above the ground. The worm was in its death throes, cut almost in twain. What remained was still dangerous, however. The tiny worm-brain did not yet know its body was dying. It would be some time before that fact registered on what served it as a mind; until then, Kothar must go on striking with the blue steel blade.

Then the worm-head touched the floor and the entire body became quiescent, except for a few twitches here and there. Kothar staggered back, his face wet with sweat. He drew a massively muscled forearm across his brow, grinning coldly.

"Damned shibboleth," he grumbled, letting Frostfire sink until its stained point touched the bone-strewn floor.

He turned away, toward the chests.

"Dwallka—*no!*" he bellowed, leaping.

The chests were disappearing, fading into thin mists into which he plunged his hands, letting Frostfire clang on the cavern floor. His fingers stabbed here and there, reaching for a huge emerald, a giant fire-pearl. His hands closed on empty air.

The treasure had existed only in the worm-brain! Just as a scavenger beetle dangled a bit of food before its prey to lure it nearer, so the worm created the treasure chest out of sheer mind-imagery, to attack humans for its food. Kothar rasped curses in high Cumberian and Low Solesian.

A moment later, laughter rumbled from his deep chest He could appreciate the grim humor of the jest. Well, he still had Frostfire, and that sword was worth a dozen such treasure chests.

He walked on; now, after wiping clean the blade, he carried the great sword naked in his hand, for his was the quick suspicion of the barbarian mind that saw danger in the rush of wind or the faint glint of light on metal. Yet there was no wind, no glimmer of light other than the blue slime-radiance.

Through small chambers and large he stalked, and now he noticed that he moved downward, as though to the bottom of the sea. The walls were wetly dripping, the air was humid, moist. Kothar found it difficult to breathe.

He rounded a corner of rock, stood on the stone rim of a vast pool of water. Above him, an eerie light shone, revealing a great cave that stretched away into utter darkness.

This was the cavern of the cloak. It had to be. It was all jagged rock and faint grey light and it was vast, a deep sea cavern unknown to any creatures but the magicians who saw it in the flickering flames of their ensorcelled fires, and to the sea beast, Iormungar, whose lair it was. Kothar studied the great cavern from the smooth platform that jutted out over its dark, placid waters.

The rocky walls of the cavern were faintly luminescent, giving off a greyish glow. In that light, Kothar saw a white something high above his head, fluttering faintly in the wind currents eddying throughout the cave. It was a grotesque caricature of a human being with arms and legs and head. It gave off a blue sheen as it rippled and danced like a frightened ghost.

Yes, this was the cloak the mermaids had woven.

Kothar looked at the walls of the cavern. They were craggy and afforded him handholds. He could mount up the wall close to the cloak. Ah, but when he was up there, how was he to reach it? It hung suspended in space, fully five feet or more from the closest wall.

Frostfire might be the answer.

He stripped off his mail shirt and leather hacqueton, his boots and scabbard belt. Naked but for a cotton cloth about his loins and his fur kilt and with Frostfire gripped between his teeth, he began the slow ascent of those slimy, slippery-wet walls.

Twice his powerful hands slipped on the grey-green rocks, twice he almost fell to the jagged rocks and dark waters below. Only his giant sinews kept him on the wall, clinging like a limpet. His breath burned his throat, and there was the stink of something alien in his nostrils.

Yet always he went upwards, his eyes fastened on the white cloak flapping as if alive where there was no wind. Soon, now. Soon! His fingers gripped, his toes found holds, he hoisted his giant body closer to the cloak.

Where a tongue of stone thrust from the wall, he set his hand. He would have to hang there a moment, poised above the rocks, for only from such a handhold could he reach out with Frostfire and catch that white thing.

Kothar drew a deep breath. The fingers of his left hand stretched out and closed on the rock-tongue. He let his toes slip from the slimed stone wall and hung in midair. His fingers did not have a firm hold; there was wetness under them, a slippery wetness that prevented his fingertips from gripping. A slight mistake in his balance and those fingers would slide off, and he would plummet down onto the jagged rocks below.

He risked a glance at the granite fangs waiting like the mouth of Iormungar to crush his flesh to pulp. His heart hammered inside his rib cage. They were sharp, those rocks, as if burnished by the waters flowing in and out among them.

Kothar drew a deep breath.

Gingerly he stretched out his sword arm and saw the point of Frostfire touch the cloak as it swayed to unseen forces. He put strain on his rolling muscles, seeking to inch closer. Again he sent out Frostfire.

This time the steel point clung to the cloak.

Kothar drew the sword and cloak toward him. He could not shift the cloak to his person, his left hand was clinging to the rock tongue, his right held the sword.

Far below his feet dangling in midair, he heard a gurgling, sucking sound, as if the cavern waters were running out. He heeded not the sound, all his attention was focused on the cloak that clung so precariously to the steel blade. One slight breeze and the cloak would fall.

A monstrous bellow shook the air.

A civilized man would have frozen motionless before that terrifying roar, or be startled into a fatal slip and plummet onto the jagged stones below. Kothar was a barbarian. His nerves were as solid as the rock to which he clung.

Even as his ears told him he faced danger, he was stabbing his toes toward the wall. His foot slipped, then fastened. The young giant let go his handhold, he threw his body sideways. His hip slammed into the wet rock even as his freed left hand caught hold of a stone ledge.

"Dwallka!" he breathed, muscles going rigid.

Inches from his leg, a scaled snout snapped shut.

Kothar shuddered, goggling down at the monster rising steadily up out of the waters boiling far below him. The barbarian had never imagined anything so huge. Its body was fully as large as half a dozen ships, the kind that ply the waters of the Inland Sea between Azynyssa and the southern kingdoms of Sybaria and Malakor. Its scales were a bluish-grey and glistened as if polished with oil.

Atop that immense body, half-hidden like an iceberg beneath the cavern waters, was a thick, supple neck, longer than five tall men standing one above the other. On that neck was a head framed in scales, with three bulging red eyes glaring hate and hunger up at Kothar.

Thick serpents seemed to hang from the head, twisting and turning, hissing with gaping jaws like Iormungar himself, seeking to find and pierce the skin of this rash man-thing with their own fangs. The trio of scarlet eyes, the living serpents that were a part of the titanic sea beast, made Kothar press back against the slimy stone wall.

"Dwallka—hear me," he growled. "A gold coin for your nearest temple if you get me out of this."

Aie! This was the father of all dragons!

Against him, Kothar was no more than a midget. The huge head was lowering, preparing to strike a second time. More than half its bulk was still hidden by the boiling waters, but its scaled neck could reach to the narrow ledge where Kothar had braced his heels.

Kothar grinned mirthlessly, sensing his doom.

His right hand still held Frostfire, with the white cloak caught upon its point. The youthful giant knew he could never descend that slime-wet wall with Iormungar yawning his maw to engulf him. One false move, even if the sea-beast only brushed him with his snout, and he would fall to be impaled on the sharp rocks.

Even as he waited to feel Iormungar's fangs close upon his flesh, Kothar studied the waters bubbling and frothing about the monster's hidden body. Kothar was as much at home in water as any fish. If he leaped for the sea waters lapping the stone ledge far below, the beast could pick him out of it as he might pick any other fish.

He felt the sweat wet upon his face. He was not afraid, inside he was raging mad at the thought that he had come so far only to fail.

"A golden coin, Dwallka," he reminded his god.

As if Dwallka of the War Hammer put the thought in his head, Kothar gripped the haft of Frostfire and stared hard through the murky gloom of the cavern at the three red eyes of Iormungar.

His hand moved the sword, the cloak fluttered free.

And Kothar leaped.

The great sword held rigid, he dropped full upon the uplifted snout of Iormungar. The cloak had fallen where he had aimed it, full across those three scarlet eyes, like a blindfold.

The mercenary could see those glittering rednesses through the thin cloth of the cloak, like coals visible through sea mist. Bracing his feet, Kothar stabbed sharply at the nearest eye.

Iormungar bellowed, head rearing upward.

The young giant tottered, striving desperately to maintain his balance. His footholds on the huge head were giving way beneath him, but even while he lurched wildly he drove Frostfire deep into a second scarlet orb.

The sea beast screamed and shook its massive head.

Kothar went flying.

So instinctive were his reflexes, so much the barbarian was this golden-haired young giant—that even as he felt his perch go out from under him, he slashed sideways with his blade. Deep into that third red eye he drove his edge, saw the cloak fouled by the blood running from it.

Then he was dropping like a stone, hitting the scaled sea beast and bouncing off, to splash deep into the cavern waters. Downward into cold black depths he plunged, sensing the flailing bulk of the monster beside him.

Blinded, Iormungar was still dangerous. His fangs could still bite deep, his head would be questing for this man who had taken away his sight. Bellowing roars shook the cavern walls. Even beneath the surface Kothar could feel their vibrations.

He swam upward. His head popped into view as the sea beast was crashing its scaled head into a rock wall. The gigantic body was threshing about; a hip hit Kothar and bounced him sideways. And where the head had struck the wall, there was a crack running through the rock.

Overhead, the ceiling was reacting to the body heaving madly in its pain throes. Clumps of dirt and chunks of rock fell into the water. A jagged stone hit Kothar on his shoulder as he tried to make his way to the rim that ran about part of the cave.

Something reared high above the barbarian and slapped downward, hitting the water flatly. Thunder rolled in the closed chamber as the monstrous tail struck inches from the Cumberian. Had it landed on him, it would have crushed his head and shoulders to red pulp.

Kothar knew the serpent was hunting for him. Its snout was dipping downward, its nostrils flared as it sought out the man-scent. The salt water hid his smell, for Iormungar was searching blindly, helplessly, while its frightful bulk threshed and twisted.

The mercenary kept his left hand on the scales that rubbed his flesh raw, feeling his way across that body and through the water until he was behind the sea beast. More and more rocks and dirt were raining down from the cavern roof. Glancing up, Kothar saw that soon, unless Iormungar stopped his floppings, he would bring the entire cavern down upon him.

There was no feeling in the scales upon which Kothar half stood, staring at the collapsing cave. The beast would not know where the man was, if he made no sound.

He let the scaled body sweep him toward the rock rim. He poised an instant, then leaped. His bare feet hit wet stone and slid.

Kothar went down on all fours to keep from sliding back into the waters. A dozen yards away, the limply wet cloak was draped across the very edge of the stone platform. He would have to get the cloak, right from under the fangs of Iormungar.

He ran like a deer for the cloak. His hand stabbed downward, tangled his fingers in it, yanked it up. The cracks in the cavern walls were widening, whole chunks of the stone ceiling were crashing onto the rock platform and into the green spray of the frothing cavern waters.

Iormungar roared and snapped.

Kothar saw that maw opening for him and dove. His shoulder hit the platform and he rolled just as part of the rock rim broke off where the sea beast bit into it.

The entire cavern was falling in now.

Kothar ran as he had never run, angling his body at the stone archway. Behind him the sea beast would have smelled him out, would be darting its head straight at him.

There was no time to turn and fight. If he paused to swing Frostfire, the ceiling would come down and crush him. Time was an eternity of flying feet and a great sword flashing in the air in his right hand.

A fetid stench touched his nostrils. He felt hot breath searing his back. Kothar left the stone floor in a savage leap. Only his rolling muscles could have carried him across that last twenty feet of space and through the archway before those fangs closed down upon his flesh.

He went through the arch, turning slightly and seeing the great mouth stretched wide to swallow him. His spine hit the floor beyond the archway just as Iormungar's snout closed on empty air and rammed into the arch itself.

Stone cracked. The cavern rumbled.

Kothar was too mesmerized by the catastrophe before his eyes to move. He lay and watched the roof fall; he saw the walls cave in upon the bellowing beast that threshed madly in its death agonies. Even Iormungar could not withstand those uncountable tons of rock and stone thudding down upon him.

The powdered dust from those rocks choked the barbarian. With a snarl, he got to his feet, brushing the stuff from his lips. He could see a long, forked tongue emerge from between huge white fangs and slither across the stone. It quivered a moment, then lay still.

Kothar let the breath out of his lungs, snatched up his mail shirt, his hacqueton and his boots. "Thanks, Dwallka," he grinned. "I'll buy a woman from your temple in Shrillikar, first chance I get—along with that gold coin I still owe you!"

He turned and ran for the outer world.

CHAPTER 4

Once again he stood before the flayed wizard.

Standing on widespread feet he lifted the cloak and held it high for the red thing that had been a man to see. The cloak quivered in his grasp as if it were alive.

"Kazazael!" Kothar roared. "I have the cloak."

His hand held the living stuff, not letting it get away. Above him, swaying in the wind currents, Kazazael stared down with glassy, disbelieving eyes. Three times he blinked those eyes into which his agonized sweat dripped, before understanding touched his mind.

"The cloak!" he screeched in hoarse tones. "Filatha maganow! Akk sograth temetto!

As Kothar stared, the cloak tore itself from his clasp and soared upward toward the flayed wizard. It hovered above him a moment, then settled down about him. There was a blurring in the air; an instant later, Kazazael had his skin back.

The wizard descended slowly to the ground as if a demon hand were lowering him. His face was hard, it might have been carved from wood, and Kothar scowled blackly when he saw his wild expression.

"Now let Red Lori beware," the sorcerer snarled. "I wear the cloak of Iormungar and so I am protected against her enchantments. Now my ensorcelments shall bring doom to her—and to King Markoth!"

His newly fleshed arms rose high. Sounds thundered from his throat. Overhead the sky darkened. Kothar could see stars through this unnatural blackness. The words seemed to shape themselves in the air, in letters of red flame.

Instantly, a wind rose. It blew about Kothar, flapping his fur kilt, whipping his legs. The barbarian snarled, putting a hand on Frostfire's hilt; he did not hold with magic, he would rather put his trust in the blued steel blade at his side. But Kazazael was a friend, and he had promised Elfa the queen to do what he could to help.

The wind grew stronger. Kothar felt his body raised into the air. His feet sought to find solid ground under him, but he could not. The wind was carrying him skyward, along with the grinning wizard.

"Let Red Lori try her tricks. My magic will fend them off." His eyes glared balefully under his shaggy brows as Kazazael glanced at Kothar. "I'll need you, mercenary. My magicks must be very strong to fight and defeat those of the witch. They will take all my concentration, all my powers. During that time I shall be helpless against non-magic—like soldiers."

Kothar grinned. Soldiers he could deal with. Apparently he was going to like what Kazazael had planned for him. Gods! He was in a mood to do a little slaying, after all this sorcery he'd been encountering. Give him honest steel and honest human-flesh to fight, and he was happy.

Far below, the countryside went by as the whirlwind carried him and the magician on their headlong course.

Kothar could make out the edge of the sea and the great escarpment beneath which the sea beast Iormungar had guarded the cavern of the cloak. He saw the distant battlefield from which he had stumbled, and the dead bodies still lying there.

The wind blew faster, faster.

In the distance, Kothar saw a high black tower rising from a rocky island in the sea. This was the home of Kazazael, from which he sent out his enchantments. Rumor said the tower was protected by the demons Bathophet and Asumu, who served Kazazael.

Downward they dropped. The stone walls of the tower parted and through this opening Kazazael and Kothar were blown. The barbarian felt his senses spin dizzily, then a stone floor was underfoot and he was rumbling words in his throat, words that were half curses, half prayers to all the gods he knew.

Kazazael sprang to a brilliant red pentagram which was inscribed with ancient sigils in solid gold, in bright silver and in bits of oricalc. Inside the scarlet star, the sorcerer lifted high his arms.

"In the sacred names of Eudor and Dakkag, I entreat protection from the demons who serve Red Lori! Throw about my tower, about my person and that of the mercenary warrior Kothar—the protection we shall need!"

A great calm fell upon the island.

For the first time since he had gone into battle on the plain of dead trees, Kothar felt at ease with his world. His stomach rumbled, telling him he needed food. His empty belly seemed to be rubbing against his spine and the mere thought of a steak cooked over red coals and served with its juices dripping, made his senses reel. Ah, and with that a beaker of cold midlands ale.

As if Kazazael understood his wants, he growled, "Go below. My maidservants will attend to you. Leave me to work out the spells that will defeat Red Lori."

Kothar was glad to abandon the wild-eyed wizard. He thrust open a wooden door and went down stone steps to the floor below. The smells of cooking food came to his nostrils.

A hand lifting a leather curtain permitted him to see into a large hall that held a huge trestle table and a dozen high-backed wooden chairs. In the shadows were four girls who came forward at sight of him.

Kothar grinned, knowing how to deal with pretty maidservants when he required food. He kissed one, pinched the plump buttock of another, stroked a third on her smooth bare side, and winked at the fourth.

"Fetch meat, pretty ones. Meat and cheese, good barley bread and ale. I'm starving to death—but you can bring back my strength."

They ran to serve him, carrying heaping platters of smoking meats, sharp cheeses, bread steaming from the baking ovens, and ale so cold the leather jack that held it was coated with drops of water. Kothar was a giant in stature, and he boasted a giant's appetite. He grinned when he saw those wooden platters, and hooked a chair toward the table with a toe.

He ate until the platters were almost empty. With bread he scooped tasty gravies off a dish spiced with a wedge of cheese on the bread, and swallowed beakers of cold ale at a gulp. When he was done, he leaned his head back against his chair back and wiped his lips with a hairy, bronzed forearm.

"Come, now, you girls," he called, beckoning the giggling maids closer. "You've served me well, and it's only right I serve you four the same."

Kothar had appetites for other things than food, and they were just as vast as the needs of his belly. His huge right hand was drawing a willing brunette toward his knee when his keen ears heard the pound of heavy footsteps trampling across the island stones.

The big barbarian growled deep in his throat. Instead of the brunette, his hand sought out Frostfire, dragging it from its scabbard. Kazazael had said he was weak against hired soldiers while working on the spells that would defeat Red Lori. He, Kothar, was not weak against fighting men.

His laughter rumbled as he brushed past the girl, clapping her behind with a big hand. He stalked like a hungry panther across the great hall and out into the chamber where the oaken, iron-barred tower door was hung. With his free left hand, he threw open that door.

A dozen men in mail shirts and metal caps and with the viper device of King Markoth sewn onto their cloaks were moving across the rocky shingle toward the tower. Kothar grinned. Red Lori would have sent them by a trick of magic, knowing Kazazael's weakness.

Men like these had chased him from the Plain of Dead Trees. Men like these had hunted him down like a dog. His long brown fingers twisted about the sword shaft they held. It was time to pay back the indignities he had suffered.

It was not the custom of Kothar to wait for battle. With a bull bellow, he leaped from the doorway, blade swinging through the air, straight for the mercenaries. One man went down and then a second, blood gouting from their wounds, before the others could react.

The ten soldiers who were left fanned out into a big circle. They would close that circle slowly, with Kothar in its center. The barbarian would be forced to fight in front and in back and at both sides, all at the same time. It was a clever plan. Against any other man, it might have succeeded.

Kothar laughed, head flung back, long tawny hair blowing in the wind. They were going to make a battle of it! Praise to Dwallka of the War Hammer! He was in the mood for a good fight.

He leaped sideways, sword flashing in the sunlight. The blued blade clove through neckmeat, a man screamed as he felt the steel bite deep. At the same instant, Kothar gripped a second man and flung him sideways, bowling over the two men nearest him.

Before the death circle could form again, the barbarian was blooding his blade in the three men closest to him. They dropped, the red gash of their wounds spurting blood. Kothar never stopped, he was a tiger on the prowl among a herd of lambs. His sword was his talon, cutting, stabbing, slashing.

As well try to hold the wind as hold the Cumberian when the blood lust bubbled in his veins. The mercenaries of King Markoth shouted to one another but the answering cries were gurgles drowned in bloody throats. Frostfire drank at blood, its keen edges starved for the red liquid which was the food of life to it.

Eight men down in minutes, only four mercenaries left. They stared in dismay at their dead and dying companions; they turned to run.

Kothar howled his glee, going after them in great leaps that carried him across ten feet of island rock at a bound. His sword rose and fell, once it thrust forward, again it slashed sideways into human flesh. The last man he caught thigh-deep in cold sea water and made his head fly through the air to splash in the ocean as Frostfire cut through his neck.

The big barbarian felt let down. The fight had lasted only a little while, scarcely long enough for him to work up a good sweat. The water at his legs was cold, so he trudged upward across the shingle, hoping Red Lori would send more men to kill.

The thought of the four maidservants made him walk a little faster. After a fight, there was nothing like soft lips and smooth flesh in his arms to make him forget the berserk rage in which he battled. There were four wenches waiting to make him happy.

"Not yet, barbarian!"

This was the voice of Kazazael drifting through the air about him. Kothar grumbled—the brunette was a shapely siren—but a promise to help Queen Elfa was a promise he meant to keep.

"What now, wizard?" he growled.

The bodiless voice said, "As I am weak against non-magic-things—so also is Red Lori. Go to her, sellsword! Slay her with the blade Frostfire!"

A black cloud came down from the sky and caught Kothar in its mists. Instantly the barbarian was swept up off the island of the thaumaturgic tower and whirled across the sky like a golden slash of lightning in a summer rainstorm.

His booted feet landed solidly on stone.

Kothar shook himself, growling curses at all magicians who treated human beings like dogs to be picked up by the scruff of the neck and hurled where the sorcerer wanted them to go. His eyes took in the long corridor, flanked on one side by a windowed wall and on the other by a rounded length of black obsidian.

He knew where he was, high in the tower that belonged to the witch, Red Lori. Behind that obsidian wall she worked her necromancies. This walking space between her thaumaturgic chamber and the windowed wall overlooking the city of Commoral was narrow, made only for two men to walk abreast; or, as some men whispered in the taverns, for the thing that was Red Lori's familiar to stalk down its prey. And that prey was anyone rash enough to come uninvited to the doors beyond which Red Lori wrought her wizardries.

Kothar let anger rumble from his throat and tightened his grip on Frostfire. He was no prey to anyone. Let him who thought so, be rash enough to attack and—"Queen Elfa," he breathed.

She came striding forward, head lowered, the sunlight streaming through the windows striking red fire from the garnets in her golden hair. Her stride never faltered as her champion cried her name. She came on steadily, staring at the ground before her, nearer and nearer.

The instincts of a barbarian are akin to those of an animal. Kothar stepped to one side and lifted Frostfire. This was not Elfa of the flirting eyes.

As a matter of fact, because she walked with head down, he could not see the eyes of this simulacra of the queen at all. The skin prickled along his spine as the woman came close enough to touch with his long sword.

"Look at me, Elfa," he rasped.

Her head came up just as she flung herself at him with a scream of utter hate. Where laughing blue eyes should be, was only black emptiness. This was no woman. This was the witch's familiar, Slothann. Her claws were out, raised to scratch. Where those poisoned claws fell, death would come hastening.

Kothar moved like a striking panther. His bulging thigh muscles worked as he leaped to one side and away from the screeching woman-shape, and while he dove, he drove the flat of his blade against the familiar.

Blue steel hit her body, sparked like lightning.

Slothann screamed shrilly in pain at the touch of bare steel to her body. The outlines of her woman-shape shimmered, blurred. Instead of the queen—a great black leopard crouched before Kothar, feral green eyes staring at him, long furry body tensed to leap.

"Damned harpy," snarled Kothar.

He did not wait to see the cat come through the air at him. He had hunted leopards in the rain forests of Azynyssa when he served in the guard of King Thycideus. He knew those cats never stood for a fight, but liked to pounce from ambush. The barbarian slashed out with Frostfire. The familiar dodged the blow and sought to strike back with a claws-bared paw. Kothar cursed and swung his blued blade in a return sweep.

The keen edge bit into fur and flesh, lopped off the huge paw. Once again lightnings sparked and flashed, as if the magic in the blade warred with the evil in the cat.

The familiar shrieked in agony.

Slothann was merely a black cat, now, that ran on three legs, trailing blood. Kothar watched it scamper out of sight among the shadows. He grinned, chuckling.

There were no soldiers in this edifice. No honest mercenary would serve within a mile of Red Lori. Every man and woman in Commoral feared her and her black arts. They had to obey her enchantments, as witness the dozen men she had hurled onto Kazazael's island, but they had no love for her and unless she commanded them by her spells, they gave her a wide berth.

Kothar began his walk along the obsidian wall.

Somewhere here, there was a door.

Halfway around the black stone pile, he came upon it. It was fashioned of bronze carved in a thousand representations of the evil demon, Omorphon. Omorphon was a serpent-god out of the ancient legends of the planet Yarth. It was said that Omorphon had come to the call of the first wizards from the gulfs of demonaic space, that it brought with it dark, wicked powers by which those early necromancers worked their evil. Kothar sensed the evil in that door, realized it was protecting Red Lori in some unimaginable way.

Ordinarily, the barbarian would have hurled his muscular bulk at that bronze slab to bring it crashing open. But the very barbarism that would have made him do that made him cautious, as a wolf is cautious about a trap where the man-smell lingers.

Kothar studied the carvings. There might be a clue in the bronze bas-relief, some little hint as to how the door might be opened safely. His hard eyes saw the intricate serpent coils form subtle patterns. They seemed to blur, to offer anyone rash enough to touch its surface a chasm waiting to catch his body, to let him fall endlessly throughout eternity in some special hell known only to Omorphon.

Only Red Lori could pass that doorway unharmed, he decided grimly. Or her familiar, Slothann.

Kothar grinned mirthlessly. Slothann had run away from his sword, but she had left something of herself behind. The barbarian moved along the hall corridor until he came to the black paw he had severed. With the paw, he might be able to open that devil's gateway.

Furry paw in hand, Kothar braced himself for instant action. He raised the paw—hurled it. And then he leaped.

As the fur touched the bronze door, the metal seemed to melt. Kothar had a flashing glimpse of an abyss opening under him as he dove forward. Had he not thrown the paw, he would be tumbling through that abyss right now, hopelessly lost from the sight of men forever.

Instead, there was something buoying him up and over that awful chasm. The black magic still in the severed paw? Kothar did not know. He did not care.

For now he was inside the chamber and the bronze door was firming back into shape behind him. His great body was poised on booted toes, ready to leap to left or right or straight ahead. Frostfire was in his hand, quivering to strike. His eyes stabbed across the room.

The chamber was empty.

He could see the phials and alembics containing the magic brews and potions of the witch, the jars and canisters holding the dried herbs and powders necessary to her magicks. Against the wall, velvet draperies embroidered by golden threadings contained the formulae for her black arts. Overhead a domed ceiling flashed sigils in silver, sigils that moved oddly back and forth as he stared up at them.

But of Red Lori, there was no sign.

Had she made herself invisible, knowing Kazazael might send Kothar to hunt her down and destroy her? The barbarian moved his blade here and there in the empty space closest to him.

Foot by foot, he advanced into the chamber, sword out and always sliding back and forth before him. Magic was being done in here. He could feel it by the raised hairs at the back of his head, by the smell in his nostrils that was not the clean smell of forest or seashore but of something musty and incredibly evil.

Kothar leaped back.

To his right, where his sword had passed through the air, stood a black cauldron. A pale green steam rose from its bubbling contents. It seemed almost as if his sword had painted a black kettle upon tripod legs above a little fire.

His nose wrinkled. Ptahhhh! He could smell that noxious concoction now. It stank like the fabled pits of Achollos, where the dead and rotting bodies of sinning sorcerers are said to lie unburied, waiting for the demons to come and reanimate them as their playthings. Through the verdant steam from the cauldron, he made more passes with his sword blade.

And now—Faintly he could see other things in this conjure chamber. What had seemed empty space was filled with rune-encrusted onyx tablets, necromantic screens of chalcedony carved in the hundred faces of dread Omorphon, witch-drums made from human skin, and with smoking braziers.

Kothar grunted. He could see Red Lori too, now.

She was all white flesh and creamy skin, clad only in a red velvet panel before her loins and a similar panel behind her. Her arms were lifted high, making her full breasts quiver, her red hair waving where there was no breeze as she stood between seven athanors fueled by demon fixes. Her sole garment was held to her loins by golden links shaped in the forbidden words of Belthamquar, father of demons.

Red Lori was a witch, but by Dwalka! She was a woman, as well. Kothar stared, tightening his grip on Frostfire to strengthen his will. Kazazael had sent him to kill her. He could not do so.

His eyes drank in her beauty. It seemed to Kothar that the red velvet that hid her body contained other words from the forbidden almanac that was attributed to Belthamquar himself, dictated eons before to a mage as great as Afgorkon. Those evil symbols protected her, they hid her body from human eyes. They also furnished the eldritch energies by which she worked her necromancies.

Slay her, man of Cumberia!

This was the voice of Kazazael whispering to his mind. Kothar growled low in his throat. Against that voice he was powerless. He must obey it.

Slowly he moved forward.

Red Lori was unsuspecting, her mind was too deeply sunk in the incantations with which she battled Kazazael to react to the sight or sound of the big barbarian. He strode forward, reaching out his left hand to catch hold of the woman.

Thunder exploded around him. He stood there with his shoulders bowed as sound swept like a maddened wind around his body, buffeting him, lashing out in frightening explosions that racked every bone in his body.

"Back—stay back, barbarian!" the sound commanded.

Kothar shook himself, lunged forward. It would take more than a noise to keep him from the witch. He staggered through waves of vibrating air that hit him with the fury of ten thousand whips. Dimly he sensed this was the demon Belthamquar defending his priestess. Belthamquar, who permitted an extension of his diabolism to seep through into this world of Kothar, was determined to keep his own.

The big youth slashed at the sound as if it were human. He heard the whistle of the steel, felt the hilt quiver in his huge hand. His dazed eyes caught glimpses of another world, an evil megacosm where gods and daemons lived, where wickedness was a way of life, where the humans trapped in that cosmos were tormented beyond endurance every moment of their lives.

Something caught at Kothar, sought to drag him from the chamber and toward that lethal land of Belthamquar, to imprison him in its deepest hell for this sacrilege he was working upon the priestess of the demon-god. Kothar fought back, he used Frostfire in sweeping slashes, listening to agonized screeches from that distant land—as if in some psychic manner, his blade could cut across the chasms of space and eons of Time to injure the hobgobs who served the father of demons.

The sound was a painful shrillness in his ears as the giant staggered sideways, struck with his sword again and yet again. The muscles of his mighty arm bunched and bulged to his movements, he was an animal battling with Belthamquar for something more precious than life itself.

Sweat ran down his face and chest, it trickled along his thickly thewed legs. "By Dwallka—no!" he roared, swinging the great sword. The pain throbbed in his chest and in his ears, then ran along every nerve-end. He fought to stay here, in this world he knew, panting and sweating, until the pain abated slightly.

Unseen hands fell away.

He swayed there, staring at his stained blade that ran with something not unlike blood, but a whitish blood that might have dripped from cacodaemons. As its droplets hit the floor, they turned to a sickly green mist that rose upward like the smoke from an ensorcelled fire and faded into nothingness.

Beyond the green mist, he saw Red Lori.

Still she stood with her bare arms raised, still her voice cried out in ringing tones the enchanted evokements of her spells. With those invocations she fought Kazazael, by their dread power she sought to penetrate his diabolic defenses. Kothar saw the muscles strutted in her shapely legs, in her bared belly, and sensed the deepness of her concentration. She did not even know that he was here.

He leaped like a panther for his prey.

With a hand he caught her arm, whirled her. He lifted Frostfire to strike her sweat-wet temple with its jeweled hilt, reversing the blade. Red Lori swayed, her blued eyelids still shut against reality. Her full red lips were slightly parted, her thin nostrils quivered against this desecration.

Her eyelids lifted.

Fury blazed out at him from her green eyes. A rage so intense it was almost palpable beat at him, like the wings of some invisible bird. Kothar growled and lowered his head, tightening his finger-grip.

"Girl—come on," he snarled.

"Get away—fool! Go back to your forests—and live! Stay here—and die!" She screeched at him like any fishwife, maddened by her interrupted incantations. Her hands rose up, beat against his face and throat and shoulders.

"Belthamquar—aid me!" she screamed.

The smooth flesh under his handgrip changed to slimy, squishy rottedness. Kothar gaped and almost released her. This was not Red Lori he had hold of, it was some boggart from beyond, all fetid flesh and slimy skin that writhed and jiggled in his palm.

Retching against the fetid stink, he came close to letting her go. Only the realization that it was the demon-god helping her kept his fingers where they were. And now his own barbaric anger surged to life. He shook the girl-demon, rattled her teeth with the fury of his jerkings.

She wailed, and instantly she was Red Lori again.

But now she was a different Lori, she was a woman whose body was an irresistibly fleshy temptation to a man. Her smile was lewd, her green eyes flared with promises of erotic delights no man born of woman had ever known. Against his chest she thrust her breasts, her hips, her bare arms closed about his neck and her lips widened for his kiss.

Kothar drew her against him. Aie! This was witchery he could understand. Yet in some dim corner of his mind he heard the voice of Kazazael.

No, Kothar—no! Beware the daughter of Hastarth!

Hastarth was the she-demon who brought madness with her illicit caresses, with her succubus-like visits in the dead of night, to tempt men's minds and bodies to her worship. In her temples, men and women adored her by offering up money with their bodies to casual passersby.

Kothar was a barbarian, with the impulses of a savage on whose bronzed hide the niceties of civilization were no more lasting than the effect of a sunburn. His mightily thewed arms crushed Red Lori to him, his lips fastened to her mouth in a kiss.

Aie! Fool that he was!

A lassitude came upon Kothar, a sweet lethargy in which his muscles became as water. As a fever sapped strength, so too did this embrace of the witch-woman. He rumbled anger deep in his chest as he loosed his arms and gripped Red Lori by her long red hair. Desperately he sought to tug her lips from his, but she knew the secrets of Hastarth, she clung to him as any limpet. And his muscles were weak. Weak!

Visions came to him like phantasms out of nightmare. He saw himself in a garden filled with lovely, fragrant flowers, and with even more lovely women who ran to do his bidding, who slipped beside him where he lay on his flower-bed to teach him the forbidden caresses of the Orient, of Johunga and Callath.

Kothar stood enthralled, staring upon unendurable pleasure even as the lips of Red Lori drained him of his life forces. His great body shook to the delights his bemused eyes were seeing, offering no more struggle to the sorceress. His hands still tangled their fingers in her hair but now they caressed, they stroked.

A city man would have succumbed. His spirit was not the restless savage thing that lay inside the yellow-polled barbarian. Inside Kothar, something—his soul, his *arete*—shrank back from such a life of ease and comfort. A little of this loveplay in a garden—yes! But a life devoted to his own sensual pleasures—no!

There was more to life than beautiful women.

Even as he lazed with female flesh on his flower bed, he wanted the clash of arms, the fierce shouts of men fighting to kill that they might stay alive. From somewhere deep inside him, the Cumberian summoned up that *arete,* strengthened it with his iron will.

Sensing his opposition, Red Lori writhed closer.

The very slight shifting of her smoothly skinned body woke the barbarian nature of this man she kissed. Kothar growled, his hands dropped to her hips where the golden chains encircled them. Those chains—each link carved in a representation of Balthamquar's demon-words—stung his palms like fire.

The pain sent new energy flooding his giant form.

His fingers closed on those golden links, his mind told him he must suffer, he must endure this agony, because by it alone could he break free of this terrible thralldom. His fingers tightened, tightened.

Red Lori cried out in the pain of that finger-grip.

And Kothar pushed her backward.

With the flat of his big hand he caught her cheek, drove her sideways and away from him. The witch-woman screeched curses, she sought to break free entirely, but his stabbing hand was like lightning. It caught her wrist, held her.

Now Kothar could see the great chamber in which he stood as if a veil had been riven from his eyes. Awful forces warred here, along with him and the redheaded sorceress. Demons bit and scratched and battled, rolling upon the ground or standing upright. Behind them, like glimpses of hell-fires, he could see the worlds out of which they had come at the summons of Red Lori and of Kazazael.

Bloody rains fell in the room, splashing and bubbling all around the barbarian. Fire rose upward from the ensorcelled floor, red tongues lapping at the demons who writhed and cursed and twisted in that magic conflagration. The blood-rain met the fire, sought to extinguish it, but the rains were feeble, the flames were strong.

Kothar sensed that by distracting Red Lori, he himself had weakened those rains, enabled Kazazael to make strong the hellflames. The demons summoned up by the wizard did not suffer from the red tongues, they only ate at the servitors of Balthamquar.

Red Lori fought him, but his strength was back in his body and he held her as though she were a child. Her bare heels pummeled his booted ankles, her fingers showed their scarlet nails as she tried to scratch him and could not. She wept, she begged, she sought to bite his wrists with her sharp white teeth.

The barbarian laughed. "Look, Lori! Watch Kazazael hurl your friends back to the hells out of which you drew them!"

"May Belthamquar—father of demons!—sink his red-hot teeth in your soul, Kothar! May he torture you to the end of Time with his terrible powers! I curse you! Curse you!"

The forces struggling in the chamber—spirit-forces that the Cumberian could see but not quite feel—swayed like smoke in the wind, all around them. Evil beat out in waves of horror, causing Kothar to grind his molars against the chill of superstitious fear rippling like ice-water down his spine.

He stood like a tree, gripping the sorceress and holding her still, while the struggle went on. Slowly, slowly, the forces of the wizard won out. The fires grew larger, brighter. The demons of Balthamquar began to shrivel, weakened by their struggle with the servitors of Eudor and Dakkag, on whom Kazazael called.

Red Lori sobbed, sensing defeat.

The Cumberian said gruffly, "Somebody must lose in a struggle for a kingdom, Lori. You're a beautiful woman but you're not queen material.

Let Elfa have Commoral, she was born to it. You have your kingdoms—in those demon worlds."

She screamed curses at his golden head.

In a little while, they stood alone in the room. The demons were gone, together with the blood rains and the hell fires. There was a smell of fire, steam and wizardry in the chamber, where the scarlet pentagram was losing its outline, running as if wet across the floor to merge with and sink into the rugs and carpets thrown here and there.

"Come," said Kothar.

Red Lori would have scratched him but his hand caught her a back-handed blow under her chin and she sank senseless in his hands. Grunting, the barbarian stooped, threw her over a shoulder and turned to leave.

The bronze doors were gone, drawn back into that realm where Belthamquar reigned. Kothar walked with firm strides along the corridor and down the narrow stone stair. As he went, he sensed a differentness about this black edifice. It blurred in his eyes; beneath his boots, it seemed less substantial.

Only when he reached the cobblestoned street and turned to stare back the way he had come did he realize that the tower was fading into nothingness, that the only reality that existed were the ruins of what had been a wizard's habitation long and long ago.

As Red Lori was finished, so was the dwelling her magicks had raised up to house her and the equipment with which she worked her spells. With her dwelling gone, so was her sorcery. Red Lori was no more than a woman, now, whose body made a pleasant weight on Kothar's shoulder.

He angled his steps toward the palace, which Kazazael would have possessed with his incantations by this time, and where Queen Elfa would be waiting. There was a sense of accomplishment in the big barbarian, but it was mingled with sympathy and something of sorrow for the girl who lay unconscious on his shoulder.

CHAPTER 5

Queen Elfa sat upon the golden throne of Commoral and watched Kothar move toward her along the aisle left free by her ladies and her courtiers. It was five days since Kazazael had defeated Red Lori and had taken over the palace, putting the Lord Markoth in wizard chains none but Kazazael could unlock.

As he advanced up the aisle, Kothar studied the golden cage that hung from the rafters, high above. The Lord Markoth crouched inside that cage, a prisoner, banished to this vantage point where he might see the throne he hungered for occupied by his wife, the rightful queen of Commoral.

Beside that cage was another, formed of silver bars on which thaumaturgic signs and symbols were graven. In that cage was Red Lori, silent, staring with her wide green eyes at the woman who sat where she, Lori, had fought to sit. When she saw Kothar walking below her, the witch-woman put her lovely face closer to the bars.

"Welcome, Prince Kothar," smiled Elfa, holding her ringed hand out for him to kiss. "It is to you we owe our throne, it is to you we intend to show our gratitude. Prince I declare you, prince of Commoral, entitled to the baronies of Davron and Larkshire, to the dukedoms of Arkyll and Hammet, to their rents and entrails as long as your line endures."

Kothar was uneasy. Prince? Duke? Baron? These were words. His mind could not envision the wealth, the power which was to be his. And there was one more thing that troubled his thoughts.

"My thanks, highness," he growled, uncomfortable before the eyes of the lords and ladies of the kingdom. He wore white velvet and gold garments, with a matching cloak dangling from his massive shoulders. The gleeful eyes of Queen Elfa flirting with him did not add to his comfort.

Elfa was talking. Kothar roused himself from his broodings to pay attention. There was laughter in the soft voice of the queen, gentle mirth as if she teased a child she loved.

"Of course, you will have to make a sacrifice to gain all this wealth and these honors. I have created you captain-general of my armies, as well, your grace. And I am having medals struck to be hung in clusters on your big chest."

The lords and ladies murmured approval of their queen and her decisions. Kothar merely wished he were somewhere else.

"Aren't you curious as to this sacrifice, Kothar?"

"Your will is my will, your majesty," he muttered.

"Oh, how sweet we have become since we were named a prince! Where is the rude, unmannerly boy I met in that hut?"

She might had added, "…and who sought to rape me!" Kothar realized, flushing. He shifted from one foot to the other and scowled at the floor.

"Frostfire!" Elfa laughed.

The Cumberian lighted his head at that. "What about Frostfire?" he rumbled. Here it was, the thing that had troubled him. He had not forgotten the words of Afgorkon. He must possess no wealth if he would own the sword.

"You have to give the sword back," Elfa said sweetly. "It was in the terms of—your bargain. I see you have bought yourself a new scabbard, too—all red velvet and gold filigree work, very handsome—in which to keep your blade. A shame, all those deniers wasted."

"I keep the sword," the barbarian rumbled, putting a huge hand to its jeweled hilt. His chin lifted defiantly, even as Elfa let her soft laughter trail out across the audience hall.

"What? Keep Frostfire? And give up a princedom?"

"Frostfire is mine. It stays with me."

"What about your baronies and dukedoms, lord prince?"

"I give them back to you, Elfa."

Her ringed hands clapped her pleasure as her blue eyes touched the counselors and courtiers who flanked the throne. They looked a little sick, Kothar thought.

Elfa cried, "I knew it! I knew it! I have won my bet with my followers, Kothar. They claimed no man was fool enough to trade a princedom for a length of steel. I told them it all depended on the viewpoint, and that in your eyes, Frostfire was worth more than my entire kingdom. Am I right?"

Kothar nodded grimly, "You are; it is. I keep the blade."

From high above the hall, where a silver cage swung on silver chains, a sweet voice called. "You keep more than the sword, barbarian! You keep my hate, my enmity."

Red Lori knelt in her cage, staring down at the giant youth. "My vengeance on your head, Cumberian. They can keep my body here—but my spirit can roam the world. It shall roam the world—after you. I will haunt you, Kothar—haunt you with the hate of a woman who might have been a queen and will not, thanks to you."

Kothar shivered. The green eyes glaring down at him seemed to fill the room. As in a dream, he heard her worlds. "No matter where you go, what you do, I shall be with you, guiding your feet in the wrong direction for ease, stirring up trouble where you rest your golden head. You shall pay, barbarian—you shall pay!"

Red Lori drew back into the depths of her silver cage and crouched down, faintly breathing. She was quiet now, but her words lingered in the air.

Elfa said, "She shall be punished, Kothar."

"No—let her alone," the barbarian rumbled. "If someone took Frostfire from me, I'd feel as she feels. Let her have the pleasure of her vengeance—it if makes her happy."

Red Lori was silent in her cage.

Queen Elfa sighed, "Be it so. I hope you'll not regret your mercy. Apparently your heart's as big as your body, which is large indeed."

An hour later, Kothar the barbarian rode out of the city gate on his war-horse, Greyling. His heavily muscled body wore his dinted mailed shirt, the leather hacqueton beneath it, his fur kilt and the fur-flapped war-boots on his feet. A worn cloak stirred to the breezes on his back.

Yet—Frostfire made a firm weight in its battered scabbard, hanging from his broad leather belt. From time to time as the city of Commoral grew small with distance behind him, his hand touched the jeweled hilt as if to reassure himself of its presence.

Ahead of him lay his world, waiting to be adventured. With him, trailing his every step, were the green eyes of Red Lori. Angry. Vengeful. Hating.

Kothar wondered when she would demand her revenge.

THE TREASURE IN THE LABYRINTH

CHAPTER 1

The tavern was alive with smoke and the smell of spilled wine. Torches flaring on the stone walls showed a naked woman dancing on a tabletop where platters of meat and cheese had been pushed together with leather mugs to give her wine-wet feet the room she needed. Her long black hair flew like whips as she strutted and posed for the greedy eyes feasting on her pallid flesh.

In the corner of the room, a huge man with golden hair caught in a bun at the nape of his neck in the manner of the barbarians from the northern wastes, sat hunched above a jack of cheap midlands ale. His face was burned bronze from the touch of sun and sea-wind, his brawny shoulders and thickly thewed arms rose upward out of a leather jerkin stained and spotted from long use. His only evidence of wealth was the massive longsword hanging from a broad leather belt, in a dented scabbard.

There was a red jewel set into the pommel of the sword that glittered like frozen blood in the scarlet flares of the wall torches. Angrily, the jewel glittered, as if it reflected the mood of its giant owner.

A woman tiptoed across the tavern rushes, bent to plant her red mouth close to the ear of the barbarian. Her laughing words roused the man from his broodings.

"And how would I pay you, girl?" he growled in his throat, lifting a limp purse from his belt and tossing it on the tabletop. "It's flatter than my belly, which rubs against my backbone. So be off to find a richer customer for your embraces."

The woman cajoled the big youth, sliding a smooth palm down his bared right arm. "For such a one as you, I would offer my pallet freely—but even Elorna needs to eat."

Kothar only grunted, staring down into the leather jack that held one last swallow of cold ale. He had been putting off the drinking of that ale, relishing its taste, wishing he might have a wedge of sharp cheese to go along with it, or a slice of steaming meat from the platters the serving wenches were carrying past his nose.

He thought he heard soft laughter, and looked around for Elorna, but she had given him up as a bad risk and was even now sliding her rump down on the lap of a plump currier. Kothar turned back to his lonely table, but still that eerie laughter persisted.

"I haven't drunk enough ale to float a beetle in my belly, let alone addle my wits," he snarled and reached for the tankard to finish off the last inch of ale in its bottom.

The face was there in the ale, looking out of the tankard at him. It was a beautiful face, that of Red Lori herself, the sorceress of Commoral who hung in a silver cage in the palace of Queen Elfa. Visions of her face had come to him in his campfires beyond the borders of Commoral, when he had ridden out of that country and onto the flatlands that mark the southern reaches of Zoradar.

He had sought employment from Prince Zopar of Zoradar, offering for sale his skill at swordplay and his experience as captain of the Foreign Legion, but Zopar was at peace with his neighbors and in no need of a sell-sword. With a few coins clanking in his purse he had walked Greyling into this town of Azdor, half starving, his throat parched for ale or wine.

Since ale was cheaper than red Thosian, he had settled for a single jack. His belly rumbled, his middle ached with the need for food. Now Red Lori was here to torment him again as she had done ever since he had ridden Greyling out of Commoral City.

Can you hear me, barbarian? I hate you!

Kothar shrugged his muscular arms. He was too hungry to care about Red Lori. She was in a silver cage, well cared for and fussed over; her body was there for Elfa the queen to gloat upon, and the queen wanted her alive and well to suffer the indignities which she heaped upon her from time to time. He even felt a little sorry for her.

As if she sensed his thoughts, her mood changed. Kothar read understanding and an odd kind of sympathy in her green eyes.

Elfa has me. I have you. But the queen lets me eat. What good is a starving enemy to one who has the upper hand, as Elfa has over me? And as I have over you, sell-sword!

Would you eat, Kothar?

The face tossed laughter out of the bottom of the tankard at his gloomy features. To his amazement, those ripe red lips were blowing him a kiss! Kothar opened his eyes wide.

You are like a pet, barbarian. Or a slave. And even a pet or a slave must have a full belly to feel the pangs of ownership.

And so…

A male voice drowned out the words of the sorceress. Kothar felt irritation of sorts. He had been alone so much in these last few weeks that even the face of his enemy was preferable to his own company. So he was turning to glare at the man who had spoken when the man clapped his shoulder.

"Ey? What do you say to that, warrior?"

"I say, to the outer darkness with you!"

The man chuckled. He was a merchant, overly plump of figure and wearing a rich fur mantle over a brocaded houppelande. There were jeweled rings on his fingers, a gold chain about his throat, a leather belt about his middle, the buckle of which was fashioned from Phalkaran silver.

"Wench! Wench!" he bawled, lifting an arm and crooking a fat finger. "Over here with that tray."

A redheaded girl came running with a wooden platter on which were heaped slices of meat steaming sweetly from the tavern ovens, bunches of fruit, and several triangles of cheese. Kothar eyed the food with wolfish eyes.

"Eat, eat," grinned the merchant, pulling back a chair. "Wench, bring more ale for my friend, and a flagon of chilled Thosian."

Kothar put out his hands, filling them with bread and meat, clapping the hot lamb between the slices of barley bread. He ate without thought, relishing only the taste of food to his tongue and the happiness it brought to his belly. He finished off the platter while the merchant eyed him in amusement.

"My name is Menthal Abanon," said the plump mercer as the barbarian used his worn jerkin sleeve to wipe grease from his mouth.

Kothar was in a more pleasant frame of mind. He reached for his refilled tankard and swallowed half the cold ale before he replied.

"So?" he asked. "What's your name to me?"

"I come to offer you employment."

The Cumberian thought about Red Lori. She had promised him he would eat, that she would see to it he would stay alive to be her plaything. Maybe a spell of hers had sent the merchant.

"My sword is always for sale," he growled.

"Excellent. I felt we could do business when I saw you sitting here staring into your mug. I watched your eyes move from the ale to the plates of food the girls were carrying to other tables."

"I was hungry," Kothar admitted.

And now he was full. Thanks to Red Lori? What did it matter who was his host or hostess? The meat and the fruit and the bread lay solid in his belly and he was at peace with his world.

The merchant hitched his elbows onto the table, leaning across its wooden top with confident ease. Greed made his blue eyes shine as he licked his thick lips with a wine-reddened tongue.

"There is a treasure to be had, not far from Azdor," he murmured softly. "No man knows what the treasure is, except that is must be very valuable because it is hidden inside a labyrinth."

A treasure? The Cumberian nodded and swung Frostfire around between his thickly thewed thighs. His poor purse could do with a bit of treasure. Even if he could not enjoy wealth and possess his sword at the same time, maybe with the help of Red Lori, he could scrape together enough gold coins to keep himself in food for a few weeks.

"Jewels," guessed Kothar. "And fine gold coins."

The merchant waved a perfumed hand. "More than that, surely! I myself own black pearls from Isthapan and red rubies from Mongrolia. My strongroom floor creaks under the weight of six chests filled with the golden coinage of Zoradar.

"No, no. Ulnar Themaquol would never have built a labyrinth to hide a treasure unless that treasure were the greatest in the world."

"How did you discover it?"

"Oh, Ulnar Themaquol boasts of his treasure whenever he shows himself outside his maze, and the castle that guards it. He is a great wizard, this Ulnar Themaquol. His necromancies let him look into other worlds than ours, you know.

"I have the feeling that in one of the demon worlds with which he is in cantraipsal contact, he saw a treasure and brought it to the center of the labyrinth, which he constructed especially to contain it and hide it from people like—ah, from thieves."

Kothar grinned, showing strong white teeth. "From thieves like us, you mean. Why not speak out, merchant? Admit the truth. Your soul suffers agonies because you can't own his treasure, as my belly suffered a while back because there was no food in it."

Menthal Abanon seemed to relax. His thick lips widened into a smile. His ringed hand tossed back a flap of his miniker fur pelisse that had slipped from place.

"We'll get along, Kothar. We're men of the world and we know what tail makes it wag, hey?"

His hand went into a velvet almoner fat with silver deniers. A handful of coins he drew out and placed in a heap on the wooden tabletop. "A man needs money to care for such a fine horse as yours, so take this as an indication of my good faith. Such a sum will let you live at ease for a few days, at least, while you consider coming into my service."

The barbarian eyed the coins. "What about the treasure in the labyrinth of Ulnar Themaquol?"

"Do you dare go into that maze?" questioned the merchant eagerly. "I—I must warn you, nobody's ever come out of it. And no man knows what takes place inside its walls, or where the brave men go who risk its intricacies."

Kothar waved a hand. He was a barbarian, he thought little of taking risks when something was worth the danger. Such a treasure as Menthal Abanon spoke of, was worth any hazard.

The fact that he would become a thief if he stole the treasure troubled him not at all. If rich men owned rare treasures, they should protect them. Evidently Ulnar Themaquol protected his wealth with supreme skill, because many men had died in its quest.

"I dare," he rumbled. His big hand half lifted the blued-steel blade of Frostfire from the worn scabbard. "I dare anything, with such a sword."

He saw greed in the eyes of the merchant as he looked at the weapon. His chuckle was cold, deadly, and made Menthal Abanon shiver.

"Feast not those pig eyes of yours on this sword, man," Kothar snarled. "Unless you'd feel the sharpness of its edge on your soft throat. Frostfire was forged to be used by a man—not a fat sapling."

The merchant flapped his perfumed hands in the smoky air, protesting he but admired the weapon. "Besides, I'm more interested in what lies deep in the maze than I am in what hangs from your belt. Come with me. I'll show you where Ulnar Themaquol lives."

The Cumberian quaffed the last of his ale, scooped the silver deniers into his purse, and rose to his feet. He towered above the merchant, as the scarewood tree rises above the lowly breech. His shoulders dwarfed those of the smaller man. Admiring eyes touched his great frame as he strode behind the mercer and between the tables.

Elnora came with a rush of slippered feet to catch his jerkin in a hand. "I saw him give you silver," she whispered. "Stay and learn the softness of my cot."

"Later, later," Kothar grinned, clasping her on the rump. "I'll be hungrier then than I am now."

The two small moons of Yarth were overhead, hurtling across the night sky in their eternal race against the coming day as the tavern door closed behind the two men.

Kothar stared up at them, breathing deep of the chill air. It was fresh outside the tavern, for the wind was moving from the forested slopes of the Ebon Hills, carrying the scent of pine and fir.

Greyling tossed his head, ring-bits jingling, as his master passed a hand across his neck. Unstrapping the reins from the tie-iron on the cobblestoned street, Kothar slid a booted foot into the stirrup and swung into his high-peaked saddle.

Menthal Abanon was stepping into a gilded litter supported by four dusky Lobans from the desert world of Oasia. Slavery was not unknown in the land of Zoradar. Kothar did not hold with slavery, he felt everyone should be his own man, but he believed that a slave should earn his release. No man would keep *him* slave!

Greyling paced along the cobblestoned streets between small houses tilting their timbered bulks outward over the narrow walkways. Behind their windows, candle-flames fluttered and flared. It was near the middling hour of the night and the good burghers of Azdor were readying themselves for bed.

For close to a full hour, the Lobans walked at a steady pace. The town gates were far behind them, the last few candle gleams were flickering out. On either side of the dirt road, tall poplons grew, half obscuring the few stars with their leafy upper branches.

Now the Cumberian could make out a dark bulkiness up ahead, on the left-hand side of the road. Crenellated towers, thin spires, blunt merlons were spaced atop that castle wall like the gaping teeth of some monstrous demon. Here and there in keep and tower, he made out the red flare of a burning torch.

The dwelling of Ulnar Themaquol was built upon solid rock. Spreading outward from that twisted heap of stone was a walled close with a flat roof that gave the appearance of extending inward under the huge stone supporting the small mansion.

"It does not look so dreadful," Kothar grumbled.

The voice of Menthal Abanon answered from behind the brocade drapes of his litter. "No man knows how dreadful is that labyrinth, except Ulnar Themaquol himself. That it is dreadful, the unknown fate of all who have gone through its door, and the dire warnings of the wizard himself, give testimony."

The barbarian hunched his shoulders against the cold night air. The wine and the ale he had drunk were still warm in his belly, but he seemed to see the face of Red Lori floating in the air before him, and his ears heard her laughter as from a great distance.

"I'd best be at it," he muttered, swinging down from Greyling. To the merchant he added, "I'll leave my horse here. If I come not back by dawn—take him to your stables. Keep him for me."

"And if you never come back?"

"He is yours—if you can keep him."

Kothar turned and studied the simple oaken door that was the only barrier to the labyrinth. An iron latch kept it shut. All a man had to do to enter was lift the latch and step through. The Cumberian hitched Frostfire closer to his right hand and moved forward in his panther-like tread.

The latch-iron was cold to his fingers, but it lifted easily. His hand shoved back the wooden door. He stepped forward into a brick-walled chamber, small and windowless, in which a blue lamp burned on the small table which was its only piece of furniture.

Kothar swung about to face the street. Menthal Abanon was holding up a brocade curtain so he could watch his partner vanish into the walled maze. There was a frightened expectancy on the plump face that made the barbarian growl in his throat. Had he delivered himself into some kind of trap?

It was easy enough to step back out of that trap. His big hand held the door open. One pace of his booted feet, and he would be breathing the chill night air instead of the faintly musty odor of this entranceway to the unknown.

"By Dwallka, no man names me coward," he rasped to his thoughts. He slammed shut the door, blotting out the sight of the litter with its fat owner and its four slaves.

Across the brick floor was another door, a door fashioned of rare woods inlaid to form a pattern. Kothar grunted, studying the sigils shaped from teak and ebony. It was an incantation in three dimensions, he realized, but in the words of a dead and forgotten language.

The Cumberian pushed the door open.

CHAPTER 2

He was staring down a long corridor of smooth metal, where the floor was tinted pale blue, the walls a faint ivory, and the ceiling pastel blue. The ceiling glowed, casting out a bluish light and illuminating the entire corridor. He walked forward, ready for the slightest breath of danger, huge hand resting lightly on Frostfire's hilt.

The corridor rounded into a shorter tunnel. This gave way, after twenty feet, into a forking of the walk. Kothar chose the left tunnel and strode along it, impatient for some activity.

A large room opened to his stare.

Eerie laughter filled that room. Was that Red Lori mocking him? Or Ulnar Themaquol? To Dwallka with them both! Laughter was only sound, it could not harm him.

He strode into those torrents of mirth with Frostfire half out of its scabbard. Added to the laughter, the lights began to dim. It grew dark slowly, so that it was not until he was at the far door of the chamber that it became as black as the fabled world of Cereeth.

His hand drew out his sword.

Before his eyes the door shimmered, grew red, then white, then a rich purple. All he could see through that shimmering was a darkness shot with streamers of light. The door melted away in the shimmering, and a cold wind came out and blew about the barbarian.

He discovered now that the wind was wrapping itself about his legs and middle, his chest and arms. It was blowing back into the eerily lighted blackness and it blew him along with it.

This was no ordinary wind; it was a gale out of some demon world, and the barbarian refused to struggle against its tug and so waste his strength. He let the stiff breeze waft him through the shimmer and into a velvet blackness where colored ribbons blew to give his eyes a chance to see the manner of his doom.

Outward from between one red streamer and two pale golden ribbons came a human skeleton, bones clicking, jaws clacking. Its long sepulchral arms reached out for Kothar, touched, tightened as it sought to drag him into its icy embrace. The barbarian saw long, glittering teeth in those parting jaws as the skeleton reached to catch his throat between its fangs.

Kothar roared thickly and brought his massively muscled forearm around, slamming it against that grinning skull. From the neck bones he drove it, through the air in a long arc, so that it hit the wall and shattered. Still the skeleton fought to catch his thickly thewed throat with its claw-like phalanges.

His barbarian instincts—trained on the clean, snow-swept wastes of the northern world—were clamoring for flight. Run from this necromantic abomination! Flee from this feat of dark wizardry!

Yet his brain told him there was no going back. The wind that roamed the doorway into this labyrinthine tunnel would never permit him to return. It was win out over this shibboleth—or perish!

The Cumberian scorned to use his sword. Frostfire was made for better foes than this gibbering ghoul! Instead his hands swept inward, outward, slapping those bones with the impact of twin hammers.

He crushed ribs, he separated hipbone from lumbar vertebrae. In a swirling nausea, he battered femurs and crushed ulnars, with his every muscle bulging.

When the skeleton lay shattered at his feet, Kothar drew a deep breath and moved between the fluttering ribbons of spectral light. Their touch was cold, but they did not harm him; perhaps with the death of the skeleton, he told himself, the streamers had lost their powers.

He moved on down the corridor until he came to a wall dividing it. He moved right, knowing one choice was much the same as another. He had no hope of solving this maze, he must go on and on until—

A man stood at the far end of the passageway, a man clad in armor of a kind Kothar had never seen. Bronze strips girded his chest and middle, a bronze helmet with a red crest towered above his hard face. A short sword hanging at his side and a long, rectangular shield weighting down his left arm told Kothar he was a soldier trained to kill. The man was eying him warily, turning slightly away from another division of the tunnelway.

Kothar grinned, "Friend, if you seek the treasure, choose one path. I'll take the other. No need for us to fight."

The soldier sneered, "I am Honorius, centurion of the Avalonian Ninth Legion. I have never met defeat in battle. The only defeat I've ever known is in this damned trap!" His right hand slammed the metal butt of his swordhilt against the wall so that echoes from the blow ran up and down the covert-way.

His eyes stared at Kothar from under the rim of his helmet. They were mad eyes, the barbarian thought. He would have to kill this soldier of the Legion. He said gruffly, "How long have you been here?"

"A year. Two years. How do you know time in this place?"

"Where did you find food?"

"Nowhere. Something about the place keeps me alive and well. As it will keep you, should you kill me. But you won't." The shield with the lightning-bolt etched in gilded metal on its face came up to confront the barbarian. "Come, then. I'll make it a swift death."

The short sword flickered behind the shield like a tongue about to dart at the Cumberian. The man was a veteran, there was evidence of his skill at weaponplay in his manner of using shield and sword together while he advanced.

Kothar shrugged. Skeleton or man, what was the difference? He must destroy each threat to gain the middle of the maze, where the treasure lay.

Frostfire rang on metal as Kothar flailed at the shield. The man behind the targe grunted and fell back a step in testimony to the strength of that blow. The shortsword stabbed.

Kothar leaped sideways, grinning coldly.

Aie! This would be a duel, down here in this nightmare-haunted labyrinth, between this soldier and himself.

He parried the stabbing sword, drove forward with Frostfire a deadly finger out before him, seeking a weakness in the defense he faced.

Steel rang on steel as the legionary parried.

Slowly they settled into their pattern of attack and parry, parry to riposte and counter-attack. Both men were quick on their feet, each was master of the blade he held. The veteran centurion carried a shield and Kothar did not, but after a time the soldier learned his targe was a weight he must bear, a heaviness that made him sweat with effort, while Kothar was a hunting leopard with only his sword to slow his movements.

Frostfire blazed in the eerie light as the Cumberian swept it sideways and around the shield. Its tip scratched human flesh and the centurion cursed.

Now he held the shield lower, his shield-arm bloodied. His eyes that glared from under his bronze helmet were glittering in mingled rage and madness, but there was no hint of surrender in their black orbs.

"I don't seek your death," Kothar rasped.

"Only one of us can win that treasure," panted the soldier. "I mean to be that man."

The barbarian shrugged his massive shoulders. He had killed all his life, both animals and men, and the centurion was just another foe to him. He would have spared his life—he admired bravery in anyone—but the veteran scorned his mercy.

They circled, swords clashing. Kothar knew the shield was slipping lower, lower, as his opponent lost blood. He could keep him fighting until he became so weak the shield would be no protection, but this was not the way of the barbarian.

He moved forward, his eyes seeking out the weakness in the man before him. He saw feet that shuffled where they had danced, fingers that had loosed their grip on the shortsword. He studied the drops of sweat that beaded the tanned, hard face in front of him.

When the centurion stumbled, Kothar knew he had his man. There was a small puddle of sweat on the floor where the soldier fought. A quick attack, a shift of foot-position on that sweat-slick floor and—Kothar leaped with a savage bellow.

Frostfire circled like blue fire in the air above his head. The legionary gave ground as his targe came up to protect his head. His right heel hit a pool of sweat. He reeled backward, shield rising to help maintain his balance, thus exposing his torso to the full length of Frostfire.

Kothar drove his sword forward.

Impaled by that blue steel while still struggling to stay on his feet, the centurion screamed, muscles going lax. He staggered back, his helmet hit the corridor wall with a metallic clang. Then he slid downward, his legs unable to hold him up.

He lay dying as the barbarian yanked his sword free.

His eyes were sane again. Kothar saw. His lips quivered into a smile. "I—I thank you, man. I have been here—too long—..."

The soldier died, propped against the wall. And as he died, Kothar cried out, for his very flesh was dissolving, fading away before his eyes as if the man were eons old and now his body was freed of the spell which held him prisoner. Gone was the flesh, only the bones remained, with the armor and the sword rapidly rusting.

The Cumberian shuddered.

How long had the legionary been in this place?

Would he himself go on like that, never dying yet dead to the outer world? Rage made a hot tidal wave in his throat. No! By Dwallka of the War Hammer! He would win the center of the labyrinth and put his hands on the treasure it hid.

A thought touched his head. In his boyhood years, he had learned the art of tracking in the forests of the north-lands. He would use that art now, to help and guide him.

Kothar knelt down, studied the floor. A faint dust lay upon the tiles, a dust that showed where the centurion had walked this way along the right-hand tunnel. He himself must go to the left, then. Quite obviously the right-hand tunnel went nowhere near the treasure chamber.

He stepped forward confidently.

For a hundred feet he walked, until he came to a fork in the tunnel. Which way, now? His knowledge of tracking could not work where there were no tracks, no evidence that a man had ever come this way before. Kothar snarled in his throat. If he could not use his tracking prowess, what of his deep-grained barbarian instincts? His homing ability to tell direction, so much a part of any Cumberian who hunted in a vast wilderness where there were no signposts, might aid him here.

He threw back his head, heavy blond hair moving gently as he turned his quivering nostrils to left and right. The middle of a maze is in its geographical center. Where was he now, in relation to that point?

Mentally he retraced his steps. Always since entering this ensorcelled enclosure, he had been veering to his left. Then he should go to his right, which should lead him deeper inside the labyrinth.

He stalked on, eyes turning and suspecting attack at any moment. In this mood, he came to a round chamber with a floor of white sand and for a roof a vast golden dome high above the sandy floor.

Kothar halted. His barbarian soul suspected danger, but he could see no threat. Shifting his wide shoulders, he thrust away his premonitions and stepped out upon the sand.

He went five paces before the storm struck.

CHAPTER 3

Up from the base on which they rested rose the sands in tiny little dustdevils, whipping about the bare, bronzed legs of the Cumberian above his fur-framed war boots. The tiny white grains stabbed like the stingers of ten thousand bees.

No enemy this, against which he could use Frostfire!

Kothar roared his fury, bent his back, and lifted his heavily muscled forearm before his eyes to protect them from the swirling sands. The dust-devils were bigger now, joining together to form larger cones of rotating madness like whitened whirlpools. Into that cyclone, Kothar plunged.

He wanted to scream out his agony. His bare skin, where unprotected by jerkin and boot, felt burned and blistered. However, he was used to the whipping, slashing snows of his northern home, and this sand spray was not so different as to be completely unendurable. He grunted, ground his teeth together, and ploughed on.

Above him the golden dome was becoming red-hot to add an intolerable heat to the savage sandstorm. Kothar drove on and on, a moving mote in a seemingly endless eruption of searing heat and stinging sands. Only his giant body could have endured such punishment. Only a barbarian used to the cruel storms of the northern wastes could have withstood that awesome blast.

Yet stand he did, and his legs churned in the stabbing agony of the biting grains, until—The roaring in his ears died away.

The heat was gone from his head and back. Drenched in sweat, Kothar swayed drunkenly as he realized he stood on the far edge of the sand pit, that his weight, coming off the sand itself, had served to shut off the mechanism that worked it. He let the sweat drip down, breathing heavily.

"Gods of Thuum! I couldn't have taken much more of *that*," he growled. He stared down at himself. Grains of white sand still clung to his fur pelisse and leather jerkin, but to his surprise, his skin showed no effects from the whipping, stabbing sands.

Like a dog shedding water, Kothar shook himself.

The maze corridor yawned before him, invitingly. What other dangers did it hide? What other inventions of a fiendish mind lurked to entrap him? No matter what they were, he must go forward!

Kothar showed his strong white teeth in a mirthless grin. Nothing could tempt him to go back into that sand storm, assuming that he could. He turned his broad back to the hell-pit and strode forward.

Where the tunnel ended, three corridor mouths began. By the process of sheer reasoning, he should go down the middle way. But he mistrusted the magician who had fashioned this maze. It would be like Ulnar Themaquol to make of that middle lane a death trap ending in a blind alley. The right-hand passageway appeared to twist away from the maze center, as did the left.

"Dwalka, guide me," the barbarian muttered.

His hand touched his swordhilt, tightened about it. "Which way, Frostfire? Left or right? Or is it to be the one between?"

He drew the blade, held it out before him. Afgorkon had said there was no magic in the blade, but he had not been sure. It was possible that this length of blued steel had absorbed magic in its past, in the time that Kothar had carried it, as a sponge absorbs water.

As a sponge drips out that water when squeezed, perhaps Frostfire would give him some signal when put in contact with magical forces. Kothar grunted. The only way to find out was by doing.

With the blade before him, he stepped into the left-hand alley. He walked for ten feet, but there was no reaction from the blue steel. Kothar retraced his steps and moved into the center way. There was still no sign from Frostfire.

Glumly, the barbarian decided his plan was nonsense.

And yet, there was one tunnel left to test.

Ten feet inside the right-hand way, Frostfire began to glow. Kothar stared down at his blade, a big grin plastered on his mouth. This then, must be the way into the heart of the labyrinth.

He walked on and on.

Suddenly, he heard a scream, a wail of utter horror and despair. It came from up ahead, and it was the voice of a woman crying out her fright.

Kothar began to run.

He realized with each pounding footfall that he might be racing to his doom. The cry might be a lure to bring him into the clutches of some unimaginable monster against which even his gigantic sinews and his sword might prove no match. Yet he knew also he wanted something at which to strike, some foe against whom he could pit those muscles and his steel.

He wanted no inanimate sand pit. He wanted flesh to bloody, meat to slash. His teeth grated together in the fury of his mood.

Full tilt he ran into the huge chamber that opened before the maze corridor. Like a giant cat, he stopped his forward progress to stare upward into vast shadows, into a blackness cobwebbed with glittering strands of sticky stuff running from one end of the chamber to the other, from the tall ceiling even to the rocky floor.

A woman hung in those strands, fifteen feet above his head. She was screaming, head thrown back so that her long brown hairs were caught and held by the gluey substance, as were her bare arms and legs. She wore what once had been a simple peasant dress, but it was now shredded so that her creamy skin gleamed through its rents.

Above her, moving leisurely across its webs, came a gigantic arthropod. It was no spider, though it was of the arachnid family; it possessed eight legs, a bristle-haired bulbous body, three glaring white eyes, and twin antennae that twitched and quivered as it neared its helpless prey.

The woman was screaming with mindless terror. She had not seen Kothar, but the hesitant advance of the giant arachnid told her something new had come upon this stage that was to be her death trap.

Her mouth closed. Instead of screaming, she sobbed as she ran her stare across the vast chamber. Her brown eyes widened at sight of the giant Kothar.

"Go on, flee from here," she cried. "He won't harm you while I am here to—to eat. But beware the webs—they swoop down like living things at anything that moves."

Her voice rose to a shriek. "Behind you!"

Kothar whirled, sword up, as alert to danger as only a barbarian or an animal can react. Frostfire was above his head, ready to strike as he saw the glittering web sweeping toward him through the air like a sticky net.

The blade swung. Its keen edge bit into the web.

And the web parted.

The woman cried, "The sword should be caught in it; its juices are so sticky and so strong they can hold anything!"

Kothar boomed laughter. The monster on the eight spindly legs appeared to quiver as its web was cut, almost as though a part of its own body were being slashed.

The Cumberian lay about him with his steel, cutting and slitting the web until it hung in thin shreds. From time to time he glanced above him where the arachnid huddled, clinging to the sticky strands and emitting faint squeaks of pain.

"Run," cried the girl, "run! It's too late to save me!"

"By Dwallka! Do you think I'm an ingrate? You warned me of the web—I'll do what I can to save you." He chuckled grimly, his big hand working on the haft of Frostfire. "If the treasure is all it's supposed to be, there's plenty for all of us!"

The creature on the web was running swiftly toward Kothar, now. Its great mandibles clicked madly as though it savored the taste of the meat it was soon to dine on. The barbarian crouched, never taking his eyes off the oncoming monstrosity.

"The web to your left!" the girl screamed.

Kothar snarled, whirling to slash the sticky stuff as it swept toward him. Out of the corner of his eye, he saw the arachnid hasten its pace, huge stinger poised to stab. The Cumberian sensed that once the stinger drove into his flesh, its poison would paralyze him into a complete helplessness.

The arachnid raced closer.

Its stinger rose—stabbed forward!

Kothar dropped flat. His blade darted upward, full into the soft underbelly of the monster. He turned the blade savagely a moment before yanking it free.

One of the creature's legs hit him a glancing blow, sent him rolling over and over along the floor. Webs rushed upon him from above. One strand caught a mighty leg, another his left arm. He was swung upward, stretched as if on a torture rack as the two webs fought for possession of his body.

The Cumberian bellowed out his agony.

He swung five feet above the floor, being pulled apart by those sticky strands. He could feel his arm being twisted from its socket, his leg turned out of his hip. Desperately he swung about, knowing the arachnid was moving sluggishly toward him.

The creature was dying, but it was not yet dead. Its stinger was a slender lance filled with enough poison to render him helpless. He dared not let that lancet break his skin!

Kothar swung his blade. Its tip could just reach the strands that held his leg. Some of the web parted before the steel, but not enough to free him. He hung there, swaying back and forth, wrenched apart as the dying monster dragged itself closer.

The thin stinger lifted.

Kothar gripped Frostfire in his fist. He must time his blow to the precise moment when that lancet stabbed at him. He would have only one opportunity to slash it.

The arachnid towered over him. Its eyes were filled with blood from the gaping wound in its underside, but the stabbing part of it was clean and white. It came downward, blurring with its speed.

Kothar swung his sword.

At the same instant, the web that held his left arm gave a tug, enough to throw his aim off. Frostfire slammed into the stinger with its side, not its biting edge. The fury of his barbarian muscles whipped the lancet to one side, drove it into the sticky webbing.

Kothar could not defend himself, now. He hung parallel to the floor in webs too taut to allow him to swing Frostfire at the arachnid. He swore between teeth clamped tight, and went on struggling. His muscles swelled and throbbed with the savagery of his battle, but it was a losing one.

And yet—The webs were shaking wildly. Could even his giant frame cause such a tossing? Kothar fought on, striving to arch his huge body, to free his leg, his arm. It seemed his leg was slipping just a little, with the gluey web sliding ever so slightly.

The girl cried, "Its stinger is caught! Look!"

The Cumbrian stared to one side of him. Frostfire had hit the stinger, had driven it into the strands that clung to his leg. The arachnid was trying to free itself, was bucking and twisting its huge head as its own sticky mucilage clung voraciously to the lancet.

"It's one part that is not impervious to the webbings," sobbed the girl, spread-eagled on another section of the webbing. "It is caught fast. Now, now free yourself."

But Kothar was already slashing at the webbing that held both his leg and the arachnid's stinger. The sword clove apart the sticky strands that left some of their grey matter on the blade. Panting, calling upon his northland gods, the Cumberian fought the web as he might a living enemy.

He was helped by the desperate arachnid shaking its monstrous head in its own attempts to get loose so it might kill its killer.

Kothar won the struggle. The webs parted, both his feet hit the ground, and now he could turn Frostfire on the strands that gripped his left arm. In a few moments he was free; some dripping strands were still fastened to his flesh, but he could move about; he was no longer a prisoner of the webbings.

He ran for the arachnid.

The blade flashed, dug deep into the thorax.

The arachnid died in convulsions, still caught by its stinger to its own webbings. The barbarian wasted no more time on it, after a hard look to make sure the head was almost severed from its body. He turned and ran for the webbing where the girl hung, legs and arms flung wide.

His sword cut enough of the webbings so her weight dragged the rest of the strands downward where he could reach them. Then she flung herself against him, head bowed, face pressed into his leather jerkin.

Kothar let her sob out her relief, an arm about her soft middle. He could understand and sympathize with her reactions. He himself knew something of this fierce delight at being alive and free.

Free? Well, hardly.

"What are you—a girl—doing in this rat's nest?"

Between tears and laughter, she looked up at him. She was a pretty thing, with smooth white skin the color of ivory, and big brown eyes, with a full mouth ripe for kisses. Her loose brown hair hung down her back and across her forehead, so she had to put her hands up to free her face.

"I am handmaiden to the wizard Pthoomol, who built this maze," she replied. "I helped fashion it, as a matter of fact, while under his spell."

Kothar blinked. "The wizard Pthoomol? But I thought Ulnar Themaquol had made it to house a treasure."

"No, it was not made by Ulnar Themaquol, though it was made for him." Her large brown eyes appealed to him. "You must ask me no more questions. When he condemned me to the maze, Pthoomol removed a little of the sorceries with which he held me subject to his will—but not all. I cannot tell you any more."

She reached out and caught his big hand in her small fingers. "What I can do for you, I shall. I can lead you through the maze to the middle chamber—where the treasure is."

Kothar followed where she led, scowling blackly. "If you knew the maze so well, why were you caught in the webs?"

She laughed delightedly, turning her pretty face over a shoulder to flirt with him. "Because—while I know each turn and twist in the labyrinth—I am as helpless as anyone else in avoiding its dangers. I was halfway into the lair of the webbing beast before I realized I'd taken a wrong turn. The strands caught me."

Her bare shoulders shrugged. "I hung there a long time, watching the creature devour its other victims—before it turned to me. There are not so many searchers in the maze, any longer. Once there were a great many. Now—few come to try their luck and skill."

Brown eyes regarded his huge frame admiringly. "You may succeed where the others have failed. None has come in here as big and as strong as you, nor as brave. It was a courageous thing you did to linger to save me, when you might have gone on. I appreciate what you've done. I'll try and repay you."

She smiled sadly. "We could live here forever, you and I. No one ever dies of old age or of lack of food within these walls. The magic of Pthoomol is very strong. I have prepared a little chamber with furniture, with some simple wines and edibles—for the taste values, not to stay alive—where we could be very happy."

Kothar thought of the outside world, of its dangers and its problems. He was no mole, to bury himself in this underground installation for the rest of his life. He hungered for the wind off the Salt Sea, for the chill blasts that roamed the forest world of Cumberia, for the sight of stars glittering with pale blue fire in the night skies above Grondel fjord.

Slowly he shook his head. "No, it cannot be. I am sorry, but I cannot stay here." His face brightened. "But you can come with me. I'll steal a horse so you can ride with me and Greyling—"

Her soft fingers touched his lips, silencing them. A sad smile distorted her own mouth. "It's impossible. I cannot leave the maze. If I do—I'll die."

They stood close together, brown eyes pleading up at blue eyes. Miramel took one forward step that brought her up against the barbarian. Her bare arms went about his neck and she kissed him hungrily, as if he were the lost love of her life come back to her.

Gently, she drew away. A film of tears blurred her vision so that her hand reached blindly for his hand. Almost angrily, she brushed at her wet cheeks.

"What is to be, must be," she murmured brokenly, and tugged at him. "Come! Stop teasing a poor, lonely girl. You want to find the middle of the maze? I shall show it to you."

He ran with her along the tunnelways. He turned where her hand and whispered word guided him. He caught glimpses of deadly traps in certain sections of the labyrinth, a flashing of razor-sharp swords swinging pendulum-like from a ceiling, a great man all made of metal standing motionless waiting for victims to walk toward its huge axe, a blackness shot with red lights that seemed the more dangerous because of the threat its blackness hid.

Miramel knew the ways to escape these traps.

"Sometimes, Pthoomol would condemn a favorite wench to spend three days in these tunnels before he gave them to Ulnar Themaquol. At the end of the three days, when the poor girl was thoroughly broken in spirit, he would send me in after her, to fetch her out."

"Did Pthoomol put the treasure in the maze?"

Miramel hesitated. "You might say so—in a sense."

"You're damned mysterious!" he grumbled.

"Only because the spell is still on me," she exclaimed, staring upward as if begging him for understanding. "I would tell you all—but I've been forbidden to do so. You'll have to trust me."

They ran for what seemed hours to the big barbarian, before Miramel drew back against a wall and pointed ahead of her. "You go straight ahead," she breathed. "The maze center lies at the end of this passageway, just around the bend."

Kothar looked down at the girl. "This is no trick, is it?" he asked. For a moment as he looked at her, her brown hair changed to flaming red and her features formed into those of Red Lori.

His hand stabbed out, caught her arm. Red Lori was gone, only the frightened face of Miramel remained. Slowly, seeing the pain in her eyes, he let his fingers relax.

As if to make amends for his suspicion, he let his palm rest on her head a moment, stroking her long brown hair. "Wait for me. There will be more than enough treasure for you, believe me. I'm no miser, I'll share it with you."

Her smile was sad. "Neither you nor I can use the treasure hidden in the maze, Kothar. But you must find this out for yourself."

The barbarian stared down at her a long moment. Mystery piled upon mystery! Was anything sane and normal in this cabalistic catacomb? Her face was innocent of guile, but then, she was under an enchantment.

Kothar kissed her cheek, drew Frostfire.

He walked down the tunnel, his great bulk dwarfing its dimensions. The answer to all the mysteries lay before him. In moments, he would know the truth.

CHAPTER 4

His booted feet stilled on the edge of a large, square room. At first he thought the room was empty, for there were no chests of golden coins, no caskets of rare and priceless gems, nothing at all but the floor and the four walls and the high ceiling, and—

It crouched in the corner, sniffling.

Kothar felt the hairs rise up on the nape of his neck. Was this the treasure for which men fought and died inside the labyrinth? Was this hairy man-thing any kind of treasure—even to Ulnar Themaquol? He could not believe it.

The thing lay in a ball of reddish fur in a far corner of the room. It sniffled and gurgled, it bleated. Of all the traps through which he had passed, this one—if it were a trap, that is, in a kind of cosmic joke—seemed least dangerous.

Disbelieving what his eyes told him, he scanned the room again. Still he saw no chests, no piles of jewels or bars of gold, no suggestion of wizard-hidden wealth, only the reddish creature mumbling to itself. Kothar rasped soft curses as he moved across the room with his lion-like tread.

Suddenly, as if aware of Kothar for the first time, the ball of reddish fur uncoiled itself. A horned head rose up, the body straightened, two hairy legs bent, and one thing stood up.

"By Dwallka!" the Cumberian breathed, awe-struck.

The man-body was covered by reddish hair, it was even larger and fully as muscular as himself, with the head of a bull tipped by wide, flaring white horns. The bull-eyes were red, mean. The muscles of chest and arms and legs—

Kothar grunted. The legs were the legs of an animal, ending in split hooves. He could see them fully, now that the monster was no longer huddled in a ball. His hand lifted Frostfire, held the blade at the ready as the bull-man lowered its horned head. Out from behind its hips lashed a thin, hairless tail.

The bull-man bellowed.

Sound was an ache in his ears from that thunderous roar. Kothar supposed it was meant to frighten him, to freeze him motionless for the few seconds the bull-man needed to reach him. Because as that cry left its throbbing throat, the being charged, head down and horns poised to gore.

Kothar swung his sword.

The beast-man lifted a huge hand, closed a leathery palm about the blade and tore it from Kothar's grip. The blued steel flew across the room, clanged against a wall. Kothar snarled, felt something touch his thigh.

Too late, he moved. The sharp horn about to dig itself into the thick sinews of his mighty thigh only grazed him, scratching a bloody furrow in its wake. Kothar was leaping sideways, his fist balled into a fleshy sledgehammer.

And striking!

His knuckles knew the thud of contact, his eyes saw the bull-head whipped sideways and away from him. Kothar sought to follow up that first blow with a second, but the bull-thing turned on its hooves and lashed out with a fist.

Kothar saw the fist, and ducked. He did not see the tail that wrapped itself about his ankles and tugged. The barbarian went backward, silent even in his surprise. No need to waste breath on a cry, he had no ally in this maze, it was his own strong body and great rolling muscles pitted against the human bull. And he needed all the air his lungs would hold.

Catlike, he turned in midair, landing on the balls of his booted feet. The bull-man was charging, head down and hooves beating out a tattoo on the floor. Kothar crouched, hands outward.

He slid sideways out of the horn-path, fingers reaching to grip the furry hips of the beast. Upward he surged, lifting the creature off its hooves. With a grunt of straining muscles, the Cumberian raised him high above his head and flung him. An instant before his body left his hands, Kothar felt the slither of that hairless tail across his middle.

This time, the tail had no time to tighten. It flailed the air as the furry creature flew through it, upside down. The bull-man hit the wall and slid down it, momentarily dazed.

Kothar leaped, leaving his booted feet and diving a yard above the floor. His hand shot out, closed on Frostfire as his bending legs took the shock of his landing. Blade naked in a fist, he turned snarling toward the slowly recovering beast-man.

"Let's see you tear my sword away this time, you necromantic nightmare!" he roared.

Bull-man and giant barbarian came for each other. Forgotten was the treasure and the fact that Miramel knelt on the very edge of the chamber, staring at this battle of Titans, gnawing on her knuckles. For the barbarian, all that existed was this fearsome foe as strong as he was himself.

Frostfire made a blue blur in the air as Kothar swung it.

The bull-man shrieked as he dodged. For while he avoided that slashing sweep of steel with his head, his tail was not so dexterous. The keen edge severed it, it fell to twist and writhe about on the floor.

Before Kothar could recover his balance from the blow that was meant to decapitate the monster, the furry creature leaped. Its fists thudded together into the northern giant's thick chest. As Kothar staggered, the beast-man hit his sword arm with a horn.

The ivory did not cut the flesh, but it numbed the great bicep muscle. The blade fell from his paralyzed fingers, clattering on the floor. Kothar shook himself, seeing the man-bull coming for him with his head sideways, one horn curved to gore.

Kothar leaped, but not before the horn drove deep into his thigh. Blood spurted as flesh ripped. Pain lanced from his torn thigh into his groin. He bellowed as if he were a bull himself. His great hands locked together and drove downward into the red-furred bullneck at his thigh-level.

His balled hands felt bone and flesh crack beneath the blow. The bull-man staggered, flailed the air with its arms, and went to its knees.

The broad back was before him, invitingly. Kothar fell upon it, locking his legs about the monster's chest. His hands fell to those twin horns even as the monster came to its hooved feet.

The beast lifted its head, sending out its trumpeting challenge while Kothar tightened his great fingers around its horns. The bull-thing raced on pounding hooves for the nearest wall, intending to scrape the barbarian off so it could horn him a second time.

Through a red haze of pain, the Cumberian twisted the horns until his arms quivered and his muscles leaped in massive bulges. Slowly, slowly, that great head was turning. Unable to stop its gallop, the monster thudded into the wall, ramming it with its own shoulder and its rider's one good leg.

Teeth grated as Kothar exerted his gigantic strength against the brute force of the bull-man, gnashing his molars together as if the sound would add to his power. The head was halfway around, now; the monster glared over its shoulder as it stumbled about the room on weakening legs.

On the rim of the chamber, Miramel stared with disbelieving eyes. No man could kill red-furred Minokar! The wizard Pthoomol himself had created the bull-man out of—"Aiieeee!" she screamed.

The horned head with its open, slavering jaws and rolling, agonized eyes from which blood slowly dripped, was facing Kothar now. The barbarian was shivering in the strain of his awesome task. A single inch more, and his foe would die. *Craaaaack!*

The neck snapped, the bull-man fell.

Kothar leaped free, half falling as pain lanced up his torn thigh when his full weight came down on his left foot. He was wet with sweat, his lungs were bellows breathing in air. His golden hair had come loose of its fastening and hung to his shoulders. He was primordial man, standing above the beast which would have slain him.

For long minutes he sobbed in near exhaustion, but with the recuperative powers of a wild thing, he felt his strength slowly seeping back into his aching body. The pain in his ripped thigh was frightful, but he was used to enduring pain.

He bent and was about to tear a strip of cloth from his kilt when a voice said, "There is no need for that, Kothar. I will cure you in return for what you have done for me."

A tall man stood in an open section of the wall, clad in purple vestments heavily braided with gold symbols. A carefully trimmed spade beard showed below a saturnine face, handsome despite the wickedly glowing eyes and the triumphant smile on thin, curving lips.

The Cumberian straightened, every sense alert. His eyes touched fallen Frostfire on the other side of the room. The man laughed softly.

"There is no need for bared steel between us," he murmured, and throwing back a flap of his cape, he disclosed a number of purple bags hanging from a chain of golden links about his middle.

His slender white hand went into a bag, lifted out a pinch of yellow powder. His fingers tossed it through the air at the barbarian.

"Let powder heal, let flesh be weal," he murmured.

There was no more pain. Wonderingly, Kothar stared down at his left thigh, at the blood gouting from his wound. Before his eyes, that wound was closing over, the blood was drying, flaking, turning into brownish powder that was slowly falling from his body. In a moment, there was no mark to show that he had ever known the bite of the ivory horn.

The man said, "Look you, Kothar."

The delicate hand gestured at the corpse of Minokar.

Kothar swallowed hard. The red fur was fading, the very shape of the bull-thing was changing! The horns were gone, the bull snout was receding, the legs were reforming themselves. Where hooves had been, were now pale white feet.

"Gods," the barbarian breathed.

"Not gods," demurred the tall man in the purple robes. "Just magical enchantments losing their powers."

Kothar sidled past the dead body which was becoming something else. Frostfire lay there at the base of the wall. His palm itched to hold that sword against this living nightmare. He bent and picked it up, held it in his hand, aware that the man was smiling at him.

"If the sword contents you, then hold it," the man said softly. "I am too happy to deny any other man his own kind of pleasure. As you may have guessed—I am Ulnar Themaquol. Yes, yes—the necromancer supposed to have built this magic maze in which to hide a treasure. Well, the labyrinth holds a treasure, true enough—the one thing dearest to me in all the universes known to my wizardries."

The bull man was gone.

A naked girl lay on the cold tiles, pink of skin with long black hair forming a glossy waterfall down her back. She was moaning, stirring, her fingers quivering with returning life.

The mage dropped to a knee, lifting off his cabal-sigiled cloak and spreading it about her nudity. There was a tenderness in his action that made Kothar wonder. As if he sensed those thoughts, Ulnar Themaquol lifted his handsome head.

"She is my beloved, barbarian, the Lady Rosannia. Long ago, the sorcerer Pthoomol and I quarreled. When he sought to cast his spells upon my person, I broke them with my necromantic wisdom. To protect myself and mine—and my Rosannia, here—from Pthoomol, I cast a conjuration from runestones taken from the ocean bed of the great Salt Sea, out of the ruins of a dead magician's castle.

"Pthoomol died from those conjurations—but before he did, he dealt me a blow that came near to killing me with grief and loneliness.

"This labyrinth which Pthoomol had used to protect his gold and jewels, he now used—to hide my beloved. Her fair body he changed into that of a Minokar, a furred bull-beast that tried to slay every living thing it saw. On girl and maze he laid a spell I have never been able to overcome.

"That spell required a man to enter the maze, to find his way to this inner chamber—and slay the Minokar. Until now, no man has ever been able to do that. Only one man before you ever penetrated to this hidden heart of the maze. Him the Minokar slew."

"Ulnar," said the girl, widening her eyes.

He kissed her soft hands, then helped her to her feet, his arm holding the cloak about her body. She lifted a hand, put back her ebony hair, stared at Kothar with a happy smile.

"You slew me, you freed me. My eternal thanks," she whispered.

Ulnar Themaquol chuckled. "I am afraid, my darling, your eternal thanks are not enough. Our barbaric friend appreciates gold and jewels more than he does the babbled murmurings of a girl, no matter how beautiful."

The wizard gestured. Kothar stared as a small casket came floating through the hidden doorway out of which the mage himself had stepped.

"The casket and the jewels in it are real, not formed by the necromantic arts, barbarian. You can spend them in any tavern from here to tropical Oasia. Take it."

The Cumberian sheathed his sword, caught the casket. It felt reassuringly heavy, but Kothar took the hinged lid in a big hand and raised it. His eyes widened at sight of the green and red and white gems that filled the coffer to overflowing. Gods! Such a fortune could make him a baron in the lands where the robber lords reigned.

He said slowly, "You are a great wizard, Ulnar Themaquol. There is a spell on my sword, Frostfire. I will give back the jewels in exchange for a counter-spell to remove it."

Ulnar Themaquol smiled happily. "I shall be glad to remove it. And keep the gems. Just tell me the name of the mage who placed it there, and let me touch the blade."

He removed his arm from about the Lady Rosannia and stretched both palms out toward the hilt, even as Kothar rumbled, "It was the lich of Afgorkon who put the spell on it. He—"

Kothar halted as the magician drew back, a look of utter horror on his face. "Afgorkon? Afgorkon? Speak not his name, man—he is the greatest necromancer Yarth has ever known! None but he can remove his curse. All but he would be blasted into the seven hells of Eboron were he to attempt it!"

The magician paused, breathing hard. He licked his lips, his eyes sliding about the room. "It may be that I have incurred his anger by giving you that casket. But no—I would sense his rage if he were angry. His spell will prevent you from keeping those jewels, barbarian. How it will come about, I do not know. But you will never keep that fortune."

Kothar sighed. He put his big hand on Frostfire. Sword or jewels, for him there was no choice. Somewhere, somehow, he might lift the enchantment on the blade. Until then, he would rather have the sword.

"Here, take it," he growled, holding out the coffer.

"Not I," murmured Ulnar Themaquol, shaking his head, putting his arm about the waist of the woman he loved. "I leave it to you, it may be the will of Afgorkon that you keep it—for a little while. In any event, his spell will prevent you from holding it very long."

The sorcerer and the Lady Rosannia turned toward the section of the wall through which he had stepped. An instant later, they were gone. The wall smoothed over, and Kothar stood alone.

"Pssst—Kothar!"

Miramel stood in the doorway on the other side of the room, gesturing at him. Her fear of the maze-heart was written on her pretty features, and her stare went from wall to ceiling to floor as if expecting more dread visitants to appear.

The barbarian walked toward her, the coffer clamped under a muscular arm. "You shall take half the treasure," he grinned. "I can't keep it, and it irks me to see Menthal Abanon get it all."

"No, no—what need have I of jewels in such a place?" her hand indicated the labyrinth all about her. Her smile was wistful. "If I could, I would wish for a man—or even a number of men—to keep me company in here through the ages until the labyrinth becomes as dust." She sighed. "It is very lonely for a girl without a man."

The Cumberian grinned, "I'll do what I can. Right now, all I want is to shake this maze dust from my boots."

Her warm little hand caught his fingers. "Come, I will show you the way. The sooner you step into the outer world, the sooner you can send a man in here to me."

Her bare feet seemed to race along the maze corridors. Her long brown hair floated behind her on the wind. Within seconds, it seemed to the bemused barbarian, he was once more at the gateway to the outer world.

"Farewell," Miramel whispered, and flung her arms about him. Her lips, as she kissed him, were soft and sweet.

Then her palm pushed him into the darkness of early morning. He could see Greyling at a little distance, cropping grass. The stars were lower in the sky, and to the west, a faint tint of crimson was coating the distant spires and rooftops of Azdor town.

"Remember—bring me a man," Miramel called.

Then he was alone. Kothar gathered up the reins, raised his huge body to the high-peaked saddle. A touch of his toes at the ribs sent Greyling into a canter. Kothar let the cool morning wind brush against his cheeks, as if it might wipe away the last trace of the magic with which he had come in contact this night.

Elnora was waiting at the tavern door when he reined in the grey warhorse. She saw the coffer and her eyes went wide. She whirled and called, "He's back, he's back—and he has one of the treasure chests with him."

There was a rush from inside the tavern, led by the merchant, Menthal Abanon. With him were three burly men in armor and leather, but without their helmets. Kothar wondered if they were to stand bodyguard for the plump man, if they had been hired to kill Kothar so Menthal Abanon might have all the treasure for himself.

In a moment they were about him like hounds yapping at a great stag. Kothar boomed out his laughter, hooked Elnora with an arm at her soft middle, and walked with her through the wooden doorway. A few torches still glowed, lighting the wooden tables and chairs, the sleepy ostler behind the scot counter, the walls hung with rare furs from Mongrolia and the Haunted Lands.

Kothar plunked the coffer down on a table, bellowed for cold ale in a leathern jack. Elorna he pulled onto his knee, and with the greedy faces of Menthal Abanon and his three guards staring, he threw back the lid.

Green fire, red fire, white fire! Flames trapped inside great jewels the least of which was worth a small kingdom. There was a hushed, awed silence in which the sobbing breath of the plump man could be heard.

"If this is just a part of the treasure," the merchant panted, "What must the rest be like? I shall be richer than fabled King Midor of Sybaros!"

"This is all of it," Kothar said, reaching for his tankard.

"All?" gasped Menthal Abanon, eyes bulging. "But—"

Kothar told them the story between gulps of midlands ale and kisses from the wine-sweet lips of Elorna. He was vaguely aware that glances passed between Menthal Abanon and his three warriors, but he was too preoccupied to pay them any heed. It was enough for his barbaric body to be here with a woman on his lap and chilled ale for his lips.

When he was done, Menthal Abanon murmured, "So then! There was no treasure—just a bull-beast that changed into a pretty girl. What a story!"

Kothar found himself surprised at the passive acceptance of his tale by Menthal Abanon. He had expected the merchant to call him a liar. He watched carefully as the plump man lifted a massive diamond and held it to the torchlight flaring on the wall.

"A perfect gem. Absolutely flawless! It is worth ten thousand times ten deniers." His soft voice was almost hypnotic as he stretched out pudgy fingers toward a great emerald. "And this gem—priceless! Never have I seen its like. These two alone would make what you have done profitable."

"We share and share alike," growled Kothar.

"Of course, of course," nodded the merchant agreeably.

A hand set a refilled jack before the barbarian. He reached for it without taking his eyes from the mercer, raised it to his lips, quaffed half the ale in one long gulp. He set the tankard down.

"Now to divide our prize," he grunted. He put his hand on a ruby, lifting it from the pile of jewels within the casket. As he did so, a lethargy came upon him, his head nodded and the red gem slipped from his grasp.

"I must be more exhausted than I thought," he muttered. His head felt so heavy, he laid it on the tabletop, half in and half out of a puddle of spilled wine.

In a moment, he was asleep.

Menthal Abanon got to his feet, breathing a relieved sigh. "He will be like that for hours. Elorna, you stay with him. Tavern keeper! Shut and bolt your doors after we depart. Fail me not! Let the barbarian sleep off the drug we placed in his ale tankard. I have no stomach to taste that sword of his! When he wakes, tell him I have gone into the maze. I'll check his story of no treasure for myself."

The merchant counted out two diamonds and slid them across the tabletop at Elorna, who snatched them up and fitted them in a small velvet purse that hung between her breasts on a bronze chain.

One emerald each, Menthal Abanon gave his guards. Then he caught up the coffer and holding it against his side, walked from the tavern toward his litter.

Kothar slept on, dreaming of his boyhood and of the small boat in which he had sailed the near reaches of the Salt Sea where it beat against the rocky walls of Grondel fjord. He woke to the taste of its spray on his lips, and found his yellow head wet with a dousing of water from the hand of the ostler.

"It's near my time to open, barbarian," the tavern keeper complained. "You've slept the time-candle around. Best be off with you."

The Cumberian was instantly awake and in full possession of his every faculty, like an animal. His big hand darted out, caught the thonged shirt of the ostler.

"Where are they? The others? Menthal Abanon and his guards? The girl, Elorna?"

"Elorna has left town," squeaked the terrified tavern keeper, shivering. "She says her two jewels will let her live like a great lady in Clonmall to the east."

Kothar growled, "And the merchant? His guards?"

"They went to the maze of Ulnar Themaquol."

The barbarian brooded. He would go back into the maze, he would search out and kill Menthal Abanon despite his three soldiers, and retake the coffer of jewels. It was his courage, his muscles, that had won them. The merchant had forfeited his claim to the casket by his treachery.

With a heavy hand, he thrust the ostler out of his way. Rage was a wildness inside his huge body, rage cleared his mind and flesh of the last dregs of the drug he had taken in the ale. On thickly thewed legs he walked from the tavern to his grey warhorse.

The iron hooves of Greyling pounded a tattoo on the cobbled streets of the little hamlet as Kothar galloped between the houses leaning over the narrow road. The smell of cooking meats was in the air, the sun was lowering to westward. It was late afternoon; soon, it would be dusk.

Before the sun dipped from sight, Kothar was reining in the big grey horse, staring. "By Dwallka! What happened to it?"

The castle and the great, walled maze were mere shards of blackened stone and marble, as if blasted by Time itself. The walls were jagged, black teeth thrusting up against a darkening sky. Where the labyrinthine traps had been, little flowers blew in the evening winds.

An old man was seated on a stone to one side of the road, munching on a loaf of bread and a wedge of cheese. He looked up at the muscular young giant, his rheumy eyes blinking.

"The maze be gone," the old man mumbled, nodding his head. "Of a sudden it were there, and next it were gone. Nothing remains but what you see. Seen it with my own eyes. Seen it disappear like water in dry sand."

"Magic," Kothar muttered.

"Aye. Magic. It had served its purpose, the treasure that was in the maze be no longer there, and the spell upon it be lifted."

Kothar thought a moment, nodding. "Saw you anything of four men, one a fat mercer, the others all warriors?"

"I did. Went into the maze a little after daybreak, carrying some kind of small chest. They'm were talkin' of the rest of the treasure them might find. Fools, all on 'em. The treasure be no more."

Vanished also was his casket of jewels, Kothar told himself. Ah, well. He had known it would happen, one way or another. He sighed and stared at the bread and cheese the old man was eating.

The ancient one held up his loaf and wedge of cheese. "Care you to dine wi' me? I have plenty more in my knapsack, and my appetite be nothing like it were, years back."

"My thanks, old one, I'll gladly share your meal."

The barbarian swung down from his saddle, thinking of Miramel inside the maze. Did she have her men to keep her happy now? Did the labyrinth exist in some different time zone? Were Menthal Abanon and his men trapped forever in its corridors? He would never learn the answers to his thoughts, he decided, but he did not care.

It was enough for him that he could feed his belly with barley bread and goat's milk cheese. There was always a distant horizon to ride over in his eternal search to escape Red Lori's hate and to learn a way to amass some gold for his flattened purse.

THE WOMAN IN THE WITCH-WOOD

CHAPTER 1

The stone tower was dark and gaunt in the rays of the setting sun. Through the gaps which had been arrow slits long ago, red fire seemed to dance as if it were a living thing behind the dark, forbidding stones. Kothar the barbarian reined in his grey warhorse and sat a moment, staring. There was an evil aura about the stone tower that seemed almost tangible.

Uneasiness touched him between his wide mailed shoulders so that he reached to shift Frostfire at his side, bringing it closer to his hand. The countryside around him was unfamiliar. He had chosen a wrong turn in the road on his way to the land of the robber barons, where he hoped to find employment under the banner of one lord-baron or another, but the day had been so filled with sunlight and the air with the scents of grapes on their vines that he had let the grey wander as it would.

Now the sun was dying in the west, and he did not like the look of the forest about him. Its underbrush seemed to stir as if alive, twigs appeared to writhe and ripple in some fey manner, and where the topmost branches swept the sky, an alien darkness lurked.

Kothar reached into his leather pouch for one of the parchment maps he carried on his travels. From Azdor, he had ridden Greyling across the flatlands of Zoradar, through the hill pass at Maalbek, and down the gorge of an old riverbed intending to come into the lands of the robber barons. A lucky toss with the dice in some border tavern, and an occasional deed for a man or woman willing to pay for his skill in weaponry, had put food in him and in his warhorse.

Sometimes he saw the face of Red Lori in his lonely campfires, sometimes he even dreamed of her, wrapped in his saddle blanket against the chill winds of some hilly slope or out of a forest glade. Yet her memory was slowly fading; she was becoming nothing but a pretty face as his great horse carried him eastward.

In one castle or another of those feudal overlords, he hoped to find employment for his blade. They were always warring, those barons, one with another, or perhaps with some small kingdom nearby, or even when they staged raids on the caravans making their way from city marketplaces to the unknown regions east of the Sisyphean Hills. They could use a man skilled in weaponplay and in the command of warriors.

His fingers spread out the map, studying its marks and sigils with furrowed brows. Odd! This forest where he rode was not delineated here. There was only a vast grey nothingness where this rutted road should have been a thin ink line, and as for the tower—why, surely old Gwalith in the marketplace stall in Exekonn where he scratched maps for any land in all the world should have known about it!

Wryly his lip twisted in a grin as he folded the parchment and slipped it back into his almoner. There would be poor forage in these woods. Sticks for a fire, maybe. Yet no food worthy of the name.

"Well, we've had lean bellies before," he told the horse. His mailed toe nudged the big grey to a walk. Perhaps with luck he would come upon a charcoal burner's hut where one of his five silver deniers might buy a loaf of bread and a wedge of cheese.

As he rode, swaying gracefully in the saddle, his eyes turned at their corners every so often to study the dark stone tower. The redness in it was not unlike some queer hobgoblin dancing widdershins about a demon flame. Surely the redness was not the result of the setting sun sinking beyond its merlons. The redness moved and leaped and danced. It seemed almost to call out to him.

Ah, and then—

The voice was sweet as the silver bells of Clonmall, pealing out above the jagged rocks where the sea lapped in eternal rhythms. It sang a song the barbarian had never heard, yet there was a response to those words in his flesh and in his bones. His breath hushed in his throat, and he tightened the reins to slow the hooves of the war-horse. With the small of his back against the high cantle of his saddle he sat like a man bemused.

As the Sirens might have sung to Ulysses, or the maidens of the Rhine, the Lorelei, to weary travelers, so that voice called out to the Cumberian. When it was done, he roused himself with an effort. His eyelids were heavy and sleep was a soft warmth wrapping his tired muscles in its clasp.

He drew his sword half out of the scabbard and clanged it back inside. The metallic echoes stirred his blood to wakefulness. The great grey horse shook its head, making its white mane fly.

"Ho, Greyling! Now I know why old Gwalith knew nothing of this place. It's haunted by ghouls and goblins."

He was about to urge the warhorse into a canter when a different kind of enchantment caught him in its spell. He paused, sniffing the air. Surely that was the smell of roasting hare, slow-turned over a bed of coals. Hare and newly baked bread, yes. His empty belly sang its own song to his senses.

Kothar grinned and rubbed a palm over his thick yellow hair. What a siren voice might not do, a food scent might. Aie, a weak thing was a man with an empty stomach. It would do no harm to walk the horse toward the tower, to see for himself whether a hare roasted on a spit.

Some poacher or outlaw, mayhap, was crouched over that fire. The barbarian feared no man alive. His sword Frostfire had taken him in and out of dangerous places in the past. It would do so again if there was danger in the stone pile.

"Come, Greyling. There may be oats or at the least, a little hay for the munching. Lift your hoofs and be careful where you step."

As if the beast understood him, it tossed its head to make the ringbits jingle and moved daintily between the berrybushes and the hazel growths. Kothar sat straighter in the high-peaked saddle, standing at times in the stirrups to help his keen eyes search out the ruin.

It was then that he saw the woman.

She was bent above the flames, clad all in black that clung to her supple figure and revealed her hips and the high mounds of her breasts. She did not look at him, all her attention was on the hares she was turning above the fire with the end of a forked stick. She had long white hair that fell down her back and merged with the color of her simple gown, like flecks of seaspray across dark shore rocks.

Kothar let the warhorse walk to the edge of the stonework where once had been a wall, and waited, shifting restlessly in the saddle. Twice he almost came down out of the kak but something restrained him.

At last he said, "Mother, I ask your pardon."

The woman turned her face and now the Cumberian saw that she was young and fair and that her hair was not white but so pale a yellow it was almost platinum. Her eyes were purple, slanted and with long silvery lashes. Her face was white, her lips the color of new blood.

"Mother?" she wondered, and laughed.

Her wise eyes assessed his giant frame with eager interest. She saw his deep chest framed in a thonged leather jerkin and mail shirt, his hugely muscled, sun-bronzed arms bare below the short sleeves of his loose bliaut. A fur pelisse framed yard-wide shoulders, held by a silver clasp below his throat. A magnificent sword hung in a worn scabbard at his left side, a dagger to the right of his broad leather belt. His thighs were naked between the edge of his homespun kilt and his war-boots trimmed in miniker fur.

Her eyes told him she found him attractive as a man to her womanhood. Her breasts rose a moment as she sighed, and he read her honest opinion of him deep in her slanted purple eyes.

Kothar flushed, for he was young and the woman very beautiful. He looked at the hares on the spit, at the black stones of the tower, at the sky that was now dark with a few stars shining in it. Very gently he lifted out of the saddle and put his feet upon the ground.

"I would buy a hare from you, and a little of the bread I see baking on the flat stones," he growled. He took two silver pieces from his almoner and held them out.

She rose to her feet. She was neither tall nor short, but the top of her pale hair came to his heart and her body was slimly rounded. A golden chain belted her waist and from the hem of her black gown, little slippers peeped.

"I have no need of silver. You are welcome to the hare—in return for a favor."

"And what favor would that be?"

"You must listen to a story."

Kothar grinned and nodded. Her eyes were brilliant; little devil flames danced deep inside them, but they did not frighten him. No woman ever born could frighten Kothar of Cumbria. And if she were in trouble, if she needed his sword to set matters right for her, then perhaps his service with the robber barons could wait a day or two, or even three.

She sensed his agreement and clapped her hands, then waved him to a flat stone. Without glancing at him again, she drew off the hares and placed them on wooden platters with bread and a little cheese and a handful of berries for their sweetening. She moved gracefully and lightly on her feet, like a forest dryad, and when she brought her own platter she sat beside him so closely that the warmth of a soft shoulder pressed his arm.

They ate, sometimes staring at the flames, sometimes at one another. Kothar would have lost himself in her purple eyes, sensing no evil in them, but she only smiled and shook her head and made him understand that all she thought of was the telling of her tale.

When the platters were clean, when she had brought a skin of properly chilled wine from the old well and filled two leather jacks with the rich liquor, she looked at him. Her pale hands clasped a goblet until her knuckles showed whitely as she began to speak.

"My name is Alaine. Once this tower was mine and all the land around it, as far as the towns of Murrd and Kolaine, for I was the lady of Shallone, a countess in my own right. Until a time when a lord stronger than I came to Shallone and drove me from my inheritance."

A twig crackled with blue flame as the fire ate into it. The woman called Alaine turned her head to stare at it. "He used weaponplay and witchcraft to dethrone me. His soldiers slew my guards and with the incantations of which he is a master, he imprisoned me here in these woods."

The barbarian rumbled, "There are no bars around the wood. I came riding its roads only this afternoon. I saw no iron nor even a wooden fence."

Her smile was gentle. "The fence is a magic one. Were I to cross the barrier my Lord Gorfroi has drawn, I would be destroyed as the flame of a candle is destroyed when someone blows it out."

Kothar nodded. He had come in contact with wizards and witches. Few men made war from Makkadania in the north to Mantaigne in the south without paying for the sorcery that would insure a victory.

"So I remain in this ruin day and night," went on the woman, "with a little food to last me and a few string traps in the underbrush to catch the harcs that feed me with their meat. Sometimes a woman comes who knew me in the old days and brings me flour or a bit of mutton. I live. No more."

She looked at the barbarian who shifted uncomfortably beneath that purple stare. "I would help you, if I could. But I'm only one man."

Alaine smiled. "My lord Gorfroi has discharged his warriors and his captains, since he no longer needs them, having other—helpers. He lives alone in the castle which once was mine. A brave man might enter that castle and kill him and—bring to me my lock of hair which Gorfroi took from me."

"A lock of your hair?"

Alaine smiled and placed pale hands to her thick white hair, lifting up its heaviness so that it seemed a helmet above her lovely face. She smiled on the Cumberian with her slanted purple eyes as she shifted that hair about, giving herself a less regal, an almost wanton look. He thought her lips were very red where she touched them with her tongue, like blood.

"He took a single strand of my hair and placed it in a golden casket marked with the sigil of Belthamquar, who as you know is king of the daemons. Until that hair is destroyed, I am his prisoner in this witch wood."

Kothar drew a deep breath.

The Lady Alaine moved closer to him, touching his arm with her soft fingers. She was perfumed—where in these woods did she acquire those scents of Araby?—and very seductive. The young barbarian leaned closer, as if to touch her lips with his own. She breathed upon his mouth as her hand tightened on his arm.

Kothar was helpless to resist the magic of the fair shoulders her black gown revealed, the curving red lips, the firmly rounded body beneath the thin cotehardie which was her garment.

His tongue stumbled in its speech.

"He keeps no men-at-arms, you say? And lives alone in your castle? These helpers! What are they?"

"Daemons," she said simply, shrugging.

Alaine reached out to touch the hilt of his sword. "If my touch could give your blade the strength to slay those familiars, I would. Yet I know no magic, except that which calls from a woman to a handsome man."

Her eyes slid sideways at him, promising him love if he should be her champion. "Love can do much, Kothar of Cumberia." It did not puzzle him that she knew his name, so lost was he in her beauty.

He sighed, "I travel to seek service with the baron lords, but I travel the road to Murrd. In Murrd I'll ask the way to the castle of Shallone."

She stood up and moved back and forth before the flames. "I would not send you to your death. I asked you to listen, not—to act. I would not be the death of any man."

She was no witchwoman, yet she wove a magical spell about his senses, blended of the sight of her slim ankles under the swaying gown and of the roundness of her hips and the silvery laughter that came from her soft lips. She clasped her hands and flirted with him over them, eyes brightly gleeful.

"And yet—and yet, were you to win past Gorfroi and take back my lock of hair, I would be the lady of Shallone again. Then I would need a strong man to be my lord, a man—such as yourself."

She spread her pale hands. "I can offer no gold or silver, nor anything but my love. And my promise that if you free me, you shall win my hand."

Alaine pointed at him, frowning prettily. "But no unnecessary risks, do you understand? If Gorfroi or his daemons are too deadly, let them be and ride away to forget me."

It would not be easy to forget such a woman. The Cumberian was quite sure he could not do it. And besides, the coins in his purse were few. His sword had been a long time without employment. He owned enough for a meal and a night's lodging at an inn, and not much else.

She came three steps nearer, then four, and reached out her soft mouth for his kissing. He held her and his brain was bemused by the joy of their caress. After a moment she drew away and walked into the shadows.

"I sleep here, barbarian. You shall slumber there, on the flat rock with your cloak beneath you and your saddle for a pillow. In the morning, I shall cook again for you."

She danced deeper into the darkness of what seemed to have been the entrance to a crypt at one time long ago. The Cumberian stood watching her until the weariness came through his pleasure and into his muscles. He sighed. First he must rub down the warhorse, and see that it was fed a little of the hay he could see beyond the woodpile.

After that, he would sleep.

Aie, and perhaps dream of the Lady of Shallone.

And as he slept he did indeed dream of the Lady Alaine. She came out of the vault where she slept and walked with gracefully flowing strides to his great long-sword in its worn, blow-dented scabbard. Around its hilt she put her hands and drew it forth. When Kothar would have protested—no hands touched Frostfire other than his own—his muscles were frozen and his tongue clove to the roof of his mouth.

He watched her fingernail scrape blue fire along the shining length of the blade and write with rune-like, mystic characters there upon the steel. As she did this, she chanted oddly in an unknown tongue.

As he watched in his dream, the black dress and white hair of the Lady Alaine blurred, to be replaced by the shape and face of Red Lori. Yes, it was the sorceress scratching fiery letters along the length of Frostfire, Red Lori who sang that weird song.

Did she want to keep him safe for her own vengeance? In her mind, she considered him her property, hers to do with as she would. To Red Lori, he was no more than a slave on whose ultimate punishment she had not as yet decided.

Suddenly her beautiful face lifted as she laid her stare on the sleeping yet wakeful barbarian. Her red lips parted and her mocking laughter stirred the hairs on the nape of his neck. When her laughter stilled, only a taunting smile remained as she bent once again to touch the blue-steel blade and whisper incantations over it.

When she was done, the longsword was bathed with flames. Deep in his mind, Kothar knew that the Lady Alaine—or was she Red Lori?—practiced great enchantments on its length. For good, for evil, he did not know.

Yet he did know that by morning, he would forget his dream. It would be as if it never had been.

The night wore on.

CHAPTER 2

In the dawn mists there was a little cheese melted over a bit of bread from the night meal and a sip of wine to allay his hunger. Alaine walked with him to the road and watched as he mounted into the high-peaked saddle. She put out her hands to seize his fingers.

"Be careful, Kothar! Gorfroi is a dangerous man."

He let the grey horse go as it would for a little way, while he swiveled about to stare back along the dirt road at the woman with silver hair waiting there so quietly. When a bend in the road hid her, he turned his face toward Murrd.

There was a queer emptiness in his middle. He supposed it was the pain of parting which caused it. Later, as the sun rose higher into the sky and the forest road wound in and out between oaks and towering chestnut trees, he admitted to himself it might be hunger. Yet if that were so, on what food had the Lady Alaine fed him?

He would have turned aside to find a farm and hot sausages and biscuits, but in the distance he could see the forest road edging into a wider thoroughfare and the spires and rooftops of a town. This would be Murrd, and there must be inns and taverns.

The hoofs of the grey warhorse beat a thunder on the hard packed dirt of the town road. Kothar galloped past a cart carrying produce to market and sent a glance at the pinched, frightened face of the driver. A little past the wagon he saw three women walking with shoulders bowed under heavy firewood. They did not look up except for one, the youngest, who showed terror in her wide eyes before she closed them.

They are frightened, all these people.

They fear something. Baron Gorfroi? It might be, since the Lady Alaine lost her castle and her towns, that Gorfroi had proved a cruel master.

He cantered into Murrd sometime past the noon hour, and found the streets almost empty of life. A boy ran up as he swung the grey into the courtyard of a large inn—there was a wooden sign in the shape of a tankard hanging on rusty chains at the roadside gate—and came down out of the saddle.

Without speaking, the boy turned to lead the big grey warhorse toward a stable. Kothar noticed for the first time that the lad shivered every now and so often, though the day was warm and the sun hot upon his shoulders.

In the tavern common room, he had to pound with a fist upon the keg counter before a pretty maidservant came running from the cellar. She curtsied after a moment, staring at him with wide green eyes in which that same terror was deeply mirrored.

"There be so few travelers," she whispered, to excuse herself.

"No wonder, if everyone acts the way the few people I've met have acted," he snorted. "What's everybody so frightened about?"

She shivered as the boy had, looking to left and right before touching fingertip to lip and leaning close. "It be the castle and what lives in the castle now."

"Only the baron Gorfroi lives there," he pointed out.

She tried to smile. The barbarian thought she should smile a lot for it gave her gamin face a rare prettiness. Her hair was long and black and a spray of freckles lay across her nose. Her mouth was red, but the fear in her turned her cheeks to a waxen pallor.

To calm her, he suggested she fill a tankard with brew and bring him a wedge of cheese. When that was before him and he was eating, he realized how hungry he was, almost as if Alaine had fed him nothing last night and this morning. During this time he continued a conversation with the girl, who was not reluctant to wag her tongue.

"Ever since the Lady Alaine left, there's been ill times on the land," she said, leaning closer. *"She* was bad enough—but the baron!"

Kothar was surprised. "The Lady Alaine—bad?"

The girl sniffed. "A witch, she was. Aie, a witch-woman. Full of spells and all that. But at least she left the villagers alone and never once bothered the farmers around the countryside."

The barbarian smiled. "Then how do you know she was a witch?"

"She cast spells. She admitted it, even bragged about it when some of us took extra days to pay our rents and land fees. Threatened to curdle cows milk or ruin our ale. Though she never did, I must admit."

The cheese was gone. He said he might do with some roast meat and bread and when this was set before him he ate like a famished man. The girl Mellicent stared at him with her great green eyes, rounded hip propped against a nearby tabletop. He squirmed under her steady gaze but ate on, steadily and purposefully, using his dagger to cut his meat.

When nothing remained but the pitcher of beer, he poured that into a leathern jack and sipped it. "And now? This Baron Gorfroi: what manner of man is he?"

She said simply, "I daren't tell. He'd come for me if I did and I don't want to be took."

"Come for you? In what way?"

"He'd send something for me. Seen it come for Giraldus, I did. A black, squidgilly thing in the dark of the night that poured itself in the window of his downstairs room—Giraldus used to be a scribe before he was took—and carried him off in its arms. If it had arms, that is."

"You only dreamed."

Her eyes were frightened. "I've had dreams. This was no dream. Kept my lips closed about it, though. Until now."

"Then why tell me?"

"You aren't one of the villagers, nor come you from a farm. The mark of the baron bean't on your skin." She rolled up her left sleeve. On her white forearm, an inch below the elbow, was a black mark. "Baron done this, after he drove out the Lady Alaine. One night it wasn't there, come morning and it was. All us folks got them, as far away as Kolaine."

He examined the mark, which looked like a black crescent. A birth-mark, in all probability—yet Mellicent seemed to speak the truth. The Cumberian scowled.

"Thing itches, it do," the girl offered. "When it itches real bad and begins to hurt, one goes to the castle."

"Have you ever gone to the castle?"

She shook her head, eyes wide. "Not yet. Some night I will."

"What happens at the castle?"

"No one knows. No one ever comes back."

There was despair beneath the fear, he saw. "Why don't you leave Murrd, you and all the others?"

She tapped the mark. "Can't. It won't let us. It keeps us here, like we were branded property."

When the villagers sought to flee, the brand burned so badly that there was no relief until they returned to their homes. As she spoke, Kothar studied the crescent mark; it would be easy enough to duplicate. If he were in the employ of the Lady Alaine, it might be time now to earn his keep.

He would sleep first. He was unexpectedly tired, as though the afflictions of the villagers in Murrd created a lassitude in his own muscular body. His hand lifted the leather jack, he drained the ale, he stood up. He understood she would not be averse to making his stay in Murrd more enjoyable, but he was more concerned with sleep at the moment than with seduction.

He hefted his leather carrying-sack to a shoulder and followed her handsome legs to the narrow wooden stair. There was gloom in the hang of her head with its loose black hair that told him the girl was anxious for him not to leave her. She felt safe with him. It was this, rather than her desire for lovemaking that had made her flirt with him, he decided.

His arm banded her slim middle, hugging her against him as he kissed her. "Later," he promised. "I have things to do this night."

She smiled tremulously, nodding, then slipped past him and ran up the wooden treads. There was a quality of breathlessness about her, a sense of intimacy which he understood to be a reaching out for companionship. Mellicent was lonely in Murrd; he was as a breath of life to her spirits. The barbarian was a contact with the outside world, and there was a fresh new strength in him which made her feel strong in turn.

The room to which she showed him was small, with a bay window thrusting out above the street. Its leaded panes permitted him to see north to the edge of the forest and south along the road he had come between the rolling hills and farmsteads. In the distance to the west he made out a black bulk against the afternoon sky. The girl stepped to his elbow, close enough so he felt her warm breath on his cheek.

"The castle," Mellicent whispered, shivering.

"Where the baron lives? Where the people go—and never come back?" She sidled close, her hand cool where it pressed his arm. She nodded vigorously, long black hair swirling.

His eyes touched the winding road, seeing a great oak tree towering upward and gorse bushes and clumps of hazel bordering the narrow footway. He could not see all that path, but he saw enough of it to know it in the dark. In the castle was Gorfroi, the baron who possessed the strand of silver hair that gave him an eldritch power over the Lady Alaine.

Mellicent lingered at the door, resting herself against its post as if to call attention to her curves. She let her lips smile, but her eyes were shy. Against hope, she wished that he would keep her with him. She did not want to spend the night alone, dreading the summons to the castle. The barbarian looked at her with pity in his eyes. If it were not for the fact that he expected trouble in this inn room, he would have bid her stay, and welcome. She stared deep into his eyes, read his admiration for her pert features, flushed, bit her lip, and slipped out into the hall to close the door gently behind her.

A moment Kothar waited, until he heard the brush of her poulaines moving toward the stair. Then he turned to his traveling sack and slung it up and over an ironbound chest. Fumbling inside it, he drew out a slender needle. He had often patched his torn garments or his quilted hacqueton rent in battle. This night he would use the needle on a different sort of material: his own skin.

For an hour he sat by the edge of the bed, dipping the needle point into black inkgall which he kept with him in a little vial, tightly stoppered, and driving that point into his skin. It was a tedious work, and painful, yet when he was done a black crescent showed on his arm as it had on that of Mellicent.

He put away the needle and the inkgall, then threw himself upon the bed. He was fully dressed in belted jerkin, hose and boots and his long-sword rested in its scabbard close to his hand on the covers. His shirt of interwoven chain mail still lay in his carryall, for mail would not help against sorcery.

Sleep did not come at once. He lay staring up at the tester with its tied curtains, telling himself he was a fool to be here at all when he could be galloping out of Murrd into the world where people did not wear black crescents which gave warlocks command over their bodies. With Greyling and his sword Frostfire, he could be earning good golden besants from the robber barons. Instead he was risking his life against the dark powers of wizardry.

CHAPTER 3

A musty smell brought him out of his deep slumber. It was everywhere in the little solar room, as if mummies held high revel on its sanded floor. The odor of cerements and mummifying liquids, of grave mold and rotting flesh, made a noisome stench in the air.

Kothar came up on an elbow, his skin crawling.

Through the leaded panes of the window, moonlight was a silver mist that showed the lavabo on its wooden stand all white and glazed. The solid dark weight of the familiar furniture, the chest and aumbry, the chair and the priedieu stood out against the wainscot paneling behind them. His carrying sack and his long woolen military cloak lay over the ironbound chest.

His fingers tightened on the braided hilt of his long-sword. The familiar grip was reassuring. His nostrils told him death walked close by this room. Against death even Frostfire was of no use, yet its great weight and solidity was like a friend.

"Who comes in the night?" he breathed.

He was alert as any animal to spring left or right. Now to his ears came the soft slush-slush of soft leather or long-dry skin rubbing over wood. There was a—something—in the hallway outside his door. The latch lifted.

The hairs on the nape of his neck rose up.

A black silhouette was all he saw at first, bent over and in the vague shape of a man wearing tight garments. Then a candle flickered in its wooden sconce beyond his door and now he made out winding sheet, cerecloth, and the mummified body of what had been a man, long and long ago. It held a basin and a brush in its mummified hands.

The cadaver shuffled into the room. A breeze swept the passageway, made its white seculchrata flutter like pennons in the wind. The odor was stifling in the little room, and the barbarian gagged.

Dead hands fumbled with brush and bowl as the lich neared the bed, dipping in the brush-hairs and bringing them out dripping black liquid. Kothar sensed that this liquid would burn deep into his flesh once it touched him. Just so had the people of this village been branded as they slept.

As it would have marked his flesh with the black crescent, had he not been awake and waiting. Slowly he slipped to one side of the coverlets, bringing his sword out of the scabbard without sound. His foot fumbled for the floor, he was off the bed and rising with the long steel blade in his hand.

The cloth-wrapped hands came away from the brush and the bowl and left them hanging in midair. The lich hurled itself upon him, snarling. Its forearm slammed into his neck where his undertunic and his leather jerkin did not cover him. The Cumberian was flung backward over the ironbound chest where his carrying sack lay with his cloak.

The thing came for him, diving. He rolled away, felt it crash into the chest, then slither sideways and grope for him. The mummy garments touched him, making his flesh crawl. They seemed empty, save for blue flames in the eye-holes. The dead hands inside the cerements tightened on his arm.

The thing was intensely strong. Kothar was a brawny young giant, and his mighty shoulders were heavy with muscles. Those thick muscles developed from boyhood in the arts of war bunched and quivered as he fought that grip, but vainly.

The thing drew him toward the brush and bowl. There it would hold him and splash a crescent of that black fluid across his flesh and he would be one more of the branded prisoners of Baron Gorfroi.

He made no sound, though his lips writhed back to show his teeth. The sweat stood in beads on his forehead and his eyes flamed almost as hotly as did the empty sockets behind the burial garments of this lich which held him. His feet pushed at the thin layer of sand on the solar floor to try and slow his progress.

Then out of his deepest memory came the recollection of that dream in which the Lady Alaine had written runes in blue fire along the length of his longsword. Magic! Aie, but for good or bad? It made no matter.

He lifted the sword, thrust clumsily at the thing that held him. It was little more than a push, yet the dead one gave, and its fingers loosed a very little. Kothar jerked free, whipped up Frostfire in a length of glittering steel.

High above his head he held the sword.

The silence in the little town was intense. Everyone was asleep in the tavern, sharing a drugged and uncanny slumber, helpless to fight the will of the warlock in the castle. Lips twisted in disgust, the mercenary slashed downward with the edge of the blade, saw it slide through cloth and—utter emptiness. At the same moment, a tingle of magical forces unleashed from the blade ran up his sword arm and into his shoulder.

A wail lifted from those burial garments as they were halved and fluttered to the sanded floor. The brush and bowl fell, the bowl rolling on edge and spilling its black contents into the thirsty sand that sucked at that moisture until it was no more.

The barbarian growled in his throat, an uncivilized sound, a throwback to the days of his distant ancestors in the presence of that which could not be understood. It was the challenge of the barbarian and the warrior to the unknown and terrifying.

Kothar stood panting above the heap of burial garments crumpled on the floor beside the brush. The grave garments musty with age and interment were sickening to see and more sickening to smell. The barbarian felt the sweat dripping from his forehead and lifted an arm to draw the sleeve of his woolen undertunic across his face.

That was when he heard the cry. It was muted, half-smothered, coming from behind him. He wheeled toward the window, leaped catlike through the moonlight to crouch, peering down into the silent street, his sword still naked in his hand. A sign creaked lazily on rusting chains. There was no one on the cobblestones.

Ah, but wait! Beyond the sign, where a street shrine made an angle with a building wall, he saw the movement of a shadow. It was black and quivering at first, and then it went away as a man stepped into the moonbeams. He was a tall man, and strong, to judge by the width of his shoulders. He began to walk dazedly and with feet that were unsure of where they stepped, like one under a thaumaturgic spell.

Kothar nodded. So! The castle called and one of the villagers responded. Perhaps he himself would have responded to that eldritch summons one night—if the black liquid in the bowl had touched his skin. Shivering, he turned his head. The rotting cerecloth still lay in a pitiful huddle beside the brush. The bowl was on edge against the chest where it had rolled, and the sands were stained with an ebon dampness. No threat waited for him there.

His eyes went downward.

The man was at the far end of the street, walking more strongly, though as clumsily as ever. The Cumberian drew air into his lungs, and reached for his scabbard on the bed. Softly he eased his blade into its sheath and buckled the great leather belt about his middle. It was now or not at all. He must go after that villager and take his place. With the palm of a hand he thrust open the leaded window.

The night air was cool on his face as he leaned out to grip the casing and use it to pivot his body outward. Slowly he eased himself over the sill, let his muscular hands take his weight. He dropped to the cobbles, his boots of soft Norgundian leather making only a faint slapping sound as they landed.

He was up and running, bent over, gripping his scabbard with his left hand, regretful that he had not kept on the mail shirt, cursing the streak of romanticism in his nature that made him champion the weak and helpless, like the Lady Alaine and pretty Mellicent. They were no concern of his; at best, what he did here was only a gamble. He should be galloping for the domains of the robber barons, where money would be easy to win for such a warrior as himself.

Instead he hurtled through the shafts of moonlight along the trail of a sacrifice to sorcery. Far ahead he could make out the man lurching past a berry bush. Beyond him was the great black oak. Kothar sprinted faster, like a wolf on the scent of prey.

He caught the man in the shadows of the oaken branches, swung him about. "Look I'll help…" His voice broke, for the man had no pupils to his eyes. Or perhaps they were retracted back inside his skull, for all Kothar could see was the glistening whiteness of his eyeballs. Moonlight shone upon them and they glittered with pallid fire. Too, his lips were twisted in a grotesque leer.

"Get away. None can help Bouchard, the son of Piers the chandler. It is my time to go to the castle. Stay back."

The man turned. The barbarian acted without thought. He drove his fist into the side of the man's head. The man stumbled but recovered; he swung about, snarling as might a wounded cat. His arms lifted, fingers spread to grasp and rend.

Kothar ducked. No use hitting him any more, he was under the grip or spell of wizardry. Yet he must do something, if he would save him from the brand of the wizard. He drew the long dagger hanging at the side of his sword-belt. There was a ball pommel at the end of its hilt.

Up under the chin of the young villager he drove that metal ball, rocking him back on his heels. In that moment of his dazedness, the Cumberian leaped, caught his arms, wrestled him toward the bole of the great black oak. From his middle he yanked free the belt the man wore, used it and the torn cloth of his sherte to make a tie-rope. Swiftly, expertly, with the practice of years in taking war prisoners for ransom, he bound him to the bole.

The man howled like a trapped wolf, ululating screams that woke echoes in the gorges beyond the path. A froth ran out upon his lips as if he had gone mad. Kothar was certain there would be candles lighted in the village, windows thrown open, curious calls ringing in the night. There was only silence; apparently the villagers had learned not to interfere when the castle called its quarry.

In a few moments, the task was done. The man lay in a circlet of leather and torn clothing, his back to the tree bole, his head hanging from exhaustion. He could stir neither arm nor leg, and the breath whistled faintly in his throat. Bouchard would not follow him, this night.

The barbarian saw where the brand lay black against the skin of the man's forearm. Just so would the undead thing have branded him, if he had let it have its way. He rolled up the sleeve of his jerkin as the sleeve of Bouchard's bliaut was drawn back to show the crescent. Then, stumbling and staggering as the youth had stumbled, he went on up the narrow pathway toward the castle.

It was not a large castle, he noted as he drew closer. The moat was narrow, the water in it was at such a low ebb he could make out objects half buried in the silt on its bottom. There was a wooden bridge lowered over the moat and beyond it a rusted portcullis raised to permit entrance to the keep.

A round stone keep, a bailey beyond it that he could see was bare and empty in the bright moonlight, and low stone walls: this was what he saw first as he came along the dusty road. The donjon tower was to the left, rising perhaps fifteen feet above the wallwalk. Joined with it was the two-story building enclosing what had been the chapel, and a kitchen. The great hall was to the right.

His boots echoed with hollow thumpings on the bridge planks. Something stirred in the darkness near the metal grille and moved out into the moonlight. The barbarian grunted. It was another lich in winding sheets.

It came toward him, caught his arm and studied the black crescent; then moved back into the shadows near the winch.

He was a little surprised that no more care than this was taken to guard the castle. Then he reflected that so many villagers had come here, all of them with the genuine black marks on their flesh, that the lich who guarded the portcullis gave it only a casual glance. The fact that Kothar was here at all was proof enough that the black mark was genuine.

He moved on into the bailey, past an overturned cart that had long ago held produce from a farm. He was surprised at the decay he saw, at the lack of evidence of habitation. Once this must have been a busy place, now it was a tomb for—what?

He went on, turning toward the great hall for only there, behind its high windows, was there any light. A green radiance flared and flickered, and he wondered if it had been set ablaze in this world.

He stepped through the doorway.

His dusty boots carried him forward onto a floor made of green jade tilework that appeared to glow with inner fire, giving the great hall its ver-dant brightness. By its eldritch light he saw walls hung with faded banners captured in battle by arms long since gone to rust. Beyond the glowing tilework was the stone stair to an upper chamber. To reach it he must cross over the green jade floor.

His boots rang out with hollow echoes in the hall. The warlock baron should have struck by now! He moved onto the jade floor, took two steps and—

The walls, dusty drapes, and ancient banners shimmered in the pallid moonlight filtering through the high windows. They seemed to draw back away from the jade tiles which flared anew with misty green flames; Kothar stared at magical brass sigils inlaid within the jade as they writhed and twisted and all but came alive in some strange ensorcelment.

A wind howled far off, wailing.

He was no longer in the great hall, but somewhere out in space and time, alone in greyness that pressed close about him. Sweat stained his jerkin, but his hand about the braided hilt of Frostfire was dry and firm. A slowly gathering anger was building in his middle.

Something stirred in the greyness far away, something that was coming nearer with each thumping of the heart. Kothar felt his blood run more quickly as he saw the thing of nightmare and of horror striding along in this world where he could see no ground below. The thing was gigantic, a beast-man with eyes that bulged in a scaled face and white fangs jutting from lips—each taller than a man.

A cockscomb of wattled flesh flared upright from its reptilian head, pulsing as the monster came walking. From its gross chin narrow tendrils hung like purple pendants, shaking to its stride. Its chest was massive, its arms thick and long and heavily scaled, and its fleshy middle hung in giant folds from the gnarled and twisted body.

Kothar growled, lifting his sword.

The beast-man roared and sprang.

Its clawed hands reached out to grasp, to bring the Cumberian upward into the open mouth and sharp teeth waiting for his blood and bones. A lesser man would have quailed and shrieked and run amuck across the jade platform. The barbarian swung Frostfire and brought its keen edge down across a taloned hand.

The being shrieked as that cold steel sliced into its flesh, as it cut through bone and sinew, slicing off two fingers and part of a third. Kothar realized that this must be the manner in which Baron Gorfroi fed the daemons who served him in the castle. Bring a man or a woman to the jade tilework, and when he stood upon this green platform, send him into this world where only greyness and this awesome beast-man dwelt, to be devoured.

He felt the tingle that ran down into his arm when his sword met that beast flesh, the same tingle he had felt when he stabbed into the lich in the solar above the inn common room. The glamor in the sword had enabled it to cleave into those dry cerements just as it slashed open this nightmare being in the grey mists. An ordinary sword would never have penetrated that purple flesh; only a blade filled with magic could do that task.

The monster drove an arm above the jade circlet, to sweep him off his feet and knock him into the greyness where only the beast-thing could live. The barbarian leaped high as he could, as if to evade a battering ram in siege warfare. His blade drove downward. Again it drew blood, an ichorous, bubbling substance that welled black in the grey mists.

The thing bellowed, its wrist hanging by threads of sinew to its arm. Blue fire leaped along the length of Frostfire, evidence that wizardry had met with wizardry in this nether world. The Cumberian crouched, staring upward at the gigantic daemon.

"Ifn thagn Gorfroi!" the daemon screeched.

A foot lifted—a scaly, taloned paw five times bigger than the Cumberian—and kicked at the edge of the jade tilework. Upward tilted the green platform, higher at one end than the other, and now Kothar could no longer keep his balance but rolled and rolled, over and over to the rim from which he would drop into the grey mist, to be caught and swallowed.

He came to rest at the edge of the castle floor. The walls were firm about him, their hangings still as dusty. His longsword was in his hand, and he was growling deep in his throat, still half-mad with the urge to sell his life as dearly as possible.

"So then," he said, getting to his feet. "The daemon could not harm me on the platform, nor could he tip me off into the grey fog, though he came near to doing it."

On his feet once again, he moved across the green jade tilework to the stone staircase. Up it he mounted slowly, brushing the chamber behind him with narrowed eyes, seeing no threat now but only rusting weapons and war pennons long since faded by the passing years.

He faced forward and came to the top of the stair and found himself looking into a chamber almost as large as the great hall out of which he had come. Its walls were of stone, wetly dripping for some reason he did not know, and no moonlight came through its recessed windows. There was a smell of salt in the air, as of the sea where it lapped against the fjords of distant Grondel Bay.

And in the floor of the room was set a white alabaster circle, a great flat disc inlaid with silver runes, much like that green jade platform off which he had rolled. From wall to wall the alabaster ran, so that he could not reach the black wood door at the opposite end of the chamber unless he stepped upon it.

Beyond the black door he might find the Baron Gorfroi. Or at least, the silver hair in the golden casket which gave Gorfroi power over the Lady Alaine. Treading like a wary panther, he moved out onto the alabaster, his sword ready for what might come against him.

He was halfway across when he sensed that the walls were changing, glowing bluish green. They looked like sea-water fashioned into a gigantic tidal wave. There was a sense of rising upward, as though the alabaster were soaring——into a pale yellow sky far above his head! Kothar brought his eyes away from those clouds to stare at a vast ocean lapping at the edges of the alabaster platform. And off near the horizon he saw little dots that jumped and leaped upon the waves like faery lights.

The dots grew larger; he could see that they were sorcerers and wizards in long black cloaks and pointed caps, with surfaces emblazoned with secret formulae for wickedness and all manner of corrupt spells. They ran lightly on the sea, chanting their cantraips as they came.

Their laughter was harsh and discordant, though obviously gleeful. Here was a human come to feed their bellies. Here was food from the world they had deserted to live in Daemonia and to work their spells in immortal psychomachy. He would fall victim to him who ran the fastest across these waves, crying out the spells that made him light as air.

A tall lamia in a cloak so darkly purple it seemed black was the first to come at him. The warlock could not put flesh upon the alabaster because its silver runes were inlaid in a pattern of high sorcery, and so it leaped upward, reaching down to clasp and lift this helpless man-thing off the alabaster that it might rend and eat him.

"Steel cannot harm me, by the powers of the god Astrol," it cackled as it jumped.

"This steel can," snarled the barbarian, and swung his longsword. It cleaved the air like a bright sunbeam. It drove into the cloaked wizard and clefted him from head to foot, and as it did Kothar felt his arm tingle, though not so strongly as it had at the inn solar or on the jade tilework.

The lamia screamed once as that magical blade went into and through his body, a high-pitched cry of horror and despair and disbelief. Then his body fell apart and a thick black substance rained down upon the alabaster and its silver runes. As that fetid gristle touched the circle it hissed, became as purple liquid and ran off into the sea.

The barbarian had no time to gaze at the purple waters. The other lamia were upon him, leaping high and screeching, clawing down with long arms to tear him from the surface of the alabaster platform and fly off with him to the black towers and the scarlet domums where they practiced their ancient wizardry.

He drove the keen edge of his longsword this way and that into demon flesh, cutting, slicing. Parts of the screaming sorcerers rained upon the platform and disappeared. Others ran off across the waves brandishing handless wrists or footless legs, or cured themselves of deep but not fatal wounds by crying out their eldritch spells.

At each slash and cut of the blade, Kothar felt less and less of the tingle that told of its magical prowess. By standing here and stabbing into these warlocks, he was using up the sorceries which the Lady Alaine—or had it been Red Lori?—had put into it. A coldness settled in his middle at the thought that he might run out of that magic before coming face to face with Baron Gorfroi.

He never knew how long he stood upon the circle in that nameless sea, battling the wizards of Daemonia. His thickly thewed legs were quivering and his giant muscles ached with tiredness when he let the point of his blade drop at last, as the last cloaked lamia drew back and away from him, hissing in his dry and wattled throat.

"Sota afraila Gorfroi!" he screamed.

Then all the necromancers turned and fled away, but now they went more slowly, for the haste that had brought them toward their meal of human flesh was only an empty failure in their middles. The Cumberian shuddered, seeing their inhuman forms, hearing their screamed curses in that unknown tongue.

The sea was going too, fading out before his eyes to form the wet, dripping walls of this second chamber in the castle of the Baron Gorfroi.

He waited, still leaning on his blade, for those walls to turn solid. He was tired, he ached with overmuch fighting, he hungered to rest, but there was no rest for him.

The black door beckoned.

With Frostfire in his right hand, its magic all but gone, Kothar put his left hand to the iron latch-handle of the black door and lifted it, pushing inward. He did not know what he might see before him; he was prepared for anything.

And yet—

He stood paralyzed with surprise.

A red mist floated about the chamber, hiding walls and furniture and every other thing but its own swirling crimson fogs. Dimly as he strained his eyes, he thought to make out vast gulfs of interstellar space, deep abysses of awesome wonder between the stars and the many planets of the universe. Here and there between the flecks of brightness that were the stars, he seemed to see dark, flapping shapes of things no man should gaze upon.

His skin crawled and his throat tightened as if he might retch. No mere mortal might traverse this barrier to the other side of this third chamber. The barbarian strained his eyes but nowhere could he see a stair or doorway that might lead on to where the Baron Gorfroi waited. Even the last remaining bits of glamour in his sword would not avail him here.

Far below his feet there was only nothingness through which the red mists swirled. No floor. He stood on the doorsill and peered out into realms of galactic space so infinite that his brain reeled before its magnitude.

"Rash mortal," said a voice.

A face swam in the crimson fog, a face of infinite evil, bearded and with thick red lips, with bright black eyes, heavy-lidded and scornful. It was an intelligent face, one born to command not only the services of mere hirelings and servants but also the demons and warlocks of all time and all space. Intuitively, Kothar knew he stared at Baron Gorfroi.

"What do you here?" asked the face.

"I come for the hair of the Lady Alaine," Kothar snarled.

The heavy eyelids lifted, the black eyes stared hard at his muscular figure and the great sword he bore between his fingers. "You are a fool. Go hence quickly, while you can. Thus far you have been fortunate. Your good luck cannot continue."

"The hair," Kothar rasped.

Gorfroi laughed thickly. "By which you mean the white body of the lovely Alaine and her inheritance, this castle of Shallone and all the lands and towns about it. So-ha! I strike truth, to judge by your face. Pah! You are only a mercenary, a sellsword. If it be wealth you hunger for—feast your greeds right here!"

The red mists were gone, and the barbarian stared before him at an ebony marble floor that stretched backward into infinity, into emptiness. Yet piled on all those interminable, unguessable miles of marble flooring lay the treasures of a million worlds.

Here were great chains of gold and mounds of red rubies and white diamonds, sculptures wrought by the finest artistic hands on a million planets, in forms and figures to make the breath catch in the throat, to cause the heart to pound in admiration, to evoke a cry of delight from the tongue. Chests and coffers held coins of gold and silver and other metals Kothar had never seen. There were so many of them, they ran back into infinity. And with them were vials and beakers and retorts, each filled with a liquid more pleasing to the sight than the last.

"The elixirs of immortality, of invulnerability, of eternal youth, of beauty, of wisdom, of happiness. They are the dreams of mankind reduced to a chemical formula, translated into a fluid which, once quaffed, can bring any happiness the mind of man can conjure up."

Kothar shivered, his every muscle tensed to leap, to drink those necromantic fluids and stuff his belt pouch full with jewels and gold until the almoner should almost burst its seams. His hand loosed the hilt of the longsword and he heard its clang as it struck the marble floor.

A blue flame leaped where sword and marble met, leaped high and blindingly before the dazed sellsword. Dumbly he stared into a room that was carpetless and barren of anything but a single high-backed chair where a man sat sleeping. Gone were the golden chains, the jewels, the elixirs and the chests.

The man opened his eyes and looked at the Cumberian. He laughed bitterly and stood erect, swaying a little, putting a hand to his forehead.

"I came close to succeeding, mercenary. A moment more and had you not dropped the sword—curse Alaine for her trick of filling it with magic!— I would have had you. Your own self would have been your downfall.

"Aye, aye—your very nature would have succeeded where ghouls and demons out of the nethermost hells of Daemonia could not. You would have run to the jewels to scoop them up and cram them into your almoner—and at first touch they would have blasted you to dust."

There was a little silence in the room. Kothar bent, lifting the sword Frostfire, seeing the baron Gorfroi fumbling behind him for the sword that hung over the cathedra where he had been sitting. With that blade in his hand, he turned once more to the barbarian.

"Long have I sat here in this ancient castle, stripping it bit by bit of all its treasures, paying them over to the wizards and warlocks of the interstellar and intergalactic abysses, that they might teach me their spells and cantraips.

"In a little while I would have been the greatest magician on Yarth! Then nothing could harm me. I have sat here without stirring for these many months. I have studied and learned, and my brain teems with sorceries with which to turn you into a mouse—to drive you mad with unguessable horrors—to hurl you screaming forever around the galaxy, carried along on wings of light, an eerie mote destined to ride all space and time without dying until your very soul cries out for the rest and surcease of the grave.

"But—you have angered my teachers!

"They blame me for what you have done to them. You cut a hand off Ophorion, and several fingers. He will be in great pain until they grow back. And in Daemonia itself, that world the warlocks built with their incantations, you killed many of the foremost lamia. Their dead souls scream out for vengeance—on you, on me!"

The baron Gorfroi paused, raising his sword.

"I could blast you, as I say—but my teachers will not permit it. They say I tried to trick them, that I allowed you into the castle and upon the jade and alabaster platforms to weaken their magic and increase my own. Who knows? Perhaps I might have done some such thing, were my studies in necromancy complete. But they are not. I am not yet empowered to use magic without the help of my demon friends, and so—I must meet you in a trial by combat."

Kothar nodded. A trial by combat was a part of his world, an accepted tenet of its laws. In the past, he had served Queen Elfa of Commoral as her champion, and had fought a number of battles in her name. The right went with the might of the victory sword in his world. Though a claimant should be correct in his claim, if he could not win the trial by combat, he must fail. It was the common belief that justice always triumphed.

That it did not, he did not need to be told. He swung up Frostfire, remembering those fights when his heart and mind told him he should lose, that the claimant had a better right than did lovely Elfa, but his fighting arm was too much to overcome. The right was his, here: he fought for Alaine and justice, to put down the threat of a wiccked sorcerer named Gorfroi. But would right win out where it had so often failed in the past?

Gorfroi came to meet him, great sword swinging. The steel blades clanged and parted to meet again in metallic fury. Back and forth went the blades in a deadly shuttlecock of edge and point. The barbarian had long ago learned the use of his sword as shield and now he plied his knowledge as he had for most of his life, fending off the bull-like onslaughts of the baron, turning the forte and foible of his blade with clever parryings of his own.

The clangor of that meeting steel filled the bare room, building a hard cacophony in the ears. Gorfroi was a huge fleshy man, who would tire easily. Kothar fought with a cool detachment that bespoke a man who made his livelihood with this weapon. His sword arm, for all its past use in Daemonia, seemed almost as fresh as ever.

Slowly and grudgingly, Gorfroi gave ground. Back he stepped, past the cathedra where he had sat so long, until the cloth of his tabard was pressed to the paneled wall. Here he made his last stand. The awareness of his doom stared out at the Cumberian from his black eyes even as it whistled in the breath he drew into his laboring lungs.

He lashed out with his blade, was parried. He thrust and was turned aside. He gripped his hilt in both hands now, for one was not enough to hold the weight of the blade and hilt and pommel, and he beat back death until he began to welcome it.

"Now damnation to all demons," he cursed, and leaped to strike his last blow at Kothar. That too, the mercenary turned aside, even as he slid to the attack and drove the point of his blade deep into the chest of the baron.

Gorfroi stood impaled a moment, mouth twisted and eyes bulging outward, before the barbarian yanked free his steel so that the baron might fall facedown upon the floor and lie inert in death. For a little time he stared at the dead nobleman, panting in his weariness.

Then with fresh strength he went past the warlock and stepped into a small room where a few cloaks and garments hung on pegs, where a counter was fastened to a wall on which rested a golden casket.

Kothar put his hands to the heavy lid and lifted it. The interior of the coffer was lined in blue velvet on which rested a single, solitary lock of silvery hair. This was the grail of all his dreams.

He carried the casket out of the castle into the early morning—the lich who customarily guarded the barbican lay in a pile of grave-cloths near the winch, now that Baron Gorfroi was dead—and out across the drawbridge. When he came to the great oak, Bouchard was trying to free himself, sane and clear-eyed.

"The mark is gone," he said as the barbarian cut his bonds with his dagger. "Something happened in the castle last night. I heard screams and outcries, I saw terrible lights flickering and glaring, and caught glimpses of red mists as if the castle burned." His eyes touched the golden casket. "What have you there?"

"A bit of hair on which has been laid a spell, no more. So the mark is gone, is it? Good."

Bouchard grinned, "I think you did this, I think you took my place and fought with demons. I won't ask what happened. I'm just grateful you came here."

The villagers grew grateful, too. They laughed and wept and the girl Mellicent ran to hug him in front of everybody and the linkboy who had stabled Greyling last night brought him out all curried and would take no money for the work. The men and women showed their arms bare of any black mark, and they would have pressed money on him, but he would have none of it.

He went to his room, to gather up his carrying-sack and his cloak. Mellicent followed him, stood in the doorway with a hip leaning against the jamb. Her face was oddly troubled, the barbarian saw.

Twice she opened her lips to speak, until finally she muttered, "Don't trust the Lady Alaine, barbarian. She be a witch, herself. She may try to pull some trick on you."

Kothar grinned, hooked her slim middle with an arm and kissed her. "I'll be back, never fear. When I come, we'll celebrate the downfall of the Baron Gorfroi."

"I'll be waiting," she promised.

With the coffer holding the silver hair from the head of the Lady Alaine resting on the high pommel of his great saddle, Kothar walked Greyling out of Murrd and toward the forest road which would bring him to the abbey ruins.

CHAPTER 4

She was waiting between the black stones of the dry well and what had been a chapel wall, long ago. Her hands were clasped just under her breasts and her purple eyes appeared to burn. The wind caught her silvery hair and blew it as it blew the silver mane of the grey warhorse. She cried out softly at sight of him and ran to meet him.

"You killed Gorfroi!" she exclaimed, clapping her hands. "I felt him die this morning just as the sun was rising."

"I have you to thank, and the magic you put into my sword," Kothar told her, swinging down out of the high-peaked saddle. He lifted the golden casket and set it in her hands.

Alaine carried the coffer to a flat stone and putting it down, raised the heavy golden lid so she might peer in at the silver hair that lay upon the dark blue velvet. She sighed, she laughed, she reached down and drew forth the hair, turning to smile at the sellsword.

"By burning this, I am free," she caroled.

"I should have thought that when the baron died, you would be free," Kothar said. "His lich died, the black mark on the villagers faded out."

"Ah, but this enchantment was on the hair," she explained, crossing swiftly past the broken chapel wall to where a fire burned redly in a circle of stones. She bent and dropped the hair into the flames. "And so the hair must be burned to drive away the spell."

He watched the fire catch the hair and burn it, twisting as flame ran all along its length so that it fell a thin black thread of char into the glowing wood and was no more.

Alaine lifted her white arms and whirled, the black skirt of her gown flying outward. Her laughter rang wild and merry, but Kothar thought there was a hardness in it. She turned then and looked at him, and her purple eyes were oddly malicious.

"My warlike barbarian with his great sword!" she laughed. "You want to claim your reward. I promised you my love, did I not? My love you shall have—aye, and the free run of my castle of Shallone!"

Her hand lifted and her white forefinger pointed. "By hair of head and nail of toe, by human love and human woe, by spell and cantraip I declare: be dog you look, be dog you are."

The Cumberian tried to cry out, and only barked. His body was shortening around him, his two legs became four and there was thick grey hair all over his body. His jaws had elongated, his tongue enlarged, and his ears were atop his head. The lady Alaine appeared three times as tall as before.

"Good dog," said the witchwoman, laughing.

Kothar sat back on his haunches and looked at her. His garments and his sword lay on the ground beside him. His mouth opened and his tongue ran out as if he laughed. Alaine eyed him dubiously. He ought to be barking wildly and running around the old ruin, mad with hate, mad with despair.

Of course, he could not harm her. The spell that had altered his physical body took care of that, but just the same, the Lady Alaine was oddly disturbed. The dog did not act as it should act. It was as if it—waited.

Her shoulders shrugged. The barbarian posed no threat. He could not speak, he could tell no one how she had rewarded him. He could only follow and obey her commands.

She crossed to the grey warhorse and placing a slippered foot in the wooden stirrup, rose into the kak with graceful ease. She sat sideways in the saddle as befitted a noble lady, and lifted the heavy leather reins. Greyling walked as she urged it, along the forest path.

Alaine chirped, and the dog came to its feet and trotted slowly after her. Was it her imagination, or were his eyes so sad they seemed to weep as they looked upon her loveliness? No matter! Alaine shook out her silvery hair and let the breeze blow it here and there across her face and shoulders.

They were almost at the edge of the forest when the witchwoman stiffened and lifted her arms as if to ward away a blow. She turned her head to the left and to the right, and now the dog saw the little black flames that ran all over her body, eating it away.

She screamed in her agony of understanding. "You tricked me! It was not my hair you gave me—but that of...that of..."

Greyling reared in animal terror, though he could not feel those black fires which ate the woman on his back, but only sensed them. Swiftly shrank the witchwoman, swiftly she withered and was consumed there in the saddle, until an errant breeze came and blew away the powder which remained.

Kothar stood on his two legs, once again. He stared at the black powder and he sighed. From his almoner he would take out the silver hair that had been from the head of the Lady Alaine and he would give it to the wind.

At the last he had taken the advice of Mellicent to beware, and had pulled a hair from the silvery mane of Greyling, that was as soft and smooth as that of any woman, and placed it in the coffer. It had been his own spell against witchcraft.

He was no richer, but he was alive, and service with the robber barons was waiting for him. One thing troubled him. Just as the Lady Alaine had touched the unseen barrier that hemmed her in, the barbarian would have sworn his oath on the war-hammer of Dwallka himself—that it had not been the Lady Alaine but the sorceress Red Lori riding upon Greyling! Had the sorceress sent out her spirit to inhabit the flesh of the Lady of Shallone? If she had been able to pass the unseen barrier raised by Baron Gorfroi—would Red Lori have gone on living as the Lady Alaine, safe from discovery inside her body?

The Cumberian shivered. He would have been only a dog, unable to speak, unable to tell of the dual personality within the shape of the Lady Alaine. Red Lori would have had her vengeance, she would have been able to mistreat him as much as she wanted, as her dog.

"By Dwallka!" he growled, the sweat beading his forehead.

Impatiently he brushed the wetness away with his wrist. Mellicent was waiting in Murrd for him to return. With the pretty maidservant he would forget about magic and wizards and sorceresses who stole female bodies to their use.

He hoped she kept her promises better than the Lady Alaine.

KOTHAR OF THE MAGIC SWORD

FOREWORD

These are tales of Kothar, barbarian swordsman, and of the blade Frost-fire, the sword given to him by Afgorkon, the living-dead wizard. His world is a dying one, for the planet upon which he lives, in the pagan splendor of a land sinking toward oblivion, is hurtling back upon its beginnings. The entire universe is collapsing now, instead of expanding.

In his world are to be found wizards, witches, warlocks and much magic, as well as the clash of swords that can withstand spells and cantraips, together with the mighty men who hold them. Across that land, from the ice wastes of Thuum to the desert lands of Oasia and beyond, he stands like a colossus, brave to the point of foolhardiness, a thief when his belly is empty enough to demand he satisfy it, a maker and an unmaker of kings and queens, a brash lover of women, a warrior when it suits his needs.

Above all else, he is an adventurer.

To see a new temple on the horizon (which may hold treasure to loot), to kiss new lips (since he admires pretty new female faces and the bodies below them), to ride where death beckons and a maytime happiness waits, Kothar will risk much. While it is true that, because he carries Frostfire, he can never be otherwise wealthy, it is also true that he never quite gives up his ambitions to be rich.

Locked behind the bars of a silver cage hung on chains high up in the palace of Queen Elfa of Commoral hangs the witchwoman Red Lori, beautiful and deadly, who yearns to punish Kothar for having hung her there, yet can think of no vengeance satisfactory to her feminine fury. And so her green eyes brood on Kothar as he travels across his world, and sometimes she reaches down to touch him, to remind him he is human and belongs to her for her punishing. Upon occasion, it pleases her to travel with him, in spirit, and even, at times, in body.

For, since she thinks of Kothar as her property, belonging to her for her revenge, she wishes nothing to happen to him until she herself is ready to determine and execute that vengeance. There are times when she will lead him into danger, into the clutches of a human monster or a demon out of some forgotten Hell, just to tantalize him, to see if he is worthy of her hatred.

And so, battling men and succubi, snarling and savage, equipped only with his wit, his brawn and his magic sword Frostfire, Kothar strides like an elemental through the lands of his world. Those lands teem with wizardry, with greeds and hates, with men eager to pit their strengths against his own, with women who sense the pagan deviltry in this giant of a man with the golden mane and find themselves attracted to it.

My sociological and archeological friends assure me that man himself can sink to such savagery, such primitive ways of life, in the last years of his existence. Crude civilization will rise and fall in mimicry of those which have gone before and now lie as dust on the planets of the universe. In short, man suffers a second childhood, when things known at the very beginnings, are known at the end.

Frostfire in hand, Kothar strides across this segment out of Time…

THE HELIX FROM BEYOND

CHAPTER 1

Two men swam steadily through the cold waters of Lake Lotusine.

One man was small, with the dark skin and curly black hair of the true southlander. He was naked except for a white loincloth about his middle and a belt that held his curved knife. He swam without strain; he was part water-rat, Rufflod liked to boast in the waterfront taverns. He was on his way to steal the greatest treasure in his world, and so he swam through the lake waters as he had never swum before.

The man who moved beside him, great muscles rolling under a sunbronzed hide, was almost twice the size of Rufflod. No southerner, he: his long yellow hair floated in the water when it was not plastered to the face he thrust out of the rippling waters at his every second stroke. His was the fair skin of the northern man, the yellow hair, the blue eyes and muscular bulk.

"Where away, Rufflod?" the big man growled.

"Not far, not far," the other called softly.

"By Dwallka! If you've lured me on a fool's errand, I'll use that khanjar you carry to flay the skin from your bones!"

"Just beyond the point—look!"

Kothar wallowed in the slight waves. Ah, he could see it now, like a golden nimbus beyond the trees and the few buildings there on the point of land jutting out from the warehouses lining this corner of the city of Romm. There was a glow in the night, low down beyond the trees silhouetted against that yellow radiance. Beams of lanthom-light shafted upward toward the stars. With it came the sound of harps and flutes, where the emperor Kyros made revel in his golden galley.

Kothar had never seen Kyros, emperor of Avalonia, though rumors of the fat, half-demented little man had crept across the Roof of the World and the Haunted Regions into the land of the baron lords, where he had been employed for a little while as a mercenary. Thinking of the wealth of Avalonia, of the green emerald rings worth kingdoms, each of them, of the pale emerald eyeglass through which the emperor looked at the world about him, tempted the juices of cupidity which lay close to the surface of the barbarian swordsman.

I will go into Avalonia and see this Kyros emperor, he had told himself over a campfire on the edge of the Unknown Land. And if by chance his emerald eyeglass or one of his emerald rings falls into my hand during my visit, I will use it to buy a little castle and a few acres of land around Grondel Bay, which is my homeland.

He had been in the great city of Romm, where Emperor Kyros held court, for close to three weeks. His purse had shrunk steadily in those days. He had never been much of a money-grubber; and when he ate, Kothar feasted like a northern troll in his cave-home, gluttonously and against the bite of coming winter winds. It was over a haunch of venison and a goblet of chilled Salemian wine that Rufflod had sighted him.

The little thief had been hunting for a partner. He was sly of wit and mind, and his body was tough as rawhide, but he needed more muscles for the job he had in mind than his arms and legs possessed. To his hot dark eyes, where they peered from the shadow of a leather curtain on the feasting barbarian at the Inn of the Seven Furies, the Cumberian looked like the man he had pictured in his mind.

They had struck their bargain quickly enough. Rufflod was a convincing talker, and he was free with the silver pieces in his purse.

"Come with me to the home of the merchant Nestorius," Rufflod invited. "He is a wealthy man, he furnished this silver as a handfast of his good will. He will tell you what he wants us to steal from Kyros."

Kothar pulled his sword Frostfire around from his side so it stood up tall and magnificent between his thickly thewed legs, bare under his fur kilt. The sword was a gift from the dead magician Afgorkon, given him when he had come staggering and bloody off the field of battle at the Plain of Dead Trees to fall by sheer accident into the crypt which had sheltered the lich Afgorkon for fifty thousand years.

The sword was the only wealth he owned, the only wealth—according to the words of Afgorkon—that he could ever own, so long as it hung by his side. To Kothar, Frostfire was riches enough, though he hungered at times for a bit of gold or a jewel or two with which to buy a particularly attractive wench's favors.

"What has Nestorius to do with this treasure?" he growled.

"Sssst! Not so loud. It was Nestorius who told Thaladomis the magician where he might sell it—to the emperor. Thaladomis did not give Nestorius his commission."

Kothar grinned, showing even white teeth in his handsome face, topped by a mane of shaggy yellow hair. His blue eyes burned in his skin like balls of cobalt. "So Thaladomis cheated him, did he? Well, that's the way of magicians."

Rufflod grinned. He liked this big man in the mail shirt and the fur tunic, with his wide shoulders and long arms rippling with heavy muscles. The size and apparent strength of Kothar made Rufflod shiver, however, whenever he looked into those blue eyes, hard as northland ice and cold as the wind called Borean.

"Now Nestorius wants his own back, and hires us to get it for him."

The barbarian frowned. "What is this helix?"

Rufflod shrugged. "I don't know. It does—strange things, things that terrify me, if what Nestorius has whispered to me be true. However, if you like, he can tell you that himself. Come along."

They went by way of the cobblestoned streets of ancient Romm, past wine shops and taverns where naked women danced to entice customers to buy their favors. They shouldered past little knots of men in heavy all-purpose cloaks who lingered in the shadows assessing each passer-by with eyes that took in wealth, extent of drunkenness and ability to fight back, all at one raking glance. Romm in the torchlights of its nights was no place for the weak of spirit or body.

The merchant Nestorius lived on the edge of the great palaces of the Romm nobility. His town house was set flush to the street, and extended for almost an entire block with a high wall about its gardens, where a woman made sweet music on a flute beneath a flowering tree. Rufflod knocked, the music halted. There was the sound of slippered feet running on garden paving-stones.

"Who's there? This is Crylla, slavegirl to Nestorius."

"Rufflod here—with a friend to see the great merchant."

An iron latch clicked. A bolt was drawn back.

A pretty face set with hanging brown hair, with eyes made brilliant by the rich green kohl tints of distant Sysyphea and a red mouth that made Kothar think of kisses, peered out at them. She frowned at Rufflod, but dimpled a smile at the barbarian where he towered in the background.

"He's been expecting you. You're late." She swung the door wide, so that the men could step into the garden. There was a sweetness in the air, suddenly, making the Cumberian wonder if it were the girl or the flowering shrubs and trees behind her.

"It wasn't easy to find him," Rufflod jerked a thumb at Kothar. The girl flirted with the barbarian, lowering and raising her lashes, smiling breathlessly as her bold eyes raked his muscular bulk.

"He's a big one, all right," she admitted.

"Just the man to help me in the job," Rufflod nodded.

The merchant Nestorius agreed with his hireling, for he beamed on Kothar like a father welcoming a rich prodigal in an upper chamber that was his study. He was a tall, lean man with a saturnine face out of which wise eyes studied his world for its taking. Clad in a brocaded garment trimmed in fur, he stood beside a long table on which were spread parchment maps of the lands of Avalonia, Aegypton, Vandacia and Oasia to the south, the unexplored lands and the vast steppes of Mongrolia to the east, Commoral to the north. To far-distant lands went the caravans and safaris of Nestorius, and his finger moved along those maps with every horse, every camel, every hired mercenary and trader in his employ.

"You made a good choice, Rufflod. This one looks like a fighter." To Kothar he said, "I assume you can fight?"

The barbarian merely growled in his throat. "What do I get out of the venture—except bruises and cuts?"

Nestorius chuckled, turning to a shelf behind him where a number of fat leather purses stood. "This," he murmured, and tossed a bag to Kothar.

The Cumberian pulled the purse-strings. Out of the almoner tumbled a dozen big jewels, tiny bars of solid gold, a few coins of Romm. He blinked. By Dwallka! This was a fortune to make a man mad. For an instant he was tempted between the wealth in his palm and his ownership of Frostfire, but only for the moment.

Secretly, he wondered if he would be able to keep this hoard, or if the spell on Frostfire, cast there by Afgorkon, would compel him to lose it, in one manner or another. His big shoulders moved restlessly. Let the Fates send their wills, he would walk his road as he saw fit.

"I'll go," he nodded, placing the jewels and the little gold bars back inside the leather bag. "For this much wealth—ask for the emperor or his emerald eyeglass or this thing called a helix, and I'll bring them to you."

"Boaster," snorted Rufflod.

But Nestorius nodded gravely. "Aye, I think you will—if it's possible. You speak the word 'helix' as if you think it nothing but a toy to please an old man's whim, as compared to the emerald eyeglass or the rings that Kyros wears. Well, think what you will, if you bring it back to me, I'll demonstrate for you what the helix can do in the hands of a man wise enough to know its use."

Kothar placed the almoner on the tabletop, beside the map. Nestorius raised his eyebrows questioningly. The barbarian said, "I wouldn't want to lose my fee during a fight. It's safer here. When we bring you the helix, I'll take the purse."

The merchant nodded approvingly. "It will be safe."

Now as he swam toward the great golden galley of the emperor, Kothar thought about his purse and the pleasures it would bring him. He did not think the water cold, he had spent his boyhood bathing in waters far icier than these southern lakes, in Grondel Bay. He was as a seal in water, huge and frolicking and utterly without fear, appearing to slither rather than swim, whereas Rufflod, for all his water-rat ability, seemed to labor ever so slightly.

They were out beyond the Point.

They could see the galley clearly, huge and massive, with its fore and aft bulwarks like walls of solid gold. At the prow a magnificent swan's head towered upward, beak half-open as if sending out its trumpeting call to battle, while at the stern, a smaller head upon a smaller neck seemed to rest as if asleep. Between one head and the other, a covered deck held two banks of oars, worked by galley slaves close to the waterline. The oars were red, gilded at their blades, and they hung motionless now while the nobles of Romm made sport with their women and their emperor on the gilded deck planks.

Kothar could see nothing of the deck itself, his attention was fastened on the aft section of the ship, where the bulwarks dipped in a half-circle toward the water. The golden galley had been built to drift on Lake Lotusine, it had never been shaped to toil in the waters of the great Salt Sea where the storms were gusty and terrible; the royal triremes were made for that, and for defending the coastline.

His eyes, as he swam, went often to the pale lights visible in the golden stern. There was a cabin there, well-lighted, and by the reflection of those oil lamps he could make out the corrugations in the hull of the galley, where it swelled like the breast of the swan it imitated. Those indentations that resembled swan's feathers might give him the handholds he needed to reach that cabin.

Rufflod had told him the emperor kept the helix in the after cabin, illumined by votive lamps and with guards posted outside the bolted cabin door. "It will not be easy," he had muttered, shucking out of his clothes near a great piling from the quay, just before they had begun their swim. "Kyros guards the helix better than he does his empress."

Kothar knew what the thief meant, now. The rails were lined with soldiers in the gilded helmets and cuirasses of the Prokorian Guard. Tough men, specially selected for their fighting abilities, all of them.

He began to understand why Nestorius had wanted him along as a bodyguard to Rufflod. Those javelins glinting in the torchlight looked very deadly; so did the short swords hanging in the gilded scabbards close to the brawny hands of the guardsmen. Around his neck on his swordbelt, Frostfire made a good weight. Though the great blade dragged on him slightly, like an anchor, it was a reassuring thing to know it was there within his own finger-reach.

They were nearer to the galley, now.

Rufflod moved closer. "Fetch!" he breathed, and dove.

Kothar was after him in a moment, his brown skin glistening with water where moonlight touched it, shaking his yellow mane and making the water drops fly an instant before he too disappeared in the murky dark waters. Underwater, his huge lungs filled with air, he was a shadow slipping past the little thief.

His outstretched hand felt cold metal beneath the surface. Kothar came up silently, poking his head out like a curious otter. His fingers went over the gold feathers fitted into place on the rounded stern.

Rufflod said, out of the darkness, "Can you climb that?"

The barbarian snorted.

Rufflod grinned, "All right, I only asked. We must mount to the aft figurehead, to the swan's beak. It is the only place where curious eyes will not be able to see us. Here, let me go first to—"

He spoke to empty air. Like a cat, the Cumberian was swarming up that round bow, fingers and bare toes clinging like limpets to the golden feathers. He moved upward with graceful ease; Kothar had climbed the great glacier of Thuum as a boy and young man, and the muscles in his mighty back tautened and loosed to his every few feet of progress.

Rufflod grunted and went after him.

Naked but for the wet cloth at his loins, the sword Frostfire in its belt and scabbard about his neck, Kothar clung to the swan's head. Below and behind him he could hear the thrumming of the harps, the wild piping of the flutes. Turning his head slightly he found he could scan the galley deck, where fat Kyros was perched on a small ivory throne over which had been flung half a dozen leopard pelts.

Sipping from a golden goblet, Kyros watched an almost-naked Oasian temple girl swing her dusky hips and shake her shoulders, stamping with bare feet on the gilded deck planks as she performed a lewd dance common in the temples of her southland. The emperor, as well as every other man and woman on the deck, could not have torn his eyes from the smooth flesh of the lithe, lovely dancing girl.

No one was thinking about the aft cabin.

Rufflod pulled himself up beside him. "I've got to get inside the cabin. Can you support me while I do, holding my ankle, and letting me get a look inside?"

"Can I hold a sack of meal?"

Rufflod nodded, content, putting his head down first and sliding over the beak, letting his palms rest on the golden feathers for support. Kothar put a huge hand over the slim ankle and gripped it. He crawled along the swan's head, letting Rufflod down more and more, so that he dangled here, fumbling at the open cabin windows.

"I see it," Rufflod muttered. "Gods—how magnificent!"

The little man was even with the window, gripping the sill, tightening his fingers ready to kick free of the barbarian. His voice came oddly muffled as he murmured, "Let me go, let go!"

Kothar opened his fingers.

Like an agile monkey, the small man dropped, catching his weight with his fingerhold on the sill and hitting the gold stern with his bare toes in a silent jar. Then he was pulling himself upward and bobbling in through the window.

Kothar lay quiet as a hunting tiger, listening. He could hear no sound from below him, no voice of an aroused guardsman, no warning bell clanging in the night. His barbarian instincts were up and flaring, for Rufflod should be at the window, lifting out the helix so that Kothar might grasp it and fasten it to his sword-belt.

By Dwallka! Where was the man?

What was happening below him in that cabin lighted by the pallid glow? There were no guards in there, they would have shouted the alarm, their swords would have made metallic sounds coming out of their scabbards as they hurled themselves on Rufflod.

Only an eerie silence in the darkness greeted his straining ears. Like a snake and as quietly, the Cumberian shifted position.

He was just beginning to slide downward to have a look for himself when the scream erupted in the cabin. It hung a moment in the air, filled with terror, full of that dread of the unknown gulfs of time and space that effect every human being…

"Aiiiigghh-ahhhhh!"

The music and the singing stopped on the deck. The emperor lifted his head, forgetting the Oasian and his wine goblet to stare at the aft cabin that held the helix. His hand made a swift gesture.

Kothar heard the guardsmen running across the deck planks in answer to that moving hand. They would be flinging open the cabin door in a moment, looking inside to see what it was that had screamed in such a bitterness of fear.

He, Kothar, also wanted a look inside the cabin.

Faster he slid downward along the golden feathers, feeling them cool to his flesh. His toes he hooked into the beak of the swan figurehead so that he dangled upside-down. His head dropped toward the cabin window.

He saw a room filled with white smoke, swirling and eddying about as if alive. Set on an ebony tripod in the fog stood a twisting spiral of thin, fine wires rising from a round blue metal base. To Kothar, it was nothing more than a toy about two feet in height. Other than the helix, the room was empty.

Where was Rufflod? Why had the thief screamed, and in such apparent agony? If the guards had not caught him—*what had?*

Kothar felt the cold sweat come out on his body. He did not hold with the forces of wizardry, and his keen nostrils smelled the stink of sorcery at the moment. The muscles in his forearms bulged as he held his grip on the cabin windowsill. All he had to do was let go his perch, and vanish in the waters below, with one supple dive.

His every barbarian instinct clamored that he flee.

But a savage determination to avenge Rufflod—if he were in fact dead—and to bring the helix with him to the merchant Nestorius, made him grin mirthlessly. He shifted position slowly, putting more weight on his big hands.

It was then that the cabin door was flung open.

Upside-down, the Cumberian could see the captain of the Prokorian Guard in gilded armor, his hard brown face surmounted by a tall golden helmet Peering in past his arm was the emperor Kyros.

The emperor squealed, "Look—the window! There's a thief hanging outside there! Somebody grab him. Grab him!"

The guards captain ducked out of view.

Kothar gathered his muscles like the tiger before his leap. One more moment and he would be safely away in the cold waters. To Dwallka with the helix!

Something caught his ankles.

The barbarian let go his hold, but whatever it was that gripped his ankles, did not. He hung upside-down like a slab of beef in a butcher stall, trying to double up his body to reach his feet with his hands.

Harsh laughter rang in his ears.

"Caught ourselves a crab, we have!"

"At least—some crabmeat to feed the fishes!"

"Aye—after the emperor finishes with him!"

The piping voice of Kyros could be heard from deckside. "Bring him down, bring him down! I want to see what manner of man dares steal from the ruler of the world. Fetch him, I say!"

He was being raised upward on the end of a pair of powerful ropes. An agile guard must have crept up on the stern figurehead, dropped a noose over his feet. Cursing, struggling, Kothar was lifted upward to the great swan's head, scrabbling with his huge hands all the time for a purchase on which to cling while he kicked his feet free of the rope.

He was yanked off the swan's head. He landed with a teeth-rattling thud on the planks above the cabin. His hand shot out for a railing spoke but before he could tighten fingers on it he was jerked along, bumping and bouncing, toward the steps leading from the stern deck toward the main deck.

"A giant!"

"Yes, a barbarian from the northern lands."

"And his sword—see his sword!"

Kothar was aware that the emperor and his nobles, surrounded by guests and guardsmen, were pressing closer as he thumped and was jounced down the slanted steps to the main deck. His lips parted, baring his strong white teeth. They would not be so complacent when he kicked loose from the bindings at his ankles.

His right hand went to Frostfire in its scabbard that hung about his neck. The great blade came into the torchlight even while he was flat on his back.

A guard lunged forward, to step on it.

Twisting upward, Kothar slashed savagely, cutting into flesh and tendons as he sat up. The guard screamed, legs cut from under him.

The bloody blade sliced through ropes, freeing his ankles. Kothar came to his feet.

Everyone was crying out in terror now, except the well-trained Prokorian Guards. Fat Kyros was shrinking behind his guards captain, screeching for his men to take the giant barbarian.

Kothar yanked the belt and scabbard from around his neck, tossing the encumbrance to one side. Frostfire gleamed like blue fire in his right hand, except where its glittering length was wet with red blood.

He made a truly barbaric figure, heavily muscled, deep of chest and wide of shoulder. His long yellow hair hung down to those shoulders, and his blue eyes flared like northern ice under morning sunlight. His smile was merciless as he crouched, blade out before him.

"I want him alive," screamed Kyros.

"Forward, shields up," rasped the guards captain.

Kothar did not wait for the attack. He hurled himself sideways, toward two guards who were a little slow about raising their rectangular shields. His blade flew like a stab of lightning across the sky. Its edge bit into a soft neck, thrust sideways and darted its point into a face.

He was back where he had stood, his spine against a wall of the stern cabin, but two of the Prokorian Guards lay dead or dying at his feet.

The other guards were disciplined men, they had seen comrades die before. Their shields went up, forming a fence of metal behind which their owners half-crouched, short, stabbing swords poised in their hands.

Kothar shifted his balance. He had fought soldiers in the shield array before. He was hampered on a galley deck, he would have liked more room and firm ground under his feet, but there was enough for what he meant to do.

He ran forward. He left his feet.

His bare soles thudded into a shield. Overbalanced, the man behind it lost his footing and went down. Kothar came with him, Frostfire slashing left and then right, into the exposed backs of the guards on either side. They grunted and went down.

Kothar landed catlike on his feet.

Kyros and the guards captain were right in front of him, the emperor with his mouth open trying to scream and too terrified to make a sound. Behind him the guards were wheeling, coming for him. The big barbarian did not wait for them.

He was in front of the emperor, grabbing his flabby arm and thrusting him hard into the guards captain, stooping and getting his left arm and shoulder under the fat body of the man who ruled Avalonia. He heisted him upward easily and ran lightly toward the galley railing.

"Hold! Don't harm the emperor!" a voice roared. "Stay your blades, stay your blades!"

Kothar gathered himself for a leap onto the railing. There, with Kyros as his hostage, he would be safe for a little while.

His feet left the deck.

In that moment of his leaping, something thudded against his head. It was not a hard blow, but it caught the big barbarian off stride. His leg buckled and he fell forward, unable to break his fall.

He saw the rail too late to avoid it.

His skull slammed hard into wood.

CHAPTER 2

Kothar shook his head. He was on his feet, still dazed from the double blows his head had taken. His eyes opened and closed as he sought to focus his blurred vision. Gods, but Frostfire was heavy! It seemed to weigh him down as might an anchor chain.

His eyes cleared.

He was standing in front of the emperor, who sat grinning at him while his pudgy fingers fondled the great hilt of Frostfire. Kothar blinked. If Kyros held his sword, what weighted his hands so much?

He looked down at a heavy iron chain. His wrists were manacled to it, it dangled there before him, black and thick and cumbersome. While he had been unconscious, the Prokorian Guards had fettered him.

"So," Kyros said softly, "we have captured ourselves a tiger."

Kothar stared at him unwinkingly.

"What were you after, stupid man? The helix?"

Jeering laughter struck his ears. The nobles and their women crowded about, echoing the royal mirth. The barbarian stared at them, seeing the pasty faces of the men and their soft bodies hidden behind silken robes that had come by the caravan roads from beyond the Sysyphean Hills.

His eyes touched the women, flickering. Aye, these women of Avalonia were fair, their flesh smooth as satin. They did not hide their bodies behind silk, they showed them proudly, half-naked in breastplates of thin gold and golden belts from which a few transparent garments floated. Their faces were regal, proud, their breasts stood up firmly, only slightly hidden by the golden cups. Excitement flared in their eyes, the desire to see a man baited, tortured and slain before them.

Kothar rumbled angrily, "I came for the helix. It will fetch me a fortune in the trade marts." He said no word of Nestorius; he felt he owed the merchant that much loyalty, since he was here to earn his gold.

Kyros barked laughter. "Fool! If you dared go into that room—but never mind that. You laid hands on my person, and for that you must die. And yet—I know not how to order your death."

"Torture him! Give him the death of the thousand cuts!"

"No—the water torture! Kyros, the water torture."

"Lash him to death at the mast!"

"Drag him below the keel as a starter."

Kyros leaned chin on fist, elbow on the arm of his throne as he studied the big barbarian. He shook his head petulantly. "No, no. None of these methods please me. I have seen men die that way. I want—something new."

Behind the emperor stood a tall, lean man, robed in black velvet covered with mystic signs and sigils. His black hair hung free to the breezes sweeping the galley deck, and there was a dark, evil look about his thin lips and narrowed eyes. Kothar knew him for a magician; probably that great necromancer Thaladomis, on whose prophecies and stargazings the emperor so depended, he whom Rufflod claimed had cheated Nestorius.

Thaladomis stirred. His dry voice rasped, "Slay him out of hand, sire— or he will be your doom! I vow this, on the silent voices of the stars which speak to me."

"I heed your counsel in all things, Thaladomis. But not in this. No! My party was lagging, that dancer from Oasia ruined it with her stupid posturings. Where did she run to, the slut? Eh? Fetch her, someone!"

Thaladomis shook his head glumly, but he made no other protest except to make a sorcerous sign in the air. Gazing steadily at him, Kothar saw the air turn faintly red about that moving finger.

Bare feet padded on the deck planks and the Oasian dancing girl was flung forward by a Prokorian Guard. She was very lovely, Kothar thought, staring down into her dusky face and the thick black hair that framed it. Her red mouth, full and open in her fear, was enriched by henna. Her slanted eyes touched the big barbarian, then she went to her knees before the emperor.

"Great lord, I did my best," she whispered.

"Your best is not good enough for Kyros. For the ruler of the world, you must do better than that!" Kyros was leaning forward, eyes bright. "What? Still in that cloak that covers you from toes to head? You wore enough clothing while you danced, but to see you shrouded like a mummy out of Aegypton turns my blood cold. Are you too lovely for my eyes and the eyes of my noble men and women to see?"

"No, lord," she whimpered, head bent low.

"Then off with the cloak. Off with it, I say!"

Her trembling fingers loosed the strings. A hand reached out from the crowd and caught it, yanking it off her body. She knelt there in her dancing costume, fine legs bare to hips, a mere length of silk tied about her loins and dangling between her thighs.

Kothar blinked. The girl was all but naked.

Kyros gestured impatiently. "The rest of it, the rest of it! Am I served by dead men? Strip her down, the clumsy slut!"

A hand caught her thick black hair, tugged her to her feet. Other hands seized the tinted dancing silks that were her only garment. In a moment she shrank naked against Kothar, as if imploring him for help.

"Look at them—beauty and her beast!" Kyros jeered.

He paused suddenly and lifted a great, flat emerald to his eye. Through it he squinted at the couple, his thick lips curving into a smile.

"I have it, I have it! We shall sentence the both of them together. Hey? Is not your ruler a genius? A twin death for twin annoyances!"

Excited voices babbled praise for Kyros, ruler of the world. The emperor sank back against the high back of the ivory throne, a pleased smile on his petulant mouth, nodding to himself. Two soldiers stepped forward in answer to his gesture.

"Seize the wench, strap her to his back," he ordered.

The numbed dancing girl was lifted high, swung down so her body fell atop the broad back of the Cumberian. Kothar quivered at that touch of female flesh, but he made no other move, standing as might a giant rock while straps were brought and her wrists and arms fastened to his own thick wrists and heavily muscled biceps.

A broader strap was brought and her middle was tied against his own, just above the loincloth he wore. Smaller thongs were used to fasten her shapely legs to his thickly thewed thighs and calves.

They stood there, when the Prokorian Guards were done, like some strange and monstrous beast. The men and women crowding about were interested, all of them eager to see the sharp edge of the imperial whimsy. They waited almost breathlessly.

"You can protect your back, barbarian—by letting Laella take the punishment while you try to save both your skins. However, if she is harmed, the fight shall be stopped and you shall be strung up and whipped.

"Now—bring out Gorth!"

A roar went up from the courtiers and their women crowding about the throne. To one side, there was a creak of rolling wheels, a deep rumble, and then a cage with silver bars came into view.

A sob sounded in Kothar's ear. "Gorth! He will kill us both together! He will fasten his claws in my back and—"

Kothar tried to stare between the pressing bodies of the men and women. What manner of beast was this Gorth? There was no sound, no snarl nor coughing rumble that might tell him whether the thing inside the bars was leopard or lion.

Two women drew apart, suddenly.

Through the space where they had stood, the barbarian could see the oncoming cage and the huge, hairy body inside it. A bear! A great brown bear from the mountains known as the Roof of The World. These brown bears were gigantic beasts, and although Kothar had never seen one, he knew they towered eight feet from claw to furry ears when standing on their hind legs.

His skin crawled. Alone and unburdened, he would have had a hard time staying alive against such an opponent. Tethered by chains in front and by a naked woman on his back, his task was all but hopeless. Yet a savage rumble began deep in his throat as his eyes met the small eyes of the giant bear, standing erect behind the silver bars now, sensing its momentary freedom.

The bear made a small, angry thunder in its hairy chest as it studied the big man it was to slay. Other times, other faces, Gorth had known, when his master had brought him out to fight picked slaves for the amusement of the men and women his master entertained. Gorth shifted uneasily on its paws, he had never fought on a ship before, and though the waters of Lake Lotusine were calm and placid, the galley did roll slightly, and this troubled the big bear.

A grate of metal, and the barred door rose. Gorth lumbered out onto the deck planks, its huge head turning this way and then that, as its nostrils grew to know these man-smells and female perfumes. Then its head lowered and its ears pricked forward. It eyed the strange thing it was to kill.

Gorth rose upward, eight feet and a few inches of furred savagery, studying the man and woman fastened together, rumbling angrily in its throat. They did not look so dangerous. True, the man was crouching, putting his hands together to gather the heavy iron chains in his hands so it made a dangling length of black metal, but otherwise he did not seem so formidable. At least, he did not hold one of those shining lengths of sharp metal whose bite Gorth had tasted in the past, during a fight.

The bear dropped to all fours, shuffled forward.

Kothar waited quietly, tensed and motionless on bent legs. He must not let the animal put its arms about him. It might well crush both Laella and him to death, if it were allowed to—"Hai!" he bellowed, leaping.

The black chain whipped like a leather thong in his great hands. Its links drove down and onto the furred head. There was a crunch, a ripping sound, and when the chain was yanked away, a strip of fur and red blood went with it.

Gorth reared up, roaring with pain and fury.

"First blood to the barbarian!" screamed a woman.

Kyros was leaning forward on his throne, eyes brilliant. His spirit thrilled to such unequal contests, because his was not the soul of the sportsman who reveled in a battle between well-matched opponents, but that of a weakling who delights in seeing another human being, more powerful and braver than he, go down before too-great-odds.

Kothar bounded catlike away from a return swipe with a huge paw that Gorth sent out at him. He circled on bare feet, making the animal turn. The chain was ready in his hands, it was a great weight but it was not too much for his muscles. For a little while, at least.

He knew he would tire in time. With Laella on his back and the chains about his wrists, he could not long continue this fight.

There might be a chance, however.

If he could madden the beast, divert it from its primary target, it might go berserk and attack anyone within claw-reach. Kothar tensed, leaped again.

His foot hit a little pool of blood, landing on the torn bit of fur the chain had ripped from Gorth's head. Kothar lost his balance, fell heavily on his side.

Laella screamed, taking part of that fall.

Gorth dropped toward his victims, long claws extended.

Kothar rolled over, under the extended forelegs. His hands shot up, gripped the fur on the side of the bear, yanked upward. Gorth swiped at him, but missed, and then Kothar was rising, planting himself on his bare feet.

The bear lifted into the air, towering above the man-thing.

Fast was Kothar, like lightning his movements. He had fought the great white bears of the northern ice wastes in his youth, with spear and club, he knew the speed of the beasts and their weaknesses.

In this moment of its rising, the bear could not protect its face. The heavy chain whipped sideways, through the air like a flail, cutting down across the little red eyes.

Gorth screamed in agony as those links bit deep.

Kothar was in and out, gathering up the chain, waiting as he panted for the beast to come for him again. The bear was in too much agony for this, it rubbed at its bleeding eyes with its paws, it made small, whimpering sounds from its froth-flecked jaws.

In a moment, Gorth would feel the pain, when the shock wore off. Then indeed, would he go mad. Slowly, step by step, the barbarian backed away from the beast. On top of him, Laella moaned. Her long black hair hung over his shoulders, tickling his sweating flesh when the wind blew. Her body shook steadily.

She stirred, moving her head. The Cumberian could hear her indrawn breath rasp in sudden terror.

"What happened?" she asked.

"I've blinded him—I think."

"Even if you kill it, what good will it do?"

Kothar showed his teeth in a cold grin. "Can you swim, girl?"

"Like a fish, usually. But this way—fastened to you—I am not sure. You cannot carry me—and the chain, in the water."

"Hsssst!"

Gorth was making roaring sounds now, lifting a bloody face and opening its jaws. The bear could see, faintly, as through a bloody film, but it felt far more the stabs of pain driving like red-hot pokers into its skull, taking away its reason.

Forgotten were its opponents, all it wanted at this moment was to pay back humankind for this agony it had given him. It sniffed the air about him. Humankind was everywhere, soft and weak and perfumed.

Gorth lunged. Great jaws opened and closed on a man in the bright silks of a nobleman of the court of Kyros. Flesh and bone cracked as he bit deep. At the same time, a right forearm shot out, claws bedding themselves in female flesh and ripping.

Kyros was on his feet, quivering in terror.

"Slay it, slay the beast!"

A dozen Prokorian Guards leaped to obey, spears out and stabbing, shields up to protect themselves from the clawed fury that ravened on the deck planks. Everywhere, men and women were turning to run, witless in their terror.

Nobody remembered Kothar.

The barbarian had backed up until Laella's spine was rammed into the cold metal of a guardsman's shield. He felt her stiffen from that contact, then he was whirling, setting both hands to that shield and the shield to its left, yanking them apart.

Kothar was between and past the startled guardsmen, running on bare feet for the rail. He knew he risked a thrown javelin that might impale both the girl and himself, but if he did not make this attempt, certain death remained for him on the galley deck.

He did not bother to put foot on the rail molding.

He dove over the balustrade, flattened out.

A spear went past his shoulder. Then he was falling for the blackish waters, arms out in front of him. Atop him, he felt the softness of Laella's naked body tighten as she steeled her flesh to the shock of entry into that water.

They hit the water and went down into Stygian blackness. Deep they went, dragged along by the heavy chain, but Kothar and Laella were used to swimming, each had taken a deep breath before splashing down. They began to swim in unison, as if their minds were locked together; actually, the dancing girl took her cues from the powerfully muscled body of the blond barbarian, as if she danced with him.

They moved upward, slowly, slowly, for the weight of the chain was awful, and their human lungs could scarcely contain enough air to counter-balance its drag. Yet they succeeded, their wet hands bobbing into view a few yards from the galley.

They could hear the screams of the women, the shouts of the men aboard the galley, and the more thunderous roars of Gorth, biting, striking, slaying as he moved through a red haze of pain against these man-things, one of whom had hurt him.

To Laella's amazement, Kothar struck out for the galley.

"Are you mad?" she asked, moving arms and legs with his.

His hands went up, stabbed at an oarblade. Hand over hand, he moved along the oars, knowing full well that the slaves chained to these oars were deep in sleep, snatching what slumber they could while their owners were busy overhead with their entertainments.

"We have to cut free of each other," Kothar growled.

He reached the last oar, sought for a handgrip on the carvings decorating the apostis, that part of the galley jutting outward above the bulwarks. He swung on these carvings, his body straining to the utmost with the weight of chain and girl, until he touched the lower part of the ram, which thrust forward a foot above the water.

"Hang on, now," he panted.

The girl did her best to fasten fingers on the carvings. Her breath sobbed in her throat, her long hair floated in the cold waters. She managed to get handgrips, and she sought to hang there, freeing Kothar's hands. He had tossed the heavy chain over the ram, so it did not drag on them too much.

He was working his long, strong fingers on the strap fittings. The straps were buckled, she saw, and after a moment of fierce tugging, the buckle parted. She sagged downward, her strength hardly enough to keep her body afloat. Luckily, her middle and her legs were still tied to those of this giant barbarian.

Her other arm was free; she felt his feet fumbling for toeholds on the rough boarding of the beak; to ease her weight on his back, she threw the arm over the ram. When he got his feet securely wedged into niches, it made it easier for him to undo the buckle on his left wrist.

"I belong to you," Laella whispered, kissing his shoulder.

Kothar grunted. "You belong to yourself, girl."

"You freed me from my master. They would ha-have tor-tortured me up there, if the bear hadn't killed me. Kyros does that at times, claiming that certain slaves of merchants do not please him and demanding they be punished by some sort of awful death, to amuse himself and his court.

"Of course, afterward, he makes a recompense of sorts to the merchants, for he enjoys his little entertainments and he knows if he is too severe, no traders will bring any more trained animals or dancing girls to Romm."

Kothar felt her breasts move as her shoulders shrugged. "That does the dead slave no good, but it insures that Kyros will have plenty of pretty slavegirls to make die in convulsions of agony before his gloating eyes.

"I hate Kyros!"

Kothar grinned, "Good. I despise him, myself. That is why I am going to take his precious helix away from him."

He felt her body stiffen against his as he unbuckled the strap about their middles. "Take the helix? You must be mad! Do you know what that is, that helix? I heard the mage Thaladomis speak of it, to my master."

She shivered. He waited, then muttered, "Well? What is it?"

His fingers worked on the straps holding their legs together as she breathed, "It is a magical doorway into—into some other world. It gives off a white radiance. Wrapped in a cloak, Kyros can enter that radiance, which destroys human flesh and bones, otherwise. He disappears, still wearing the cloak, and wanders amid lands of strange and terrible beauty. Inside the cloak, he is safe from danger in that other world, which Thaladomis calls Nirvalla."

The last strap fell away.

Kothar put his arm about the shivering girl and hoisted her up to the ram, plopping her down so she sat there, both hands fastened to the bronze plates covering that long wooden beak. Her eyes were enormous, staring down at him.

"You don't mean it? You're not really going after the helix?"

"You're safe, you can swim to shore from here."

"I can't leave you. I belong to you."

Kothar grinned and clapped her wet thigh with a big hand. "Then wait for me, girl. I won't be long. If Kyros has a cloak, I mean to take it away from him just as I'll take away the helix."

Like a big cat he began to climb the curving prow of the golden galley, hand over hand and with his toes seeking holds by stabbing blindly. Upward he went with pantherish ease as the naked girl clung to the ram and watched.

His head lifted above the cabin window. Not daring to enter the cabin where Rufflod had disappeared so mysteriously, he waited, patient as a tiger on the prowl. He heard the sound of voices, the sharp cries and grunts of fighting men, the bellowing of a wounded, blinded bear as it sought to take as many human lives as it could before the stabbing swords of the guardsmen reached its heart.

Now he could hear the emperor, babbling with fright.

"Around me! Form a ring around me, get me to the stern cabin," Kyros cried.

A man screamed as the bear clawed his face. Then the measured tramp of disciplined guards told Kothar the emperor was being herded toward the cabin door. The Cumberian shifted his weight on his bare feet. His hands raised the long chain to which he was still manacled.

The cabin door opened.

Kyros stood framed for a moment against the torchlight visible through that long rectangular doorway. A thick scarlet cloak, marked with mystic symbols worked in silver thread, had been tossed about his shoulders. A cowl, decorated by runes and amulets pinned to its surface, shadowed the emperor's face until only a white blob was visible.

Kyros moved into the room of the white mists. From the window, Kothar watched with wide eyes, half-expecting him to vanish as Rufflod had vanished. The emperor walked straight forward toward the helix, cloak wrapped tightly about him.

Balanced on his toes, his hands and arms free, Kothar waited.

The chain of black links was gathered in his two hands. Kyros was close, now. A long sweep of that chain would hit him, stun him.

Another few steps, and Kyros would be in range.

The barbarian rose up, hurled his chain. Below him the water rippled at the stern. A false move would overbalance him, send him down into those cold waters. But Kothar had a body trained to cling to small perches since boyhood, when he had hunted mountain goats in Cumberia. His leg muscles swelled. He hung there, casting that chain into the room of the white fogs.

The links hit the cowl.

The cowl crumpled, caught in the black links. It leaped as Kothar made the chain leap backward toward him. The cloak with the magic sigils seemed almost to fly through the air at him.

Where Kyros had been—was nothingness!

Only the white mist floated there. The emperor of Avalonia was gone. Kothar gulped, catching the cloak and dragging it through the window.

Hurriedly, he threw the cloak about him, feeling its material send a tingling shock through his flesh. Grunting against this seeming result of magical incantations, he drew the cowl down about his head, wondering if Kyros still had the sword Frostfire, if he had suffered Rufflod's fate, or if he wandered somewhere in that hidden world Laella had named Nirvalla.

He threw a leg, protected by the cloak, over the sill. He stepped into the room. Kothar saw, as he wrapped himself deeper in the folds of the cloak, that the mists seemed thinner. The helix still blazed with a golden refulgence, looked at from the shadowed recesses of the cowl, but the white fog was dissipating.

He strode forward.

Hands outstretched, he reached for the helix.

There was a blaze of white-hot brilliance, and Kothar felt the floor go out from under his bare feet. He poised a moment in that yellow radiance, floating between the opening corners of reality.

And then—

A face appeared before him.

"Red Lori!" he bellowed.

Mocking laughter shook him, inside the protective cloak. Her eyes were wide, gleeful, taunting. He noticed her long red lashes, like tiny fans, that seemed to regard him as if he were some kind of pet.

"Yes, Kothar, my hated one, my foe! I am Red Lori. Oh, don't worry—I'm safely locked behind silver bars, I still hang from the ceiling in Queen Elfa's audience hall. But my spirit can go where I will it—and I will it now to let you see it.

"Foolish man! Did you think the words I spoke were empty as the breeze that sweeps across the meadows? I meant them, Kothar!

"When you overcame me and put me here, you earned my hate. You belong to me, barbarian—to be punished. I have not chosen yet to punish you—but be punished you will, in time. So for now, go into Nirvalla—but know that I go with you in spirit. What happens to you will be the result of what I want to happen!"

Her laughter rang out again, from the red mouth that formed a wide oval, so that Kothar could see her tongue. Her slanted green eyes blazed with mockery.

Then she was gone.

Kothar felt something firm into existence under his feet.

CHAPTER 3

He stood on a flat rock, above a rolling grassland that stretched away toward low hills and a forested slope in the distance. Closer, where he stood with the cloak flapping in the warm wind, rocks were piled high as though a giant hand had flung them together in a playful mood.

The sky was yellow here, and the wind seemed to whisper as with many soft voices. Almost, it seemed he could understand those voices. They warned him, they counseled him, but he could not understand their words, only the mood they wrote across his mind with their faint suspirations. A shadow moved along the ground. Looking up, he saw a giant eagle soaring along on the wind currents, with widespread wings.

Kothar shook himself.

There was a black tower in the distance, and a narrow roadway leading to it, past the rock pile where the barbarian stood. He moved down, walked along to the road. There would be someone in the tower, he hoped, who could tell him where he was and how to get back into the room with the helix.

It seemed he had walked for only a little while, then the tower loomed before him, squat and low, with the mark of ineffable age on its dark stones. There were no windows in the tower, none that he could see, at least.

Only a great oaken door, hung with an iron knocker, showed that there was any way in or out of that tower.

Kothar gripped the knocker, banged it hard.

The door opened soundlessly. A woman in a tight black kirtle stood there, her face white as chalk, her lips the color of fresh red blood, her eyes behind long black lashes and thin brows like burning black coals. She did not seemed surprised to see him, her lips curled into a faint smile.

"Whom seek you, stranger?"

"The emperor of Avalonia, Kyros. He has my sword Frostfire. I would win it back from him."

The woman stood back, nodding. "Enter, then. I am Leithe, of this land Nirvalla. I know of Kyros and his golden galley where he keeps the helix."

Kothar moved into the hall, his bare feet touching the curious stones that formed the tower floor. Though they appeared cold, the flaggings, each one marked with a magical sign, were quite warm and comfortable. The walls were draped in thick brocades of scarlet and black, with the signs of the Seven Sisters of Salathus worked into their materials. An iron torchere on the wall held a length of glowing wood that gave off a surprising amount of bluish light.

The woman walked ahead of him, her rounded haunches swaying with catlike grace as she led the way into a room beyond the hall. Here was set a long banqueting table, with crystal goblets and platters of earthenware.

"Eat, stranger. While you dine, I will tell you a little tale," Leithe murmured, moving to the table, lifting the cover from a platter and revealing steaming meat, gesturing at a salver piled with bread, removing the top of a plate that held several cheeses.

She poured red wine into a crystal goblet for him as Kothar seated himself on a bench. Her black eyes studied his great body, nodding from time to time as she mentally assayed the strength in his rolling muscles.

"You may be the one," she told him as he reached for meat and bread. "Long have I waited for you to come walking down that road."

"The one for what?" the Cumberian asked, between bites.

"The man to break the spell of Thaladomis."

Kothar blinked, head lifting with surprise. "The emperor's magician? What's he got to do with Nirvalla?"

The woman seated herself at the table, reached for a crystal goblet and sipped at the red wine it contained. Her eyes brooded as she looked back into the past.

"This world of Nirvalla was created by the archmage Phronalom.

"Phronalom was the greatest wizard of his time. Only the almost mythical Afgorkon was his better, it is said. Phronalom lived in the kingdom of Althasia, long and long ago, perhaps forty thousand of your years."

The barbarian nodded, wiping his wine-wet lips with the back of his hairy forearm. "I've heard of Althasia and of Phronalom. They tell fairy tales about them in Vandacia."

The woman began to talk.

Althasia in those days was a world of tyrants and warlords, of armies marching to conquest, of soldiers in little bands breaking into the homes of citizens, carrying them off with their wives and children to serve the desires of King Drongol. To King Drongol, his people existed only to pleasure his royal whims and fulfill the needs of his kingdom.

He established breeding farms where his most valiant warriors acted as studs to the healthiest and loveliest women of the kingdom. Children and more children, demanded the king. Male children, to train as warriors, female children to bear more future warriors.

Phronalom lived in Althasia, content with his magic and his beloved wife, Ayatha. Ayatha was reputedly the most beautiful woman in the world at that time. On her, King Drongol cast a wanting eye. Not for himself, he had concubines by the hundreds to assuage his lusts; he wanted Ayatha for his breeding farms, for she was as wise as she was beautiful.

By his spells, Phronalom learned of this plan, and decided to thwart it. None could match him for his esoteric knowledge, his understanding of necromancies and the dark wisdoms. Though King Drongol had surrounded himself with wizards, Phronalom was the greatest of them all.

On a wild night, when lightning shredded the sky with yellow flashes and the rains poured down like the tears of the gods, Phronalom summoned up the demon spirits who served him. On these incubi, he asked a simple question. How could he escape the evil schemes of Drongol?

The demons told him he must build a helix.

The helix would be the doorway into a world that the helix itself, by means of the necromantic spells and cantraips by which it was formed, would create. Into that world—Nirvalla—Phronalom and Ayatha could flee, and with them such retainers and acquaintances as might choose to make the journey.

In his sorcerous sanctuary, Phronalom performed the rites to make the helix. It took seven hours, even with the demons of Ebthor and Nixus to help him. During these seven hours, the soldiers of King Drongol came for Ayatha. To the pounding of their spear-butts on the door, Phronalom finished his incantation.

The golden helix glowed for the first time.

Into Nirvalla, this land of magical enchantment, stepped Phronalom and his wife, with many of their servitors and their acquaintances. It was a lush, young world, as Yarth itself might have been before the coming of man. The winds were sweet, the grasses rich and lush, the trees heavily leaved so that when the wind stirred them their branches made music like that of a thousand harps. The water of this magical world was sweet, the meats of its animals tasty.

Here lived the great mage, happily untouched by human hates and greeds and lusts. The land he gave freely to his friends. There was so much of it, no man or woman would be crowded, and with his cantrips, Phronalom could always extend its borders.

"There is no age in Nirvalla, no Time," smiled Leithe, refilling their crystal cups. "For close to forty thousand of your years we have dwelt here, in a kind of paradise.

"We can conjure up what we want, out of the very air, for Nirvalla is a land of sorcery, and that very sorcery seems to be alive in the air."

Kothar swallowed his wine and pushed away his empty platter. His hand went automatically to where Frostfire usually hung in its scabbard, but when his fingers closed on empty air, he frowned.

"What of Kyros? How did he get the helix?" he asked.

Leithe smiled sadly.

"Thaladomis is a mighty mage. He was born in Vandacis, in that land which was known once as Althasia. He had heard of the great Phronalom, and devoted his early years to tracking down old parchments and palimpsests which told of his enchantments. In dusty cellars and forgotten tombs he came upon these relics of a forgotten age."

Studying the scrolls, Thaladomis realized that he could himself venture into Nirvalla, perhaps even steal the helix. However, he was magician enough to know that the helix would be guarded by terrible spells, and first he must find a way to counteract those sorceries.

Long he hunted, until at last, beside the white dust of what had been a skeleton centuries ago, he came upon a length of parchment which, protected by necromancies, had endured through the years. The parchment told how each member of the little group who had gone into Nirvalla with Phronalom and Ayatha wore magic cloaks that protected them from the baneful influence of the helix.

Creating such a cloak for himself with the aid of certain demons who hated the demons of Ebthor and Nixus, Thaladomis went himself into Nirvalla. He found the helix, and spoke the word that would enable him to touch it.

With the helix, Thaladomis went from Nirvalla into his own world. The prize was his, but when he had finished gloating over it, Thaladomis realized he was no better off than he was before. He could go in or out of Nirvalla, but what good would that do him? He was a man who enjoyed life, the kisses of women and their caresses, the taste of rare foods and fine wines, and the helix would give him none of these.

Still, there must be a man in his world who would pay him well for the helix, for the privilege of going into Nirvalla and enjoying its eternal youthfulness. For two years, Thaladomis pondered, then he decided on a prospective buyer, at the suggestion of a merchant named Nestorius.

Avalonia was the richest kingdom in all Yarth.

The emperor Kyros was its richest man.

To Kyros then, went Thaladomis, with the helix. He permitted Kyros to don the cloak and walk into the hidden lands, and when he emerged, Kyros was exultant. He offered Thaladomis a fortune in gold and jewels, he built

Thaladomis a palace only slightly less luxurious than his own. The magician was given his pick of the beautiful women of his court.

Leithe laughed harshly. "That fat man, coming here and going when and where he would, in perfect safety! Phronalom does not dare harm him, for fear Thaladomis might destroy the helix in retaliation.

"And if that happens—"

"Nirvalla is no more!"

Leithe stared down into her empty goblet, turning it around and around with her slender fingers. "You might think forty thousand years is a long time, stranger. It is no more than the winking of an eyelid to us who enjoy the pleasures of Nirvalla."

Her black eyes rose to study his big, muscular body. "We have all we want here, except age and misery. If I want a youth for my enjoyment, all I need to do is—"

Her slim white fingers made certain signs in the air.

A young man in a short chiton stood before them, golden locks on his head, a small harp in his hands. Leithe stared at him with warm eyes.

"Vathik," she smiled. "He loves me. And he plays the harp beautifully, almost as well as fabled Otheron." Her fingers wriggled, the youth disappeared. Leithe sighed.

Kothar grinned at her bent head. "I can see why you enjoy this kind of life—but it isn't for me. I'd rust from idleness. Give me Frostfire and a way back to my own world and time, and I'll be grateful."

Leithe lifted her head, staring at him.

"You could be the one," she said at last. "You see, when Thaladomis stole the helix, he was forced by the very nature of the demoniac magic that went into the creation of the helix to cast a spell in its place.

"By his spell, Thaladomis placed Ayatha herself in thrall for the helix. If the helix is returned to Nirvalla—Ayatha dies!"

Kothar growled, "Then how in the name of great Dwallka can I help? How can anyone help?"

A scarlet fingernail traced a little sign on the bare wooden tabletop. "There is a way," murmured Leithe. "It needs a brave man, a man with a crazy, mad kind of courage. But it can be done."

"The spell involves the demon Warrl. By trickery, Thaladomis imprisoned Warrl inside a great ruby on which the necromancies that control the return of the helix to Nirvalla as well as the life or death of Ayatha are engraved. Shatter that ruby—and you release the demon inside it and render useless the incantations that prevent the return of the helix. Shattered, the ruby spell that decides whether Ayatha lives or dies is also rendered null and void. The trouble is—no one knows where the ruby is hidden but Thaladomis himself."

Kothar nodded, "That's easy to understand—but first I must find Kyros."

The woman frowned. "Why Kyros? He is nothing!"

"He carries Frostfire," Kothar grinned coldly, showing his big white teeth. "And I mean to have my sword back."

Leithe laughed softly. "I can show you a dozen swords, give them all to you—come with me!"

She rose with a supple twisting of her slim body beneath the clinging black stuff of her gown. A beautiful woman was Leithe the enchantress and at another time, Kothar told himself, he might be interested in teaching her how a man who did not disappear at the flick of the fingers might please her fleshly needs far better than Vathik.

Following her twitching buttocks out into the hall and up a flight of wooden steps, Kothar came to the round tower room where Leithe performed her own incantations. There were vials and parchments here; in the cabinets about the walls were the dried wings of bats, the hairs of cats, the many artifacts needed for her spells. On several prie-dieux were open volumes containing the lore of a thousand wizards.

On a golden tripod, set into a velvet-lined ring, was a large silver ball. The surface of the globe was highly polished, so that it hurt the eyes to gaze upon it. Leithe crossed to the ball, touched it with her fingers. Kothar saw that high gloss vanish so that the ball became transparent as crystal. In it, little black wisps of smoke appeared to float.

"Gaze, stranger!" Leithe whispered.

There was a tiny sword inside the globe, a great, two-handed weapon with a glittering blade that glistened as if sunlight touched it. "Jortos swung that blade, Jortos the hero of Alvia, in his defense of his homeland. It is yours, if you say the word."

Her fingers moved again and the two-handed sword was replaced by a curved scimitar with a red velvet-wrapped hilt in which gleamed a blue jewel. "Salamor used that sword when he destroyed the demon gods of Oasia. If you want it, nod your head."

"Frostfire was made by Afgorkon," the barbarian rumbled. "Afgorkon gave it to me to help Queen Elfa. I feel naked without it. I want only Frostfire."

"And Kyros carries that sword?" Leithe asked.

Her palm went down on the globe, pressed it. Her blued eyelids closed so that her lashes made little black fans on her cheeks. She seemed almost not to breathe, to be no more than a wax mannikin of a woman for a few seconds.

"Look," she breathed.

Inside the globe, Kyros sat on a flat rock that bordered a limpid pool in which naiads swam, laughing and sporting with one another. Two of them, naked, were holding bunches of purple grapes to Kyros' lips, bidding him swallow this fruit of Nirvalla.

Leithe whispered, "The grapes give him youthfulness to carry into his world. He has been here before, that man. He is almost as deadly as Thaladomis, for he intends to bring soldiers here—and to make Nirvalla his own where he will rule forever.

"He is a wicked, evil man. He would destroy our peace." Leithe sighed, nodding. "Yes, perhaps it is best that you go to Kyros and take Frostfire away from him." She held up a warning finger. "But I must tell you one thing. You cannot kill Kyros in Nirvalla. He is protected by the same spell that keeps us all young. There is no death here, and the man who tries to kill another—dies himself."

Kothar growled, "By Dwallka! You try a man's patience with all these limitations on what a man may do. Very well! I'll heed you—but can I choke him, just a little?"

The woman laughed, throwing back her head.

"Yes, Kothar—choke him, but not unto death!"

Her right hand lifted. It made signs at the giant barbarian. Kothar felt cold, as if he were embedded inside the great glacier that lay astride parts of Cumberia and Thuum in his northland home. In that cold, his chains turned to powder, blew away.

He gasped for breath—Kyros was five feet away, nibbling at the grapes the naked naiads fed him. In its jeweled scabbard, Frostfire lay propped between his knees. Kothar tensed on the rock where he stood, about to make his leap.

The emperor looked slimmer, stronger, to his eyes, and he realized that the grapes were feeding his flesh with youth and strength. He was not so much the fat fop now as he was a younger, more vital man. The jewels he wore on his fingers, the great emerald hanging in its golden circlet from his throat, seemed almost out of place.

Kothar began his leap.

Kyros saw him from the corners of his eyes. He sprang aside, thrusting a naiad between himself and the barbarian. At the same time his right hand moved down to grip Frostfire's hilt and yank free the blued blade.

The naiad screamed as her falling body hit Kothar just below the knees, toppling him forward. The barbarian fell heavily, almost at the feet of the youthful emperor.

Up came that great blade, poised to strike.

Kothar cried, "Wait! There is a curse on that steel, Kyros!"

The wind had been knocked from his great body so that the Cumberian could only lie there and drag in mouthfuls of air into his lungs as Kyros lowered the point of the blade and touched it to his throat.

"What curse, barbarian? Tell me before I slay you—and tell me also how you came into this hidden land! I paid Thaladomis well for that privilege! If every thief in Avalonia can cross over into Nirvalla, I'll begin to think the mage cheated me!"

Kothar grunted against the point digging into his neckflesh. "I hooked the cloak with my chain, just as you disappeared. But that's of no importance. What is important is the fact that no man who owns Frostfire can own any other wealth!"

The emperor laughed, quite good-naturedly. "Liar! See my jewels. Study the emerald eyeglass I carry about my neck. Men would die to own those things, they are worth small kingdoms, of themselves."

"They are glass," grinned Kothar.

Kyros, slightly startled, glanced at his left hand where he wore three rings. At the same time he pressed the point deeper into Kothar's throat, so that it drew a speck of blood from his sun-bronzed flesh.

"Liar! They are—"

Frantically, Kyros held his left hand higher so the yellow light of Nirvalla struck it, showed the jewels in his rings to be lusterless and dull. Flushing with disbelief, the emperor clawed at the great emerald in its golden filigree work at the end of his neck-chain.

And Kothar struck.

His arm hit the blade, knocked it sideways.

He came rolling off a hip, driving his massively muscled body into the emperor's legs. Back went Kyros, to thud down hard on the grassy bank. Before the man could move, Kothar leaped. His powerful fingers went deep into his fat throat as he flung himself astraddle across his body. Those mighty fingers tightened.

Kyros tried to scream, but could not.

His eyes bulged, his fat cheeks shook, his mouth was a huge, distorted circle of bluish lips. The flabby hands that had been caressing the naked naiads were now writhing at the iron-hard wrists bearing the weight of those suffocating hands deeper, deeper into his throat.

Then Kothar grinned, and let his fingers relax a little. Kyros made a whistling sound in his throat as he dragged air into his lungs.

The barbarian growled, "Do you want to die?"

Frantically, Kyros shook his head. "No," he whimpered. "No, no— have mercy, Kothar!"

"I will have mercy, Kyros—if you tell me of the spell Thaladomis wove to enable him to keep the helix out of Nirvalla."

It was a long shot he was betting on, the Cumberian knew, but he understood men, and as sly a ruler as Kyros would never have committed his precious person into the safekeeping of as strange a world as Nirvalla without some assurance that he was safe. Kyros would have demanded, when he paid the price for the helix, reassurances that he would be unharmed in this magic land.

Thaladomis would have told him of the ensorcelled ruby and of the spell the mage had put upon it which would make the helix safe from removal back into Nirvalla. The necromancer would have boasted of his slyness in hiding that jewel so its spell could not be removed but the emperor would have wheedled the information out of him. The flicker of understanding in Kyros' eyes told him he was right.

Kyros panted, "I—I don't know."

Iron fingers tightened once again. Kyros beat the air with his plump, perfumed hands, making movements with his blue lips. "Wa-wait," he gasped. "Perhaps I do remember."

Kothar took away his hand. Kyros lay there gasping, moving his head from right to left and back again. There were big purple blotches on his neck.

"Thaladomis locked a powerful demon inside the ruby gem of Gwanthol," Kyros babbled. "The jewel he hid in the—in the belly of Skrye, the great eagle of Nirvalla."

"An eagle?" Kothar rumbled.

Kyros nodded, smiling a wicked grin. "Yes, an eagle created by a spell of the magician, an eagle nothing can harm. Skrye flies high, barbarian—in the cold reaches of the clouds, where no man and no arrow can go."

As if in mockery, an eagle screamed, high up where the sky made a blue vault, specked with distant clouds. Kothar knelt astride the emperor of Avalonia, and knew disgust. He could never hope to catch and slay that eagle. His keen eyes picked out the tiny white dot soaring there, and he sighed.

His quest was hopeless.

CHAPTER 4

Leithe laughed when he told her what Kyros had said. They sat once again in her dining hall, Kothar eating meat and quaffing great gulps of the chilled red wine at which Leithe merely sipped. Her black eyes were alight with triumph.

"There is a way, now that we know where the ruby is hidden," she comforted him. "All we need do is make a plan to catch it."

"And then, what?" the barbarian growled. "Nothing dies, here in Nirvalla! You told me so, yourself. How do I get the ruby out of Skrye except by disemboweling him—and if the bird is to live on in agony—well, I don't know."

Leithe laughed again. "Only those who crossed over with Phronalom are protected by his magic. Skrye was created by Thaladomis, and no such protection clings to him. No, no. You may slay Skrye—if you can."

The woman frowned, suddenly thoughtful. She repeated softly, "If you can. Yes! For Thaladomis must have placed a powerful spell on Skrye, to save it from some such venture as you would attempt."

"If I could not slay Kyros for fear of dying myself, why can I kill Skrye?" Kothar wondered.

"Kyros is a man, Skrye is but an animal. There are different rules for each." Leithe smiled faintly. "If we could not kill animals here in Nirvalla, what would we do for our meals? No, no, if you can slay Skrye, you may, safely."

She brooded, forgetful of the man, until at last she sighed and shook her head so that her long ebon tresses danced. "I do not know the way," she confessed.

Kothar chuckled, putting a hand on the jeweled hilt of Frostfire, drawing it upward in its scabbard until the woman could see its polished blue blade. "My Frostfire will find a way. Afgorkon made it, there is magic in that steel—a rare and terrible magic."

He swallowed more wine, pouring it this time himself, from the big silver pitcher. He muttered, with his goblet halfway to his lips, "All I need to do is find Skrye, to get him down to the ground. Dwallka knows I can't go flying through the air the way he does."

Leithe nodded, "In that, at least, I can help. When Thaladomis left Skrye in Nirvalla, it was as a real eagle, with the wants of an eagle. With something like our present needs in mind, we of Nirvalla have been feeding young lambs to Skrye, so that by now he comes unsuspectingly to a farmstead some miles from here, to feed when the hunger moves in him.

"He does not always feed at the farm, but he does come more or less regularly, seeming to know that tender food will be there for the mere taking. You shall go there, Kothar—and wait for Skrye."

The barbarian yawned. "I'm tired," he confessed.

Leithe rose to her feet. "You shall sleep in my bed, stranger. I have me a mind to test the muscles of your body, and its strength."

Kothar grinned, wiping his wine-wet lips with the back of a huge forearm where golden hairs glittered in the torchlight. "I'm tired, Leithe. When I sleep, I sleep. But I do thank you for the offer."

Leithe merely stared at him, thin eyebrows lifted.

Her bed was warm, soft. The coverlets were light, but they made a nest for his huge body and he slept without dreaming, but then in the night a red light made him open sleepy eyes and by the reflection of the fireflames in the greystone hearth, he saw Leithe standing, slipping down her black garments, revealing her pale skin, the heavy breasts and smooth slopes of hips and thighs. She seemed a succubus to the drowsing giant.

Through his lashes he saw her approach the bed, smiling down at his recumbent figure. Her hand caught the coverlets, threw them back. She knelt on the bed, bending down to kiss his lips with a mouth that was fire and velvet.

"As Afgorkon put magic into your steel, so I shall put a little magic in your body, barbarian," she whispered.

Her hand ran down his chest…

Kothar woke to morning sunlight, wondering if he had dreamed last night, when Leithe had stripped off her garments and had come into this bed with him. She was not there now but the pillow beside his own was indented, where a head had lain. A long black hair rested on the pillow.

With a chuckle, Kothar reached for it, tied it on a knot about a lock of his yellow mane. "For luck," he told himself. He felt renewed in his strength and cunning, and wondered idly if there had been any truth in what the sorceress had whispered to him about putting magic in his flesh.

Leithe was nowhere in the tower but there was food on the dining room table, hot and tasty, and outside the tower door a black horse stood, caparisoned in silvered bridle and reins, with an ornate saddle of silver and ivory for his sitting.

Drawing the cloak of Thaladomis about his great shoulders, he kicked the black stallion to a gallop.

Along the narrow, dusty little roads of Nirvalla the iron hooves of the great warhorse carried thunder in a rolling tattoo as its long strides ate up ground. Past a hillside where a small farm lay, leaving a small castle behind on distant hills, the stallion ran on and on.

The twisted ruin of a great tree, its limbs and twigs black against the yellow sky, told Kothar he was near his destination. He drew back on the reins and the horse slowed to a canter. A narrow trail led up into the low hills past the tiny farm buildings. Kothar chose that pathway, letting the stallion walk.

Where a stone fence bordered a field where young lambs browsed, the Cumberian swung out of the saddle. His eyes took in the scene, saw also a small shed that held tools, and he found, upon investigation, a number of sheepskins for the tanning. One of the sheepskins was supple to the touch; Kothar dropped the cloak, tossing the woolly hide about his broad shoulders.

On hands and knees he crept into the meadow and mingled with the lambs. The sight of him did not startle them, they were reassured by the sign of the hide atop his back.

Neither was Skrye surprised, an hour later, for from the air, Kothar looked to be no more than a big ram. Downward from the clouds floated the big eagle, wings widespread as it glided like a ghost, ever earthward. Kothar saw him, grinned coldly, and crept forward like a sheep nibbling the grass.

Skrye floated thirty feet above the flock.

Under his hide, the barbarian sweated. Would the eagle drop near him? Or would it swoop down for a tiny lamb on the fringe of the flock, too far away for him to reach it? He waited with the patience of the animal he so much resembled.

Skrye screeched and fell.

Straight downward he dropped, talons spread wide for a small, woolly back. Kothar grunted gratefully, edged closer.

As those talons closed, Kothar sprang.

His hands went into feathers and across a golden leg. Skrye screamed, startled, turned its head, drove its sharp beak at this oddly shaped sheep. Kothar flinched and cursed as his flesh tore and blood showed but his fingers merely tightened. He rose upward to his feet, and now both hands were about the legs of Skrye as he swung him around and around over his head.

Kothar bent, drove Skrye downward at a big grey rock half-buried in the meadowland loam. The bird bounced when it hit, but it fought back, contorting its body, tearing with its beak at the big gash in Kothar's forearm its first attack had caused.

Three more times Kothar swung the bird. It did no good, and now he realized that the magic of Thaladomis protected it. Perhaps not even steel could harm Skrye.

Ahhh! But he carried more than steel.

Frostfire!

He let go the eagle. Instantly it was up, away. Yet Kothar was whipping out the blue blade of his sword, and in that same movement, cutting upward so that the blade made a blur in the clear air.

The edge slashed into a wing of the rising eagle, it sheared away flesh and feathers. With a cry of stark fury, the bird fluttered weakly to the ground. Kothar was after it, using the point. He jabbed, impaling the eagle, holding it, screaming and still struggling, to the grass.

Skrye took time to die, but when it was dead, Kothar knelt and fumbled until his bloody fingers closed on something ovoid in shape and hard to the touch. He brought it out into the sunlight, and saw that it was the ruby of Warrl. He wiped the jewel and his hands clean on the meadowland dirt, then crossed the fields to where a little trickle of water came along the spillway of the farm springhouse.

He washed the blood and dirt from the ruby and from his hands. He slipped the jewel into a fold of his loincloth and tightened the rope belt that held it.

Then he rode to the black tower.

Leithe washed his badly gashed forearm with soapy water and a soft cloth and spread a salve on the flesh which healed it within the hour. Her lips twitched from time to time at sight of the single black hair knotted into his yellow mane, and her beautiful features assumed a satisfied look.

"Without that strand of my hair, you might have died," she told him, and broke into soft laughter. "Or if I had not come to sleep with you last night, to give your flesh a little of my own magic. I'm glad to see you are a sensible man. Now let me see the ruby."

She took it into her palms, cupping them so the blood-red jewel glinted evilly. Long she looked into its red depths, sighing and nodding her head, before she spoke again.

"Yes, the demon is trapped inside it, where Thaladomis put him," she murmured. "And he begs for freedom. His name is Warrl, and he burns to have revenge on the magician."

"Dare we free him?" Kothar asked, staring at the jewel.

"We must free him, if we ever hope to get the helix back into Nirvalla. The spell that keeps the helix in your world will be broken when Warrl is loosed. But since there will be incantations on the ruby, so that it will not crack like an ordinary jewel, we must make preparations."

In her incantation chamber, Kothar watched Leithe light the coals and toss certain herbs on them when they glowed red, so that a pungent, pleasant smell rose into the air. From one of the opened volumes, Leithe studied the magic formula that would enable her to set Warrl free.

In a golden mortar, she ground up with a golden pestle the dried hide of a frog, the eyes of a cat, nard and wolfbane, poppy seeds and black water from a witch pool, making a rich paste. Lifting the ruby, she smeared the paste over it.

"Fetch the warhammer, Kothar," she commanded. From its peg along the wall above a cabinet containing the gall bladder of a dog, the liver of a boar and the other herbs and spices which Leithe employed in her necromancies, the barbarian lifted down the long-handled weapon and Leithe, using a silver mortar and pestle this time, ground up purple foxglove mixed with henbane and the roots of dried Kolor beans with water, forming a purplish liquid. Kothar came at her gesture, dipping the flat end of the warhammer into the mixture.

Leithe placed the ruby on a flat slab. "Strike!" she cried.

Kothar raised the warhammer, brought it down upon the ruby. The jewel cracked to the sound of a thousand bells clanging, and from its red interior, amid the shards of shattered ruby, lifted a blackish smoke.

Leithe made a sign in the air. "Peace between us, Warrl—and peace between you and this warrior."

Red eyes glowed in the midst of the black cloud, and a deep voice said, "Peace between us, Leithe, and with you, warrior. My quarrel is with Thaladomis!"

"Go, Warrl. We have freed you."

"I shall go. My gratitude to you both."

The black smoke whirled, fluttered a moment, and was gone. Kothar let out his breath slowly, aware that the hairs on the back of his neck were stiff, and that his sun-bronzed flesh crawled. He did not like demons or wizards, but they were a necessary part of his world.

Give him the cold wind blowing across the ice wastes and a white bear at bay to his hunting spears, and he was content. Give him a horse beneath him to ride, Frostfire to swing at a human foe, and he was happy.

As for warlocks and their spells—"Fauggghh!" he growled, shaking himself.

Leithe smiled, put a pale hand on his hairy forearm. "It was necessary, Kothar. Now you can leave Nirvalla, but wear your cloak. Much of the black magic has gone out of the helix, but it is still dangerous to mortal hands. Go now, with my gratitude, and that of Phronolom and Ayatha."

"What of Kyros?"

"He stays here." She shrugged. "He is harmless without his soldiers and Thaladomis, being nothing but a fat little man. Let the naiads keep him for their plaything, if they will. He cannot harm anyone, now."

"And Ayatha? Didn't you say she was in thrall? That she sleeps in her bed like a dead woman?"

"The ruby has been shattered, Warrl freed. Ayatha too, has been freed. She is alive, and in the arms of Phronalom at this very moment."

Kothar grinned, nodding. His big hands hitched at Frostfire, drew his cloak closer about his giant frame. "I'll be gone, then. But—how do I get back?"

Leithe said, "Speak these words, 'krthnol abbatt sorgik.' Ah, and when you take the helix from the galley, say the single word 'horthidol'!"

The barbarian nodded.

As if at a sudden thought, he stepped forward, caught Leithe in his arms, and mashed her lips with his, holding her close in his embrace. He felt a fire in his flesh at the touch of her soft body to his, but this woman was not for him.

He let her go. She laughed happily and whispered the words that he repeated after her.

"Krthnol abbatt sorgik!"

Leithe and her room of incantations was gone.

CHAPTER 5

The helix gleamed in golden splendor in front of him.

Kothar saw that the room was bare of the white mists; probably, he reasoned, because the evil emanations of Warrl no longer touched the golden spiral. Kothar put out his hands toward the glistening helix.

"Horthidol," he breathed, and the helix lifted easily into his fingers. Gently he carried it to the window, where he wrapped the cloak about it.

He slid a foot through the cabin window and stepped out into the night. Below him, naked and cold and wet, the Oasian dancing girl shivered to the cold night winds blowing across Lake Lotusine. At sight of him, she gave a glad little cry.

"I was afraid," she panted, reaching up toward him as he came downward, toes and fingergrips supporting his big body. "There have been terrible sounds and cries from the deck."

"There may be even worse ones, soon," he rumbled.

The girl rose up to press herself against him, her hands caressing his shoulders and back while she pressed her lips to his chest. Kothar grinned. Aie! The sorceress Leithe had been every inch a woman, but this dusky daughter of the southlands was all the woman any man might need, and the witchery she possessed had only to do with her beauty and not with spells and incantations.

He kissed her with the savagery of the northlands in his mouth; she moaned and squirmed against him.

"They killed Gorth finally," she told him when he let her go, "and just tossed his body overboard."

"We'd better get away," he growled. "A demon's coming for Thaladomis—and I don't want to be around when they meet. By Dwallka! I've had my belly full of magic for the nonce."

But he was too late.

Already an eerie wail was rising from the deck. Kothar caught the girl to him, shifting her onto his broad back where she locked legs about his middle and arms about his neck for easier riding. She caught the cloak-wrapped helix in a hand so he could use both arms for climbing.

"I'll take one look," he rasped.

He went up the side of the gilded galley as a monkey might run up a tree branch in the vast jungles south of Ispahan. His head lifted above the rail, followed by her own.

A dark smoke was writhing on the galley deck. To one side of it a noblewoman, dark of hair and stripped to a tiny girdle during the carousing following the killing of the great bear, shrank back at sight of it. Her eyes bulged, both hands were lifted palms outward as if to halt its progress. Her mouth was contorted in a grimace of stark fear as she made little whimpering sounds.

"No, no—stay away! Whatever you are—stay back!"

At her cry, men turned from the tables set with fruit and meats and cups of fine Salernian wine, where the courtiers of the royal court feasted and made merry in the absence of the emperor. The women who were being disrobed as the night wore on, who perched on laps or leaned against men flushed with wine, were forgotten. And Thaladomis, who sat at the end of the table, waited upon by two rich noblewomen, stark naked, whom it was his amusement to humble and degrade, paused with a fruit halfway to his lips.

As that black cloud grew and took shape, the magician leaped to his feet, scattering a bowl of fruit and a wine cup. His face was white as the snows of Thuum, there was utter terror in his gaze.

"No!" he screamed. "You are safe in—"

The dark cloud firmed into shape, towering upward into the semblance of a winged man, a man with heavy, rolling muscles and long, furry ears. The blazing red eyes, filled with hate, with the lust to slay, froze every man and woman motionless at that banqueting table.

"I come, Thaladomis! For your mean, arrogant soul I thirst! You shall attend me at *my* banqueting hall—for all eternity! Between the tortures fallen demons suffer, you shall wait on me day and night, without food— what need has a spirit for food?—and without rest from the blows and buffets which shall be your pay in my employ!"

Thaladomis screamed. He alone of all the feasters understood what the demon meant, how he spoke truth, that he reigned in a sub-world out of which Thaladomis had summoned him, to entrap him in the ruby.

The magician could not move. It was as if he had been turned to stone. He watched, as did the others but with greater terror in his soul, as Warrl became massive reality on the deck planks and stepped forward to claim his slave.

His arm went out, lifted Thaladomis into the air.

Gripping the body of the magician in his left fist, Warrl caught his left arm and twisted it savagely. Thaladomis screamed in agony.

"Stop! Stop! You're twisting off my arm!"

"What need has a spirit for arms, mage?"

He ripped loose the arm. As Thaladomis came close to fainting in his agony, Warrl turned his attention to his other arm, turning it, yanking it, until it flew through the air out over the waters of Lake Lotusine.

Behind him, Kothar felt Laella shuddering in horror, whispering, "I cannot look! It is awful. He is a wicked man but—"

"He would have kept Warrl inside the ruby forever," Kothar rumbled. "The demon seeks only just vengeance. And the ways of demons are not our ways. We might show mercy, not a demon!"

A leg fell to the deck. A second leg was flung into the night. Thaladomis was no more than a mewling torso of a man.

In his vast hand, Warrl lifted him high, shook him in the air. "What? Not dead yet? Come, Thaladomis—yield up your spirit to me, or off comes your head, as well!"

"Yes, yes!" cried the wizard. "Anything—to end this agony!"

Something thin and grey fluttered where the armless, legless torso hung in that dark, ebon hand. A shriek, and the torso fell, and now Warrl gripped merely a struggling length of—emptiness—in his fist.

The demon flung back his head, hailed laughter to the sky.

"I win, Thaladomis! You are mine—for all eternity!"

The wind blew across the deck.

A woman wept softly in the night.

The deck was empty where Warrl had stood.

Kothar lowered himself away from the rail. In moments he was dipping his feet and then his body into the cold waters of the lake. He took back the helix in the cloak, and with Laella beside him, struck out for the nearest shore.

The dancing girl kept good time, trailing him by only a little on their way toward the stones of an old quay jutting out from a small dock. Behind the dock was an old warehouse, its doors closed at this hour of the morning. Dawn was still an hour away, and soon the cobblestoned streets would know the rattle of cartwheels and the tramp of early risers on their way to work.

Kothar put a hand on a piling, yanked himself upward. He put a hand down, drew the shivering, wet dancing girl up onto the stone to stand beside him. She was naked, but Kothar dared not remove the cloak from about the helix for fear it would blast them both. He himself only wore his wet loincloth and Frostfire in its scabbard. He shifted the belt about his middle to make running that much easier.

"Running will warm you," he told the girl.

Hand in hand they sped away across the cobblestones.

They met no one on the way to the walled gardens of Nestorius the merchant, and the big stone house flanking it, where a single window glowed golden with light behind its curtain. The barbarian held the shivering Oasian close against him as his hand made thunder with the knocker.

To his surprise, the street door was opened almost immediately. The same girl who had opened it when Rufflod stood beside him smiled at him and looked with surprise at the naked Laella.

"I'll fetch clothes," she said, and fled.

Moments later, the Oasian dancing girl was slipping into a woolen kirtle that came to the middle of her thighs. Her feet went into sandals, and then she stood and shook back her long black hair, letting it dry in the wind sweeping across the garden. Kothar put on a dry loincloth, a fur kilt, and a heavy woolen shirt.

"Nestorius is awake," the girl said. "He waits for you."

She brought them across the garden and into the big stone house. The night was very still around them, the flapping of the girl's sandals were loud in the otherwise silent house.

Nestorius was standing in his library, tall and saturnine, his dark face flushed with expectancy. His eyes went at once to the helix wrapped inside the cloak and he put his hands together, rubbing them.

"You have it," he cried, and there was both surprise and excitement in his voice. "I never thought you could do it, despite what Rufflod said. Where is he, by the way?"

"Dead," answered Kothar. "The helix killed him—as it will kill you if you stand in the same room with it, while not wearing this cloak. Let the cloak dry, put it on—and you can step into a strange world beyond our own."

He told of his adventure while Nestorius listened.

When he was finished, the merchant said, "Then I have sent you on a fool's errand. What good is the helix to me, if this Phronalom may send a demon to take it back?"

The barbarian shrugged. "I brought you the helix, that was our agreement. I made no promises as to what the helix was, what treasure it might bring you. That was your concern."

Nestorius smiled coldly. "I pay for services, barbarian. Why should I pay you good gold for something I won't be able to keep?"

Kothar put out his hands and closed them on the fur-trimmed cotehardie the merchant wore. Easily he lifted the man into the air, shaking him gently.

"Nestorius, I like not your cheating ways. I would as soon kill you as let you trick me out of my money. Now hand over the leather bag with the gold and the jewels in it that I earned this night, by Dwallka!"

The trader read the hard blue eyes of the Cumberian correctly and sweat came out upon his brow. "Let me down," he cried, "or I'll have my guards in on you to toss you in one of the emperor's jails."

Kothar grinned. "If you do, you'll be dead before they get here! And the emperor won't be coming back. Now—which is it?"

Nestorius nodded his head, smiling grimly. "Very well. Set me down. I'll give you the gold."

The barbarian lowered him. At the same time, the merchant broke free and leaped toward the shelves that lined his study. His hand went out toward the leather sacks piled there. Instead of lifting a sack, Nestorius put his hand on the bell and yanked it off the shelf.

In a moment the clangor of the bell would alert his guards. Triumph shone in the face of the lean, dark man and a grin revealed his teeth.

Suddenly, the room was cold.

No blast of freezing gale from the ice wastes of Thuum could have been more frigid. Hoarfrost formed instantly on the shelves, the books, the paintings and draperies on the wall. Icicles hung from the ceiling as the moist air froze under that arctic blast.

Nestorius froze too, eyes wide with horror.

A demon writhed into being in the room, white, coated with rime, pink eyes glowing in a face which seemed made from ice. Its pink eyes touched Nestorius, the barbarian and the dancing girl, then settled on the helix in the sodden cloak.

It moved forward, and Kothar heard the sound of ice crunching, a sound he had heard many times when he had stood atop the great glacier of his northern homelands.

"No!" screamed the merchant, and leaped.

"Stand back!" the ice demon warned.

Nestorius took no heed of that icy voice. He caught the helix in his arms, wrapped them about the cloak-shrouded spiral. "It's mine," he panted. "I paid good gold for its delivery. That makes it mine!"

"It belongs to Phronalom, it is not yours."

"Besides, you paid no gold," Kothar grated. "You denied your debt, which means the helix does not belong to you—but to me, the thief who took it. And I give it away freely."

Nestorius stared from the man to the demon. "I will pay. I was but jesting. Take the leather sack—take two!"

Inexorably the demon moved on the merchant who went back two steps, then three, until the draperied wall permitted him to go no farther. The ice-being advanced, white arms held out. Its frigid fingers it placed on Nestorius.

The merchant stiffened. Hoarfrost covered his cotehardie, his body; icicles formed on his face. He was dead, frozen, propped up against the wall.

The demon took the helix and the cloak away from his nerveless fingers. For a moment he stared down at it. Then he was gone.

Laella shook herself, pushing back her long hair. "Gods of Oasia—I'm freezing! Kothar—let's get out of here!"

The barbarian stared at the rigid body of the merchant, nodding. "Yes. I don't want to be blamed for Nestorius' death."

Laella ran to the shelf, snatched at two leather bags fat with coins and jewels. "I'll take these to pay for all the trouble you've been through. We both deserve something, and Nestorius has no further need for gold."

She ran for the door, clutching the bags.

Kothar followed after her, pausing only for one long, last glance at the dead merchant. Strange. If the merchant had played honest, there would have been no trouble. He might still be alive.

Laella was in the doorway, waving a hand.

"Come, Kothar! We can buy passage to the southlands with but a small part of all this gold."

He ran after the girl, wondering how long he would be permitted to keep the gold and the jewels. The girl, now, was another matter. It would be a long trip to Oasia. The nights would be dark velvet and the girl warm and fragrant in his arms.

Kothar grinned and ran the faster.

A PLAGUE OF DEMONS

CHAPTER 1

For three days, on the long ride from Romm to Clon Mell in the land of Gwyn Caer, Kothar the barbarian had seen the face of Red Lori, and heard her threats.

The first time she appeared to his eyes, he was making a campfire on the border region between the misty swamp and the lands of the baron lords. There was the smell of salt in the air from the dying sea that had beat against the shore of what was now Avalonia, eons ago. Cattails swayed to the cool wind whipping the swamp waters into tiny ripples. Laella was off gathering twigs and he was alone with the red flames his flint and steel had sparked.

Red Lori was a part of those flames, laughing up at him, her slanted green eyes narrowed, her red tongue showing between her teeth.

"Two days, barbarian. Two days of life remain!"

She was lovely, Kothar thought, staring at her image in the fire. Too bad she was a witch—or had been, before Kothar had hung her in a silver cage in the palace of Queen Elfa of Commoral—for she was a disturbingly beautiful woman. Long red hair fell to her curving white haunches, and her breasts were full and tilted. Naked she stood in her cage, naked she appeared to him now.

Then she was gone; only her taunting laughter remained.

The second time she appeared was as he bent above a pool inside the mountain barriers of Gwyn Caer, hands cupped to lift cool mountain water to his lips. The Oasian dancing girl was changing her garments behind a stand of pines that protected her from the cold boreal breezes. The witch-woman stood on the bottom stones, a tiny figurine with arms upraised to him, eyes flaring.

"One day of life is yours, Kothar! Only one remains!"

Then she faded from view, and Kothar drank the water in his cupped hands with a worried scowl on his craggy features. Well he knew and understood the hate of the redhead, he was aware of her ability to talk to demons even if most of her necromantic powers had been stripped from her by the wizard Kazazael before she had been imprisoned in the cage. Still, the demons might obey her and send their dread familiars to slay him to satisfy her need for vengeance.

And then, last night in the Inn of the Cross and Keys within Clon Mell itself, within range of the bells that rang like sweet music from church spires and temple cloisters, she had come again. Laella sat across the wooden tabletop from him in a woolen tunic hung with chains, her red mouth babbling comments on the people around them, and there was the smell of roasting meat and midlands ale in the air.

He was lifting the leather jack that held his own ale, tilting it to drain the last remaining mouthful, when she was there, a tiny imp inside the leather, up to her knees in cool liquid.

"No day remains! You die this night, Kothar!"

Her laughter rang in his ears.

He marveled that Laella did not hear it, but she was too intent on the dancing girl who had stepped out on a cleared section of the floor to pay other sights and sounds any attention. The dancing girl was from Makkadonia, dark of skin, with long black hair swaying to her movements. A girdle of coins ringed her bare middle, strings of bells fell from that girdle almost to her ankles. A pair of castanets between her fingers kept rhythm to the jangle of the bells and to the strings and drums of the musicians in a small alcove.

Laella would criticize the dancer, he was sure. She herself had danced, in those days when she had been a slave, before kings and emperors, and would find easy fault with some tavern belly dancer. The barbarian turned his eyes to his leathern jack.

To his surprise, Red Lori was still there.

"Beg me, Kothar! Beg for your life!"

"Not me," he growled.

"Then you die!"

He grinned down at the tiny figure. "Do you think to frighten me?" he jeered. His hand raised the jack, he swallowed the ale, half-expecting to find the woman in his mouth.

She was still inside the jack when he lowered it, laughing up at him. "Then I'll kill Laella! I'll kill both of you!"

"You're afraid," he said suddenly. "That's why you threaten me. Either that—or you have a plan. And Laella doesn't play a part in it. You want her out of the way."

The witchwoman was silent, glaring up at him.

When he put his eyes on the Oasian dancing girl, he saw she was still raptly eying the belly dancer, but with a shade less interest. Red Lori said, "Oh, she can't hear us, she just sees you gawking into your empty ale mug, like the barbarian boor you are. You're free to talk."

Kothar shook his head. "I won't get rid of her, just to pleasure you. I enjoy her company."

"Then die! I'll be well rid of you."

She faded from view, making an angry gesture.

Kothar sighed and turned in his chair, hand upraised to signal a passing serving wench to come and fill his jack. To Dwallka with Red Lori! He would feast and drink and later he would bed down his Oasian dancing girl in a soft bed in the upper room he had rented that afternoon. The ale and the wanton wisdoms of the Oasian would make him forget the witchwoman and her threats.

Let Red Lori strike—if she could!

CHAPTER 2

They came in the dark of the night, three killers from the thieves' market section of Clon Mell, daggers in their hands. They moved as their shadows moved, silently, yet their feet made little sounds where they trampled down the rushes covering the floor of the little bedroom.

Only the animal senses of the big Cumberian saved his life, and that of the Oasian dancing girl curled up against him between the soft sheets. Kothar had been trained to sleep since boyhood with his ears alive to strange sounds. As those rushes crackled ever so faintly, he was off the bed and rolling with Laella in the grip of an arm, flinging the bedsheets behind him to distract their attackers.

His eyes were not bleary from sleep. He saw the dark shapes of the trio of killers, clearly enough, and remembered the threats of Red Lori. The bedsheets he had flung at them entangled their heads. Kothar dove over the bed at them without thinking, putting his hands on the bed, kicking out with his bare feet at the belly of the third man, doubling him up in pain.

Kothar reached out, grabbed the sheeted heads of the other two assassins and rammed their skulls together so hard Laella could hear the sound of their splitting, like overripe melons dropped on a paving-stone. The men sagged, and Kothar let them go, grinning so that he showed his white teeth in his sun-bronzed face like pearls in dark sand as he reached for his great sword.

The blade came free just in time. The man he had kicked in the belly was on top of him, swinging a slim scimitar. Kothar got his sword up just in time, the steel blades rang with a sharp clangor. Then, with a movement so fast Laella could not follow it, Kothar slashed sideways with the keen edge of Frostfire.

Through flesh and blood he drove his steel, cleaving deep into the assassin who stood a moment, mouth open, eyes wide, before he realized that his body had been cut almost in half. He made a mewling sound, then was silent as he died.

Over the bed and the three dead bodies, Kothar stared at the naked girl. "They might have killed you," he told her.

"They didn't," she pointed out.

He lifted the sheet that covered the two dead men and wiped his blade on it, very carefully. His face was twisted in thought, and then he shook his head.

"If they had killed me, they wouldn't have let you live. I can't let you die, Laella. I've got to send you home to your people."

She argued all the rest of the night but the barbarian would not listen to her. "Enough that you were almost killed! Another time, I might not hear them as they came."

"Why did they try to kill you?"

His brawny shoulders lifted in a casual shrug. "Who knows? Maybe Kyros' uncle sent them, for having done away with the emperor."

He did not tell her about Red Lori.

Early next morning, the chiming of camel bells made sweet sounds in the air as they walked through the merchant bazaar toward the stalls where Althassar the Miser was forming a trade caravan for the southern lands. Kothar strode along with a black scowl on his face, Laella with the traces of tears recently dried.

To Althassar the Miser he growled, "I'm sending her back to her folks. She's too much for me. She drains me with her embraces."

Well, Laella thought, it's as good an excuse as any.

The bearded merchant grinned knowingly while Kothar poured out gold pieces from his leather sack. He was about to make a quip about barbarians and Oasian girls but the hard face of the youthful giant before him made him bite his tongue.

Kothar was not happy about this parting. He would miss the dancing girl, but he was determined that Red Lori would not get the chance to strike at him through her.

Ah, well. A lonely campfire and life was preferable to a soft bed and loving female flesh, when a dagger-stab might come with it.

It had been a pleasant interlude.

Now it was over.

Kothar took the girl into his arms for a farewell kiss. She wriggled her soft flesh against him in a desperate attempt to remind him of what he would be missing, once she mounted her camel and became part of the caravan being formed by the bearded merchant.

Then he pushed her away, and strode off between a pile of Vandacian carpets displayed by two old men. Kothar walked swiftly, not looking back.

He would miss the girl. By the gods, he would! She had made a most pleasant traveling companion.

It was for her own good, this parting.

But—was it?

Kothar admitted he felt a sense of freedom he had not known since he had taken up with the Oasian wench. He could go where he would now, without worrying about finding a bed to sleep in and a wooden tabletop off which to eat. He could hunker down beside a twig fire and cook his meal and eat it, and let the wind blow free about his fur-clad shoulders.

He walked purposefully through the bazaar, his mind on the little shop of the trader Pahk Mah. Pahk Mah dealt in silver and strange weapons, in gold wares and in the spices of the Orient, in slavegirls and in jewels. He asked no questions of the men who brought him curiously carved little statues or jewels that might have been taken from the rings women wore, for Pahk Mah was known to the brotherhood of thievery as a fence.

Not that the jewels in his little leather bag were stolen, Kothar reasoned, though Laella had snatched them without permission. It was just caution that made him turn into the little cobblestoned street at the end of which the shop of Pahk Mah made itself known by a wooden sign hanging on iron chains above its recessed doorway.

His hand pushed the door, but it would not open. Kothar peered in through the grimy glass, seeing ivory statuettes of naked women in lewd poses, candlesticks carved from solid gold, ebony trays and bowls, ivory canisters, weapons fashioned by the ironworkers of Abathor who were reputedly among the finest ever known.

The interior of the shop was a hodgepodge of miscellany.

It was also empty.

With the flat of his hand, the barbarian pounded on the door. "Pahk Mah!" he bellowed. "Pahk Mah! Open up."

He saw movement in the dark recesses of the shop, near the long wooden counter, where rare books on demonolatry and necromancy sat binding by binding alongside ceremonial bells and incensories in which the forbidden scents of Ikrikone might be burned by initiates to the dark rites.

His hand beckoned. The figure in the shadows scurried forward. When he passed a beam of dying sunlight, Kothar recognized the man for Ishral, the assistant to Pahk Mah. Ishral made flapping motions with his hands, indicating that the barbarian should go away.

Kothar grinned, lifting out the leather sack and shaking it. He even poured a couple of the jewels onto his palm where they sparkled as if with inner fires.

Ishral came close to the door.

"Go away. The old man is ill."

"Then somebody must have cheated him in a trade. The old man hasn't known a day of sickness in his life. Now let me in, Ishral, or I'll kick down your door and all the thieves in Clon Mell will be here within seconds to loot and steal."

Ishral shook his head, but his hands went to the latches and the bolts behind which Pahk Mah barricaded himself. As the door opened, his quavering voice protested, "He will beat me for this. I ought to have my head examined."

The Cumberian clapped his bony shoulder with a hand. "I bring rare jewels to the old man, jewels he will be delighted to see."

Ishral shuffled ahead of him, grumbling denials. He was even older than Pahk Mah, Kothar thought, following him. Men said Ishral had been a slave, long ago, who had made love to a queen of Aegypton and had been caught in the process by a jealous lover. As a result, Ishral had lost that which made him a man.

It was probably just gossip, but the man did speak in a high voice, and he had no use for women, as far as anyone knew. He was bald, with a forked beard and piercing black eyes, and his skin was a fish belly white.

Altogether, an unlovely specimen, but he was shrewd, as grasping and as clever as Pahk Mali, and there were some who claimed he was a partner to the shopkeeper.

Ishral paused at a leather curtain.

"Wait here, I will tell the old one," he said.

"Nonsense, he'll be glad to see me," Kothar grinned, and swept aside the hanging. He paused, honestly shocked.

An old man Pahk Mah was, he knew. But this bag of bones who sat hunched on a stool before this backroom fireplace, thin and with white hair, eyes rheumy and shivering steadily, was something more than old. This man was absolutely terrified.

The barbarian strode forward.

He felt the warmth of the flames on his booted legs, and his brawny body made a shadow that fell across the bent, shivering figure.

"What's wrong, old friend?" he asked quietly.

"I am cursed by the gods," the old man wailed.

"Nonsense. What gods there are only exist in the minds of men. Now speak out, tell me what's bothering you."

"It's my daughter, Mahla."

"Pretty little Mahla of the gold hair? Has she died?"

"Not yet. She dies tonight!"

Kothar reached for a three-legged stool, dragging it forward and settling his rump on it, frowning. He remembered Mahla from the last time he had been in this shop. She had been little more than a child, slimly curved but with a sweet face and long yellow hair that fell to her hips.

"Who kills her, old one?"

"The worshipers of the dark god, Pulthoom. They celebrate his rites in the ruins of the old abbey outside the city, where the old city used to be before it was razed because of the magicks performed within its walls."

Kothar growled, "I'll save her. I'll go at once."

The old man shook his head, staring blindly into the fire. "It's no use. I offended the priests of Pulthoom by not giving them a sacred golden bowl my agents found in the ruins of Allakar. For nothing! They wanted it for nothing!"

Pahk Mali turned his head and stared hard at Kothar. His eyes were suddenly bright and keen, hard as agates. The hair on his head was white, but his face was carefully shaved. He had been a tall, powerful man once. Now he seemed wasted away.

"You can do nothing, Kothar," he said softly. "I have offended Pulthoom and I will be punished. So say his priests. They took Mahla away with them, as evidence of what my punishment shall be. They intend to sacrifice her this night at Thistem Abbey."

"They have to wait for darkness. It isn't dark yet."

"I thank you for your intentions, but you can do nothing against a god. I have sinned, I shall be punished."

"Why didn't you give them the bowl?"

The old man snarled, "What? And lose money?"

"Isn't your girl worth more than money?"

"Yes, but at the time, I didn't know what the priests would do. After they took Mahla, I offered them the bowl, but they said I must pay for my sins. My dearest treasure—my Mahla—must die, they said. Only in such a way would I understand the power of the dark god."

"Hogwash," growled the barbarian. They were just taking advantage of an old man. Besides, they needed a living sacrifice to Pulthoom and only a female would do.

His hand hitched Frostfire between his legs.

He held no love for the priests of these dark gods.

They were cunning, cruel men, for the most part, and they used Pulthoom and his godhood as excuses to take what they wanted in the way of wealth or womanhood.

Kothar doubted that they would kill Mahla. More likely they would throw a scare into her and keep her as a plaything for their lusts. After they tired of her, they could always stick a dagger between her ribs.

"Pahk Mah, let me leave this with you for study."

Kothar handed over the leather sack.

The old man came to life, nodding and undoing the pull cord, letting the jewels roll out on his palm. His eyes blazed, he made a little sound with his lips.

"They are excellent gems, they have been selected for size and color by an expert. I'm not going to ask where they come from, enough for me that they'll be mine." Placing the jewels back into the sack, Pahk Mah pulled tight the strings.

"Now tell me, what do you want in exchange for them? Money, I suppose. All you wanderers are the same."

Kothar smiled grimly. "I don't know what I want, as yet. I'll know more about that, after I get your girl back."

Pahk Mah opened his eyes wide. "You'd dare do that? Leap in among the worshipers of the dark god and grab her?"

"If it means I'd get you to judge my jewels and give me fair recompense for them, I would. I can't have you sitting here moping away your days. I need money for my travels. If this is the only way to get it, I'll do it."

He rose to his feet, towering above the old man. In his fur jerkin and mail shirt, he made a giant figure, his bared arms bulging with muscle, his legs naked between his kilt and his warboots.

"How do I find this abbey?" he asked.

It was Ishral who answered, from the leather drape where he had been standing. "You follow the Street of the Silk Sellers down a slope and then out across the heath. You can scarcely miss them. The ruins are the only things on the heath."

The man turned and walked away, letting the leather curtain rustle into place. Kothar went after him, turning once to study the old man who was shaking the jewels out of the little leather sack and studying them. The barbarian nodded, apparently satisfied.

From the old man, his eyes went casually to a length of wrapping out of which protruded a length of obal horn. Intrigued, the barbarian stepped closer, gripping the wrapping and throwing it back.

"What's this? I never knew Pahk Mah to treasure anything so much that he wrapped it up like a babe in swaddling clothes."

The wrapping came undone. Before him lay a horn bow perhaps five feet in length, polished and gleaming as if new. Beside it lay a quiver, filled with arrows.

"By Dwallka! No wonder he cares for it so tenderly. This is a weapon fit for a king. Here, let me test it."

Ishral mumbled, "It was the bow of Krangor of Abathor, he who lived two centuries ago and carved out a kingdom for himself in the southlands."

Kothar grinned, "Stolen, no doubt, from the temple where it rested by some quick-fingering thief. I'll take it as part payment for those jewels."

Ishral shrugged.

With the bow in a hand, with the quiver over a shoulder, the barbarian strode out into the dying sunlight. Behind him, he heard the bolts and latches click into place.

Outside the shop, the wind had sprung up. It ruffled the fur of his jerkin and swung the wooden shop-sign on its iron chains. Here and there a man hurried along, head bent. The sky was darkening, the cool chill of coming night was already in the air.

Kothar walked the Street of the Silk Sellers like a lion padding along a jungle trail, not noticing the glances his giant bulk received, intent only on finding Thistem Abbey and rescuing the girl who would be flat on her back on the sacrificial stone.

It would not be an easy task, her rescue. The worshipers of the dark god were fanatics, half-crazy men who would not think twice about sticking a dagger in his back, even as he made his escape from the ruins. Kothar grinned at his thoughts. By Dwallka, he was no fat southlander to accept cold steel gracefully. He would kill first, laying about him with Frostfire until he cleared a path for himself and little Mahla.

And yet, he could not run forever with Mahla in his arms, not with the hue and cry after him. He would need horses. He had stabled his warhorse Greyling and the white mare on which he and Laella had ridden into Clon Mell, at a blacksmith shop not far from here. It would be best to make a small detour, and get them.

He paid over two copper coins to the smith and swung up into the kak. Holding the reins of the smaller horse, which had belonged to Laella, he moved eastward toward the vast stretch of heath.

He did not see the man Ishral, who had come to a street well and paused there, watching Kothar as he cantered away from the Street of Silk Sellers. Under the grey hood of his cloak, that he wore against the gathering wind, Ishral was smiling grimly.

Kothar would not live to see the rites of Pulthoom.

CHAPTER 3

The heath stretched like a corner of fabled Aedenn across the world. Overhead the stars were flicking into life in a grey bowl of sky, and where the bluebells and the heather stretched their petals, the wind moaned and whistled as if to announce the coming of the dark god.

Kothar rode with his head bowed, aware that on such a night as this, Pulthoom the Black Lord would find it easy to penetrate the barriers between worlds and make his dread presence known. Kothar had no doubt of his ability to steal Mahla from the frenzied worshipers, but the dark god himself was another matter. He did not like to fight with gods or demons.

He could see nothing but the vast wasteland on either side of him. Due to the gathering dusk, the spires and rooftops of Clon Mell were nothing but a haze on his back trail. He felt alone, but this fact could not account for the coldness rippling up and down his spine.

Kothar had been alone too often for that.

No, this uneasiness was the result of that animal instinct which was so much a part of him. As might the wary wolf near a trap, Kothar sensed danger.

He did not shift position, he kept Greyling to a steady walk. But under his hood his eyes raked the heath in front of him. No need to look upon his back trail, his ears would hear the sound of hooves galloping, if there was danger behind him.

What danger there might be was in front of him.

He was nearing a group of jagged rocks, jutting upward from the heath floor like the gnarled fingers of some half-buried giant. A man or two might hide among those rocks, very easily.

Kothar reined in the roan.

He reached downward blindly, his fingers fumbling for the horn bow he had taken from among the weapons in the shop of Pahk Mah. Its tip he put on his foot in an iron stirrup. His muscles rolled, bulging, as he bent that length of obal horn, bringing its catgut string up over the rock and setting it in place.

His fingers touched the feathered shafts hanging in the hide quiver, lifting one out and nocking it to the bowstring. His laughter rode the wind as he tightened his grip on the bow.

He would not walk blindly into any trap.

The dark worshipers might well post guards to keep the soldiers of the king from harrying them. They might consider Kothar such a warrior. If so, he did not intend to make a sitting target for them.

He slid from the saddle.

He walked across the heath, still wrapped in his cloak, but he had brushed the flaps of that cloak back to free his arms for the firing. His angle of walk would carry him to one side of the rocks.

It was dusk, so he almost missed seeing the touch of black cloth against the grey rock. Only his keen barbarian eyes, trained since birth to see sudden movement, could have picked out that betraying color.

He crouched lower so that the tall grasses hid his huge bulk. Bow in hand, arrow to the string, he sidled forward. The night was still around him, there was no cry of bird or beast, only the faint slither of his war-boots on the grass told of his movements.

A man in the black and red robes of a priest of Pulthoom rose upward. His hands whirled. A *something* flew through the air at Kothar. The big barbarian could not see it clearly, it was too dark.

The horn bow bent. An arrow flew faster than the wind.

The priest in the ornate robes stiffened, jerked. His head whipped back as the arrow shaft buried itself in his chest.

The *something* burst into flames, fifty feet from the barbarian. Kothar stared, slightly awed. What had destroyed that thing? He had not done it, and his animal instinct told him the priest who flung it had not intended his weapon to be destroyed before it reached its target.

The Cumberian ran forward. In the high grasses, he saw a burning length of rope with two round stones attached to each end. Kothar had never seen a bolar before, but he knew the hunters of Gwyn Caer used these weapons to hunt down the long-necked deer that sometimes ran upon the heath.

Bending closer, he saw a face inside the flames.

"I destroyed the bolar, Kothar! I have another fate in store for you!"

"Your killers failed in the inn bedroom, Red Lori!"

"They were not sent to kill, but to warn you! I wanted you to rid yourself of the dancing girl! Where you are going—there shall be women enough for you to handle!"

Mocking laughter made the hairs on his neck bristle.

Then—Red Lori was gone.

He stood with the wind howling about him, frowning. His eyes raked the heath, the jutting rock pile. A dead priest lay on those rocks. Did he have a companion? The barbarian moved forward, still alert, yet somehow relaxed. If Red Lori were protecting him, she would let no harm befall him until it was her whim to strike.

Yet he did not abandon his caution. He came upon the rocks from the side, seeing the dead priest with his shaft in his chest lying huddled on the stones. There was no one else in this hiding place.

Kothar bent, yanked out his arrow. These handmade shafts were too valuable to leave lying about. He cleansed the arrowhead in the dirt between the stones while his eyes considered the dead bulk of the priest.

Then his hands were out, stripped off the priestly cloak. Shrugging out of his own grey chlamys he draped it across the dead body. The red and black robe he tossed about his own shoulders. It would be a disguise, of sorts.

He ran down his two horses, mounted Greyling and catching up the reins of the white mare, brought them at a walk toward the abbey ruins.

A red light shone where Thirsten Abbey stood. A sound of voices raised in song came faintly with the wind. The worshipers of the dark god were beginning their evil rites. Where that red light made the darkest shadows Kothar dismounted and tethered the reins to a granite column that leaned sideways against another.

Kothar studied the ancient ruins. Here had been the almonry, yonder the rest rooms for the pilgrims and poorer folk. Behind these had stood the courtyard, that glimmered now in the dim moonlight shining through low, scudding clouds. Grass had grown between the paving stones, and an occasional flower nodded its head to the darkness.

On soundless feet, Kothar moved across that courtyard toward the church. Behind what was left of the church walls, through the openings where once had been stained-glass windows, were the red flares of many torches and the believers gathered to adore Pulthoom.

"Hsssst—Aldred! Over here!"

Kothar shifted the direction of his walk toward a blackness half-hidden in the shadows. A pale face looked up at him from the rim of a cowl.

"Did you kill the barb—ohhh! You aren't Aldred!"

Big hands went out, drove into the grey wool of the cowl, tightening like claws about a corded throat. The man in the woolen cloak gagged and gurgled, swung off his feet and slammed into the stone wall of the cloister.

"Ishral! By Dwallka—so that's where the treachery lies!"

Kothar released his hold on Ishral to let him speak. When he could, it was with a croak that told how painful it was to drag air into his lungs. "I—I thought to have you killed!

"You went roundabout so as not to be seen while I galloped here as fast as I could! May the dark god claw out your vitals—"

Before he could scream for help, the barbarian swung him up, held his toes inches from the ground while his fingers choked the life silently from the vainly struggling man. A moment later, he let him go. Ishral slumped to the flaggings, lay dead.

Gathering the red and black cloak about him, Kothar stepped forward, moving between two stone abutments that towered overhead. He could see more clearly now by the light of the many torch flames.

On the flat altar where the god Mizran had been worshiped long ago lay the white body of a naked girl. Golden chains held her wrists, golden links her ankles. Bowed before that altar were fifty men and women, keening out their blasphemous hymns. Behind the altar, arrayed in a robe much like that worn by Kothar, stood a priest with a silver bowl raised high. A glittering scythe with a golden handle lay tucked into his white rope belt.

The girl on the altar—could she be Mahla?

Kothar had seen the blonde daughter of old Pahk Mah more than two years ago. He scowled darkly. She had been a scrawny thing then, with little meat to her bones nor shape to the meat that was there. Yet now she was a woman, it seemed, with finely curved limbs and breasts that formed twin bowls.

She was petrified with fright—or drugs.

She lay with blue eyes wide to the bowl that was being turned by the priest so that a drop of blackish fluid could drip onto her pale skin, between her breasts. Mahla threw back her head, screeching in agony. Her body strutted its muscles, her legs and arms flailing, causing the golden links of her chains to jangle.

The worshipers raised their heads, their song growing louder as if to drown her cries.

"Thy blood accepts her, dark Pulthoom!" droned the priest.

"Glory to thee, great god," intoned the worshipers.

"Appear before us, feast upon thy gift."

"And do honor to us who worship thee."

They were too intent upon what was happening to the girl to heed the shadowy figure that moved between their kneeling ranks like a panther creeping through veldt grasses. Kothar had seen with a single raking glance that these were no warriors gathered here but fat merchants and lean traders, with their serving maids or shop assistants, pretty girls who were being kept, no doubt, by the same monies they helped earn at their tasks.

Another drop spilled, and again Mahla screamed.

There was a rustling as the woolen paenulas slid down from the heads and shoulders of the men and women. Kothar chuckled, suddenly. Except for those heavy woolen cloaks, everyone was naked.

Kothar held no sympathy for demons. He did not enjoy the supernatural manifestations of the eldritch beings who inhabited his world from' time to time. Nor did he relish the spells and incantations of the wizards and sorcerers who summoned up those fiends out of Hel.

He knew that they maintained a grip on their followers by reason of the orgies which followed every rite, being an integral part of it. When female flesh was offered to male flesh to be enjoyed, there were few men who could resist its lure, no matter what its trappings.

The merchants and the traders were here with their pretty assistants to break the humdrum routine of their daily lives. Forgotten were their wives, snugly asleep in their beds. This was a night for revelry.

With complete confidence in his rolling muscles, with an awareness that his only opposition would come from the high priest with the bowl in his hands and the two acolyte priests behind him who led the obscene chantings, Kothar stepped forward.

Sensing his presence, the high priest raised his eyes.

A look of absolute horror made those dark orbs bulge. The worshipers were standing now, their cloaks pooled at their feet. Each man and each woman was naked, ready for the orgiastic rites with which his worshipers greeted Pulthoom. Against this nudity the cloaked figure of the giant barbarian stood out boldly.

"Blasphemer!" screeched the priest.

He drew back the bowl to hurl it.

Kothar leaped. The horn bow went out, hit the bowl, tilting it as horn rang against silver. That dread fluid gushed from the bowl, splattered across the face and throat of the high priest.

His scream was shrill, agonized.

The two other priests leaped forward, sharpened scythes drawn. Kothar rasped a curse, put a palm on the altar and leaped, slashing sideways with the horn. The hard horn hit their faces, drawing blood, as the barbarian drove both feet against the chest of the closest acolyte.

A wail of horror and awe broke from the naked worshipers.

Kothar landed catlike on his feet, the fallen priest on the broken sanctuary floor. Beyond the altar and the priests, a blackness was gathering in the sanctuary, a rolling darkness that sent a stab of abysmal terror into the huge blond barbarian.

Instinctively he dropped the bow, reached for Frostfire.

Red eyes glared down at him from that blackness, at the blasphemer who dared to interrupt these wicked rites. For a few seconds, Kothar crouched frozen, hardly breathing, aware only of his heart hammering away inside his rib cage.

Hate glared at him, and dire threat.

Slowly, then, the blackness dimmed, the red eyes grew pale and lifeless. A wind blew across the sanctuary and the blackness wisped into nothingness. The rites of Pulthoom had been interrupted too soon for the dark god to maintain life in this world.

Kothar came out of his trance in time to see the second acolyte leaping at him with his keen scythe raised high. His arm lifted, drove Frostfire forward, full into the throat of the priest.

Blood spurted. His knees bent, the priest fell.

Kothar swung about, blood dripping from his sword. The naked men and women glared at him but they were unarmed, even had they been willing to stand against this shaggy giant. The barbarian whirled his sword so that the blood-drops flew.

"Begone!" he bellowed. "Lest I slay more than the priests of Pulthoom. This girl—is mine!"

As one, they bent to retrieve their woolen cloaks. They babbled helplessly to one another, from time to time casting their eyes at the naked girl and at the barbarian who meant to take her. They fled when they saw the hard, rocklike bronzed face and the cold blue eyes watching their every move.

When he stood alone in front of the altar, Kothar stooped, fumbled in the belt purse beneath the robes of the high priest, found a little golden key. With the key he unlocked the manacles holding Mahla's wrists and arms ankles.

She moaned, head moving left and right.

"Poor thing," he breathed, bending to lift her.

She opened her long-lashed eyes.

Kothar halted, frozen. There was a glee in those eyes, a wickedness that touched a chord of loathing deep inside him. These were not the eyes of Mahla! And yet—this was her body!

"Greetings, barbarian," she breathed. "My thanks for rescue."

"Who are you?" he whispered.

She shrugged, lying shamelessly in front of him on the altar top, making no move to rise. "What does it matter? I am Mahla, if you must have a name."

"Not you!" he snorted.

Her laughter rang out, lewd and evil.

"No, you are right. Though this is her flesh, her spirit wanders in the cold grey wastes of Nifferheim. Ah, you start! You know Nifferheim, then?"

In the northland, Nifferheim was that limbo where the spirits of those whose bodies had been displaced by spirits were doomed to wander eternally. If they did not return to their bodies within a certain time, they must spend all eternity in the grey spirit world.

"I see you do," she mocked, lifting a hand. "Here, help me."

Almost unconsciously, his big brown hand went to her small, white fingers, aiding her to sit up. He was staring at her with new eyes, discovering that the sweet lines which had been the face of Mahla were altering subtly. The cheeks were not so full, the eyes seemed slanted, the mouth more boldly curved.

And her body!

Where before Mahla had boasted the clean virginal lines of a girl upon the threshold of womanhood, now her breasts were fuller, heavier, the lines of her hips more rounded. The girlish legs were meatier, more shapely. This was a woman who sat before him naked on the edge of the altar.

"Who are you?" he growled a second time.

"Ahrima. I am a female demon."

His puzzled frown made her smile. "Why does a female demon concern herself with the rites to Pulthoom, you are wondering? Because I was asked to do so, I was promised as reward to take over this body of little Mahla."

She slid off the stone altar and danced a few steps, here and there, her taunting eyes never leaving the scowling face of the big barbarian. She was temptation incarnate in her evil nudity, and that part of him that is in every man was responding to her shameless allure.

"Who?" he blurted, to take his mind off her flesh.

"Red Lori," she laughed, and dancing up to him, threw her arms about his neck. She kissed him hungrily and despite his iron will, Kothar felt the reins of his control slipping badly.

He put his hands to her bare sides to push her away and found himself caressing her soft flesh instead. Against her mouth he muttered, "What does that witch want now?"

"Freedom, Kothar!" cried Ahrima, leaning back to stare up into his face. "And you shall be the man to free her."

"Not me," he grated. "You've wasted your time."

"Have I? What of Mahla who wanders in Nifferheim? Will you let her stroll eternally in that terrible grey wasteland?"

"What do you mean?" he asked hoarsely.

"When you free Red Lori, I shall go back to my own spirit realm, and the true Mahla shall return into her body. It's that easy to understand, barbarian. Now fetch me a cloak—by the ten eyes of Beeltheer, that wind is cold!"

Her palm chafed her arm as she moved inside the red and black cloak he wore, gathering its flaps about her nudity. She cuddled closer to his big body, her blue eyes gleeful as they stared upward.

"You may be used to these boreal blasts, but I'm a girl demon, and ordinarily I don't feel things like cold and heat. Damn Red Lori, to have induced me to take this task! When I put on human flesh, when I take over a living body, I feel with all their senses."

Kothar pushed her back, reached down and yanked free the rich robes of the high priest. He threw them about her with a snarl. "Here, take this cloak—it goes well with your demon spirit."

She held up a bare foot, smudged with dirt from the altar paving-stones. "And boots for my feet?"

One of the acolytes had feet small enough to possess boots that fit her, he discovered as he knelt to put them on. She stood above him, regal and evil, her brooding eyes and wicked smile acknowledging the fact that she boasted powers that could make this man her slave.

"I am almost jealous of Red Lori, you know," she said softly, wriggling her bare toes to make it harder for him to slip on the second boot. "You might be fun to annoy, to work up into a mad rage upon occasion."

His powerful hands wedged the boot on, making her wince. He growled, "I serve no woman."

"Foolish man," she laughed. "You shall learn."

He glared into her eyes, wondering if he might choke her to death and what the powers of a female demon were, inside its human cage. She was lovely, tempting in the very evil that had altered the features of little Mahla. The wind whipped her long yellow hair, the red torchlights made intriguing shadows on her full red lips.

It took all his will power to keep from gathering her into his arms and crushing her lips with kisses. He was only a man, he thought, and she boasted not only the body of a beautiful woman but the soul of a devil out of Hel.

"You see?" she asked softly.

He shook himself, whirling on a heel and plunging through the night to gather up the reins of the horses. She followed after him, pacing slowly, yet it seemed her footfalls were echoed in his middle.

He held the iron stirrup so she could slide a boot into it and mount into the saddle of the white mare. He felt the touch of her hand on his shoulder as she aided herself to rise.

"You need fear no ambush with me beside you," her voice said above his head. "I am your protection. Now—ride for Commoral!"

He could do nothing else, he decided.

CHAPTER 4

Where the high hills of Gwyn Caer merge with the rolling flatlands of eastern Commoral, there is a mountain pass, a narrow trail of worn rock wedged between twin masses of rock and mountainside. It is cold here, the boreal winds blow without ceasing, and the traveler constantly shivers inside his fur-lined clothing.

It was late in the day, the sun was sinking to the west, and the horseman and his female companion found that their tired horses could not carry them as swiftly as they might have wished. Their slow pace annoyed the man, who wanted to reach the lower slopes of these high hills before nightfall.

"You might use a spell to warm the air," he growled, half-turning in his kak to study the woman who rode so gracefully, half the length of a horse behind him.

"I save my spells," she murmured sweetly.

"Why? Let the witchwoman cast her own spells."

"She needs my help. You shall learn why, when the time comes. For now, keep your mount walking. If we must seek night shelter in these wilds, let it be so."

Irritated—what use were female demons if they could not use their demoniac wisdom to aid a man when he needed it?—Kothar swung around to the front. He rode with angry eyes fixed upon the narrow rock path where his stallion walked, and so he did not notice the towering thing that stared down upon him from the stone wall to his right.

It was a furry monster that glared downward with red-rimmed purple eyes, a misshapen thing that resembled a man, but only vaguely, since its body was covered from the top of its skull to its feet with long, white fur.

Few men had ever seen an abominathol, but the tales spun in the ale-houses or the way stations that were scattered here and there along this rocky path into Commoral abounded with descriptions of its speed, its fury, its savage destructiveness. Men it tore apart with its huge paws, women it carried off—no man knew where.

It ran lightly on the jagged rocks as it trailed Kothar and Ahrima along the pass. Its eyes gleamed with blood-lust, its breath came shorter, it made little crooning sounds deep in its throat. This night the man would be dead, the woman would be his. And the carcasses of those horses would make good eating.

Dusk came upon the travelers just as the rocks fell away in front of a long stretch of mountain meadow where the snow lay deep. A mile away, Kothar made out the lines of a small hut. Probably the home of a sheep-herder, he reasoned, during the milder seasons. It would serve them for the night.

He waved a hand, calling the attention of the woman to the hut. Her eyes studied it carefully, and then she shrugged as if the matter of shelter were of no concern to her. Proud bitch! he told himself silently. She dies from the cold, yet she will not express what she must feel.

"I'll build a fire," he told her. "At least, we won't feel the wind in that place and the flames will warm us. You can do the cooking."

Their saddlebags held food and two bottles of red Makkadonian wine. It might be pleasant with a fire going and good food in his belly, inside that hut. It would have been pleasant, if Ahrima had not been a demon-woman.

He turned Greyling off the trail and along a narrow footpath, that showed where the snow had sunk a little. Behind the hut was a lean-to, protected from the wind, where he could water and feed the horses.

He came out of the saddle, turning toward the woman. His cupped hands formed a rest for the booted foot she kicked free of the stirrup. She smiled down at him tauntingly.

"Serve me well, Kothar—and I'll plead with Red Lori to let you live for a little while—if only to serve me in my demon world as my slave."

He grunted and turned away, stripping off both saddles, rubbing down the horses, then fitting nosebags on their heads. The grain in the bags would suffice their appetites until they reached the lowlands tomorrow.

Walking into the hut, he found Ahrima huddled in a chair, shivering.

"Why didn't you make a fire?" he rasped.

"I told you, I am saving my powers," she replied, not turning her head to look at him.

He busied himself with the woodpile in the corner, that had been built in the cool days of autumn, setting small, cut logs inside the ring of stone in the middle of the hut. Above this was the funnel of the chimney, opening up wide to absorb the smoke, with a metal spit set into it for the cooking.

Kothar lifted a pair of saddlebags and tossed them at the woman. "If you want to eat, cook!"

Her blue eyes blazed at him. "You can cook for two!"

"I can. I won't," he rasped.

Unfolding a cloth he lifted out a steak and hung it on a hook above the growing flames. Taking a cooking pot, he went outside, filled it with snow, and brought it back. In moments the smell of cooking steak and boiling kavv filled the little hut.

Ahrima shifted restlessly. Sighing, she unfastened her saddlebags and lifted out her own steak. She nudged him with her shoulder, making him give her room above the flames.

Suddenly the barbarian lifted his head.

"Did you hear that?" he asked, rising to his feet.

Ahrima chuckled. "You're as nervous as a newly captured tiger. Sit down. What is it that you think you're hearing?"

"A footstep outside, crunching snow. Listen!"

Only the wind whistling around the hut touched their ears. Restless, Kothar stalked back and forth. He had taken off his swordbelt for greater ease of movement. Now he strode forward to catch up his blade.

He never reached it.

The wooden wall of the hut bulged inward. Half a dozen planks split. A great arm, covered with long white fur, slid between the openings to catch a plank and rip it loose. An unearthly snarl echoed the sound of splintering wood. Then the abominathol was in the hut, leaping for Kothar.

The big barbarian swung a ham-like fist. It drove into the big-fanged mouth of the beast-man just as Ahrima screamed in horror. The giant Cumberian ducked under a sidewiping paw, drove his other fist under the rib cage of the furry thing. The abominathol roared, reached out both paws and lifted Kothar high.

For a moment it stood on widespread legs, holding the barbarian high. Then it flung him against the far wall. Wood creaked and cracked, dust came out like a mist over Lake Lotusine, and Kothar dropped to the ground.

The abominathol reached for the shrinking Ahrima.

"Damned beast," the barbarian snarled, and leaped.

He hit the beast-man, knocked him backward. Fingers locked in the loose fur at its throat, he rode the thing to the hardpacked dirt floor. At the impact of their landing, Kothar lifted upward and banged the abominathol's apelike head down on the ground.

The beast-man howled in mingled pain and fury.

Clawed hands ripped at the Cumberian, tearing the fur of his jerkin but scratching with futile strength on the steel links of his shirt. Kothar drove a fist into the open-mouthed face below him as the abominathol screeched.

It surged upward, carrying the man with it, it caught a pawful of yellow hair and tugged, unbalancing the man and hurling him sideways. The abominathol had never fought a man who did not cave in to its savage blows. This human who battled him growled and snarled as much as the beast-man, and his fists felt like hammers banging into its face and sides.

Man and beast-man surged to their feet and for a few seconds their arms moved like pistons as they drove fists and paws at one another, standing almost toe to toe. The terrified woman crouched beside the firestones bit her knuckles, eyes wide and frightened.

Risking death from a possible broken neck, the abominathol lowered its head and charged. Its hard skull hit Kothar in his middle, carried him backward into the hood of the chimney. He rammed that stone sheathing with his back and head, it felt as if he had been struck with a war-mace.

For an instant, Kothar sagged.

In that moment, the beast-man struck. Its paws locked together and came up hard beneath the chin of this man who would not yield. Kothar went backward and hung a moment against the bricks of the chimney.

The beast-man whirled and reached for Ahrima. Its snarl made its ugly face even more hideous, and the blood running from its lips and nose added to the ferocity of its appearance. Its huge paws caught up the shrinking woman, hoisted her over a shoulder.

It leaped for the broken opening in the side of the hut.

Kothar stood with his back propped against the chimney bricks, dragging in great gulps of air. He was growling in his throat, telling himself he ought to let the abominathol run off with Ahrima. Let the beast-man kill and eat the demon-wench, if he wanted, or add her to his harem. He would be rid of her and—

It was not Ahrima, but Mahla who was being taken, he remembered. Little golden Mahla with the sweet smile, whose spirit wandered eternally in cold, grey Nifferheim.

With a bellow, Kothar leaped.

He sprang onto the back of the beast-man, his arms slid under his armpits. Behind the abominathol's broad neck he locked his giant hands.

The beast-man staggered, dropping the woman.

The weight of the barbarian atop his back would not have impeded the massive abominathol, ordinarily. But the steel-thewed arms and hands were bending his head forward, and the massively muscled thighs and calves had a grip on his middle that squeezed his insides into a knot.

It could not reach those tightening legs to pry them apart because its arms were held out at right angles to its body by the arms beneath his armpits. And the pressure on its neck was growing more deadly by the moment. Kothar grunted, applying more of that awful pressure. The beast-man sobbed, gasping for breath, unable to do more than stand helplessly, being bent forward with inexorable force.

It ran forward suddenly, hoping to slam into the hut wall and dislodge its leechlike attacker. At the last moment, the Cumberian turned it so the top of its skull slammed into the wooden plankings.

It was not a hard blow but it seemed to rouse the beast-man to a fury of madness. Its thick lips slavered with froth, its eyes rolled in its skull, it tried to scream but could make only a mewling sound.

Furry white legs carried it back and forth at the dead run across the room. Ahrima had shrunk against the chimney bricks, eyes wide, the back of her hand to her open mouth. She knew the animal might of the abominathol, she could not believe that a mere man—even such a physical giant as Kothar—could be killing the beast-man even though she was seeing it done before her eyes.

The thing was bent double, now, like an old man crippled with age. Kothar rode its bowed back like some ghastly parasite, sapping its strength. Its red-rimmed milky eyes rolled as it sighted the girl framed against the hearth bricks. It began to stumble toward her.

By turning itself sideways, it might catch her soft throat in one of its paws and throttle the life from her. Kothar was aware of this; he roared at Ahrima.

"Out of the way! Out of the way!!"

Ahrima could not move, she stood frozen in mingled fascination and fear. Having put on human flesh, she was helpless against the human emotions that flooded her demon spirit.

Kothar growled and applied even more pressure with his arms. His muscles bulged until his sun-bronzed flesh appeared bloated to the point of splitting. The beast-man tried to scream but made only a gurgling sound in its throat. Its legs began to quiver.

Its furry paw touched Ahrima; fell away.

The abominathol sagged toward the floor. Kothar whirled it, drove its skull hard into the chimney bricks. There was a sodden sound, blood appeared on the white fur covering its poll.

As it dropped, Kothar put out one final effort.

Kraaa-aaakkk.

The beast-man went limp, its neck broken.

Over its dead body, the barbarian grinned up at the woman. "You're safe enough now," he rumbled.

Her breasts quivered as Ahrima fought for breath. Her eyes were glazed with the experience she had suffered. Her palms were wet, her heart was exploding in her chest. Three times she licked her lips with her tongue before she could speak.

"By the gods of Bandamarr! Man, you please me!"

Kothar let his eyes blaze at her. "Enough to win your help against Red Lori?"

She paused, tightening her fingers against the chimney bricks where she leaned, nodding her head until the long yellow hair that reached to her waist made rippling movements. "Yes—yes, but not now. I am under vow to her. I cannot break my promise. Ah, but when she is free—perhaps then I can help you, Kothar!"

"And in return for that help?"

She shook her head. "I do not know, yet. I find that being human has its own rewards. Fright. Pleasure—in seeing a man fight for you." Her hand made a waving motion in the air. "The smell of food cooking, the cold air, the sensation of touch, are all things I know nothing of, in the world out of which I came."

She watched him rise, catch hold of the dead body. "What are you doing with that thing?"

"Putting it outside, where it will freeze stiff against the broken wall planks. It will get colder, much colder before morning, and the mountain winds will try to get in here at us. The abominathol made that opening, let him block it."

When he returned, Kothar built up the fire, and taking the steaks off their steel hooks, handed one to the woman.

"Eat," he told her. "You'll need a full belly to keep you warm against the coldness."

She watched him sink his big white fangs in the juicy meat. With a sigh, she followed his example and found the steak to be delicious. The kavv he poured into two earthenware cups was sweet and warming. To her surprise, Ahrima decided she was very comfortable.

Only when Kothar shook out the two saddle blankets, handing her one, did she refuse. "These things stink of horseflesh. I couldn't."

The man stared at her, shrugged, and wrapped both blankets about himself. He lay down close to the fire. Outside the hut the wind wailed and snow blew in antic flurries. Ahrima wrapped her arms about herself, sitting huddled over on a low stool, trying to absorb the last bit of heat from the flames.

After a while, Kothar threw back a corner of the blanket. "Get in here," he said gruffly. "You'll freeze almost as solid as the abominathol, sitting there. My body heat will warm you."

Ahrima offered no objections. She dropped, wriggled herself against him, and let him throw the horse blankets over them. In moments, she was warmer, more comfortable.

Sleepily, she threw an arm about him, hugging him.

Kothar muttered, "Sleep, Ahrima. Mahla is like a baby sister to me—and you wear her body."

The she-demon smiled lazily. "Another time, Kothar," she promised, and began to laugh, softly and with promise in her throat.

CHAPTER 5

Commoral City was asleep, though the noonday sun hung high overhead and its streets were filled with men and women. Everywhere that Kothar looked, he saw faces and bodies frozen in the middle of a movement, eyes wide and staring, lips parted while frozen in mid-speech. Marveling, he walked Greyling onward, holding the reins of the white mare.

Ahead of him walked Ahrima.

Her body was clothed in a shimmering blue cloud out of which little lightnings stabbed. She had dismounted just outside the city gates which were wide open to permit farm carts and wagons to bring produce into Commoral City.

"It is time now to use my demoniac powers," she had told him.

Her hands had stripped down her garments even as that blue cloud formed about her flesh. Instantly, the clangor of a smith's hammer on white-hot metal ceased, there was no more talk. The heavy strides of a gate guard halted, the creak of wooden hubs and axles ceased to be.

Everywhere, men and women paused in their everyday affairs, under the spell of this wizardry. Ahrima walked forward through the gate, and Kothar had no choice but to follow her.

In front of them stood the glistening stone bulk of the palace, and to one side, the graceful lines of the Audience Hall, in which Queen Elfa of Commoral held court and distributed justice to her people. From the wooden rafters in the high-vaulted ceiling of that Audience Hall, two cages hung.

In the golden cage was imprisoned the fallen king, Markoth.

In a silver cage sat the witchwoman, Red Lori.

Kothar grinned, remembering how he had helped the wizard Kazazael defeat the Lord Markoth, how he had stopped Red Lori from completing the incantations that might have destroyed Kazazael. Queen Elfa had hung them both in cages here, as reminders to other possible recalcitrants of the fate suffered by those who opposed her royal will.

In front of the door of the Audience Hall, Ahrima paused.

Kothar swung down, went up the marble steps and gripped the door-pull rings, tugging on them. The bronze gates swung outward, and the barbarian walked into the huge Audience Hall.

"Welcome, Kothar!" cried a voice.

He looked up at the silver cage and the naked woman in it. For many months Red Lori had sat behind these pale, glittering bars, helpless. Now the time of her deliverance was at hand.

"Ahhh—and Ahrima the friendly demon!" Lori mocked.

Ahrima said in a cold voice, "I have obeyed you, Lori. I have brought the man, I hold the city under spell that he may do his work."

Kothar studied the silver cage, noting its inaccessibility. He growled, "I'll need a long rope, an iron hook."

"In the door beyond the transept, barbarian," called Lori, "you will find such a hook and such a rope. It is how they feed me, by sending up baskets of food."

He found the hook with a pulley attached just below it and a long rope by which her jailers could send little baskets up to the cages, fastened to loops set here and there in the rope. He lifted them and carried them back to the hall.

He twirled the hook, sent it flying high. It missed the first time but on his second try, the barbed end sank into the cage floor. The barbarian gathered the two dangling rope lengths in his hands and began mounting.

Like a monkey, he scrambled upward until he could put a hand on a silver bar. He dragged himself upward, setting his feet between the bars and on the bottom of the cage. Red Lori stood now, watching him with her slanted green eyes in which hope warred with mockery.

His huge hands fastened about the silver bars. There were thaumaturgic signs and sigils on those bars but they were there to prevent sorcery from harming them, they were useless against the huge muscles of the youthful giant who clung to them. Those muscles bulged, the bars began to bend.

Red Lori laughed softly, "Only you could do it, Kothar!"

He widened the space between those bars and watched as the witch-woman ducked between them and pressed herself against him.

"Hold me, barbarian. Carry me to safety!"

"I could drop you," he snarled. "I ought to drop you. There's no magic in you now, Kazazael removed all that. You're just a woman."

Anger touched her face, mingled with fear. "Ahrima would blast you!" she retorted.

"I'm not so sure," he grinned. "She might be happier if you were out of the way, Red Lori. It would give her a freer hand."

Her eyes widened, close to his. "So? You've put some sort of male spell on her? Have you made love to her, barbarian?"

"Not while she wears the body of Mahla, no."

"Then carry me!"

His arm slipped about her middle, he lowered himself gingerly until the cage floor was level with his eyes. His legs and feet twisted into the ropes below him. Then he let go his grip and stabbed fingers at the ropes.

Using the pulley, he lowered himself and his companion to the floor below. When his feet touched the stone flaggings, he released her.

Red Lori turned to the woman. "My thanks, Ahrima. I am in your debt." The girl who was Mahla merely inclined her head.

"Come," the witchwoman ordered. "The spell has lasted a long time. We must ride, now—before the people wake."

They made good time through the silent city streets. At a market stall, Red Lori hurriedly selected garments to cover her nudity, and a fur cloak to throw about her shoulders. Ahrima, still surrounded by her necromantic blue cloud out of which the golden lightnings spurted, had gone on ahead, since she was on foot.

Beyond the city gates, Ahrima halted. Slowly the blue clouds faded until she too, was as unclothed as Red Lori had been.

Ahrima gasped and bent her slim white legs, trying to cover her nudity by stooping forward and using her arms and her hands. "Mizran help me," she cried.

Kothar swung around, and grinned. The female demon had gone back to her own world; instantly, the spirit of Mahla had returned from Nifferheim to occupy her own true body. Mahla lacked the bold lewdness of Ahrima, she was dying of embarrassment and fright, finding herself naked outside the gates of Commoral City.

He tossed a cloak to her. "Cover yourself," he granted.

She did as he bid, turning her head to study the great gate of Commoral City and Red Lori where she sat the saddle of the white mare. Tears were forming in her eyes and she began to sob.

"You know me, Mahla," Kothar said gently.

"I do? Oh yes. You're—Kothar."

"Your father sent me to rescue you from the worshipers of the dark god. You didn't know that, nor that a demon spirit has been inside your body while your spirit wandered in Nifferheim."

"It was awful," she whimpered.

His hand reached down to clasp hers as he kicked a fur-flapped war boot free of the iron stirrup. "Mount behind me, girl. We've a long way to go."

"To Memphor," Red Lori said coldly.

"To Clon Mell, first. I return Mahla to her father." Red Lori sat up straighter as if to argue, but Kothar was toeing Greyling to the gallop. "The city is waking, witchwoman. Stay there—and be recaptured!"

She kicked the mare into a ran.

All that long day, Red Lori was silent, galloping behind him, but Kothar knew her mind was alive, planning what was to come. He paid her little heed, he was too interested in soothing the fears of Mahla.

"It was a dead place," she told him, arms clasped about his middle and seated on the croup of the big warhorse. "All rock and grey gravel. The sky was as grey as the stones, and there was no place to go, all I could do was wander here and there and never see another living thing."

"You're safe out of the place. Forget it!"

"How can I forget it? When I close my eyes, I see it—and me in it. I shall never be able to forget it."

"In time you will."

Her arms tightened about his lean middle and he felt the weight of her head on his back. "With your help, I could," she breathed, and fell asleep.

Kothar slowed his headlong gallop so that she might sleep in some semblance of comfort. Within seconds, Red Lori was at his side, face flushed, eyes blazing.

"Go faster," she cried. "Don't you realize they'll have discovered that I'm not in my cage any longer and that Queen Elfa will have riders out scouring the city and the countryside for me? You know what she will do if she recaptures me!" She added slyly, "And to you, as well!"

"Use your witch tricks to stop her," he grumbled.

"You know I cannot!" she flared. "My magic is gone, taken from me by Kazazael! I'm just an ordinary woman, now."

He showed his teeth in a mirthless grin. "Maybe I ought to stick a dagger between your ribs and leave you for dead. Then I'd be free of you forever."

Her taunting laughter rang in his ears. "What? And have Ahrima return to displace Mahla's spirit once again? Next time, she might not release her body so easily, Kothar. She has taken a fancy to you, barbarian."

There was enough truth in what the witchwoman said to worry him, Kothar admitted to himself. He dared not take the risk. He must find a better way to rid himself of the sorceress. He wondered what it was she wanted in Memphor.

At a steady canter they rode through the flatlands of Commoral, but instead of crossing the mountain pass between Commoral and Gwyn Caer, he angled Greyling southward, to go around those high hills. His first duty was to return Mahla to her father. Afterward, he could concern himself with the witchwoman.

They rode into Clon Mell with the rising sun, mingling with the artisans and the craftsmen of the city on their way to their shops and stalls. The smell of freshly grown vegetables and newly made cheeses and bread filled the air at this early hour. Clon Mell was a great trade city, where hungry travelers from as far eastward as Makkadonia and from the southerly corners of Vandacia and Abathor came with wine and leather goods and fine horses to sell for good gold pieces in the many marts of the city.

Red Lori hung back a little, saying, "Go with the girl to her father. I shall wait for you in the street of the booksellers, where there is a thing I want to purchase."

Kothar cocked an eyebrow at her. "And what shall you use for money? The merchants of Clon Mell do not trade for smiles from pretty girls."

"You shall pay," she nodded sweetly, "from the reward monies old Pahk Mah will pay you for having rescued his daughter."

Kothar shrugged and rode on.

His knock on the locked door of the shop brought Pahk Mah hurrying to unbolt it. Father and daughter fell into an embrace while Kothar shifted uncomfortably from foot to foot.

Then the old man lifted his tear-wet eyes to study the barbarian. "What can I give you, Kothar—to pay you for what you've done?"

"Fair exchange for my jewels. No more."

"I shall add a bonus," Pahk Mah nodded, "though it shall bankrupt me. I am a loving father, you understand, and not one to show ingratitude."

"You're an old fraud, Pahk Mah. Just give me honest value."

"In what way?"

"Pay me in silver bars."

The old man stared. "In silver? You'll need a horse to carry the weight."

"Then add the horse, and a sack of coins."

"Good silver I have, from Phalkar. Bars of the finest metal, each one stamped with the Phalkarian leopards. The bars will not need to be so heavy, because the silver itself will be purer, though you'll still need a mount to carry them."

"And saddlebags to hold them," Kothar nodded.

The old man led the way between suits of lacquered armor from distant Mongrolia, past tables heavy with porcelain masterpieces and cases of rare coins. His shop was a little sampling of the world he lived in, Kothar thought, remembering the horn bow and how it had served him. His hand brushed over the jeweled surface of a golden mask placed face up on the long wooden counter.

"I ride to Memphor in Aegypton," he said casually, as Pahk Mah made marks on a length of scroll with a quill pen.

"Into the land of tombs and crypts," the old man nodded. "A dusty land, that's Aegypton. What seek you there?"

"Service with the Pharah. I'm a soldier by trade, and I've been a wanderer too long."

"Beware the tombs, they hold ghosts," Pahk Mah grinned, straightening and pushing the scroll so Kothar could read his figures.

In minutes, two young helpers came to fetch silver bars from the basement storerooms, gleaming lengths of greyish metal that glittered where the sunbeams touched them. Kothar nodded at sight of them, and turned to Pahk Mah.

"Where's Ishral?"

"They found him dead by the Thistem Abbey ruins," Pahk Mah snarled. "I think it was he who arranged to have my girl slain in the dark rites—for a promise from the high priest that he would be made youthful once more and be given his manhood back by Pulthoom."

The metal bars filled six big leather saddlebags. The young helpers led out a roan horse and tossed the bags over a blanket resting on its back, fastening them with wires. One of them led the horse forward by a rope bridle and matching reins.

Pahk Mah handed the barbarian two bags heavy with coins.

"Go with Mizran," he murmured.

Mahla came to kiss his cheek, her blue eyes veiled in shyness. "Come again soon, Kothar. I will pray for you, every night as long as I live. You cannot guess what it was you rescued me from."

Then he was mounting up on Greyling, urging the big warhorse toward the street of booksellers. His keen eyes picked out Red Lori in her red wool cloak, standing patiently beside the white mare. She carried a small rope bag in which Kothar made out several books.

"A dozen golden dikkars," she stated.

Kothar blinked. "A dozen dikkars? It's a fortune! What sort of books did you buy?"

"Books that shall aid me in my tasks. Pay the shopkeeper."

Grumbling, the barbarian did as she bid, marveling how the words of Afgorkon always came true. No matter how much of a fortune he amassed, he could never keep it so long as he carried the sword Frostfire. When he was done, he saw that Red Lori was seated on the white mare, turning it to ride out of Clon Mell.

Seconds later, he was following her, leading the roan by its rope reins. He wondered if he were riding to his death.

They went by way of the southern passes into the lands of the baron lords, along the eastern slopes of the tall mountains known as the Roof of the World, skirting the fringe of the Haunted Lands. Their camps were lonely fires at the base of a snow-tipped mountain, or on an island in the middle of the great swamps.

At every camp, Red Lori went away from him to sit on a rock or a stretch of flat ground, cross-legged, to open her books and study them. She sat there with bent head, brows furrowed in concentration, while he cut the meat for their stews or hung meat chunks over the flames on a bent stick and a thin wire.

He noticed too, that there were maps in the books, which she spread out and stared at for long periods of time, as if she memorized their lines. Besides the maps, bits of parchment rustled as she opened them, and these too, she appeared to memorize.

He had to call her several times before she would hear him and come to eat, walking dreamily and with her eyes gazing blankly. At these times, he thought she was not so much the witchwoman as a lonely, frightened girl. He grew aware that Red Lori was groping for something lost to her.

Red Lori had forgotten her hate for him, and her determination for revenge, or so it seemed. During the days she rode quietly behind him, in his shadow. At their nighttime meals, she stirred to soft laughter after she had eaten, and told him tales of her past enchantments. She was a learned sorceress, she had come close to destroying mighty Kazazael, long ago. It was only by his own efforts that she had been overcome.

Yet now she seemed to have forgotten her desire for revenge.

Kothar could not understand it.

They left the swamplands for the long steppes that began the homelands of the Mongrolians, fierce nomad riders who raided and looted wherever there was a chance at profit. Kothar was wary of these horse-archers, he would have preferred to go over the Roof of the World, but Red Lori would have none of it.

"It would take too long," she pointed out. "And I am in a hurry. I am helpless, the way I am—and I do not like to be helpless."

Her slanted green eyes studied him across the campfire. "I need a body-guard like you, Kothar. Someone who must obey me, yet a man who can fight demons if need be."

"Where are we going?" he asked bluntly.

"To Memphor."

"But why? What's in Memphor that's so important?"

"Secrets I must master, to become as I was."

He grinned, reaching for another slab of meat. "And then? What happens to me when you're a sorceress again?"

"I haven't decided," she murmured, brooding at him, chin on fist. "I hate you, you know that. I am determined to have my vengeance on you, but I haven't made up my mind yet just what direction that revenge will take."

"I ought to lose you, maybe choke the life out of you or run my sword blade through your middle."

"You won't. Ahrima will repossess little Mahla—and you're too tenderhearted to see the girl suffer. It's amazing, really. A big clod of a barbarian like you, nursing sentimental feelings toward a girl who doesn't mean a thing to you."

She shook her head and laughed, and on that note their talk ended. She went back to her maps and her books, reading by the firelight, while he rubbed down their horses and cleaned the wooden platters and cups of the debris from their meal.

On the sixth day after leaving Commoral City, Kothar sighted a long line of men and animals moving across the vast prairie. He stood in the iron stirrups and let his gaze assess that length of moving life.

"A caravan," he said after a time. "I thought at first it might be Mongrols, but it's moving too slowly."

"We'll join them," she told him.

"They seem to be moving toward the southwest, and Memphor lies in that direction. They'll have hired mercenaries to protect them against Mongrol raids. It might be a good idea."

They toed their mounts to a gallop.

An hour before the sun set, they pulled up before a bearded trader out of Makkadonia, who listened to their invented tale of two wanderers who had lost their way. As he quoted a price, he tugged at his beard and studied the horizon.

"Ten gold pieces each," he said.

Kothar snorted. "Ten gold pieces? You ought to pay me for riding with you. If the Mongrols attack—"

The merchant whipped around, jabbing a finger at the barbarian. "If the Mongrols attack, you and your woman will be glad to have my soldiers here, to protect you both. Now the price is twenty gold pieces, pay or leave."

He paid, at Red Lori's urging.

They were assigned a place in the line toward the rear. A big wagon filled with linen and silk goods from Athenos made a soft bed for Red Lori. Kothar himself would sleep on the ground beneath the wagon, wrapped in his saddle blankets. Paying out good gold for such dubious protection—Kothar would rather have trusted to himself and Frostfire against an enemy than the over-fat mercenaries in steel caps and chainmail who served the caravan—was a waste of good gold.

The only thing he got out of it, the Cumberian decided, was that he did not have to get up during the night to put more wood on the campfires. The guards did this, so that the travelers could get an unbroken rest.

For two days, Kothar and Red Lori rode with the caravan.

On the morning of the fourth day, the Mongrols struck.

CHAPTER 6

They came riding out of the early mists that shrouded the ground in billowing white fog, like the fabled ghosts of Jagthanoy, shaking their wooden bows above their fur-flapped caps but uttering no sound. Only a faint thunder that ran along the ground told the guards that anyone but themselves were abroad on this vast flatland, and the guards were too sleepy to notice.

The vibration woke the barbarian.

Instantly he was awake, rising upward and tossing the saddle blankets aside. He had heard the drum of hooves galloping often before. He reached for his swordbelt, bellowing.

"Hoy—the guards! Hoy! Raiders coming!"

He snatched at his horn bow and quiver of arrows in the middle of a run for the wagon. A man was rubbing sleep from his eyes, blinking, off to one side. Kothar caught him by the shoulders, whirled him sideways so that he fell away from a wagonwheel he had been using as a prop and sprawled full length on the ground.

"Red Lori," he roared, lifting a strip of canvas.

She was sitting upright, clutching a robe to her shoulders. Her green eyes were enormous. "What is it?"

"Raiders, probably Mongrols! They're devils. They ride like the wind and shoot like Parphian who was chief archer to King Brabinak the Wise, centuries ago in Cumberia. Stir your carcass, girl! Up!"

Her hands dropped the fur robe, grabbed for blouse and woolen skirt. The quick fear that ran in her turned her cheeks an ashen hue. She dressed with her eyes on the big Cumberian as he strung his bow and loosened the arrows in the quiver that he carried over a shoulder by its leather thong.

"Are there many of them?" she breathed.

"Too many," he rasped. "Listen!"

Even she could pick out that thunder now, and interpret it. The guards were running here and there, brandishing their weapons. Their leader, a corpulent Macedonian, was hastily buckling on his armor and shouting commands to which nobody listened. Everywhere, women were screaming and men shouted where only the wind listened.

Kothar grabbed her arm, helped Red Lori from the wagon. "We'll make a run for it," he told her. "Our horses are rested, they haven't been extended by the slow caravan pace of the last few days."

"Are you mad?" she sobbed. "Leave the caravan's protection? Put our trust in horses? You run, if you want. I stay!"

His hand called her attention to a pair of guards running past them. Kothar sneered, "Would you trust in such as those? They're soft, flabby. What muscles they ever had, have turned to mush!"

"Nevertheless, I stay!" She twisted her arm free of his grip, panting and staring up into his face with angry eyes.

He grinned coldly, gesturing to the west. "Too late to run, anyhow. See there, where another line rides out of the rising sun." He sighed and began lifting arrows out of the quiver, digging them into the ground at his feet, point first. "Ah, well. I always knew I'd die in battle. Get behind me, girl. My body will protect yours."

"If you hadn't put me in that cage," she berated his broad back as he shoved her behind him, "I'd be able to overcome them with a spell, or whisk us off to a pleasure boat on the Outer Sea! But now I'm trapped without my wizardries. Kothar—I could kill you!"

He grunted, "Pray to your gods, Lori—that you're still alive by night-fall and me with you." He was done with his task, and studied the twenty arrows jutting their feathered shafts upward into the air. "Tell you what. If you still live by nightfall and I've saved you—call off your vendetta against me."

She ignored him to shade her eyes and watch the Mongrols gallop closer. They were short, swarthy men, heavily muscled, in chainmail shirts and woolen jerkins. Each man had learned to ride a shaggy steppes pony and wield the bow that would be his main weapon as a horse-archer, from infancy. They were reputed to be the finest cavalry in the world; each man was a separate fighting unit in himself.

The fur-flaps of their brocade caps jounced as they toed their ponies to the gallop. They came on like the kelets, the evil demons who were worshiped by the Mongrol tribes, screeching and yelling. A bow twanged. Kothar watched the flight of the arrow, dark against the sky, as it curved up and away.

"Brace yourself," he growled. "They ride right at the wagons, change direction, hit the wagons at a slant. They kill, they hurl blazing torches, they spread fear and panic."

Of its own accord, her hand went out to touch the fur jerkin that he wore under his own mail shirt. The contact sent a stab of reassurance through her. Red Lori said, "Save me, Kothar—and our feud is forgotten!"

"Your feud, not mine," he snarled.

His bow lifted, an arrow nocked to the string. No sense wasting shafts, he only had a score of them, but he would be ready if the Mongrols changed direction and came at their end of the caravan.

Up ahead, the mercenaries were firing their own bows.

"Fools," Kothar growled. "They waste their shafts."

The shafts fell far short. And then the galloping archers were within range and the air filled with their arrows. Men screamed as those points went into them. Here and there, the shrill cry of a woman told where a mis-directed shaft had found softer flesh. It was not the custom of the Mongrols to slay the women, they wanted them for slaves.

Kothar waited until the horse-archers were less than one hundred yards away. Then he bent the horn bow, felt it quiver as he released his arrow. His eyes followed its course until it sank into the chest of a rider. As the rider slid from his kak, the Cumberian was already firing his second shaft.

For long minutes, the barbarian shot and shot, until his arrows had dwindled in number to five. All around him the caravan was in a wild me-lee. Guards were down, dying. Merchants were running about from wagon to wagon as if seeking a way out of this trap the Mongrols were drawing about them.

The clang of steel on steel could be heard where the Mongrols were using their curving scimitars against the straight steel blades of the caravan guards. Fires had sprung up, red flames and black smoke rising toward the immensity of blue sky above the prairie.

Red Lori was sobbing, gnawing on her knuckles. Her frightened eyes went from a man dragging himself along the ground and dripping blood as the arrow in his side let out his life, to a woman clinging to her baby and on her knees as if to beg pity of the horsemen. To Red Lori's anguished stares, only the barbarian seemed calm, unmoved.

For every arrow Kothar had shot, a Mongrol had died. Their bodies lay on the plain beyond the wagons. Other than those dead, the vast steppes seemed curiously empty.

A rider loomed up, scimitar in hand. His face was split by a big grin as he aimed his steel at the giant bulk of the Cumberian. Kothar grunted, sent his last arrow upward into the man.

His hand yanked at his sword, ripped Frostfire free of the scabbard. He leaped for the rider-less horse, using the dead body as a mounting block to fling himself upward into the high-peaked saddle.

"Come on, girl!" he bellowed. "This is our chance!"

She ran to him, was caught by the wrist and swept upward, to land with a thud on the croup of the shaggy plains pony. The horse whinnied its disapproval of this double weight but the heels drumming its sides sent it into a headlong gallop.

Head down, Red Lori bent behind Kothar, clinging to his middle with her arms. Kothar raced away from the blazing wagons and dying men, the women who were already being stripped for the raping. Soft outlanders! he thought. With a score of Cumberians, I could have destroyed those archers. They would not have panicked as the mercenaries had done, they would have made their arrows count.

They rode in a backlash of sound from the burning wagons. The Mongrols were off their horses and moving here and there, hunting out wounded men and slaying them, dragging merchants from under wagons to run them through with already bloody steel. The women were wailing, they were seeing their babies and children slain before their bulging eyes.

The Mongrols would kill the older women, Kothar knew, or those unattractive enough to serve as body slaves. They might even save a few women for the torturing later at night when they made camp. The torturing would rouse their lusts, they would begin arguing over the females, then, in the heat of aroused senses.

He rode into the south, into an unexplored region that included the upper reaches of Vandacia and Abathor, where few men ever ventured. It was said by some to be haunted by ghosts and demons, but Kothar would rather take his chances with those than with the horse-archers. His heels banged the pony's side, making it run even faster.

"My books," cried Red Lori suddenly. "My precious maps!"

"Are they more precious than your life?"

"Almost! Turn back, Kothar!"

His laughter was harsh upon-the wind. From time to time he turned his neck, studying their back trail. No pursuit had been mounted as yet; their flight might even gone unobserved. Kothar told himself this luck could not last. They would be seen and followed. The Mongrols never relaxed their hold on a man or a woman unless death came to claim him.

Yet it seemed they might make it.

The caravan wagons were low on the horizon, the black smoke rose upward at a greater distance. The Mongrols would be too busy looting and raping to bother about a pony carrying off a man and a women, he hoped.

He set his face to the prairie in front of him, eyes ranging that wide expanse of tall grass and small rocks, hunting for a possible hiding place. There was none, he could see that at a glance; yet he went on hoping.

"Kothar!" Red Lori screamed. "They come!"

There were thirty of them, far behind them but gaining at every step. They rode bent forward in their kaks, hard of face and merciless. Their bows were on their backs, they were more intent on overtaking their quarry than in overcoming him.

Their pony stumbled under them.

In another moment, it would fall. Kothar cursed.

CHAPTER 7

Even his great strength could not keep the pony upright for very long. Its legs were wobbling, its tossing head hurled globs of saliva from its foam-flecked lips; behind them, the Mongrols were closing in fast. Already, there were arrows whistling through the air.

Pain dug into Kothar's shoulder, into his thigh. With a hoarse cry of rage he kicked his feet free of the stirrups, threw a warbooted leg over the pony's head and slipped to the ground.

"Ride on, girl!" he bellowed.

Frostfire was in his hand, it rose to deflect a shaft and then another. The Mongrols were all around him by this time; his blade flailed sideways and to the right. The arrow shafts protruding from thigh and shoulder hampered his movements, but there was nothing wrong with his sword arm and his right leg.

Blood flecked the blue steel as it slashed through mail and flesh. A rider dropped, right arm gone at the elbow, another fell back with his chest dripping redly. The wail of a third nomad gurgled into nothingness as the barbarian yanked his blade from a throat.

He did not see Red Lori, he did not know whether she had won freedom or not, he was too concerned with trying to save his own skin. The odds were fearful but he had fought and won against fearful odds at other times. Savage blood beat in his veins, a battle rage shook him, he was snarling and cursing, sobbing air into his lungs and panting as he sprang from one place to the next, plying his steel with unstoppable fury.

Six men were down on the ground, three more sat their saddles wounded. The Mongrols were cursing now, using their curving scimitars like whips, trying to get at him.

A blade slashed his arm even as its wielder died. A second sword came in, and Kothar was slow in making his parry. There was a ring of steel on steel and he caught a blur of motion to one side of his head. Then the sword hit and—

He lay for hours among the dead.

Overhead the vultures wheeled and dipped, waiting. There were eight bodies on the ground, all of those bodies were dead but one. In a little while, all eight men would be in the spirit world.

The living man stirred. He groaned. His arm lifted and fell. After a time he pushed himself upward to his knees. His face stared up at the sky where the black birds flew, and a snarl rumbled in his thick throat.

"Damned scavengers," he growled, and sought to rise.

He stared down at his left thigh when his leg would not support his weight. A broken arrow shaft bobbed there to his movements. He put a hand to the shaft, worked it gently back and forth. Pain bit his flesh and ran all through his body, but he persisted. After a time, the point came out.

He threw it aside, scooped a handful of dirt and pressed it to the wound. The dirt would help to clot the blood. It was an old trick he had learned from a mercenary in the Foreign Guard of Queen Elfa.

Kothar could stand now. He put his hand to his head, his palm came away wet. The swordstroke which he remembered only dimly had done this. Luckily, Frostfire had turned to the edge so that only the flat of the blade had struck him. He would live, even if his head ached for a while.

A more serious thing was the arrow in his shoulder. He could get his fingers on it but he could not work it out. If it remained in his flesh, it might fester and then, surely, he would die. Kothar snarled, staring around the grassy plain.

He must find a rock. He could lie down and rub the shaft against the rock, and perhaps dislodge it in that manner. It would hurt, but he was used to hurt. The hurt would go away after a time, and he would be alive.

Finding Frostfire half-hidden beneath a corpse, he cleaned the blade and sheathed it. Hunkered down, he studied the dead bodies, noting the leather purses at their sides that held food, the nomad leather bottles containing wine or water. Kothar grinned. He was not ashamed to rob the dead, especially dead enemies.

Laden down with money, food and water, he began his trek.

After two hours, he found he was weaker than he had thought. The loss of blood was making him stumble. It even made him see visions.

There was a horse out here, a brown Abathoran stallion. It stood a hundred yards away, the wind ruffling its mane and the tasseled braidwork of its reins. It posed with proud awareness of its strength, and once in a while it shook its head.

Kothar whistled softly, and moved forward. To his surprise, the stallion did not bolt; it even advanced a little toward him. Kothar grinned and began to trot. So did the horse.

His hand caught the reins, his other hand went to the soft white muzzle and rubbed it. "By Dwallka, you're a horse to equal Greyling," he muttered.

His foot went into the stirrup, he swung up into the oddly shaped saddle, the cantle of which was high, reaching to the small of his back. The pommel was widely arched. Kothar frowned, vaguely recalling pictures of such a saddle seen in old history books.

He toed the horse to a canter. He must find a way to get the arrowpoint out of his flesh, and fast. Even the movements of the horse between his thighs added to his pain. He gave the animal its head; one direction might be as good as another.

An hour later, a building loomed like a black dot on the horizon. Kothar felt his spirits brighten at sight of it. He kicked the stallion into a run. He would be able to get help, there.

The closer he came to those dark, blackened stones, the more he began to realize there would be no help at all. He had stumbled onto a stone temple or shrine to some forgotten god. The broken columns towered upward toward the sky, but there were great gaps between them, and the arches and shattered walls of what had been the nave were half-covered over with moss and vines.

He reined in, close to the first line of pillars.

His eyes made out an altar inside the domed apse. Behind the altar was a hollowed-out niche in the solid stone. At sight of it, Kothar felt a cold chill ripple down his spine.

He came to the ground and walked forward, intending to put his back against a pillar and scrape out the arrow. As he turned, a voice whispered to him.

"No need for that, barbarian," the voice sang in the wind.

Kothar looked around him, tensing. He could see nothing, but he could hear mocking laughter as he put hand to his sword hilt.

"No need for steel between us. Can you kill a god?"

A faint susurration made him turn. Where the stone had been hollowed behind and above the altar, it was filling now with—blackness. It billowed upward as from the ground itself, surging outward, with faint red lines streaming here and there in the ebon richness.

"I am Thurkaknorr, barbarian!"

Kothar waited.

The blackness sighed. "Ahhh. Have I been forgotten so soon? Have the years passed so swiftly in your world and not in mine? Is my name so unfamiliar?"

"I never heard of you," Kothar said honestly.

"No. I see as I look about me that all the world I know has changed. Where stood a city, and my temple on a hill high above it, is no more. The very dirt has covered the spires and the rooftops, hiding them from view. I remember the olden days and I long for them." There was a silence as the wind moaned, playing between the broken columns of the ancient temple. "Come closer, man," said the blackness.

When Kothar stood before the altar, the darkness reached outward, swept about the barbarian. There were tingles in his wounded thigh, in his head, and where the arrow shaft protruded from his shoulder. He heard a low chuckle, shrouded in that blackness.

"The Mongrols wounded you, left you for dead—as they robbed my temple of its almost forgotten treasures. We have a score to settle with them, you and I!"

It seemed that, within the ebon darkness, Kothar stared out upon vast plains of black sand and dirt, where crystal trees and bushes grew white against that blackness, so that it made a faery picture beneath a glittering crystal sky. Strange beings moved, here and there, and in the far distance, a magnificent building rose skyward.

"My world, man. Here Thurkaknorr reigns supreme."

The darkness withdrew, left Kothar standing motionless in front of the altar, aware of a sense of well-being he had never known. His wounds were healed, he stared at the clean, sun-bronzed skin of his left thigh, he touched palm to his head and found no clotted blood, no bruise. At his feet lay the arrow that had been in his shoulder.

"My thanks, god or demon or whatever you are. Aye, we owe the Mongrols much. I intend to pay back some of my debt!"

"How? By riding willy-nilly over these steppes?"

"Sooner or later I'll find them!"

"By that time, Red Lori may be dead."

Kothar felt his heart leap. "She lives?"

"Aye, she lives—as captive of the nomads. She is just one more bit of loot the Mongrols have been amassing on their raiding expedition." There was a slight pause, then Thurkaknorr added, "Why are you so set on rescuing her? I know from my gods—or fellow demons, if you will—that she feuds with you."

Kothar explained his reasons for serving Red Lori, to save the spirit of blonde Mahla. The demon-god listened quietly. When the Cumberian had finished, Thurkaknorr spoke again.

"So you say. Yet I know it is written in the books of Dythan that your fates are oddly interwoven, you and Red Lori. You must serve her because this is the way destiny would have it.

"Were she to be won by a Mongrol, she would bend him to her will, she would find a way to use her necromancies once again—and this must not be! Not yet, at any rate. No, the books of Dythan say that you alone have power to stop the witchwoman. Yet how, I do not know."

Kothar grinned. It was a warm feeling, knowing that, it made him draw Frostfire from the scabbard and clang it back so that the metal rang.

"What shall I do then?"

"Bring her here. With her—bring the Mongrols!"

The blackness faded. Only the viuga winds inhabited the ruined temple with the big barbarian. Kothar shook himself, turned and walked toward the brown stallion. He would have preferred to ride Greyling but his own warhorse was probably a prisoner of the nomad raiders.

Under his weight, the brown stallion reared, then came down at a gallop, racing to the north as if it knew the mission ahead of it. Kothar gave the beast its reins, an inner voice told him the stallion was the gift of Thurkaknorr, and was something more than a mere animal.

The horse ran with unceasing speed, as though its muscles were not of this world, but another. Kothar did not bother to dismount, he ate the food and drank the water in the Mongrol canteens. The wind of his passing ruffled his shaggy yellow hair and the long furs on his jerkin, but Kothar sat like a stoneman, scarcely moving otherwise, thrilling to the speed of this supernal animal.

As the sun set, his keen nose smelled cooking fires.

Through the gathering darkness raced the beast, without pause or hesitation. Now Kothar could see the Mongrol campfires, red dots in the deepening night. He drew back on the reins, slowing his headlong pace. The stallion walked now, while the barbarian stood in the stirrups and scanned the camp.

It was set in a little hollow, where the earth dipped away to form a wide hollow. In front of a big tent were the women of the caravan, roped together, standing or sitting as they ate the stew and drank the mare's milk which formed the raiding fare of the nomad riders. On a stool over which a spotted hide was thrown, sat a big Mongrol, his chest framed in mail shirt and red cloak, a peaked helmet on his head. Kothar assumed this must be the khan of the nomads.

Kothar shifted in the saddle, giving his muscles a rest against the hours-long ride. He waited patiently, being familiar with the methods of the raiders. They were about to begin the victory feasting; kettles and cauldrons hung over the flames, filling the air with the fragrance of meat and vegetables.

After the feasting would come the disposal of the treasure and the women. The nomads would enjoy their women, and get drunk. It might be best then to go down into the camp and take Red Lori away from them.

His eyes touched golden links, small coffers thick with jewels.

Yes, barbarian—that is *the treasure of Thurkaknorr!*

"How am I to take it?" Kothar wondered.

Leave that to *me! Bring the woman—and the Mongrols.*

Kothar grinned. He would be able to bring the Mongrols, all right—if he galloped down into the camp and yanked Red Lori up on his brown stallion! He could get himself killed that way, too. No, he would wait.

He waited until the feasting was done and the drinking had begun. A woman was led forward, stripped and made to walk up and down between the sitting ranks of horse-archers. A man stood up, drew his sword and caught the woman by a hand.

Another nomad rose, drew his own sword and leaped forward.

The men fought while the woman shrank back, terrified. Kothar watched with something akin to battle fury working in his veins. He was watching the custom called the mating duel, in which men fought for their females until one was wounded, or dead.

A cry came from one of the duelists, as he fell back with a slash across his swordwrist. The other man laughed, drove his blade into the ground to clean it, and reached for the woman he had won. Two men came to apply salve and bandages to the wounded man.

Three women were taken from the ropes and claimed by nomads before Red Lori was led forward. She stood proudly and unafraid, as though she scorned these men, but Kothar who knew her realized fear ate in her vitals.

The man on the hide-covered stool stood up, walked slowly forward. He put a hand on Red Lori and said something in the nomad tongue.

Go down, Kothar! Challenge him! "And get myself killed?" the barbarian growled.

Even as he spoke the brown stallion was moving forward and Kothar found he was yanking Frostfire from the scabbard. His voice bugled, "I challenge, Imkak Khan! The woman is mine!"

The seated men began to rise and reach for weapons. They had posted no guards, these steppes were their home and no body of fighting men strong enough to attack them, was within three hundred miles. They stared at the giant Cumberian as he rode the brown horse forward between the fireflames.

Red Lori stood proudly, her white shoulders thrown back. The man who held her long red hair twisted in a hand was glaring at the solitary rider.

While Kothar reined in his mount, Imkak Khan snapped, "You're no Mongrol, and only a Mongrol possesses the right to challenge in the mating duel."

Kothar stood before the khan, grinning coldly. "If you refuse, it proves you a coward and unfit to rule—let alone take a woman captive for your enjoyment."

He let his blue eyes roam the circle of watching nomads.

"You tried to kill me today, some of you. You left me for dead. I'm alive—and here to claim my own. Are the nomads all cowards? Don't they dare meet me in single combat? Or must they fight with odds of twenty to one to hope for victory?"

He let his mocking laughter boom out.

"You aren't men! Then what do you want with a woman?"

Red Lori smiled at him, then cried, "They are boors, Kothar. Fearful boors who are brave only when they fight with overwhelming numbers—or perhaps when they attack women."

The hand holding her hair yanked back, tugging her off balance. Red Lori cried out as she staggered. Before she could right herself, Kothar was leaping forward, his left fist swinging, ramming into the jaw of the khan.

The khan flew backward off his feet.

The nomads surged forward. Kothar snarled, swung Frostfire in front of their eyes. "Back! Before I kill you all! Is your khan a puling infant, that he cannot defend himself? Is he the kind of leader you nomads follow? Pah! I spit on him—and on you!"

The khan screamed in his fury as he came off the ground, his scimitar glinting with the firelight as he swung it. Kothar shoved Red Lori behind him, catching the fury of that steel and turning it.

The khan was a tall man, wiry in his strength. He fought like a burning flame, darting and dipping, falling to a knee and thrusting, employing overhead blows that changed in mid-thrust into sidewise slashes. He cursed and panted, his black eyes blazed with the battle rage.

Kothar stood like a rock, calm and scarcely moving, Frostfire turning almost of itself to ward off the blows and cuts that flew about him with blinding intensity.

Steel sang with metallic cadences, sparks flew as edge met edge.

The khan was driving Kothar back and back, to the shouted delight of his nomad riders. The barbarian let the khan turn him, because Kothar had spotted Greyling in the rope corral that held the nomads' horses. Greyling for Red Lori, the brown stallion for himself! And so he allowed the khan to turn him and he listened to the delighted howls of the horse-archers with a grim smile.

When the corral ropes touched his back and Red Lori pressed against him, Kothar made his move. He bounded away from the hemp, he slashed with Frostfire like a man freshly come into battle. His giant frame and massive muscles felt no fatigue, whereas Imkak Khan was weary from the many sword-strokes with which he had belabored the sword of the giant barbarian.

Back, went Imkak Khan. Back, until he stumbled.

The grins on the faces of his followers were gone before the scowls and glares that watched the swordplay of the Cumberian. Death for their leader glinted coldly out the blue eyes of this barbarian who watched his every move. The men sensed this, so did their khan.

"Help me!" shouted Imkak Khan.

At the same moment the great blue blade of Frostfire fell atop his skull, splitting his head from poll to chin. Blood gushed. The body of the nomad ruler swayed a moment, still on his legs—and Kothar leaped.

His arm swept Red Lori up, flung her through the air onto the bare back of Greyling, even as he vaulted the rope fence. Like a cat, the barbarian was after her, landing behind her, bloody sword flashing as he severed the corral ropes. The nomad ponies surged forward in an eruption of flying hooves and snapping teeth.

Nomad ponies are chancy beasts, at best. With the smell of spilled blood in their nostrils, with the harsh cries of the Cumberian ringing in their ears, they went mad with terror. Like a tidal wave they swept from their hempen bounds and spilled out across the camp. They rode down their masters, trampling some, less fleet of foot than the others, into bloody lifelessness.

Kothar and Red Lori rode Greyling through the midst of this flash flood of horseflesh. A cry from the barbarian brought the brown stallion galloping, using its greater heights and weight to wedge a path between the smaller steppes ponies.

Kothar leaped to the brown back. Greyling could carry Red Lori. Somewhere off in the darkness, a bow twanged. The galloping ponies had trodden down the campfires, and the stink of singed flesh and hair was all around them. In the darkness, the archers could not see to shoot, yet a shaft whizzed past Red Lori, making her cry out.

"Ride south!" Kothar yelled. "And fast!"

She bent above the neck of the grey warhorse, its white mane stinging her cheeks, urging on the beast with soft words and stroking hands. Fast was Greyling, but even faster was the demon-horse between Kothar's thighs. It raced ahead of the warhorse, its hooves barely skimming the ground.

Behind them, order was coming out of chaos as the Mongrols ran down their mounts and leaped on their bare backs. Their war cry ululated to the stars as scimitars flashed and the ground shook to the thunder of galloping hooves.

The chase went on through the hours of the night.

Long before dawn, the brown stallion and Greyling swerved to a halt before the ruined temple. Kothar leaped down, went to the grey horse and helped Red Lori. She leaned against him when her feet firmed on the ground, catching his arms and holding him.

"Let me rest a little while, Kothar. I have not your endurance. I'm exhausted. Do you have any water?"

He gave her a leather bottle and made her sip its contents slowly. The sun was rising to the east, the broken pillars of the ancient temple sent long shadows across the ground. While she sat on a plinth and got her strength back, the barbarian told her about Thurkaknorr.

"Yes, I know the name," she murmured, "from those times when I consorted with demons during my spells and incantations. He is a very potent god, Thurkaknorr."

"He'd better be a prompt god," the barbarian growled.

Red Lori looked where Kothar jerked his thumb. A line of dots on the northern horizon showed where the nomads came at the run. In minutes they would be upon them. She saw the barbarian glance at the hollowed stone behind the altar.

"He will come," she told him.

His answer was the sound of Frostfire scraping from the scabbard. "Useless to trust a god or demon," he snarled. "You do what they want, and one way or the other they turn on you."

He swung about, faced the north and the horse-archers, disdaining anything but the direct attack. Screeching shrilly, waving their scimitars—one or two were unfastening their bows and putting arrows to the strings—they ran on with a cloud of yellow dust rising behind them to tell the direction of their coming.

A few arrowshafts slid into the air. Two were close; these, Kothar knocked aside. Then the nomads were in front of him, and he went to meet them, swinging the blued blade, shouting the battle cry of the Cumberian Viks where he had served his apprenticeship to Dwallka, god of battles.

A rider went down, and another. A scimitar glanced off the barbarian's mailed shirt. Gripping a bridle, using it to support his weight, he swung from one horse to a second, driving his blade sideways into a rider and upward to disembowel a man who missed his own slash at his bared head.

"Enough, barbarian! You served to bring them close—now none may escape. Now—they belong to me!"

Every man stood frozen in horror, staring at the flat altar and the hollowed stone shell behind it, where a gathering blackness was emerging, flecked with angry red beams that pulsed and flared deep inside it. A raw fury beat outward from that ebon intelligence like a tangible thing. Even Kothar felt it lash about him.

The horse-archers were terrified. This was a king among the kelets, the evil spirits that inhabited their steppe world. Their shamans had spoken of these demons that lived somewhere in the vast wastelands over which they raced their ponies.

As one man, they screeched their fear, turned their horses to flee. But the blackness was far faster than mere flesh. It sped from the hollowed stone, raced to form twin arms on either side of the temple, extending outward.

Kothar moved steadily backward, his eyes touching Thurkaknorr and then the nomads, until his thigh met Red Lori where she sat upon the plinth, smiling dreamily.

"Watch, Kothar—and know the might of an angry Thurkaknorr!" she breathed, laughing softly and catching his hand in hers.

He was too fascinated by what was happening to shake off her hold. The nomads were galloping their ponies toward the thin line of blackness ringing them in, shouting and swinging their scimitars. One of them galloped at the thinnest section, toeing his horse for a leap.

Upward rose the shaggy steppes pony.

In the middle of their rise, the rider screamed, back arching and sword falling from his suddenly nerveless fingers. The blackness rose upward like a wall to meet him. Where his arm protruded through the blackness there was only a skeleton. The flesh had been stripped away, leaving bare bone.

"Dwallka!" bellowed Kothar.

The pony completed its leap, landing on the other side of the dark wall. Instead of a man, a skeleton sat its back, a skeleton that fell from the saddle and lay on the grassy ground—dead bones glinting in the morning sunlight.

A wail went up from the other nomads. They were going mad from superstitious terror. They glared around them, seeking a way out; there was none. They were trapped here and the blackness that was Thurkaknorr was moving slowly inward for the feasting.

You desecrated my temple! You stole my treasures! Thieves! Rapers of women! Killers of men! This day you die!

The ring closed. Men rose up in their stirrups to slash at it, but the hands that held the scimitars were bones, and the bones fell away so that only the handless wrists remained to the wildly screaming Mongrols. More men sought to ride through the blackness; they too, were turned to skeletons.

In a little while it was over. The blackness was receding into the hollowed-out stone. Shaggy ponies ran here and there, the ground was littered with human bones. Red Lori was standing, shading her eyes with an upraised hand as she stared at that which was Thurkaknorr.

And Thurkaknorr spoke.

"Go now, barbarian, with this woman. I shall recover my treasure by assembling and giving life to the bones scattered here and there, commanding them to bring me what is mine."

The blackness receded. In a moment only the stone shell itself could be seen. A steppes pony whinnied, riderless.

"Come," said Kothar.

Red Lori followed him quite meekly.

CHAPTER 8

On Greyling, the barbarian set a fast pace toward the desert lands of Aegypton. Red Lori followed on a steppes pony. When he had looked about for the brown stallion, it was nowhere to be seen, convincing the barbarian that it had, indeed, been a creation of Thurkaknorr for his needs.

Behind them, attached to a rope rein, came the horse laden with the silver bars Pahk Mah had traded to him. Without the horse and its burden, Kothar knew he was helpless against Red Lori. He had made a special point of riding to the Mongrol encampment—where only dead men remained—to secure his horse, overriding the objections Red Lori made.

They went by lonely ways, galloping along an abandoned caravan trail, pausing on wind-swept hills to eat and sleep. Sometimes they rode without a road under their horses' hooves, the barbarian trusting to his instinct and to the sun and stars to tell him he rode south by west. At every mile they galloped, Red Lori recovered a little of her arrogance.

"I think I shall keep you alive, Kothar," she told him once when they halted to let their horses blow. "I have in mind the fact that Kazazael sent you to kill my guardians when I was too deeply involved in an incantation to help them. You make a good guardian, all by yourself."

"I belong to no one but myself," he growled.

"Oh? Is it your wish to ride with me to Memphor? Or do you come because of what might happen to Mahla?"

"Yes, because of Mahla," he answered.

"What I do now, I can do again. I can always find a way to strike at you. Remember it. Be grateful that I give you life—so serve me well."

Her taunting laughter rang out, and Kothar scowled.

They came out upon the desert sands of Aegypton seeing the grim stone pyramids rising black against the red of a setting sun. Memphor lay to the west, they could not see it from these gravel beds across which they galloped. To the south lay the forgotten ruins of Xythoron. Xythoron was a city whose eerie destruction—legends say it was by a rain of fireballs out of the dark domain of the demon-gods—lay so far in the past that none had known of its existence until a century ago, when two travelers from the land of Yurj discovered it.

There were tombs in the city ruins, strange buildings of twisted, alien architecture, of a material not known on Yarth. Only one tomb had ever been opened, by a team of diggers sent from Memphor. No man knows what came out of the tomb, only the shattered, pulpy remains of the diggers were found, as if torn apart by mad, gigantic hands. The tomb had been hastily sealed up, and today no man in his right mind walked the time-worn paving stones of cursed Xythoron.

"There are ways to open the tombs," Red Lori hinted.

Kothar grinned, "You've lost your powers of wizardry. Won't you be taking a chance?"

"You'd like me to fail, wouldn't you?" she flared. "You'd like a demon to come out of the tomb and tear me to pieces!"

"There is some danger, then?"

"Of course there's danger—not only for me but for you as well!" She laughed shrilly. "They won't stop with me, if they're unleashed. They'll rip you limb from limb, too."

They rode on, their horses' hooves scratching sparks from the stones of the desert. Night was closing in, the sun was nothing more than a red reflection on the clouds.

"We ought to make camp," Kothar said.

"Not yet. We should be in Xythoron soon."

A coldness ran down the barbarian's spine. He had no wish to make his campfire on stones where demons walked. He preferred the clean air of mountain or steppe to the stink of embalming fluids. He did not hold with wizards and demonolatry, though he knew they existed.

His hand touched the jeweled hilt of Frostfire. There was magic in his sword, and he had the uncomfortable feeling that he might need all the magic help he could get before he got out of Xythoron alive. If he got out alive.

The stars were in the sky, clustered close together, as the first iron hoof rang on a paving-stone. Kothar walked Greyling here, uneasy at the brooding menace of the low stone buildings, their caved-in roofbeams, charred and powdery, at the marble mausoleums that rose upward between the houses. The odor of death was still in the dead air, mixed with the smells of natron and bitumen.

His hand tightened on the rope rein of the roan. He wanted the roan close, he did not intend for it to bolt and run, not when it had come so far. Red Lori rose beside him, shifting her weight in the saddle as her eyes roamed the tombs and houses. From the manner in which her eyes quested, the Cumberian knew she sought a sign to help her pick out the tomb she sought.

He waited for her to signal him.

"There," she cried, pointing. "That black tomb, with the spire. It is the crypt of the mage Kalikalides."

She swung down and ran for the bronze doors of the black mausoleum. Her hands came up, she ran palms and fingertips across the grotesque carvings and eerie imageries caught in metal by an unknown artisan. Kothar saw her nod her head as if satisfied.

He began walking into one building after another, ripping loose charred timbers and carrying out bits of wooden furniture. These he piled in the square before the tomb. Red Lori watched him, having turned away from the bronze doors, with a taunting smile on her red mouth.

"Are you making a cooking fire or a bonfire?" she asked tardy.

"Both. I don't like this place."

"Kothar the brave! Kothar the unconquerable! Like a little child, he dreads the darkness."

He grinned at her with quick humor. Lying, he said, "Yes, you might say I am afraid of the dark. The flames will keep the demons away."

"Not when I summon them up. And the fire will do you no good inside the tomb. But do what you will, I don't object." He saw her shiver and come closer to the little flames that began licking upward at the blackened wood chips he had broken off ancient timbers with his bare hands. She was none too sure of herself and her powers, he decided. Being human at the moment, she too, had a need for warmth.

He set a stool for her beside the flames.

"What do you hope to accomplish here?" he asked as he hung a small cooking pot above the flames.

"I shall summon up Deethra. He was the mightiest of the necromancers of Xythoron. He shall restore to me my powers."

"In exchange for what? All magicians are mammonists at heart."

Red Lori shivered, brooding down at the flames that had now reached upward to a height of five feet. Kothar watched the flames too, but he was thinking, In a few hours those charred timbers will be glowing coals, hot enough for my purpose. He looked at the witchwoman.

"When are you going to open the tomb?"

"When I have eaten. It will be a long vigil—if it is to succeed at all." Again she shivered, though the flames were hot and the wind had died down. "Deethra may oppose me, in which case—"

She raised and lowered her shoulders. "Those maps and psalteries I bought in the Street of Booksellers in Clon Mell told of the hours most favorable to the raising up of the dead age. I wish I had them with me now. I must trust to my memory or completely fail in my attempt."

"Then you'd only be a normal woman," Kothar rasped.

Her green eyes studied him. "Would you like that, barbarian?"

His hands tossed broken chair legs on the flames. "You might prove more interesting as a companion."

She rose to her feet, preening in her female pride. Her eyes touched the twin moons of Yarth moving slowly across the blue-black night sky. "There is no time to show you how companionable I might be," she murmured. "The hour of the rat is upon us, and it is time now to open the bronze gates. Come you with me, Kothar."

"Perhaps I should remain behind. Robbers, ghouls or cutpurses may be abroad."

She hooted. "In dread Xythoron? Come!"

He went with her to the gates. "Break them," she commanded.

His huge hands went to the gates, pushed inward. His muscles leaped and bulged beneath his skin. Sweat drops touched his forehead. The bronze doors moved inward, but the iron bar that held them did not break.

Moving back a few feet, he hurled himself upon them. He heard a faint crack, but the bar still held.

As he paused, breathing heavily, Red Lori murmured, "The iron bar is very old. Very old. Even in this dry air, it must be rusted through. Try again."

A third time he hurled himself at the gates. And now they gave, so that the barbarian plummeted inward, hitting a smoothly tiled floor and rolling through a mixture of noisome, charnel odors.

"Paugh!" he said, rolling over and coming to his feet.

Red Lori came racing through the doorway, a silhouette of curves and flying hair against the starlit night. She had left the cloak on the paving-stones beside the fire, she wore only the shirt and fringed skirt of the Mon-grol females, which she had donned in the nomad camp.

Kothar looked about him at the empty mausoleum. "You've ridden a fool's errand. There's nothing here"

"The floor, barbarian! Grasp that iron ring."

His eyes could make out dimly a trap door in the floor. There was an iron ring there, very rusted. Kothar bent, grasped it. His back arched; he heaved, panting. Slowly the trap door rose. As it did so a blue light came out into the vault, illuminating it.

"Kalikalides left the light," she breathed. "It is a demon-light, that can never be extinguished. By its magic aid, his body will have the appearance of true life."

She moved to the trap-door opening, where she could see narrow steps leading downward into the crypt itself. There was a hush on the world, a silence which throbbed in the eardrums as she set first one foot and then another on those treads.

Kothar trailed her down the steps, his neck itching with supernatural dread, his hand gripping Frostfire's hilt. He did not know what he would see; the reality somewhat disappointed him.

A stone bier occupied the center of the room. On it lay a body, seemingly only recently dead, wrapped in garments of gold and purple covered with necromantic sigils. The face was flushed, as if with blood. The man's alive! Kothar thought dazedly. But no, these were the things potent magic could do, so to preserve a body.

Red Lori began to chant.

The blue lights dimmed, then glowed more brightly, but now it seemed to the Cumberian that the blue light was like mist floating in the air, flecked with tiny lights. It grew harder to see; he could not make out the body of Kalikalides quite as clearly, and even Red Lori seemed to be a long distance off.

Her chanting filled the vault, grew louder.

There was no longer a crypt about them, but a metallic room, the walls of which glowed with many colors, sending out their rays of light across the vast chamber in which he and Red Lori stood. Before them was what seemed to be a throne made out of huge metal building blocks, with a grill-work of golden tracery forming its back.

A cloud shimmered on the throne.

The cloud firmed, became the mage Kalikalides. He was the same as the dead body on the crypt slab, the barbarian saw, except that he was alive. Alive? Yes—and no. For his eyelids were closed, though his eyes appeared to burn through their covering as he stared down on the woman and the man.

"Who wakes Kalikalides? Who dares this realm of the dead?"

"I, Red Lori. A sorceress—once. I have lost my powers. I seek them back, with your help."

"You know the rites to command my speech?"

"I do. 'By the wisdom of Asherol, by the might of—'"

"Wait!" the mage cried. "There is a mortal here, a man who knows nothing of these wizardries! Let him wait outside my realm while I do what must be done to give you back your powers."

Kothar felt those dead eyes studying him. Again that sepulchral voice boomed forth. "His presence can disturb the forces which I must summon up, which I must invest in you. He must go back."

The barbarian felt the scene blur before his eyes. He staggered a moment, then saw that he was once more inside the crypt. Red Lori was gone, the dead body of Kalikalides rested unmoving on its cold stone slab. Kothar growled a curse.

He turned and leaped for the stairs. On the upper floor, he lowered the trap door and dropped it into place. He ran for the bronze gates, slammed them together. There was no way to restore the bar that had held them closed for thousands of years, but he had a better way to seal them.

The charred timbers and the bits of furniture had burned down to red coals. The heat from those blue flames was terrible. The barbarian hoped it would be enough for his purpose.

He went to the roan, unstrapped the saddlebags. The silver bars he removed from the bags, placing them in the cooking pots he had brought along from the Mongrol camp. The cooking pots he placed on the coals.

Silver had a low melting point, he knew. He did not have to melt the silver completely, just enough so that he could work it. He labored mightily, throwing more timbers on the flames. Now he must stand by, and wait.

It was dawn when the silver was soft enough to pour from the pots. He carried those pots to the bronze gates and worked the molten silver in with his dagger, all along the cracks. When he was done, the pots were empty, but there was a solid silver seal running along the joints of the doors, and where they hung on their hinges.

Not so much as a breath of air could escape the crypt. Kothar hoped that Red Lori would be as helpless. He had gambled on the fact that Kazazael had used silver bars to contain her; no witch or sorceress could pass through anything covered with silver; something about the metal was impervious to magic.

The silver would hold her, or he was doomed.

As the sun came up, he rode out of Xythoron.

KOTHAR AND THE DEMON QUEEN

CHAPTER ONE

For uncounted years the mage Mindos Omthl had lived by the side of the Sunken Sea, in a gaunt black tower that had been built in the forgotten years when there had been water in that ancient sea-bottom. For all those years, while he had performed conjurations for the wealthy merchants and the noblemen of Thankarol and Niemm, he had dreamed of the lost spell of Baithorion, which was said to give the performer of that necromancy the lost secret of eternal youth.

Mindos Omthl was an old man, wrinkled and bent. He had few years left in which to find the lost parchments of Baithorion. His chests and coffers were heavy with the gold and jewels he had amassed over the years; he had no more need for wealth; the only thing he wanted, and needed with an almost insane desperation, was his departed youth. Here and there in the great metropoli of his world, in Romm and in Memphor, in Thankarol and in Niemm, he had agents searching relentlessly for some hint of those almost legendary scrolls.

At long last, in ghoul-haunted Anthom, which was little more than a city of the dead, an agent came across a forgotten passageway, discovered when the bricks of a cellar were knocked down to extend an aqueduct. The passageway, its floor thick with dust, its walls hidden by spider webs, led to a circular stone room that turned out to be a depository of much forgotten, arcane lore. Encased in an ivory cylinder were the lost conjurations of the long-dead Baithorion.

With quivering fingers Mindos Omthl unscrewed the ivory cylinder and gently removed the crackling parchments. His rheumy eyes scanned the sheets of vellum, widening in disbelieving delight. At last, he had the secret of eternal youth in his hands. The sigils and scrawlings that marked these sheets were in the very handwriting of Baithorion himself!

Eagerly he set up his alembics, the great phials which contained the gore of fifty virgins, and the golden censers which held a potent incense made from dead men's bones. He planted his sandaled feet inside the red pentagram drawn with the blood of a recently deceased high priest and which Mindos Omthl himself had extracted before the high priest had been laid to rest.

In a quavering voice he chanted from the forgotten language, known these days only to Mindos Omthl himself. His hand swung the censer, his eyes beheld the grey incense smoke rising and spreading, his ears heard—There was a rustle as of dried leather.

Ahh! Something was forming in the shadows beyond the pentagram, where all was black as ebony out of the jungle worlds of Oasia. A living presence was shaping there, a sentience which betrayed itself at first only by two blazing red eyes.

The spell of Baithorion was working!

His old heart thudded inside his rib cage as the mage leaned forward, looking toward those glaring orbs. "Are you Abathon? The demon of the ten hells of Kryth?"

"I am Abathon," was a whisper in the blackness. "Who summons Abathon from his eternal pleasures?"

"Mindos Omthl, the magician of Niemm."

"What would you of Abathon?"

"Youth! I want—youth! A strong young heart, a powerful young body to enjoy the wealth and knowledge I have amassed over the years."

There was a little silence.

When the demon spoke, it was with obvious reluctance. "Dread and dangerous are the spells of Baithorion! Be warned, mage. Better to let Abathon go back to his pleasures in awesome Kryth than to dare what has been forbidden for all men to know since Baithorion died in screaming madness. Let me go, I say, and I shall forget what—"

"No!" shouted Mindos Omthl.

His scrawny hand reached for a vial of virgins' blood. With a scream of lust greater than the lust of any man for any woman, he hurled the glass vial across the room, past the red mark of the pentagram and at the shadowy thing that was red-eyed Abathon.

The vial was deftly caught. The demon breathed in the smell of the blood and was lost. Muttering, "Long have I gone unfed on nectar such as this," he raised the vial to his grotesque mouth and drank.

"You must serve me now," the mage screeched, dancing in his triumph. "You have drunk the blood, you have committed yourself to my command."

The demon did not answer, being busy with the vial. His long tongue came out to lap away the last traces of that red substance and then he lowered the cruet.

"I have drunk the blood. I am yours to command," he said simply. Yet to the mage, there seemed to be a hesitancy about Abathon that put him on his guard.

"Make me young. Eternally young—like Baithorion!" he shouted.

"Not so fast. Young I can make you, but only for an hour. You see, there is a—"

"No," screamed Mindos Omthl angrily. "The spell is for eternal youth! I have read of it in the books of Gronlex Storbon, in his *Dialogue of Demons* and in his scarce *Nights of Necromancy*, which I possess. The spell is for eternal youth."

The demon snorted. "As if Gronlex Storbon knew everything! He knew little of the magician who was Baithorion. Ten times ten thousand years lay between their lifetimes. Gronlex Storbon worked from manuscripts as dusty as that from which you read. Some words he could not understand, some words were erased by the brush of Time that destroys everything.

"I, Abathon the demon god of Kryth, tell you this, that to complete your spell you need the aid of the god Xixthur."

The mage licked his thin blue lips. His heart, which had sunk with despair, now beat madly with renewed hope. His shaking hand he raised, to point at the horror crouching in the corner of his solar. "Tell me, how may I raise this god Xixthur?"

"By stealing him."

Mindos Omthl goggled. "Steal a god?"

"Xixthur is owned by Queen Candara of Kor. He rests within her most private bedchamber, to which she admits no one but herself—not even her lovers. In this room, hidden away at the very topmost chamber in the highest tower in the city of Kor, is Xixthur."

"I cannot enchant the god away from her?"

"Candara is part woman, part demon. She knows protective spells herself, with which she shelters Xixthur. No, no, Mindos Omthl. You cannot perform any known incantation which will release her hold on him."

"Then—then how can I get him?"

"Only a demon can steal the god, a demon who seeks the god for himself, not for any living man. And so I am afraid your quest is useless. If you should ensorcell up a demon, and order it to steal Xixthur for you, he would fail because he would not be stealing the god for his own use."

"No, I am afraid you have wasted your time. However…"

"Yes?" quavered Mindos Omthl hopefully.

"There may be a way. I can sense the conjunction of strange and eerie forces in your world. I seem to see the figure of a man striding across the mists of the Haunted Lands, a man with a great sword."

"What do I want with a man?" snorted the baffled mage.

"Do not scorn that which you do not understand! I see also, in the city of Urgal an old, old demon—a demon even older than you, magician. His strength and powers are on the wane. He may do you a favor—and steal the god Xixthur for his own use."

Mindos Omthl clapped his old hands. "Then you can steal Xixthur away from him? Is this what you are telling me, Abathon?"

"Know you anyone who can rob from a demon? No, no—don't ask me to do it. I do not prey on my own kind. You must find another."

The sorcerer wailed, "But what else is there but demons who can help me? My agents are no help, they possess neither the strength nor the will to steal from demons. And as for the race of men—bah!"

Abathon chuckled. "The man I see in the mists is big and strong, Mindos Omthl. He carries a magic sword. It may be that he—might help."

The magician needed no further hint. He whirled toward a great crystal globe, making sure not to step beyond the red lines of the sacred pentagram, for then Abathon would be under no compulsion to serve him, despite having drunk the blood of the fifty virgins; and might attack and destroy him, treachery being the main characteristic of all demons.

His withered hands made cryptic signs above the crystal, his mouth uttered harsh, blasphemous words. His old eyes watched as the crystal grew less clear, turned cloudy and became the mists of the Haunted Lands.

Mindos Omthl stared at a figure of a giant youth, small inside the crystal but huge by comparison with the stone blocks past which he walked, leading a grey horse. He wore a mail shirt that glittered as if newly polished, there was a leather kilt about his loins, and a great sword with a red gem set into its hilt bobbed at his side. A yellow mane of uncut hair hung down to his shoulders, hair that blew this way and that to the strong winds sweeping the barren plains of the wasteland through which he moved.

"Is this the man?"

The demon nodded. "I sense strange powers about him. If I knew not better I would say he is under the protection of Afgorkon himself, beside whose arcane wisdom even Baithorion was but a babe, while you yourself might as well not have been born."

At sound of that dread name, Mindos Omthl made a protective sign with his fingers in the air. He wheezed, "If Afgorkon protects him, what use is he to me?"

"Afgorkon sleeps, at times. If you dare…"

Mindos Omthl gibbered in his eagerness. "I dare, I dare," he cried, leaping from one foot to the other. "I dare anything to be young once more. Tell me what to do, Abathon. Tell me!"

The demon began to speak.

* * * *

Kothar had walked for hours through the white mists of the Haunted Lands. Beside him were the grey stone blocks which, rumor said, had been used to build the lost city of Dru in the days of its greatest glory, half a million years before. The barbarian swordsman was not interested in lost cities; his belly was too empty for that, he needed food badly.

It had been a hare-brained impulse that had brought him across the Rooftop of the World and down those mountain slopes into the Haunted Lands where lived demons and ghouls who ate the flesh from a man's bones even while he was still alive. Kothar was fleeing from the thought of Red Lori, the sorceress who hated him and whom he had imprisoned in the tomb of Kalikalides and sealed therein with solid silver along the edges of the mausoleum door. He had ridden away, leaving her a prisoner with the lich of dead Kalikalides, and Kothar felt vaguely uneasy about the whole thing.

Oh, yes. He had tricked her. But since then Red Lori had been silent. She had not appeared to him in the ale cups he had downed in the taverns of Balthogar and Romm on his way toward the high mountains known as the Rooftop of the World, nor even in the fires he set at night in his lonely camps. And this was the way of Red Lori, so that Kothar had become accustomed to it, ever since Queen Elfa of Commoral had put Red Lori in a silver cage and hung her in her audience hall.

It had been Kothar who had captured Red Lori, the sorceress. It had been Kothar who had stolen her naked body out of the silver cage to save the life of Mahla, daughter of old Pahk Mah. He had ridden into Memphor where the mausoleum of long-dead Kalikalides stood, so that Red Lori could recapture her lost magics.

Now he was fleeing from his memories.

At any time he expected to see the woman of the red hair step out from behind a boulder and confront him. His palm itched and burned to grasp the pommel of his sword Frostfire and test its steel against her womanflesh. Yet she did not appear, neither in mist nor ale cup nor campfires, and so Kothar worried.

"It isn't like her," he muttered to his grey war-horse, Greyling. "She should be cursing me up and down and through the middle. And she's silent. What evil can she be cooking up?"

The big grey shook its head and silver mane, making its ringbits jingle. Kothar rumbled laughter. "You don't know either, do you? Still, we'll both be on our guard."

All men of Yarth hated and feared the Haunted Lands, through which the blond giant strode. There were devils and worse in these mists that seeped eternally from cracks in the rocks and crevasses in the ground, and that came down from the very clouds to add their moisture to the rest. A wanderer might make only a weak fire in this wilderness of tumbled stone and gravelly ground. It was a dead, barren world, and what little vegetation grew here was sparse and stunted, and oddly distorted.

Men said there was a city in the Haunted Lands.

Its name was Kor. Its queen was beautiful Candara.

Kothar had hopes of finding Kor, of taking service with Queen Candara, whom men said was a demon. Demon or woman, it made no difference to the blond barbarian so long as she paid her soldiers in good gold. And gossip had it that she did this, robbing the gold from the merchant caravans that skirted her borders in abject terror.

The mists appeared to be thickening around him, the deeper into the Haunted Lands he went. They billowed and eddied in the wind. From time to time the Cumberian fancied he could see faces there, and that he could hear voices warning him to go back, go back, this land was not for him.

Kothar grinned coldly. Maybe this was why Red Lori was letting him alone. He was walking toward a fate more awful than any she might conjure up for him.

Now he heard strange sounds, like wet mud being squelched and trodden as if by some mighty beast. Kothar held his breath, listening. He turned suddenly and caught at Greyling, pressing his hands to its nostrils that it might not whinny out its fear.

"Easy, easy," he begged. "By Dwallka! We're in a very hell, inside this place. Be quiet, Greyling—on both our lives."

He dropped the reins, knowing the warhorse would wait patiently and silently for his return. On war-booted feet he moved forward, drawing Frostfire from the scabbard with but a whisper of steel on metal.

Past a huge boulder that bore cryptic carvings, put there by a hand that Yarth had long ago forgotten, he inched his way over wet stones and a pallid moss that grew between them. Inside him, he knew a primeval fear, the fright man has always had before the unknown, the mysterious. His mighty fingers tightened on his sword hilt.

A wind blew up, moaning about his ears.

The mists eddied around him, parting. There was a dark something beyond those mists, half glimpsed, half hidden by them. A gigantic something that moved, that made those squelching noises. Kothar felt the hairs on the back of his neck stand up. In the name of his northland god, Dwallka—what was this thing?

It towered up, higher than a city wall. It was black and scaly, and its bulk was ten times greater than a house. It was the size of a small palace! Kothar choked back a curse. The beast—dragon—behemoth—paused as if the wind that shook the mists carried with it his man-smell to its nostrils. A great mouth yawned, disclosing huge teeth. And then its bellow shook the ground beneath Kothar's war boots.

Sweat stood out on his brow. He dared not move, he was frozen motionless. Slowly Kothar backed, until his spine was touching the side of a huge grey boulder. The beast could not swallow him and the rock, not together. His fingers tightened his grip on the sword hilt.

The beast moved its head from side to side, questing for that elusive scent. Tiring of its pastime, it moved on through the noisome swamps, feet lifting from the mud and water with those loud, squelching sounds.

Kothar heaved a sigh.

"By Dwallka! This is no place for us to be, Greyling."

Catching up the reins of the terrified beast, he moved on carefully, walking always on the firmest sections of ground where the greenest grass grew, for a misstep in any other direction might mean their deaths. For miles they walked, the big man and the warhorse, but at length the mists fell away to reveal the slopes of distant hills and a grassy plain between.

Kothar swung into the saddle and rode.

Kor lay beyond the hills, not far away. In other lands, the name of Kor was dreaded and reviled. It had been founded many centuries ago by mutinous soldiers from Avalonia and Vandacia, together with a mixed crew of criminals and riffraff out of Commoral carrying the leopard banner of an exiled queen named Candara. There were women with the men, camp followers and harlots who were themselves thieves and cutpurses.

Such as these had laid the first stones of Kor, with the help of a god, some men said, named Xixthur. It was the largest city in the haunted lands, there were few who dared attack it. And so, in its way, it prospered. Oddly enough, Kor had always been ruled by a woman whose name was Candara.

The first Candara had been sister to the king of Vandacia. The demon served her whim, history said, and had suggested that she flee away from Vandacia with its malcontents and rebels to set up her own realm. She was reputedly a beautiful woman, dusky of skin with hair the tint of a blackbird's wing, and glossy, with eyes that resembled the black of pure obsidian.

Kothar came through the hills at sunset.

Below him lay the plain of Kor and on it lay the city. It was a vast, walled place with leaden roofs alternating with red tiles and blue, the houses themselves being of grey stone. The barbarian stared down at Kor and grimaced. Leaning over the saddle, he spat in disgust.

"A vile place, that stinks," he growled. "My better judgment tells me to ride on, to skirt those walls. But my belly is empty, needing food, and my mouth would not object to a washing down with ale."

He grinned at the thought, and straightened. He was becoming an old lady! He supposed it had to do with Red Lori, whom he had left sealed up in the tomb of dread Kalikalides to share eternity with the dead mage. He had been uneasy about it, ever since.

His war boot toed Greyling to a canter.

The sun was setting behind his back as it lowered over the peaks of the Roof of the World. Shadows were long and ominous as the grey horse cantered between the huge wooden gates which men were beginning to close even now, while there was still light on the plain of Kor by which to see.

Kothar asked, "A good inn? That doesn't rob a man?"

An officer in worn armor waved an arm, grinning. "The Queen's Navel, on the first street to your left past the square. Good supping, stranger!"

The Cumberian thought it a bit odd that he was not interrogated more thoroughly; he was a stranger and well armed with a longsword at his side and a horn bow and quiver on his horse, but he guessed Kor welcomed whatever visitors it might get, for it was not a pleasant place to be.

The air smelled of wine and garbage, since this was the windless season, and the mists came up to the walls of the city like an attacking army every night, as if to pen those stinks inside. Kothar blew his nose and toed Greyling to a faster run.

As he moved down the Street of Winesellers and away from the gate square, the air became fresher, sweeter. His eyes sparkled. Lovely women moved along the narrow walks, hips swinging, and sometimes one or two of them turned to smile at the huge blond stranger. Doors opened onto common rooms where the fragrance of baking bread mingled with that of roasting meats and freshly sliced cheeses.

Kothar grinned, coming to a sign that showed the supposed belly of the queen, and a deep-set navel. There was a tiny stable to one side of the inn, which a man could reach by walking below a wooden archway into an inner court.

A boy ran to snatch the reins of the warhorse and catch the copper coin Kothar flipped through the air at him. He nodded when the barbarian told him he wanted good oats, clean water, and a dry place for Greyling to rest.

Kothar lifted a muscular arm, pushed open a door.

He did not see the thing in black rags that snuffled and lurched along the corridor to his right. It stiffened at the scent of the Cumberian, lifting its head almost out of the hood of the tattered cloak that hid its body. Red eyes blazed at sight of the young giant, and what seemed to be a forked tongue ran slowly about its lips.

With something of a limp, it turned and scurried for the darker shadows of the street. The patter of its feet made oddly metallic sounds.

Kothar strode into the common room, into the smells of bread and meat and cheese. A dozen men turned their heads at sight of him; they were burly men, coopers and wainwrights and a blacksmith or two. Their eyes held steady as they scanned him. He read neither friendship nor enmity in their eyes. A woman stepped from around a wooden tun which a man in a leather apron was broaching, and advanced on him.

"Where'll you sit?" she asked.

"Is there a difference?" he wondered, intrigued.

She waved a bare arm to her left. "Over there's where the girls come to dance. A strong man like you can get the woman of your choice if she must pass by you, instead of running across half the room." She turned and gestured to her right. "That's the place where the food is served. We make plenty but there are always men to eat it and to drink the ale and such whiskey as we serve, and there are some who may take it away from you."

The woman laughed, her eyes flirtatious. She was pretty enough, but a little old and shopworn for Kothar, though there were times when he would not have scorned her body in his bed. A simple tunic covered her body from shoulders to knees and was held at her middle by a broad leather belt.

"So which is it, my young giant? Food? Or women?"

Kothar grinned. "Sit me where the women walk. I can always get what food I need. And right now, I need plenty."

The woman said softly, "Don't be too sure about the food. The men who come to the Navel are strong and fearless. They fear nothing, except perhaps Zordanor."

"Who's this Zordanor?" he asked, but she had turned on a slippered heel to march him across the room toward a small table set near an open space on the floor.

He noticed a curtain hung to one side of and almost directly behind his chair. Apparently the dancing girls came from the curtained doorway, passing by his table to reach the space where they would dance. Kothar grinned hugely. He was not thinking of wenches, but more of his empty belly; still, when he had eaten and drunk enough, he might be interested in a female.

He slipped a copper coin to the woman, who looked surprised. Then she smiled in a friendly way and said, "Pick up a platter at yonder table, go to the long counter set close to the far wall and bang on it with a spoon. I'll see that a girl attends you."

The barbarian nodded. His stomach rumbled. He growled, "Fetch me a tankard of ale. I die of thirst from a long ride."

The woman shook her head. "I seat the men, to prevent quarrels. The girl who brings you meat will fetch you ale."

She walked away. Kothar rubbed his chin thoughtfully. He was a stranger, he would follow these customs of Kor, being a polite man when it suited him. He moved like a tiger to the table filled with wooden platters and selected one, then a spoon. His dagger would serve for knife and fork.

He banged the spoon on the counter. As he did so, the door swung inward and four big men came striding in off the street. The woman hurried forward, but the men waved her away, looking hard at Kothar. They seated themselves at a table not far from the food counter.

A pretty girl with long yellow hair came running as the spoon banged. Her face was a little frightened, Kothar thought, so he tried to reassure her.

"Meat, my pretty. Roasting meat, with the blood running from it. And plenty of it. With freshly baked bread and a wedge of strong cheese. And a big tankard of ale."

She bobbed her head and ran.

Kothar felt the eyes on his back with the instinct of a wild animal. The skin crawled between his shoulder blades. Slowly he let his eyes roam about the room. The dozen early eaters had forgotten the food on their plates, they were more interested in him and in the men who sat at a table near the counter.

He stared at the men. They were big, heavily muscled. Their faces were pitted and scarred, and their eyes were the eyes of pigs, though merciless. He knew their kind. They hungered for amusement, and they had settled on him as the man most likely to give it to them, despite his muscular bulk.

The girl came back, holding his platter laden with newly sliced meat and bread, with a large chunk of cheese. She told him the price and he paid her in the silver dinars of Balthogar.

She scooped up the coins and ran.

Kothar turned, the platter in his big hands.

The four men at the nearby table were rising to their feet, grinning. They were moving apart, by two's. Kothar saw that when he walked between them, they would move in on him.

He stepped forward, as if ignoring them.

One of the men said, "Put it on my table, stranger. That is just about the sort of supper I'd have chosen for myself."

Kothar lifted his eyebrows, halting. "What table is that, friend?"

The man laughed contemptuously, pointing.

Kothar moved as does the hunting cat in the jungles of Oasia, gracefully and with blinding speed. The platter of hot meats he rammed into the face of his tormentor. In almost the same motion his big hand gripped the edge of the wooden table and drove it up and sideways into the bellies of the two bullies to his-right. They went down gasping, with sick groans.

One man remained untouched. Him Kothar caught by the collar of his woolen jerkin and by the leather belt at his waist. He swung him upward without effort, drove him downward into the man whose face was red from hot meat and scalding gravies. Then he lifted them and slammed their heads together.

"You've spoiled my meal, the lot of you," rumbled Kothar.

The heads cracked together again.

"I'm not a rich man, I can't pay for this entertainment you're giving me."

Crack went the unshaven polls.

"You'll pay for my meal, you shall, and add in some fine wine to quench the thirst you've raised."

He let the men sag to the floor by opening his fingers. They lay like scarecrows placed in a cornfield to fright off the birds. Grunting, he stared down at them, then reached for a fat leather purse attached by chains to the belt of his chief tormenter. He opened the purse, grinned when he saw all the fine silver, and tossed a handful of coins on the countertop.

"Fill me another plate, dumpling," he told the blonde girl. "And this time, add a bottle of your best wine to my mug of ale."

He carried his platter and the wine bottle to his table, and began to eat. Kothar was possessed of a barbarian's prodigious appetite, he relished every mouthful as if it might be his last. He drained his mug of ale, then scorned a glass to tip the wine bottle to his lips and drink.

By this time, the four men were stirring, rising to their feet and looking blearily about them. Kothar waved a big hand.

"Come sit on the floor at my feet, dogs. I don't want you baying to the street watch about my having stolen your silver."

The men advanced on him with a hangdog air. One of them blustered, "You can't keep us sitting at your feet, stranger."

"Sit," said Kothar, and the men sat.

When the bottle was almost empty, the Cumberian said, "I thank you for the gift of dinner. It tasted especially good because it was your coins that made it possible."

"You robbed my purse," said one of the four.

"It was a gift, friend, to make up for my meal you spilled. You gave me the silver with a free hand and a generous heart."

The man at his feet saw the cold bleakness of the eyes that glared down at him. His mouth went dry and he nodded, "It was a gift, freely given," he nodded.

Kothar tilted the bottle to his lips. He was in the act of draining the last bit of wine when the unnatural silence of the tavern alerted his animal-like senses. He glanced about him casually, and discovered two newcomers standing just inside the tavern doorway.

One of the newcomers was a man, misshaped with a huge hump to his back and a crouch to his stance. Shaggy hair hung below his shoulders and his wide gash of a mouth was rimmed with bulging purple lips through which a forked tongue showed as it ran about his mouth. He wore filthy rags, but the eyes that peered out from that grotesquerie of a face were bright and intelligent.

Beside this human travesty stood a woman, garbed in black hood and robe so that only her face and sandaled feet showed. Kothar stared into her face, seeing a sultry loveliness, dusky skin and a few strands of glossy black hair and large eyes in which the black pupils seemed like coals out of Hell.

She stirred faintly under his stare.

"Is this the one, Zordanor?"

The misshapen thing nodded its shaggy head, "The prophesying sticks said two men would come to Kor and that one of them would be of service to you. This is the other."

"Yes, the Makkadonian we already have."

Kothar felt his belly muscles tense. This woman and that monster beside her meant no good to him. He might have to use Frostfire on them before he could win free. He waited warily as the woman walked toward him, the black woolen robe faintly swinging to her stride. There was something so essentially female about her walking that his eyes tried to burn through the black wool to see her body.

She said, "I will hire you, stranger."

"I came to serve Candara the queen, lady."

"Fool! Who do you think I am?"

Kothar grinned. "All the queens I ever knew came with retinues of servants and many soldiers to protect them and enhance their glory."

Her laughter rang out. "I need no protection with Zordanor beside me. And being Candara, I have all the glory I can possibly use. Everything inside the walls of Kor is mine."

"Excepting only me."

Her black eyes brooded at him. "If you take my gold, you belong to me, stranger. Well? Do you accept my service?"

She made a gesture with a ringed hand. The hunchback put a paw into a velvet purse hanging at his side and lifted out a dozen gold pieces. He dropped them casually on the tabletop.

"A pledge of my generosity," the woman breathed.

The barbarian stared at the gold, remembering the three copper soltars in his leathern almoner, which was all his wealth. He nodded his blond head, and put out a hand to gather in the coins.

"Aren't you interested in the sort of employment I offer?"

Broad shoulders lifted and fell. "One task is much like another, when queens select them. I do what I'm paid to do." He picked up the gold pieces, one by one, rubbing them between forefinger and thumb before dropping them into his own purse.

"Come with us," Candara said, and turned on a heel.

Kothar went after them, tossing his cloak about his shoulders against the night chill beyond the tavern walls. He towered above the hunchback and the woman, and he wondered, as the wind came down the street and blew against his wine-warmed cheeks, if he had been hired as a bodyguard.

The woman ignored his presence, walking with her regal stride over swill-wet cobblestones and past little stone ditches filled with slops and water. The hunchback hobbled along at her side, ignoring the barbarian as totally as did Candara herself.

They came to a broad oaken gate set with brass studs, that formed the only opening in a greystone wall. Two men in armor nodded to the queen and opened the doors. They went into the outer courtyard of the palace of Kor, that was bounded by a high stone wall and towered high above the smaller, meaner hovels of the citizenry of the city. Here the air was sweeter, and the torches flaring in their iron holders showed neat paving stones. Some soldiers in half-armor stood at the open armory door and stared at the little cortege. Kothar fancied he could read fear and something of sympathy in their eyes when they looked at him.

They went up a narrow stone staircase and through a wooden door into a stone chamber hung with heavy brocade draperies. A fire below a hooded chimney made a warmth in the room. A large chair was perched beside the hearth, and across the room, beside a prie-dieu holding a psaltery, was a writing desk and chair.

Candara seated herself in the easy chair.

She threw back her hood. Kothar stifled a grunt of sheer admiration. By Salara of the bared breasts! This was one beautiful woman. Her face was dusky of skin, like that of a woman of Memphor, and her hair was the color of a raven wing, black and glossy, and fell to below her shoulders. Her mouth was red as newly spilled blood, and seemed made for kisses.

"Have you ever fought a demon, stranger?"

"Now and again," the Cumberian shrugged.

Her laughter rippled out. "You do not fear them, then?" She leaned forward, holding her breath as she awaited his answer.

"I avoid them when I can. I fight them when I must."

"I would order you to go to the city of Urgal and either kill the demon that protects it—Azthamur—or steal from it that which Azthamur robbed from me."

"Then I shall obey."

"Or die in the attempt?"

Kothar shrugged. The queen ran her eyes over his muscular bulk and the Cumberian fancied that he could read desire for his barbarian body in her stare. He wondered if her lust was fed on the thought that he might be a dead man in a few days.

"There is one thing I must tell you," she said slowly. "I have chosen another to do this task for me.

"Then why seek me out?"

The hunchback, who had been standing in the shadows to one side of the hooded fireplace, spoke softly. "I have recited the incantations and cast the prophecy sticks, but I cannot tell which one."

"Send him. If he fails, I'll go," Kothar growled.

She shook her head. "No. Were I to warn Azthamur that I seek Xixthur from him, he would come at night to Kor and eat the flesh from my bones. I do not—dare to do that."

"Xixthur?"

She smiled faintly. "I shall tell you about Xixthur—if I choose you to go to Urgal."

There was a promise in her eyes that touched sparks to the hot blood beating in his veins. Kothar rumbled, "Let there be a contest, then, between this other and myself. Whoever lives, shall go to Urgal."

Candara shook her head as amusement glinted in her black eyes. "You could never defeat Japthon in a combat, stranger. No man born of woman can do that. And yet, I know no other way to decide. Perhaps you are smarter than Japthon, who is a brute with the brains of a pig and the body of a war god."

"Let them fight," said Zordanor.

Regretfully, as her eyes studied the handsome bulk of the young blond giant, Queen Candara nodded her lovely head. Kothar realized she believed that she was sentencing him to death.

"When do we fight?" asked the barbarian.

"Within the hour. Zordanor will show you the way."

Candara rose and smiled sadly at him.

CHAPTER TWO

Deep within the pile of stone that was the palace of the queen in Kor was a small round chamber with a dirt floor and a tier of several seats rising upward from a ten foot wall around the small arena. More than a hundred torches glowed along the wall, so that the arena itself was lighted brightly while the tier of seats was in dark shadows.

Kothar came out of a doorway in the round stone wall, carrying Frostfire and a shield that Zordanor had handed him. He stepped onto the hard packed dirt and let his stare range upward toward the box bearing the royal arms, a spotted leopard rampant on an azure field. Candara sat there, shrouded in her black woolen robe, though the hood was down to show her glossy hair and her exquisitely beautiful face.

A clang of metal alerted him. He swung about as the largest man he had ever seen stepped from a dark doorway behind a raised iron grille. The man was a Makkadonian, with auburn hair beneath a high-crested helmet, wearing a mail shirt to his middle thighs and below that, red leggings strapped with brown leather. He towered half a foot above Kothar, and Kothar was himself a giant, while his arms were each a foot longer than those of the barbarian.

Kothar grunted. He had his task cut out for him, to stay alive this day. No pampered city soldier, this one; he was what the queen had named him: a brute. There was brutish intelligence beneath the shaggy brows, glinting out at him from dull blue eyes, but no wit, no understanding of anything beyond his own muscles.

Japthon let out a bull bellow and charged.

In either hand, he carried a gigantic battle-axe, huge weapons made especially for his titanic strength. He swung one axe; Kothar raised his shield to block it and was rocked back on his heels by the sheer power of the arm that swung it. At almost the same moment, the other axe darted for his skull.

Kothar rasped a curse and ducked. He swung the glaive in his hand, watched Japthon cross his right arm over to catch the blow on the flat of his axe helm and deflect it. Japthon brought his left hand axe upward toward Kothar's jaw.

The barbarian leaped back, feeling shame that he must yield before the awesome strength of this other man. The shame ate in him, gnawing away even as he strove with shield and blade to turn the frightful blows raining at him from either side.

Back he was pushed, and back until his spine felt the round stone wall beyond which he could not go. The Cumberian knew the black eyes of the queen were blazing down at them and thought of the promise in those eyes when Candara had looked at him.

Slowly the shame turned to anger, to that barbarian madness with which he was wont to fight. His teeth gritted together and his lips writhed back. Though he was a giant in strength and statue, this man who opposed him was a freak in his musculature. Ambidextrous, he used either hand equally well and his great battle-axes were like darting steel petrels that would slay if they could penetrate his defenses.

Kothar lunged, driving his point straight before him. He caught Japthon poised for a double swing. The monster could not move quickly enough to prevent that steel from stabbing into his side.

The Makkadonian howled in fury. Blood came out where Frostfire had sheared through chainmail and the cotton hacqueton beneath it, so that his mail ran red and the leather thongs that held his leggings changed their tint to scarlet. The wound was not deep but it would bother Japthon.

Japthon leaped, both axes swinging.

Kothar retreated, parrying every blow. He would exhaust the bigger man, cause the loss of blood to weaken him. It was folly to stand toe to toe with him and let mere chance decide the battle by a lucky blow. Better to give ground, to let the Makkadonian tire himself.

This time, Kothar chose the way of his retreat, avoiding the round stone wall, keeping empty air at his backbone and using Frostfire as a shield. The shield Zordanor had given him was a mass of crushed wood and ripped steel, somewhere on the arena floor. Above his head, he could hear Candara crying out words, but he could not understand them.

The blows came more slowly, now. The fire was running out of the bigger man with each beating of his heart that forced the blood from the torn flesh in his side. There was a glaze over the hard blue eyes that stared at Kothar.

When he was just below the royal box, Candara leaned far out and shouted down at the Cumberian.

"Do not kill him, barbarian! He's too good a man to die like this. I will keep him as a bodyguard and send you to Urgal."

Kothar lowered his great blade, but Japthon would have none of it. The man had never met defeat, he would not accept it now. He came forward, swinging his axes for the killing stroke.

The Cumberian lashed out with Frostfire.

Through a wooden haft he drove his blade, splintering it so that the axe head fell thudding to the ground. He stabbed sideways, saw his point drive into the bulging muscles of an arm, watched the blood well and spurt.

Japthon let go his axe. He stood staring at Kothar with wide, disbelieving eyes.

He growled, "Kill cleanly, man!"

His head lifted. His blue eyes blazed up at Candara. Kothar leaped, his blade flashing like blood in the red torchlights. The flat of the blade took the bigger man on top of his head, making a sodden thunk. A moment Japthon stood upright, then slowly toppled backward, the senses knocked out of him.

Candara was on her feet.

"I told you not to slay him!" she screeched.

"I dazed him only," Kothar bellowed back. "Fetch your leech, he'll have him good as new by morning—or almost." Anger at this female crowded out his barbarian sense of caution. He growled, "If you think so much of him, let Japthon go to Urgal. I'll be gone from Kor by dawn!"

The fury faded slowly from her face. She shook her head, "No, stranger. You go to Urgal to do battle with Azthamur."

"And when I get this Xixthur for you?"

She waved a ringed hand. Two men in chainmail came to the wooden door and beckoned to him. Candara called, "Come to my bedchamber, stranger. There I shall tell you about Xixthur—and why I want him back."

Kothar shrugged and sheathing Frostfire, followed the soldiers out of the arena. As he walked along a corridor, a man carrying the little black sack of a leech hurried past him to attend to Japthon. The soldiers brought him up two flights of stairs to a door before which two burly men, heavily armed, stood guard.

One of the guards opened the door. Kothar stepped into a huge room dominated by a great four-poster bed, the coverlets of which were pale blue satin. There were lounges and cushions thrown about the chamber, the air of which was lightly perfumed. Tall windows peered out over Kor toward the misted Haunted Lands. Kothar stared out at those distant mists, remembering the beast he had encountered, and shivered.

"What? Afraid after the fighting is over?"

Candara stood in a doorway leading from the bedchamber into a small anteroom. She still wore the black wool robe, with the hood thrown back, and behind her, the barbarian could see Zordanor.

She came into the room, loosening the clasps of the cloak, letting it slip from her shoulders downward. Kothar goggled. The queen was naked under a thin black thing that only pretended to hide her from neck to sandaled feet. It was a nightdress of some sort, he guessed, and its gossamer was stitched with golden threadings in cabbalistic fashion.

Zordanor closed the door behind her, remaining in the outer room, leaving Candara alone with her champion. She saw the manner in which his eyes ran over her shapely legs and curving hips; and she laughed a little, as if this worship were her due.

"What reward will you ask for bringing Xixthur to me?" she murmured.

"A hundred gold pieces," he growled.

Her thin black eyebrows rose. "So little? I was prepared to pay far more."

Her hips swung lazily, challengingly, as she moved past the barbarian to a little table of ebony inlaid with ivory. An iron casket rested on its top. With a ringed hand, the queen threw back its cover.

Kothar saw that the coffer was filled with bright golden coins. Candara turned and stared at him. "This is but a partial payment, stranger—if you succeed in your venture."

The Cumberian eyed the gold with mingled feelings. The curse of Afgorkon was still on him, he knew. So long as he carried the great sword Frostfire, which was a present from that long-dead necromancer, he could own no other treasure. To Kothar, who was a fighting man above everything else, Frostfire was enough treasure to own. Yet he did not deny that so much gold would weigh heavily in his money-purse.

He sighed, knowing that this wealth could give him everything he might ever need, plenty of fine food, enough ale and wine to quench his thirsts, a woman or two to occupy his bed of nights. He was a simple man, and so he was honestly surprised when the queen spoke again.

"You might win a crown, Kothar—and me to go with it," she said softly, lifting her bare arms and stretching, moving her fully curved body from side to side beneath the thin black gossamer, so that he saw how finely formed were her legs and hips, how full and womanly her firm breasts.

The barbarian did not laugh. He had given no thought to becoming prince of Kor, but the notion appealed to him suddenly. With this woman for his queen, he might have all the wealth any man might want, for the wealth would be in the name of Candara his queen and not in his own. It was a way of getting around the curse of Afgorkon.

He grinned at Candara, stretched out a hand toward her.

She slid aside to avoid him, but Kothar with a woman was like the tiger when it hunted. His hand veered, changing direction. His big fingers closed down on her wrists and yanked her toward him. Against his chest he crushed her, staring down into her black eyes.

"I would make you a good prince," he murmured.

"Let me go," she commanded. "You are not yet prince in Kor! And Kor is my city."

He grinned. The softness of her perfumed skin, which he could feel as his palms slid up and down her back, was borning a hunger in the barbarian. Aye, by Salara of the bare breasts! This was a woman to keep a man warm on a cold winter night.

"You're too used to a man who stands in awe of you," he grumbled, and clapped a hand to her buttock, forcing her against him. At the same time his mouth crushed her soft red lips. She stiffened in outraged pride, but she sensed the manhood of the big barbarian and her femininity responded to it. Her bare arms came up about his neck and her soft loins plastered their curves to his hips.

"And you aren't afraid of me, are you?" she breathed.

"Nor of those soft-muscled louts you call your guards. If you want me punished for kissing you, call them in."

"For you to slay them? No, Kothar. The demon Azthamur will slay you—horribly and in dreadful enough fashion if you fail. So awfully that even my queenly pride will be satisfied for your daring to kiss me without permission."

He kissed her again, slamming her against his hard body. When he let her go, she was shivering. Her full mouth curved into a faint smile.

"And if you succeed, if you being Xixthur back to me, then I shall be your queen, and no harm's been done."

"Who is Xixthur?" he asked.

"A god of strange shape and mien. Eternally quiet, yet possessed of powers to keep me young and beautiful for many, many years."

"You want me to capture a god?"

"Xixthur cannot harm you. He is a beneficent god, who confers long life to those who keep him. Which is why old Azthamur wants Xixthur, of course. For eons, Azthamur has dwelt in Urgal, where he serves the lords of Urgal with grim faithfulness.

"Let me warn you of Azthamur. He may not be slain—at least if he can—no living man knows how. Yet you must find a way to slay him, or failing that, to trick him into letting you take Xixthur away from him.

"But be warned! Unless you slay Azthamur, he will follow you to the very rim of Yarth itself, to claim your life as payment for your sacrilege. Once, long ago, as the story has it, one man bested Azthamur in battle and fled away with the royal princess of Urgal, Athalia the Angelic. Azthamur went after him and in the deserts south of Vandacia, caught up with him.

"The man put up a very terrible fight, but Azthamur conquered, and whatever fate then befell the man, no one knows except the princess herself, but she went mad at sight of it. Babbling horribly, she was brought back to Urgal by Azthamur, and given to her brother who was king in Urgal. No man ever saw her again, but the legend is told that she haunts the battlements of Urgal on moonless nights, howling like the doomed spirit she is."

"Tales to frighten babies!"

Her lovely shoulders rose and fell. "Perhaps. I but repeat what is known of Azthamur, so you may be warned. Do not hesitate. Slay Azthamur, if you want to go on living. There is no other way."

"And how did the demon steal Xixthur?"

"It was a stormy night, very dark, with only the scratchings of yellow lightnings in the sky to give light to the people of Kor. Perhaps the darkness that came upon my city was the result of a demon-spell, but whatever was the reason, men and women in Kor moved in a black fog that night. I myself was inside a fog, even in this bedchamber. I could not see my hand before my face.

"Sometime on that night, Azthamur came.

"When I went next day to commune with Xixthur, as is my habit, the god was gone from the little alcove off my bedchamber, that none can enter but I."

She moved gently and Kothar freed her, to watch her walk across the room to a hanging drape that showed the many loves of Salara. Clutching a pull-rope, Candara whisked back the drapery to reveal a door locked and bolted by chains and bars. The chains hung loose, the bars free of the metal slots that held them.

Candara put a hand on the iron latch; she tugged.

The door swung open. Past the queen, who stood to one side of the doorway, Kothar could see an alcove walled solidly with stone, the floor of which supported a stone dais. On that dais had rested the god Xixthur. It was empty, now.

"I put spells on the chains and bars of the door," Candara said softly. "It was as if the door were wide open. Azthamur went in as freely as he might walk down a street in Urgal. He took Xixthur and left the alcove. I do not know how it was done.

"Even though I am part demon, as an inheritance from my ancestors, and know many terrifying spells and conjurations, I do not know how he managed to do it. Perhaps I do not want to know, really."

She shivered. Kothar felt the hairs on the back of his thick neck rise up, bristling. He did not care for all this talk of demons. He relished a good fight with a man, but witches and warlocks were an ilk he could do without.

And yet, it was his task to slay Azthamur.

"Most demons have a weakness of a sort," he grumbled. "Has this Azthamur such a weakness?"

"None that I know."

The barbarian put his hand on his swordhilt. Ah, well! Frostfire had served him at other times, in other ways against demons and warlocks. It might serve him so, once again. His grey eyes brooded at Candara, studying her flesh beneath the black gossamer. He sighed. She was a prize worth fighting a demon to win.

As if she read his thought, she smiled. "Win Xixthur, win me. It is that easy, barbarian."

She turned toward her great bed, dismissing him with a wave of her hand. Kothar chuckled and moved toward her with his catlike tread. She turned, fire in her glare.

"I am not yet your queen," she snapped.

Kothar laughed. "With a man, I would demand a handfasting on our agreement. With a woman, I ask for something else."

He swept her off her feet with a motion of his big arms and tossed her onto the bed. Then he was with her, and though she screamed at first and fought, soon enough her arms were about him and her lips drank thirstily of his kisses.

* * * *

On Greyling, Kothar rode through the rocky wastes that lay for leagues between Kor and Urgal. The scraping of iron hoofs on stones and pebbles, the beating of the hot sun down on his chainmail shirt, were his only companions in this vast barren world. This rocky waste was part of the Haunted Lands, which stretched from Windmere Wood in Commoral as far as the rich city-state of Sybaros. It was not a kind land, to man nor beast.

Until sunset, the barbarian rode.

The black ruins of a chapel rose upward from the pebbly sands, gaunt and eerie against the redness of the setting sun. This was formerly the chapel of Blessed Randolphus, his parchment map told him when he brought it out of a saddlebag and unrolled it. There was good water here and the remains of a shed where he could stable Greyling.

He had ridden the grey warhorse from Kor, intending to leave it here against the possibility of a sudden flight from Urgal. By a long rope he had led a big roan stallion on which he would ride into Urgal. With Greyling he would leave his horn bow and his quiver of war arrows.

Kothar cooked his meat over a glowing fire and sat his rump on an overturned pedestal to eat it. The cool desert winds blew through the ruins at night like the screechings of a lost soul, but the barbarian heeded them not, other than by tugging his bearskin cloak tighter about his great body.

Next day he sat the roan as it kicked up dirt and pebbles on the way to Urgal. The roan was a good horse, the sort a wandering mercenary might own.

His possession of such an animal would not arouse suspicion.

All day long he rode, into the twilight of the day.

Then, when he was about to make camp, he saw the lights of distant Urgal. They were red and tiny in the far stretches between where he stood, about to make his campfire, and the city itself, and he recalled the tales of Urgal he had heard long ago and far away in his youth at Grondel Bay. Demons dwelled in Urgal, which was a city more wicked even than Kor, for it was ruled by Prince Tor Domnus, of whom strange tales were told.

Tor Domnus kept armed men in his palace, as did Queen Candara, but where Candara contented herself with robbing an occasional caravan, Tor Domnus sold the services of his warriors to princes in the countries beyond the Haunted Lands. If a prince wanted a man slain, that prince sought out Tor Domnus and paid his price, and soon, that man who was marked for death, would die.

For a greater fee, Tor Domnus rented out his hard-bitten soldiers by the regiment. There were many barons and smaller lords in the bordering domains of Gwyn Caer and Phalkar, Sybaros and Makkadonia, who ruled in castles won with the air of Urgalian troops. Urgal and Kor existed inside the Haunted Lands because neither was quite certain of victory in any war where the other was concerned.

As he roasted his small slabs of meat over a slow fire, Kothar pondered ways and means of entering into Urgal and spiriting out Xixthur without disturbing the demon Azthamur. A bold approach was still the best. He would ride in according to his plan and seek employment as a mercenary. Once in Urgal, he would make inquiries, learn where the demon kept itself.

He ate his meat and bread, a few chunks of cheese. His wine, in a dusty bottle that had been the gift of Candara, he tilted to his lips again and again. The warmth of the fire felt good; he inched closer to it, sat huddled before the dancing flames.

It was as he swallowed the last of the wine and was about to pitch the bottle into a small stone cairn that stood beside the firestones, that he heard the click of footsteps.

He whirled, Frostfire half out of the scabbard.

A skeleton in female garb was walking toward him. The sound he had heard was that of her bony feet striking the stones. Kothar rasped a curse and lunged upward. Frostfire came out into the firelight.

"No need for weapons between us," said a sweet voice.

"Lich!" he growled. "Keep your distance!"

Soft laughter rose into the night. "So, a barbarian out of the northern snowfields. A fine giant of a man, but too weak to slay Azthamur. Too small, too frail!"

"What know you of Azthamur, dead one?"

"Too much, too much! What would you know?"

"How to find him, how to slay him!"

"There is no way to slay him. Yet I could show you a way into his lair whereby you might have your chance at it."

"And your fee?"

"His death, man of the north. I wait for his death without hope, as I have waited these many centuries. None may slay Azthamur, yet I go on hoping."

Kothar gestured with his free hand at a flat stone beside the fire. "Come sit you beside me, lich. Tell me of this way into Azthamur's lair."

"I may not come near the fire. I dread the heat. I move best where the night winds blow with frost in their touch, out here on the barrens, or on the battlements of Urgal on winter nights."

"Ahhh! You're Althalia, who was princess in Urgal long ago?"

"I am Althalia—but no longer am I the Angelic One. Nowadays—or I should say—nowanights, I haunt the city and the castle, seeking vengeance on Azthamur who slew my lover. I have searched and searched, but none has ever come my way with any hope of victory."

"Until now," Kothar rumbled.

"Perhaps. I always hope. I'll do what I can, I promise. Keep you on your way, northman. We shall meet again."

The skeletal figure in the rotted rags turned and walked off into the night desert. Kothar stared after her. She took only a few steps, she walked as normally as any woman, yet her figure receded swiftly as if Time itself hastened her departure.

Kothar shook his giant frame.

There was no sight of the lich. He went toward the spot where she had stood, but there was no mark on the stone or in the dust to show that she had been here at all. Perhaps he had dreamed it. The wine Candara had given him might have been very strong, perhaps even drugged.

The Cumberian shrugged and rolled himself up in his saddle blankets. The roan would stand guard, whinnying if any came that way. Before he fell asleep he pulled Frostfire out of the scabbard and placed it close to his hand.

Next day at noon—Urgal being farther away than he had thought last night—he came in through the wide city gate, slouched in the high peaked saddle. His eyes went to the sellers of trade goods just outside the city gate, to the boards on which naked dancing girls postured before the flesh-tents where they welcomed their clients, to the traders in clay urns and vases, to the vendors of fruits and meats and cheeses, to the bakers of breads and sweetstuffs.

Kothar was surprised at the size and extent of the city. Kor was tiny, compared to Urgal. Urgal was closer to the borders of Phalkar and Gwyn Caer; perhaps this accounted for the greater number of traders and merchants. Besides, it was easier for a criminal to slip through the marshes of Phalkar or over the mountain passes of Gwyn Caer and arrive in Urgal, than it was to brave the empty wastes to come to Kor.

A man in armor moved from a sentry box at sight of the barbarian, hailing him. "State your business in Urgal, man. Tor Domnus takes not kindly to wanderers without a name."

"My name is Kothar, and I'm a sellsword out of Grondel Bay where the land is too poor and the sea too rough for my stomach. I like soft lands and soft women in my life."

The officer was staring at Frostfire. "Can you use that blade you carry? Or is it loot you stole from a better man?"

"Try me," the barbarian grunted.

"Not me. I'll let Evmor do that, he handles the recruits. If you've come to join the bandits our prince calls his army, that is."

"It was in my mind when I set out for Urgal."

"Straight ahead, then, until you come to the Street of Winesellers. Turn right and travel until you see a low brick building. That's where Evmor trains his rookies."

Kothar nodded, swinging the roan about. The officer yelled after him not to waste too much time and money in the stewpots. Evmor might want to test his swordplay, and an unmuddled head was a necessity against a swordsman as good as Evmor.

Kothar grinned his thanks for the advice.

A man in half-armor, lounging in the doorway of the low brick barracks, waved a hand toward the dark recesses of the building when Kothar drew rein and asked the whereabouts of the fencing master.

"He's yonder, teaching boys to use a sword. He's in a hot temper, I'd wait until tomorrow if I were you."

The Cumberian swung from the saddle. "Damn his temper. I come seeking employment as a soldier. If some ninny named Evmor can best me—with either fist or sword, mind—I'll go away meekly."

The soldier laughed. "Yours is the casket at the funeral, stranger. Do what you want." Kothar noticed that he pulled his shoulder from the door lintel and came after him at a distance as the barbarian walked toward a sunny spot in the open courtyard behind the brick wall.

There were perhaps half a dozen youths with wooden blades in their hands facing a squat, muscular man whose left eye was covered with a black patch. The short man was naked to the waist, and held a wooden sword in a hairy right hand. His voice was thickened by long years of quaffing the inferior wines of Urgal, and his face showed red in the sunlight.

Evmor was saying, "—pale pimps and sons of whores! I might as well try teaching the Naniko harlots to use a blade as you spineless spittles. Oh, come along. Line up and have at it again. I need a laugh to put me in a better humor."

Kothar cleared his throat. The squat man swung about, his one good eye taking in the muscular bigness of the barbarian. He showed small teeth in a mirthless grin.

"What's this, another babe come to cut his teeth on a sword's edge? By the Kraken! I truly earn the little that Tor Domnus pays me."

Kothar rasped, "Save your breath, Evmor. I've killed better men than you with my bare hands. I'm here to wear the boar's head of Urgal on my jacket. Just show me where the armor is so I can go to work."

Evmor gaped. "So ho! A wit who can skip the training, he knows so much. He thinks that Evmor is a—"

The man leaped, wooden blade slashing downward.

Kothar sprang inside the sweep of the blade. His left hand went up to catch Evmor's sword wrist; his right fist slammed deep into the belly of the shorter man.

Evmor rocked back on his heels, waving his arms, mouth open and eyes bulging. He sat down abruptly on the courtyard cobbles and slid for three feet.

Evmor shook his head, then stared shrewdly up at Kothar.

"You may do, stranger. It's the first time that ruse has failed to work. You have good reactions, I'll say that. Do you know how to use that blade you carry as well as you do your fists?"

"Better."

Evmor pulled himself to his feet by a hand on a weapon rack. "Do you, now? Would you care to match me with the steel?"

The barbarian turned, yanked free a blade as long as his own, with a leather wrapping about the hilt, and tossed it at the squat man. Evmor caught it handily.

"Scratch me if you can," the barbarian grinned.

Evmor flung himself at him. Kothar parried his blade with ease, for he had been schooled in use of the sword since childhood, first by his adoptive father—Kothar had never known his real father, nor his mother—and then by an old man-at-arms who had come back to Grondel Bay after a lifetime of serving the southland kings as a warrior, who delighted in imparting all his weapon-wisdom to the boy Kothar.

Three times Kothar parried before he struck back with the flat of the blade atop the skull, as he had done to Japthon. Evmor flung his arms wide, turned twice, witlessly, before he fell facedown in the courtyard dust.

Kothar reached for a water bucket, doused Evmor with its contents. Then he put a hand down and brought the man to his feet, where he swayed dizzily. "No man's ever treated me so," Evmor complained ruefully, rubbing the top of his poll. His eyes watched the recruits gathered in a group, staring with big eyes and broad grins.

"Laugh now, you whoresons," he growled. "This one's a man. You want me to turn him loose on you for weapon play targets?"

He barked laughter when they shook their heads, their grins fading. Evmor put an arm about the barbarian. "You come with me, stranger. I want to talk to you about that trick you used just then, over a mug of ale in the buttery."

Kothar rumbled, "It was taught me by a man named Svairn. He fought much of his life in the southlands."

"Did he now? Svairn of Grondel Bay? I knew him well. My treat for the ale, man of the north. Come along. You others—back to your wooden blades. And I hope you knock each others' skulls in."

Over their ale mugs, Evmor promised Kothar a jacket with the boar's head on it, and a shirt of mail to wear instead of his own. He vowed the barbarian he would be an officer in the riffraff Tor Domnus surrounded himself with, before the first fall winds came down from the hills.

Evmor complained about the recruits the prince of Urgal supplied him with, expecting him to make soldiers of them and the lack of honest fighting men in the army itself. He drank the strong ale with gusto, so much so that Kothar had to support him back to the little room that was his home in Urgal.

When the squat man invited him to share his comforts, Kothar nodded, loosed his mail shirt, casting it aside, and with Frostfire on the cot beside him, fell into a sound sleep. Time enough tomorrow, he told himself, to go hunting up the demon.

He woke to the smell of cooking meats and baking bread. Evmor was crouched at the brick hearth, busying himself with skillet and baking tins. When he saw Kothar yawn and toss his legs over the side of his cot, the squat man nodded.

"Food that sits well on an ale-tossed belly, this. Come and find a platter and heap it high. I eat best at an early hour, and enough to keep me going all the day."

"What about my uniform?" Kothar asked.

He wanted battlement patrol duty. From the battlements where Althalia was said to walk, he could learn where Azthamur laired and visit him. He could not stroll about the battlements in his worn chain-mail shirt and bear-skin cloak; he needed the disguise of the boar's head jacket.

Evmor waved a huge hand. "Later, later. Come and eat now, and tell me more of Svairn."

They feasted together, then Evmor took Kothar to the weapons room and fitted him out with a new chainmail shirt and the leather jerkin with the insignia of Tor Domnus on it.

"You wear those well," commented Evmor.

"I've lived my life as a fighting man. I was captain of the Foreign Guard for Queen Elfa of Commoral."

"Ah! Then you've good prospects for advancement here in Urgal. We've too few trained soldiers."

His duties on this first day were so light as to chafe the spirits of the big blond barbarian. He helped Evmor train the rookies, using a wooden sword, then polished his own weapons side by side with a couple of the castle guards. Kothar spoke little, except when spoken to; he used his ears to learn what he might of Azthamur.

During the conversation he swung the talk toward demons. "I sought employment by Candara of Kor, but I got into trouble during a fight at one of the taverns there. I made it out of the city two jumps ahead of her city guards."

A big Phalkaran chuckled. "Candara won't bother you much longer. Tor Domnus has plans for Kor."

"You make it sound as if I can expect good fighting. It's what I live for, a good fight."

"Her demoniac powers won't help her against Azthamur," grinned a scarred veteran of many wars. "We have our own demon, here in Urgal. He serves Tor Domnus well."

Kothar murmured, "Azthamur? I've never heard of that particular demon."

"You will if you stay here long enough."

"Azthamur lives in the caverns below the west battlement," muttered the veteran, making the sign of the axe that was the protective sign of Huldor, a beneficent demon who guarded innocent men and women from the wrath of other demons. "No one dares go there, excepting maybe Tor Domnus."

The west battlement. He was making progress, Kothar thought. He would ask Evmor for guard duty on that wall walk during the night. He had no need to stay in Urgal long; his role of soldier under the boar's head banner was but a ruse. He lifted the shirt of chainmail he had been polishing, studying it.

"Who guards the western bastion?" he asked casually.

The veteran hooted. "No need for a guard there, even if Evmor assigns one to the job. The demon patrols his own. No man would be fool enough to put his footprints there unless ordered to do so. Every so often Azthamur emerges and nobody ever sees the guard on duty again."

Better and better, the barbarian thought. This night I will walk those walks and go down the stairs to the lair where Azthamur guards the stolen god Xixthur. He felt tension creep into his muscles. Quite freely, Kothar would admit to a dislike for matching strengths with a demon, but it was his task to steal Xixthur, and this he meant to do.

Later, after the evening meal, he sought out Evmor.

"I am restless, friend. Give me a task to do that I may sleep better when I hit my pallet."

With a little persuasion, he got Evmor to agree to let him stand the watch. He ate early, of meat and bread and berry tarts, and when he moved up the narrow steps to the wall walk, he felt strong and confident.

The night was cool, the winds over the Haunted Lands were blowing northward, carrying a dampness with them that chilled the bones in a man's body. Overhead the two moons of Yarth were bright silver against a dark sky in which thousands upon thousands of stars were visible. At one time, so the legends said, these stars were few and far between; now they were everywhere, like glistening pebbles on a beach.

Kothar paced up and down a few times, slowly. He carried the boar's head shield and the spear of the watchman, and Frostfire hung at his side. He must wait until the candle lights, making the castle windows glow yellow in the night, were out before he dared leave his post and descend the narrow stairs.

It was as he was turning the corner to come back along the wall walk that he saw her. She was standing, wrapped in a long cloak that hid everything but her white skull and the bones of her skeletal feet. She was staring at him with black, empty eye sockets that were like pools of blackness, and when she moved, Kothar heard the grate of bones rubbing against bones.

"You came, northman. Good!" she said.

"I wait for the castle to sleep."

"Pah! No need for that. Nobody dares come this way to see if you're on duty. The captain of the guards is a bloated thing, fat with rich foods and ale, who likes his comfort above all else."

Kothar moved to the narrow staircase door. The skeleton was there before him, in some eerie manner the barbarian could not explain; she seemed not to walk but rather to float.

"Let me go first, man from Cumberia. Azthamur knows me. I go often to bait him, to assure him that some day there will come one who will find a way to slay him."

"He does not harm you?"

"A demon like Azthamur cannot harm the dead."

The door opened to her touch. Kothar watched her float through the opening with the short hairs on his neck standing stiffly. He liked not this consorting with a dead spirit, but Althalia was an ally of sorts, and he would accept her help if she chose to give it.

There were no torches on the stairs, only ebon blackness. But the bones of the skeleton gave off a subdued radiance by which Kothar could see to plant his feet. Down they went, ever downward, past the ground floor of the castle and into regions where a charnel smell added its odors to the mustiness of the air.

"By Dwallka! A man might rot here if he stayed very long. Get me out of this place, woman."

"Soon, northman. Soon."

The stairs led down into water. The skeletal figure floated above those waters, but she assured Kothar that they were shallow, and he moved on catlike feet through the wetness until a low archway showed ahead. Now the stink was more noisome than ever, and the barbarian, who loved the clean air of mountainside and plain, came close to retching.

Here and there, Kothar could see human and animal bones scattered about indiscriminately. There were some bodies that still had flesh upon their bones, half eaten, rotting. Kothar cursed the demon beneath his breath.

"Aye, he is a curse on mankind," whispered the spirit woman. "He has lived so long in Urgal, feasting at first on human blood, that he has acquired a taste for flesh, which is why he sometimes goes out upon the wall walk and devours a guard."

Kothar stepped under the archway, seeing a faint blue light coming from the walls. He was surprised, for the chamber before him was like a great room in the castle above, walled with woods of varying hues, with a rock ceiling overhead and a smooth floor underfoot.

A hundred chests and coffers stood about the room, thrust back against the wooden walls. Some of their lids were up, revealing ropes of pearls and golden urns, chalices and coins. He was a little dazzled by such wealth; demons had no need for riches.

"Of all the loot taken by Tor Domnus, a part is granted to the demon, who lends his help when the prince goes forth to rob a caravan. Tor Domnus, though very greedy, does not mind. Azthamur is his insurance against defeat. Besides, the loot never really leaves his castle, since the demon dwells here in its sub-cellars."

Kothar heard a footstep. His hand went to his swordhilt and very slowly, without noise, he drew Frostfire naked from its scabbard. He waited, listening to those footfalls. Beside him, the skeleton that had been the Princess Athalia did not stir.

The air in this cavern chamber was sweet, it had none of the carnal odor of the outer caves. A sweet wind swept through the room, carrying the salt scent of musk and incense. It was the lair of a sybarite and sensualist.

Then a woman stepped into the room.

CHAPTER THREE

She had been weeping, Kothar saw.

Her eyes were red, her smooth white cheeks glistened with tears. She wore a white samite gown, rent down one side so that her pale thigh and hip showed through the opening. Her hair was long and brown, and her beauty was enough to make a man stare in awe.

"Philisia," breathed the skeleton.

The woman raised her face, stared through her tears at Kothar and the dead Althalia. Her soft red mouth opened. She gasped.

"Are you victims of the demon, too?" she whimpered.

Kothar grunted, "I'm here to slay him."

Philisia looked at Althalia. "I have heard of you, dead one. Men say you prowl the battlements howling out your fury against Azthamur."

The skeleton was silent.

"Where is the demon?" asked Kothar.

"Coming, coming," whimpered the woman with the long brown hair. "He is going to eat me. Tor Domnus gave me to him. I—I was the prince's m-mistress. He tired of me and—"

She halted; whirled, putting a hand to her mouth.

It sounded as if some great, scaled being was stepping on stones. Kothar tightened his grip on Frostfire. Then the thing was in the room and the barbarian stared at a monstrous thing that was a parody of humankind and—of a fish.

Glittering blue scales covered its body. Its mouth was huge, running the width of its fishlike features, set with double teeth at the top and bottom of its jaws. Its single eye was a brilliant blue and shone with evil laughter. Wide shoulders, also scaled, and long arms, with legs that bulged with muscles beneath the bluish-white scales, spoke of the raw power of this monster.

"What's this? Another victim for my appetite?"

"Not so, Azthamur!" cried the skeletal woman. "This is the man who has come to slay you, as I have promised many times."

The woman Philisia slipped past a small fire glowing in a ring of firestones, and moved to stand beside Kothar. "Save me, barbarian!" she breathed. "Save me and I belong to you."

Kothar grinned mirthlessly. He had no need of a woman at the moment, he was too concerned with staying alive while Azthamur died. The fish-like creature was advancing on him steadily, arms by its side. Apparently he was counting on the fear that usually paralyzed the guards on the wall walks when he came for them, to keep Kothar helpless.

The barbarian heaved up Frostfire. The steel flashed in the bluish light as he drove its edge at the neck of the creature.

A man would have lost his head before that savage blow. Azthamur grunted and reeled backward, respect showing in his large blue eye. The demon showed no blood, nor was its scaled flesh marred by so much as a scratch. Azthamur shook himself, then sprang forward.

Kothar met him with the point of his sword. It did not wound the fish-man but it slowed him. The barbarian drove the hilt of his blade into the demon's face.

Then scaled arms were closing about him, lifting him off his feet. Kothar put the blade of his sword against the thickly thewed neck of the fish-man catching the flat of the blade in a hand. He pushed the edge of the sword against that thinly scaled throat with all his strength, until his back muscles were bulging out his chainmail shirt.

"I'll break your back, man!" snarled Azthamur. "I'll leave you writhing helpless on the floor while I eat Philisia before your eyes—and when I'm hungry enough, I'll start on you."

"Foulness," grated Kothar, applying more pressure.

Slowly he was bending the fishhead backward. Azthamur was grimacing with the effort of fighting the steel blade across his throat. If the demon maintained the bear's hug of his long arms about the barbarian, then his neck would snap, sooner or later.

Suddenly the thickly muscled arms loosened.

Azthamur caught Kothar by a wrist, whirled him away. The Cumberian staggered, trying to regain his balance. Then the fish-man was upon him.

A scaled hand darted out, caught up the spear Kothar had dropped when Azthamur attacked. Spear held between his fingers, the demon leaped.

One single swing of Frostfire slashed the haft of the spear. The point fell to clang on the stone floor. Yet the remnant of the long shaft rammed into the barbarian's belly, knocking him backward.

As he fell, Kothar slashed again with Frostfire, hitting the demon on the side of the head and knocking him into a coffer of rare black pearls from the depths of the Outer Sea. Azthamur stumbled, fell over the chest and rolled along the floor.

The barbarian righted his big body, stood a moment on widespread legs. He saw the gills of the fish-man opening and closing, just below his rib case on either side of his scaled body. By Dwallka, but the monster knew it was in a fight!

Kothar leaped, sword point aiming at that long blue eye.

The demon was faster, twisting away, his scaled hand stabbing for a curved scimitar from the southlands, bringing it down with a flash of blue light on steel. The scimitar drove sideways, ringing against the long, straight blade of the magic sword.

Curved blade and straight glinted in the pale azure light as demon fought with man. Kothar set himself for a battle to the death, knowing the odds against him. Azthamur might slay him with the scimitar. No matter how often and how hard he struck the demon, even the blue steel of Frostfire seemed unable to cut the demon scales.

For long moments, they fought.

Philisia stood with the skeleton woman, hands clasped before her, brown eyes glowing as they watched the play of the steel blades. The skeleton made no sound, it waited with rigid back and high-held head, staring with empty eye sockets at that one-sided duel.

It was Philisia who whimpered, "Look! Azthamur drives him back. Turn, man—run if you can. No living thing can defeat Azthamur!"

Kothar did not hear her. His every sense was attuned only to the clanging contact of the blades. Never had he fought like this, never before had there been no chance at all of victory for his sword, no matter what the odds he faced.

Against Azthamur, he fought vainly and without hope. Steel could not kill this monster. Nothing could do that. Nothing! Yet he fought on, sullenly yielding ground. He would not turn his back and run, as Philisia counseled. He would fight until the scimitar came drinking of his life's blood, like the warrior he was.

Back, always backward, the demon pressed the man.

Now skeletal Althalia and the terrified Philisia were some distance away, and Kothar battled directly under the archway leading into the charnel caverns. Even his mighty muscles were tiring by this time, and Frostfire was a terrible weight in his right hand. It took more and more effort to swing his sword to meet the sweeping slashes of the scimitar.

"Rash human," panted Azthamur. "I'll enjoy eating you more than any meal I've ever tasted."

"Kill me first, before you gloat!" Kothar rasped.

"The killing will come soon. You are beaten."

The scimitar flashed and darted. It clanged against the hilt of the straight sword, it made Kothar skip and dance to its weaving patterns. Kothar told himself steel would never defeat Azthamur. There must be some other way.

He hurled his blade, leaped sideways.

His hands went down, laid hold of a great rock tumbled among others on the cavern floor. His muscles creaked with strain but he got the rock up and above his head, and as the demon charged, he flung it.

The stone caught Azthamur on his scaled chest. Its sheer weight bowled him over so that he went backward to land on the stone floor with his spine. Before he could twist away, Kothar was on him.

A hand turned the demon.

Kothar slid his forearms under the armpits of the fish-man. His hands met behind his neck, locked fingers. In this wrestling grip, he held the panting monster for a few seconds, bending his head forward with massive strength.

But Azthamur only laughed softly, half under his breath, and his demon muscles tightened and his arms came down against the arms of Kothar where the barbarian held him. Slowly, he broke that cunning grip, pressing down with his arms until Kothar grunted in the pain of the holding.

"Were I more demon now than man, you would have died in agony long ago," Azthamur rasped. "But I have put on human guise, and that weakens my demoniac powers——just enough so that you can put up a good fight against me."

"Enough that I can snap your neck!"

"Not so, man," panted Azthamur, and broke the hold of the gripping fingers at his throat.

Kothar rolled away, the demon turning to come after him.

The pale light from the inner chamber was almost no light at all in these outer caverns. There was a sheen on the shallow waters, glinting bluely where those reflections were, and its sight made Kothar realize suddenly that in that water, the demon would be much like the fish.

As Azthamur came for him, the barbarian lifted a rock in his hand and drove it sideways at the face before him. He had aimed for the blue eye, but the demon ducked slightly and took the stone across its temple. Momentarily stunned, it was no match for an aroused Kothar battling savagely for his life.

He whirled Azthamur, tripped him with a foot.

They fell together into the shallow waters, and as that wetness closed about him, Kothar sought once again for a hold on the thick neck of the fish-man. His fingers tightened on scaly flesh, sank deep.

Grimly, Kothar hung to his clasp on that throat. Azthamur needed air for his lungs, having assumed quasi-humanoid shape. The only way for him to get that air was through his windpipe. But the demon was far too strong for the merely human hands that held him.

Azthamur reared up, dripping water, dragging Kothar with him, and his fists slammed hard into his belly. The barbarian grunted. Each blow was like that of a sledgehammer in the hands of a strong man. His finger-grip loosed, fell away.

He let go his hold with a quickness that surprised the fish-man. Kothar dropped backward and his mightily thewed legs came up to clamp about the demon's middle. Kothar heaved with all his body and Azthamur toppled forward into the water.

Like a cat, the barbarian shifted position. His legs inched higher, his hands stabbed toward the thick neck and tightened on the scaled flesh once again. With all his power, he held the fish-head below the surface of the rolling cave waters.

It was as the demon was bunching his back to throw him off that Kothar remembered a truth his adoptive father had told him once in a fishing smack out of Grondel Bay. A fish can drown in water, he had said. And Kothar blessed his memory as his legs inched further upward on that monstrous body until his thick thighs were clamped tight about the gills below the fish-man's rib case.

The demon gulped in air and water, his head still below the surface. Not until his lungs were full of water that his gills could not pass out, did he realize the trick Kothar had played upon him.

Now indeed did his back arch and his muscles bulge as he fought desperately to free himself of that death-grip on his throat. But his lungs were taut with water, and he coughed fiercely underwater and every time he coughed, he swallowed more of the brackish liquid. Kothar kept his thighs clamped tight. His fingers were like stone as they sank deep into weakening throat muscles.

After a time, Azthamur quieted.

But still the barbarian kept his grip.

Not until the skeleton woman and Philisia came creeping through the cavern murk toward him did he realize that the demon might be dead. Slowly his fingers loosened; they ached with the strain of that terrible clasping. Azthamur never moved.

Kothar rose to his feet, stood above the floating body. He panted and shivered in the aftermath of his battle. He reached down, caught the fish-body and yanked it upward onto the ooze-wet stones.

"Bind him," breathed the skeletal woman.

"No need for that. He's dead."

"Bind him, just the same," she advised.

Philisia ran with her hands filled with wire torn from a hanging orna-ment, and with this, Kothar knelt and bound the demon. When he was done, he stood and stared at Althalia and at the woman with the long brown hair who shivered in her torn court gown.

"Xixthur," Kothar said. "I must find him."

The skeletal woman went and sat on a flat rock, knees together, bony jaw resting on equally bony knees, and she stared down at the motionless Azthamur with empty eye sockets. The woman of flesh and blood crept closer to the barbarian and plucked at his fur cloak.

"Xixthur is not in the caves of Azthamur," she breathed.

The barbarian whirled on her. "What's this? Are you telling me I'm here on a fool's errand?"

She smiled and shook her head. She was not as young a woman as he had thought from his first glimpse of her, Kothar realized; yet neither was she old. There were tiny lines at the corners of her eyes and a bitterness to the quirk of her lips that marked her as a woman who had seen sin and suffering, and was not untouched by them.

Her body was heavily curved, almost overripe with wanton fleshiness. The brown hair had come loose in the jeweled fastenings that had held it; it was this that made her seem younger. Parts of her gown were torn here and there so that the pale tints of her flesh gleamed in the rents.

"Where is Xixthur, then?" he asked.

"In the apartments of Kylwyrren, the magician who serves Tor Domnus."

Kothar picked up Frostfire from the floor where it had fallen in the fight and slid the blue blade back into its scabbard. "Then I will find Kylwyrren and take it away from him."

Her smile was patient. "You would have to fight your way through half of Tor Domnus's soldiers, man. I know a better way, up the hidden stairways that only I, of all the people in Urgal am well aware of."

Kothar caught her arm. "Then lead the way, woman."

He turned to stare back at Althalia, crouched above the motionless form of Azthamur. Well, her vengeance for the long-ago death of her lover was an accomplished thing, now. He would leave her here to gloat and enjoy her triumph.

Philisia walked ahead of him with sure steps, across the smooth stone floor of this chamber that had belonged to Azthamur and, parting a hanging drapery, slipped through and up a flight of narrow stone steps. Kothar followed on her heels.

"Why do you alone know this way?" he wondered.

"My father was castellan for Tor Domnus, before Tor Domnus saw my beauty and took me into his bed." Philisia sighed. "My father objected, he did not want his daughter to be any man's mistress, even to a prince. Tor Domnus ordered my father slain."

She sighed. "Since then, I have hated the prince of Urgal, though I have continued to be his harlot. Until some nights ago when a trader out of Zoane in Sybaros carried in to him a blonde woman who caught Tor Domnus's eye and roused his passions.

"Tor Domnus bought the woman.

"Me, he gave this night to the demon."

She turned and flashed a smile back at him. "You saved me from Azthamur, barbarian. Now I belong to you."

Kothar growled, "I have no need for a woman, Philisia. My errand for Queen Candara demands that I travel alone."

"You will not leave me here to be ravished by the soldiery? Or tortured to death to amuse Tor Domnus's new bedmate?"

The Cumberian rasped a curse. "You'll have to keep up with me. I must flee like the wind once I lay hands on Xixthur."

"I will ride with you, as fast or as slowly as you like. I am not a weak woman." She slowed her upward progress, cautioning him with a waving hand. "Hush now. We approach the apartments where Kylwyrren dwells."

They were in utter darkness. They stood on a flat landing, so close that the barbarian could feel the soft body of the woman against his own. He felt her tremble, he put his thickly muscled arm about her slim middle, drew her closer to give her added courage.

Her warm hand pressed his.

Then she was slipping from his grasp and fumbling in the ebon blackness. A narrow panel slid back, revealing the back of a brocade hanging. She breathed into his ear, "This is a wall in the apartments of the mage. Step carefully, and make no sound."

She thrust aside the drapery and Kothar followed her into a stone chamber filled along its walls with shelves and cabinets that held the assorted impedimenta of a magician. Curious glass vials and oddly shaped urns and jars contained the magical properties with which Kylwyrren worked his spells.

The chamber was lighted by a reflection from a lamp in another room. Philisia held her forefinger to her lips, then beckoned him. As noiselessly as a cat, Kothar went after her.

They paused before a round tower room, where a single lamp shed its radiance upon a squat metal thing, with eyes of glass here and there in its rounded bulk, which rested on three thin metal legs. It stood about two feet in height and was, perhaps, the ugliest thing that Kothar had ever seen.

His eyes went to a cadaverous man with dank black hair, clad in a robe embellished with silver threadings woven with the names of the thousand and three demons known to man. His elbows rested on his knees, his dark eyes brooded on the metal object perched before him.

The barbarian scanned the mage more closely.

There was no sign of a weapon close to the magician, nor did it seem that he could have a dagger hidden beneath his robes. Kothar drew a deep breath.

Kylwyrren must have heard him, for he turned and his bold eyes stared out from under tufted eyebrows at the man and woman. Philisia gave a little cry.

Kylwyrren said softly, "I would never have believed it."

Philisia cried, "Tor Domnus gave me to Azthamur this night, Kylwyrren. This man from Cumberia saved my life."

It was as if the magician had not heard her. "For ages, there have been legends. To our people, they were only that, like fairy tales made to interest little children. But here before me is the proof."

He swung back to the metal thing, slapped his hand against it. "The legends say that once the race of men went to the stars, all the stars and to the planets around them. That once our universe was an expanding one, that the suns were flung outward into space by a single titanic blast of matter.

"Now the universe is old. Old!

"The star-suns are falling back upon themselves, back to that beginning of all Time and all Space. When they come together in a fantastic crash and gathering-together of all Matter—will the process begin all over again?"

Kothar listened without understanding. He knew the ways of a sword in his hand and the fury of a battle, the cry of the wolves along the frozen barrens of his homeland, but he knew nothing of stars and planets. His feet had burned in the desert sands, he was familiar with habits of hawk and eagle, deer and horse, but such things as Time and Space and Matter were unknown to him.

He rasped, "Is that Xixthur?"

The magician smiled in his bemusement. "Aye! This is Candara's god, this gross thing of glass and metal. Early men made this, barbarian. Early men, with a knowledge of matter that no man today knows anything of. Even my magic might be weak beside their wisdom. I could never make such a thing as this."

Philisia forgot her uneasiness to ask, "What is it?"

"Candara calls it a god. In a sense, I suppose it is. But I have read old manuscripts, ancient parchments that tell the legends of early men, and I know that it is a thing that gives off what early man called 'rays.' "These rays destroyed sick tissue in a human body, they killed germs, they repaired flesh and bone and muscle. Don't ask me how. They did. I have not those ancient wisdoms. No wonder Candara grieves to lose it! No wonder she wants it back. This thing will give her eternal youth."

"Eternal youth?" Philisia quavered, coming a step closer. "Will it give that to me too, Kylwyrren?"

"Assuredly. You see this tiny bit of metal? You move it so—"

Kothar saw the glass eyes in the metal hull glow with light, and heard the faint hum of the thing. The radiance from the eyes went everywhere, forming a kaleidoscope of red and blue and yellow throughout the chamber.

"—and somehow," continued Kylwyrren, "the rays given off by this Xixthur repairs the ills of the human body and reinvigorates it, giving it strength and youth. I do not know whether it would make an old person young—my knowledge extends only so far—but I am positive it will keep a man or woman from aging any more."

Philisia exclaimed, "Ohhh!"

Kothar moved forward, his hand on his swordhilt. "I must take it away from you, magician. It belongs to Candara. She has sent me for it, to fetch it back to her."

The magician nodded. "I expected some such attempt. So also does Tor Domnus. I am alone at the moment, but his soldiers patrol the halls and corridors. You can never hope to get away with it."

"I must try."

The woman said softly, "He must bind and gag you, old man. We do not dare permit you to give the alarm."

Kylwyrren nodded, sighing. "Yes, you must do that. I have served Tor Domnus for many years, but he is a hard taskmaster and I have no love for him. Why should I risk cold steel in my flesh?"

He stood up and turned, putting his skinny arms behind his back for their tying. Kothar made short work of the task, he caught the man and lowered him to the floor, and there he bound his ankles. Philisia placed a cloth between his teeth and her slender white fingers knotted the thong that held it in place.

In a moment, the barbarian had swept up Xixthur into the crook of an arm and turned to follow Philisia through the secret panel of the hidden doorway. She stood beside the drapery, half lifting it.

It was then that the arched door at the other end of the tower chamber opened. A man came into the room, calling out the name of Kylwyrren. He was tall and broad of shoulder, with a hard face burned by desert sun and mountain wind. He wore a black velvet jupon, and one black and one white velvet stocking on each leg. A dagger with a golden pommel hung by his hip.

Kothar was across the room, the weight of Xixthur like cotton batting to his muscles. His fist swept up and around. It landed on the astounded face of the startled man and drove him backward through the doorway and out into the tower corridor.

The barbarian slammed the arched door shut, dropped a metal bar across two slots on either side. "That will keep them busy for a while, trying to break down the door."

He ran for the hidden panel where Philisia stood, half-swooning in her terror. "That was Tor Domnus himself you hit," she whimpered. "He will have us flayed alive for that!"

"Then run," growled Kothar, catching her by a shoulder and whirling her around, pushing her through the narrow panel.

He went after her, waited while she closed the panel. Then she was before him, shivering and moaning in her fear, until his hand caught her shoulder and his fingers tightened.

"Don't be afraid," he breathed.

She went more surely down the stone stairs and along the floor of the chamber of the demon Azthamur. The skeletal woman was still sitting beside the unmoving body of the fish-man and did not turn her head as they ran past.

"Where to now?" rasped the barbarian. "We can't go up the stairs to the wall walk. Tor Domnus has seen my face, knows I'm wearing his boar's head uniform."

Philisia shrank against him, shuddering. His arm went around her shoulders protectingly. "I d-don't know," she told him.

"Think! The demon must come and go a secret way. He would not show himself in the streets of Urgal, would he—when Tor Domnus sends him on an eerie errand?"

"No-no. He is never seen by the common people."

He watched her thin brows settle into a thoughtful frown. Her tiny teeth nibbled at her lower lip and from time to time she sighed. Finally she shook her head.

"I'm sorry. I don't remember any hidden way down this far in the caverns."

Kothar stared around him at the wet stones and the shallow waters. He knew with that barbaric instinct that was so much a part of him that Azthamur came and went by secret ways to the castle and to Urgal. His stare was caught and held by the brackish water about his knees.

Azthamur was—or had been—a fish-man. What more likely means to travel in and out of his lair than by a water route? Somewhere in this cavern must be a subterranean stream that would carry Philisia and him safely out of Urgal.

He began to pad back and forth in the little pool, explaining his actions to the woman, who nodded her understanding. Holding her gown hip high, she walked where he did not, slowly and with searching feet. Each of them knew that Tor Domnus was a raging maniac high above their heads, seeking entry into the tower rooms of Kylwyrren.

Yet the secret waterway eluded their eyes and their feet as they went from one end of the caves to the other. By now the prince of Urgal would be inside the tower, would have freed Kylwyrren and listened to his tale. Soldiers wearing the boar's head uniform of Tor Domnus would soon be flooding these lower cellars.

And then Philisia went out of sight.

CHAPTER FOUR

One moment she was walking and the next she was sinking down into the water, crying out sharply. Kothar waded toward her, reached down, caught her by the hand and yanked her up. She dripped wetly, her gown was plastered to her body but she laughed happily.

"It's there, some sort of hole, an opening in the rock. I went down into it. But—but it's dark down there."

"I'll go. You stay here. If it leads me beyond Urgal, I'll come back for you."

They heard the sound of footsteps on the distant stone staircase. Philisia shook her head. "No time for that. We go together. I'm not staying here to be caught by Tor Domnus's soldiers."

Kothar nodded. Shifting his grip on Xixthur, he stepped forward and sank downward like a stone, vaguely aware that the woman was following after him. For fifteen feet he went straight down, then saw dim light through the water ahead. He swam as best he could with the great weight of the metal god in his arms, but the water shallowed ahead and he was soon standing up to his middle thighs in water, inside a huge stone-walled sea cave. Philisia gripped his sword belt, yanked herself to her feet beside him. "Where are we?" he wondered.

"Somewhere on the shoreline of Urgonlake, where there are many cliffs." She put her head to one side, gathering her brown hair in her hands and wringing out the droplets of water. "The lake is bordered by cliffs. This cave must be inside one of them, completely hidden from view."

"There's an opening of sorts up ahead. Come on." They waded across the cave to a strip of pale water lightened by shafts of moonlight. Kothar put Xixthur down on a stone ledge and dove. He came up in lake water with the moon low in the sky and a gigantic stone cliff rising behind him.

He went back for Xixthur, and told Philisia what he had seen. She nodded, "Yes, the face of the cliff must reach underwater a few feet, just enough to hide the entrance into this cave. This is the path by which Azthamur came and went. It will serve to let us get away."

She bent, tore the long sodden skirt of her gown until she was naked below her upper thighs. Her brown eyes flashed at him. "It makes swimming easier, with less of this thing to encumber me."

Then she turned in the water and dove.

They came up alongside the cliff face, kicking to buoy themselves in the deeper water. Xixthur was so heavy, Kothar was forced to grip a jutting section of rock to keep his head in the air.

"Certainly I can't swim with this thing," he growled. His eyes raked the sheer face of the cliff. "And that bluff doesn't afford any handgrips or toeholds to let me climb it."

He began to inch his way along the base of the cliff, holding Xixthur under an arm and using his free hand to find and cling to jutting parts of the cliff. A cool wind was blowing across the lake from the forest on the other side. It was a lonely, desolate spot, considering the fact that it was so close to the city of Urgal, which raised its walls on the other side of the cliff.

"If Azthamur used the lake for his comings and goings," panted Philisia, "no man or woman in the city would use it. Perhaps, long ago, they did come here to swim—until the demon caught and ate a few."

"It helps us, that fact," Kothar admitted.

He found a narrow trail where the cliff side ended, and lifted out of the water, putting the ray-machine on the ground and turning to lend a hand to Philisia. She sank down on solid ground at his feet, shivering. The water had been icy cold, the wind from the forests just as chilling. The myriad stars in the sky were fading from view before the first shafts of red sunlight coming from beyond distant Sybaros, which beached upon the salt waters of the Outer Sea.

"Let me rest," she begged.

"There's no time for that. This early hour of the morning is the best time to travel, for there won't be many folk about to see and report us to Tor Domnus."

He bent, caught her hand, yanked her to her feet. She shivered, wet and miserable, against him. Kothar grinned, slapped her haunch.

"The sun will dry you off in the barrens between Urgal and Kor. But first we've got to find a stable and steal two horses."

She nodded, sniffling. "Tor Domnus keeps horses not far from here that are used by his couriers to travel with messages to the lords of Phalkar and Sybaros."

Kothar heaved Xixthur to a shoulder and planted his feet where Philisia walked. She went surefootedly through these woods, and there was an aliveness about her that made the barbarian realize that, for the first time in her life, she felt truly free. From time to time, she turned to flash a smile at him.

She slowed her steps as they came to the edge of the woods that bordered on a wide road running between Urgal and Phalkar to the north. As he stood within the leafy boscage of leaves and bushes, Kothar could make out the big barns and stables, he caught the smell of horseflesh, he heard a man rattling tools about inside a large shed.

"There will be guards here and there," she whispered.

The barbarian grunted. Alone and without Xixthur, he might have risked a direct attack, simply going into the stables, snatching a horse and galloping off. With Philisia to consider, he must use caution.

He said, "There's a low roof there," nodding at a thatched section of the stable roof. "I'm going up to have a look."

He was catlike in his leap to the eaves, swinging up easily, with a bunching of muscles beneath his tanned hide. Then he was moving over the stable roof to another roof and down that until the watching woman lost sight of him.

His eyes took in the big yard, the troughs, the bales of hay piled close to the wall of the big barn. The sunlight was a hot warmth bathing fences and well-stones with their buckets resting on their cappings. The heat of this early morning sun drew the sweat from a man and caused heat waves to dance across the distant desert.

His hand touched the thatching of the roof, brushed over it. It had been baked by that hot sunlight until it crackled with dryness. Thatch would burn like tinder, he thought, as would the bales of hay just below his perch on the roof. Kothar grinned and his fingers went hunting in his belt-purse for steel and flint.

He crouched, struck a spark, another spark, then blew as it caught fire. He made a hasty torch of the thatchwork and, waving it above his head to make that fire blaze, he tossed it downward.

An instant later a thin thread of grey smoke was rising upward from the hay. Kothar turned and scrambled across the rooftop to the low edge, from which he leaped. He ran to find Philisia hidden in some berry bushes.

"I'll fetch three horses," he told her. "Be ready to mount."

He whirled and ran. By this time a stablehand had seen the smoke, had sensed the gathering flames inside the hay. His hoarse shouts brought men and boys at the run.

Their first concern was the horses. They ran inside the stables, drove out every mount. Kothar watched those horses run, his eyes taking in their legs, their glossy coats, the depth of their barrels. He selected a big roan for himself, a smaller mare for Philisia. He needed a third horse to carry Xixthur; he would use reins or straps to fasten it on.

He was up and running, bent over. His hands went to the reddish mane of the big, rangy roan; an instant later his leg was swinging over his back and he thumped down onto its bare back. The roan wore no bridle but the mare did, and so did the heavyset brown stallion he had chosen to carry Xixthur.

The men and boys were too busy inside the stables and the barns to notice him as he galloped off with the mare and the brown behind him. Only when he paused to snatch up a fallen bridle did a youngster see him and open his mouth to yell a warning.

Kothar leaped. The back of his hand took the youth across the jaw, toppled him backward into a water trough. The boy would recover soon enough, and yell the warning, but Kothar had had some few precious minutes in which to seat Philisia and fasten Xixthur on the brown horse.

The woman came at the run, bare white legs below her torn gown flashing whitely in the sunlight. She let Kothar throw her upward onto the mare; she caught the reins expertly; she was a good horsewoman, he saw. Then she called out instructions to Kothar as to how to lash the metal object inside a fold of the stolen reins. When it was done, the barbarian tested the tightened knots and nodded. Xixthur should stay put, no matter how fast the brown horse had to gallop.

He swung up onto the roan.

An instant later they were pounding out across the fields east of the stables, heading toward the edge of the farm fields and beyond them, the desert.

They rode swiftly, but not at any killing pace. It would take time for the stable hands to alert the soldiers of Tor Domnus that the man they hunted was mounted now and on his way into the desert. By that time, they should be far ahead.

Past farmhouses and hay ricks they rode, and through fields furrowed to a nicety by a plow. While they cantered through an orchard, Kothar pulled down as many apples as he could reach and stuffed them inside his boar's head leather jerkin. They would need food until they reached the ruined chapel where he had left Greyling and his weapons.

It was past noon when they came to the vast stretch of rock and sand that was the rim of the Barren Desert. Ahead lay a sea of sand and a few rocks, baking in the hot sunlight.

Philisia shivered and made a soft, whimpering sound, seeing all that desert lying before her. "I'll cook to death," she breathed, indicating the scantiness of her gown. Its low collar revealed her shoulders, white and smooth, its thinness emphasized the thrust of her breasts, the slenderness of her waist. Where she had torn its skirt, her legs showed pale almost to her hips.

Kothar barked, "Would you stay behind?"

She bit her lower lip, shook her head.

Then they were cantering out across the pebbles, seeking to conserve their strength and that of their horses. It was a long pull to Kor from Urgal; the way was broken only by the ruins of the ancient chapel where the barbarian had left Greyling. With the instinct of those who live their years in the wild, he guided the roan toward those ruins.

The blinding sunlight baked them. Sweat ran down their backs and along their faces. Kothar felt the bite of thirst and glanced at Philisia, seeing how she suffered. By Salara! Her skin would be burned red by nightfall! He yanked free his bearskin cloak, and with rough grace tossed it about her near nakedness.

She flashed him a weak, grateful glance.

They rode on through the heat.

Toward noon, Philisia moaned and swayed on her horse. The Cumberian urged the roan closer, reached out, gathered the girl up in a thickly thewed arm.

"You'll be easier, this way," he told her.

She cuddled against his chest, though the hot steel of his chainmail shirt was like fire to her skin. She pillowed her head on his chest and let her body go limp. In moments she was asleep, utterly exhausted.

Staring straight ahead, bringing the mare and the brown horse behind him at the length of their tethers, he rode onward.

Instinct made him turn when he did to survey their back trail. His keen eyes made out four dots, far away. Kothar scowled, remembering that Tor Domnus kept fast horses for his couriers in those royal stables. The men following him would be riding the fastest horses the prince of Urgal owned.

He kicked the roan to a gallop from its slow canter. There was distance between himself and the men who followed and he wanted to maintain that distance as best he could.

He was many miles from the ruined chapel. His horn bow and long war arrows in their quiver were at the chapel with Greyling. Until he held his horn bow in his hand, he would have no defense against those oncoming riders, other than his sword.

Grimly, Kothar stared straight ahead.

The soft soughing of the sand underhoof, the hot wind burning his cheeks, the constant burning of the sun on his body, were the only indications the Cumberian had that he was trapped inside a nightmare. The weight of the sleeping girl in his arms was another guidepost to reality, as was the gnawing worry in his brain.

Those riders behind him would be coming fast. Faster than he dared drive the roan and the other horses. They might overtake him before he came to the chapel. Then they could stand off at a distance and pick off the horses with arrows, and then feather their shafts in his chest.

He rode facing forward until he could hold back no longer. Then he swung about in the saddle and stared at the four men who were behind him.

"By Dwallka," he growled.

They were almost within bowshot range.

One of them, probably the best archer, was bringing his bow off his shoulder and reaching for an arrow with a hand. First shot for the brown horse, with Xixthur on it. Xixthur was more important than the man or the woman.

After that…

* * * *

Mindos Omthl was weeping softly in chagrin.

"So near, so near! Another few miles and he would be at the ancient chapel of Randolphus. Then with his bow he could stand off those men, maybe slay them so he could get away."

The demon Abathon snorted.

"You are a fool, magician," he snapped. "You pride yourself on being able to make magic. Well, make a spell to aid him. It's that simple."

Mindos Omthl stared at the creature he had summoned up. He shook his head, muttering, "I am a fool, indeed. But you said yourself that I could not steal from a demon and—"

"Kothar has done your stealing for you, mage. No need to try and take Xixthur from him. In time, he will bring that metal thing to you, I believe. But right now, he needs a helping hand. Look!"

Mindos Omthl craned his leathery neck, saw the mailed chest of the barbarian and the woman who slept nestled within his arm. As he watched, an arrowshaft flew overhead, winking brightly in the desert sunlight.

"A helping hand, yes. But I must not reveal to anyone that I've had a hand in it. I don't want Tor Domnus nor Queen Candara to come seeking me." Abathon asked, "How about a rainstorm?"

The magician took thought, finally nodding. "Yes. A heavy storm with rain like a cloudburst that will hide man and woman and horses from those who pursue."

He turned to his vials and alembics resting on a nearby tabletop. His big-veined hands darted out, closed on glass and marble. From each he poured noisome liquids into a chalcedony bowl, and into the pool of wetness he dropped pinches of ground wort-bane and hazel roots. Steam rose upward from the crucible.

Mindos Omthl began to chant...

* * * *

The black cloud was on the horizon to the south.

It came fast, and as it came, it spread out, and now Kothar could hear the rumble of distant thunder and see the flash of lightning inside that moving darkness. He had no suspicion of wizardry in the sight. Storms had been known before over desert lands. It was only the timing of the approaching storm that made him wonder.

An arrow missed the brown horse.

"By Dwallka," snarled the barbarian, kicking the roan to a faster pace "if that cloud brings rain to hide us, we may still make it."

The cloud was overhead. It came to a stop.

Those black, fluffy masses opened up and water came down. Like a flood in spate was that water, that drenched man and woman and beast, until it grew hard to breathe.

Kothar turned the roan aside, angled its walk in a slightly different direction. Now if those riders should gallop forward, blind in this drenching downpour, they would never be able to find them.

The rain woke Philisia. She lifted her head, letting the cool moisture drench her skin and hair and the thin stuff of her torn gown until the samite was plastered to her generous curves.

"Do I dream?" she asked.

"If you do, I dream myself. It's rain, right enough. And it couldn't have come at a better time."

Her laughter rang out. "I'm cool again, and not thirsty any more." She opened her red mouth and let the water drops beat down inside her throat, swallowing greedily from moment to moment.

The horses moved at a walk, now that there was no immediate reason for haste. In such a downpour, Kothar could not see the ruined chapel until he was upon it, he knew. But as long as the rain continued, he was safe, and it showed no sign of stopping.

All he had to guide him now was his instinct.

He remembered where the chapel was, and his knees turned the roan in that direction. Greyling had been too well trained to whinny at approaching horses, and so he knew he could not count on guidance from his warhorse. He did not want his own mounts to whinny for fear they might attract the attention of the four men who pursued them.

It was an eternity in the downpour, with all that wet greyness deluging the desert around them, making tiny pools where the stones and pebbles were clustered. The horses plodded, splashing through those pools, shaking their heads and blowing their delight in the cool wetness that steamed on their hides.

The greystone arch loomed black in the rain, and beside it the crumbling wall of what had been a monastery showed long and low. Kothar grinned his pleasure through tight lips.

He urged the roan toward the tiny roof of the old shed where he had stored his weapons and left Greyling. As the roan neared the fallen timbers, Kothar heard a faint nicker. He let his laughter out softly, below his breath.

Then he was lowering Philisia to the ground and swinging down, finding Greyling at his elbow, bumping his back with his Roman nose, in affectionate greeting. Kothar rubbed fingers along the grey nose, whispered words into the silky grey ears.

Philisia murmured, "This is Randolphus's chapel. I saw it once, long ago, in a picture book. What are we doing here?"

"Recovering my weapons," the Cumberian grinned.

He moved to a wrapping and unrolled it, disclosing the horn bow that he had from old Pahk Mah when he had rescued his daughter. He bent the bow, fitted the string to it. Then he set the bow and his quiver of war arrows against a well-wall protected from the rain by the leaded roof.

"If those men find us now, I'm not completely helpless. I, too, can fire war arrows—and I'm a better shot than that lout who was shooting at our horses."

She crowded against him, shivering, seeking warmth and courage from his nearness. This huge barbarian was like a rock pillar to Philisia. His keen wits and bulging muscles had delivered her from dreaded Azthamur, he had brought her safely out of Tor Domnus's castle with the metal object which Candara called a god. He had, by some trick she could not understand, made it rain, and then had found shelter here in this old chapel.

Philisia was grateful. She slipped her bare arms upward about his neck, dragged his mouth down to her soft lips. They clung together in their kiss for long moments.

Then Kothar growled, "We have no time for foolishness, girl. Much as I'd enjoy bedding you down, that is. First, we'll ride to Kor and then we'll beg a bed of Candara where we can frolic as we will."

She sighed and nodded, nestling her head to his chest but still clinging to his neck with her arms. "You are my lord, Kothar. I'll go and do whatever you say."

Kothar wondered if the prohibition Afgorkon had laid on him extended to women. This Philisia was a treasure of sorts, but as long as he carried Frostfire by his side, he could own no treasure. He sighed. He would have to wait and see, where Philisia was concerned.

The rain was letting up.

He could see a hundred yards from the chapel now, and soon, almost to the horizon. A faint white mist clung to the ground where the rain made steam on the hot desert sands. That mist would be almost as good as rain in hiding them from the four warriors who wore the boar's head device.

From a saddlebag on Greyling's saddle, he drew out cold meat and bread and a flagon of cool water. Philisia seated herself on a stone bench and munched happily, eyes glowing as they studied the graceful bulk of the Cumberian moving to and fro, preparing for their departure.

"It will be night, soon. That rain lasted all afternoon. Our horses' hoofs will make little sound on the desert sands. By dawn, if we ride all night, we ought to be in Kor."

When the meat and bread were gone and the flagon empty, Kothar rose to his feet and stretched out a hand to the girl. Overhead the stars were appearing, scattered across the blue sky with a myriad generosity that made the evening heavens brilliant above them.

"There'll be moonlight too, but the moons of Yarth don't show the desert as clearly as does the sun. I think we'll be all right."

The barbarian mounted on Greyling, he helped Philisia up on her mare. He reached for the reins to draw the brown horse after them, letting the roan trail free.

He turned the grey toward Kor.

* * * *

And in the city of Kor, Queen Candara brooded.

She sat cross-legged on a stool in the necromantic chamber of hunchbacked Zordanor watching the misshapen man as he peered into a bowl of molten silver where gleamed the night stars and the two moons of Yarth and the vast stretches of the Barren Desert.

Candara rested her dimpled chin on a fist, while her black eyes seemed to stare at far-off visions. Truly, she had never really expected the barbarian to steal Xixthur from the demon Azthamur. She had been hopeful, yes; she had counted on the magicks of the mage Zordanor, who had predicted success; yet in her heart, since she knew the strength and wicked wiles of Azthamur, she had resigned herself to defeat and the resultant aging process which would, in time, turn her into an old woman.

"What do I do with him now?" she asked querulously.

Zordanor waved an impatient hand, gesturing her to silence. "They come, the barbarian and the prince's former mistress. They will be before the city gate by sunrise. The four men who trailed them have turned back to meet Tor Domnus and the soldiers he is bringing with him."

Candara straightened. Her fist hit her thigh angrily. "To wage war with me? He would dare?"

"Who can read the mind of a man like Tor Domnus? Not I, nor any magician alive. But if Tor Domnus knows the value of Xixthur, as I am sure he must—since Azthamur will have told him of its value—then I feel confident he will hurl his soldiery at your walls, to secure the metal god for his own use."

"I must prevent him, Zordanor! I am not so strong in Kor as I would like, and the loyalty of my hired mercenaries is a chancy thing, at best."

The hunchback nodded. "Aye. But how?"

Candara tossed her foot as her brows furrowed. She was not often given to thought, she cared more for the carnal pleasures of the flesh than the cerebral enjoyments of the mind. Yet her mind was good. She was no fool, for all her follies, and when she reasoned, she thought well and thoroughly.

"I need help, Zordanor. Greater help than you can give."

His ugly face showed surprise. "And who in these Haunted Lands can give you aid that is beyond my powers?"

"Mindos Omthl, the necromancer."

The misshapen man gasped. His eyes narrowed and his nostrils flared to his breathing. He swayed back and forth, oddly toad-like, but his huge head nodded slowly.

The old mage lived in a remote corner of the Haunted Lands, beside the Sunken Sea bottom out of which the first life on Yarth was said to have crawled eons ago, in a gaunt black tower filled with the secrets of necromancy and old wizardry. No man traveled near the black tower, for an certain nights hellish fires could be glimpsed from its narrow windows and more than one traveler told of screams of fear and agony resounding from its walls.

It was common knowledge in the Haunted Lands that Mindos Omthl knew all there was to know of arcane wisdom. His vials contained elixirs and nostrums, lenitives and concoctions which had no like anywhere in the lands between the Salt Ocean and the Outer Seas. With such *materia medica,* the old mage could perform any incantation.

"Certainly he knows more than I," muttered Zordanor, "and far more than Kylwyrren who serves Prince Tor Domnus."

"You approve my choice, then?"

"I do—under the circumstances. Mindos Omthl can summon up demons from the lowest tiers of the nether worlds. Awful demons." Zordanor shuddered. "But he demands a high price for his enchantments. A price you may not be willing to pay."

Candara made a grimace. "It is pay his price—or that of Tor Domnus. I would rather trust the old man than the young."

She stood, regal in a black gown that clung faithfully to her splendid body. "You shall accompany me, Zordanor. You and Mindos Omthl can make wizard talk together. Perhaps you can make him name a sensible price for his labors."

The hunchback shook his head dubiously. "Mindos Omthl cannot be swayed by words. But we shall see."

Within the hour two fast horses were saddled and bridled at the postern gate of the castle, that faced the more desolate areas of the Haunted Lands. Zordanor came first, peering quickly with his eyes, then swinging his neck about so he could see Queen Candara, wrapped in a black wool robe, descend the two stone steps and place a sandaled foot in the ivory stirrup of her saddle.

Moments later, they galloped out across the wastes.

They rode swiftly, for Zordanor had prepared certain spells that shrank the land beneath their horses' hoofs. Before noon, they were reining up before the red metal door set in the black stone wall of the ancient tower.

"Who comes before Mindos Omthl?" boomed a voice.

"Queen Candara of Kor," answered Zordanor, "together with her court magician. We would ask help of Mindos Omthl against our mutual enemy."

"Mindos Omthl has no enemies."

"I speak of Tor Domnus of Urgal."

There was a little silence. Then the red door slid back and a brass man moved from its shadows, clanking out onto the rocky ground surrounding the tower. The metal giant made a bow and its voice boomed out like thunder muffled in a narrow gorge.

"Mindos Omthl will see you. Follow me."

Candara slipped from the saddle and walked with Zordanor across the pebbles toward the opening of the red door. Inside herself, she was frightened. She knew the powers of a mage like Mindos Omthl, she understood that by coming to see him to beg his help she well might be placing herself within his necromantic powers.

She told herself she had no choice. Well enough she knew that Tor Domnus would follow Kothar to the gates of Kor and inside them, to wrest Xixthur from his grasp. And Candara could not give up Xixthur! She would die, were she to do that. And the queen of Kor found life very sweet and satisfying to her senses.

Inside the black tower it was cool, the air was scented sweetly; by magic, she was sure. Ahead of her, the metallic man clanked up the narrow stone staircase. Slightly below her came Zordanor who was no match for Mindos Omthl in the casting of spells and wizardries. She had poor weapons to serve her, she told herself.

The brass man halted on a little landing. Its gleaming arm drew back certain draperies and Candara stepped forward into a round chamber with stone walls covered with cabinets holding any number of necromantic volumes and vials, alembics and philtre pots.

The mage himself stood grim and tall beside a golden pillar that supported a large crystal ball. He was poised within the red lines of a pentagram, at which sight Zordanor gasped and shrank back, for no magician stood inside the pentagram unless he summoned evil demons.

"Be not afraid," Mindos Omthl cried. "I have sent the demon Abathon back into his own hells. I am alone."

As if to display the truth of his assertion, he stepped over the red pentagram on the floor and advanced upon Queen Candara. His old eyes glowed at sight of her sultry beauty, for upon entering the room the queen had slipped back the hood of her robe.

She held out her hands. The magician caught them in his own, bent and kissed each one.

"I am here to serve you, highness," he murmured.

Candara admitted surprise. This old man was courtly, polite, vastly different from most of the mages she had known in her lifetime. There was none of the arrogance of someone like Kazazael, the magician who served Queen Elfa of Commoral, for instance, or even of Zordanor, for that matter.

"I must defend my city against Tor Domnus," she said simply, walking where he gestured, to seat herself on an X-chair. She threw open her robe, revealing her body clad in the scantiest of black gossamer, under which her nudity might be glimpsed.

With a faint smile, she watched the mage scan her loveliness. He was too old for fleshly desires, she thought, but no one ever really knew about such things where a magician was concerned. She was glad now that she had donned this dark flimsiness that showed so much of her beauty.

"Tor Domnus is a greedy man," the magician admitted.

"He seeks to conquer Kor. He may not stop with that. He may want all the Haunted Lands for his own, including even this black tower and the great magician who lives inside it."

Mindos Omthl paced back and forth. His long cloak flapped to his stridings and it seemed to Zordanor, who eyed him closely, that the hundred signs of the demons of Alpalonnia fluttered and writhed as if alive. When he came to a bronze amillary, he halted and leaned his elbows on a bronze band.

"Xixthur," he said suddenly, and Queen Candara started. "Xixthur is the cause of Tor Domnus leading his warriors against Kor. So the demon voices tell me."

Candara glanced about her fearfully. Demon queen she might be, for her father was Hasthar, who lived in one of the eleven hel-worlds and visited her from time to time as he had visited her mother before her, though not in such an intimate way. It had been Hasthar, centuries ago, who had brought Xixthur to her, so that she might live forever.

"Azthamur stole Xixthur from me," she whispered.

"And you would have him back—safely?"

"Yes. Without the threat of Tor Domnus hanging above my head! Tor Domnus knows that Xixthur will give eternal life, and wants my god for his own."

"I too, would like eternal life."

Candara drew a deep breath. "I will—share—my god with you, magician. If you help me drive Tor Domnus away."

His grin was wolfish. "I could take Xixthur away from you, you know. A mere sharing is not enough."

Her back straightened. "What else is there? Would you deny Xixthur to me?"

"By no means. You shall keep Xixthur in the little alcove off your bedchamber. But the man who shares your bed of nights will be me, your highness. I am sick of loneliness. I would go out into the world again."

"I would be king in Kor!"

Zordanor gasped, leaning forward from the shadows to study the dusky face of his queen. Candara was a woman jealous of her queenly rule, of the city that paid her its allegiance. She would never share her throne with such as Mindos Omthl, let alone her bed. Candara liked young lovers.

Her soft laughter rang out.

"But Mindos Omthl, you are old."

His smile was mirthless. His scrawny neck shot forward so that he seemed to Zordanor like a hungry vulture about to feast on female flesh.

"I am not so much older than you, Candara," he snapped. "Indeed, I do believe you have a few years on me, say four or five centuries. It was long before my time that you were born of a princess of Vandacia and the demon Hasthar. Long before my time."

His laughter cackled in the air.

"You have remained youthful for—how long has it been?—surely more than a thousand years. Xixthur has done that for you, Xixthur the god. Xixthur could do the same for me. I will be youthful and strong. You will be happy to have me in your arms on cold winter nights."

Candara made her face smooth. She did not want to offend this old man, even by a facial grimace that might let him know his presence would not be welcome in Kor. No, she must pretend, she must agree to all his suggestions, until the threat of Tor Domnus was no more.

Then she could deal with Mindos Omthl.

"I would be happy to share my crown with such as you, magician," she said. "And who knows? With you beside me, perhaps we might extend our rule to that of Urgal, and beyond Urgal into Phalkar and Sybaros."

Her lips smiled a promise that her heart denied.

CHAPTER FIVE

Kothar came to the gates of Kor a little before sunset. Beside him, Philisia drooped on the back of the little mare. It had been a long ride from the ancient chapel of Randolphus, her body ached from the tip of her toes to the top of her brown head. She ran weary eyes over the stone walls of Kor and told herself that Tor Domnus would take this place within an hour.

A guard challenged the barbarian, but Kothar merely pointed to Xixthur strapped on the back of the brown horse and the guard's eyes widened in awe as he nodded and gestured them through.

Kothar called down, "Keep your eyes open, man. Tor Domnus may be on my back trail with his soldiers."

Then the Cumberian toed Greyling to a canter and rode through the cobbled streets of Kor. He would find lodging first for Philisia, he did not feel easy about bringing her beside him when he faced Candara. She was worn with traveling, her shoulders drooped and rounded, her face was streaked with dust and grime.

He avoided the Queen's Navel to draw up before a door set between two jutting bay windows, with tiny panes of glass between their lead grips. There was a courtyard beyond it, through a wooden archway, and candle lights gleamed in a number of the upstairs rooms.

He half-lifted Philisia from the saddle, her legs were almost too numb for walking, but his arm about her waist guided her until she learned the use of her feet and could stagger beside him into the common room and to the scot counter where a beefy man made figures in a ledger.

A room for the Lady Philisia and a hot meal for them both was soon arranged. They dined below-stairs in a corner of the common room, watching it fill with traveling merchants and traders, with some of the city guards, with men and women from nearby houses.

Kothar walked with her up the walled staircase and waited until she was safe behind a latched door before he turned away to find Queen Candara. Suspicion and distrust were strong in the barbarian. Now that he had Xixthur for her, would Candara of Kor honor her promise to him, to reward him with a kingship?

He was expected at the palace wall gate. There was a heavy guard on duty, and as he cantered Greyling across the fountain square toward that wall-gate, the big oaken doors swung wide to admit him. Her magician could have alerted her as to his coming, he realized.

He dismounted in the inner court. His were the hands that undid the fastenings that held the metal god, his the hands that lifted Xixthur, carried him up the outer stairs.

Candara waited for him in her throne room, dark except for two towering candles on either side of the ivory and ebony chair that was her throne in Kor. Her legs were crossed under a clinging white tunic with a golden belt about its middle. She had loosened her black hair so that it made an ebony waterfall across her bare shoulders down as far as her knees. The white tunic was like a nightrail, something which she might wear to her great four-poster bed of nights. It was of sheer Vandacian linen, which was as thin as the webs of Oasian spiders. Under it, the queen displayed the perfection of her dusky body.

As his footfalls echoed with hollow thumpings in the dark hall, she broke into laughter and clapped her hands.

"You have done well, barbarian," she cried, uncrossing her legs and leaning forward, staring at the thing he carried.

He set Xixthur down with a thump before her.

"I fought Azthamur for this. I left him bound and gagged, and barely escaped from Tor Domnus's soldiers."

She nodded. "You have done well, Kothar. You deserve to be rewarded. And rewarded you shall be!"

She came off her throne, and as she passed before a tall candle, Kothar saw by its pallid light that beneath the white tissue of her gown, she wore nothing at all. As if to test the prohibition of Afgorkon he asked, "Shall I be prince in Kor?"

She was standing beside Xixthur, running her palms over his smooth metal surface. Her eyes lifted to touch Kothar. "Of course. I have given my word as queen. Gold and jewels, a crown for your head. You shall make a splendid prince, Kothar."

She sounded convincing enough.

And yet there was a laughter in her eyes that told the barbarian she toyed with him. To drive out that laughter, he growled, "Tor Domnus comes after me, to take back Xixthur."

She nodded. "I know. Zordanor has warned me."

"I saw no guards on the city walls, only a few men before the gate. Tor Domnus will bring a thousand mercenaries with him."

Candara clapped her hands. From the shadows four men came, slaves from the southlands below Oasia, naked to their middles. They bent and lifted Xixthur between them and carried him from the throne room.

Kothar stirred, scowling. He did not trust this queen and her wanton wiles. She should have been worried about the army Tor Domnus was bringing with him from Urgal. She had perhaps five hundred cutthroats wearing her leopard livery; surely not enough to defend Kor for very long, even if they were all fanatic in their loyalty.

He said, "I have some experience in leading men in battle. I would help defend Kor for you."

Her eyes smiled at him. "And you shall, my barbarian swordsman. But not this night, not yet. Zordanor informs me that Tor Domnus will not come to Kor until the morrow, a little before midday. Until then, we have the night and what is left of the morning to ourselves."

She came close, putting her arms about his neck and her body to his, lifting her lips for the kissing. As his mouth closed on hers, Kothar told himself she was a witch, that she knew how to fan the fires in a man's bloodstream with her wiles.

"We shall go to our royal bed, Kothar," she whispered, and put her arm in his.

He walked with her up a flight of stone steps covered with red carpeting to a long gallery. Despite all his suspicions, so sensually alluring was Candara in her white tunic that he found himself laughing as she laughed, whispering words of adoration for her beauty.

Her red mouth was a moist fruit promising ecstasy. Her shoulders, bare above the gown, were indicative of the smooth body that would soon be his. Her eyes glowed as they flattered his muscular bulk by telling him silently that his arms would soon be encompassing her nakedness.

And then, still in the gallery, she turned to teasing.

Catching up her tunic skirt she ran ahead of him like a wood nymph fleeing before a satyr. Her laughter and her dusky face turned back toward him over a shoulder, lured him on.

"Come chase me, Kothar—chase me!"

She was perhaps twenty feet away, dancing on sandaled feet. She was a succubus that comes in the night hours to test the male strengths of men. She was Salara and Isthis, the love goddesses of Vandacia and Memphor.

With a bellow, the Cumberian leaped forward.

His hands were stretched out for the grasping, his palms itched to stroke her dusky flesh. It was dark in the gallery, there were no torches, only a candle or two to show the way. Even if there had been a thousand torches, Kothar might not have known his danger.

For all he saw was Candara, with her body nude beneath the white linen of her gown, her head thrown back so that her glossy black hair fell behind her almost to the backs of her knees. Her red mouth was open and she was laughing, laughing, as the trap door opened under his foot.

The gallery floor fell away beneath his war boots.

"By Dwallka!" Kothar bellowed, falling.

Candara shrieked her enjoyment of the moment.

But now there was no wanton eagerness in it, to blind and tempt, there was merely mockery and a cold cruelty. She had set her royal trap and like the dupe he was, he had tumbled headlong into it! Down he went in utter blackness, and high above his head the trap dropped into place.

He landed on his feet on a sloping stone ramp and tumbled forward, heels over head, rolling downward until he came to a crashing stop on a dry rock floor. He lay a few moments, gasping, his body throwing off the shock.

He waited, blind in this darkness that was all around him. He knew there was life other than himself in this chamber: His barbarian instincts told him so. Ah, but what sort of life was it? Surely it had heard him tumble downward and roll across the floor.

Why did it wait to attack?

For it was waiting, scarcely breathing. He must make the first move, it seemed to be telling him, then it would make its rush.

Carefully, silently, Kothar drew his sword.

He was sitting, with Frostfire in his huge hand. Slowly he gathered his war-booted legs beneath him; he heaved upward.

Something rustled in the blackness.

Sweat glistened on the Cumberian's forehead. Was it a snake, slithering so across the floor? Something touched his ankle. Another something wrapped itself about his thickly thewed right forearm. A foul stench came to his nostrils. Stifling an exclamation of disgust, he slashed sideways with his blade, and struck only empty air.

His left hand went to his forearm, closed down on a long tendril, tugged at it. The tendril stuck, having sucker-discs along its underside. Kothar snarled a curse and his muscles bulged. The tendril came free.

He slashed with his sword. He heard a shrill cry. Then he was moving forward, crouched, cutting at the thing at his ankle, slashing left and right with his sword edge, blindly. Twice he felt the momentary opposition of something thin and living.

"By Dwallka! Give me a light, you gods of Cumberia!"

There was only darkness.

And now in angry haste came a score of those tendrils, darting unseen through the darkness, to wrap about his entire body. Kothar was raised upward off his feet, hung there in the air as more and more of the tendrils slipped about him.

He fought savagely to keep his sword arm free.

The thing that had him struggled just as fiercely to enwrap his arms, but it was wary for it knew the right arm held a sharp something that could hurt it. Its wariness was the one weapon Kothar had, for it gave him a chance to slash with Frostfire, to cut free the tendril that held his throat, that sought with its sucker-discs to pull out his eyes.

He felt drops of ichor touching his skin where the tendrils bled. As he went on struggling, he found that where that ichor touched him, the gripping tendrils slid and slipped.

Kothar twisted himself feverishly now, wriggled and squirmed until more and more drops rained on him. He found a sliced-off section of the thing and rubbed its oozing end over his face and throat, then over his swordarm until the tendril he held went dry.

In its struggles, the thing that held him discovered that by gripping him tightly in many spots, it could tug at him, draw his arm away from his shoulder, his legs from his trunk, about which it had twisted other tendrils. Kothar knew he was being pulled apart. The pain was agonizing, but he had suffered agony before.

He was half a wild animal, and a wild animal bore its hurts with stoic calm. Kothar gritted his teeth and endured that torment of torn flesh and bones twisted out of their sockets. For now he was able to see a thin membranous thing that crouched on the floor and extended thin feelers upward to where it held him suspended above it.

An octopus? A kraken out of the ocean deeps?

No. This was no animal but—A plant!

The plant glowed faintly in the blackness, probably a gift from Nature itself, as the deep-ocean fish are provided with lights to show them the ocean floor. The plant was filled with phosphorescent liquids, that ichor which covered parts of Kothar as he battled.

When he has first dropped here, his eyes had been used to the brilliance of the world beyond the trap door. Down here, in this ebon darkness, it took a little time for those eyes to adjust so they could see light as pale as that phosphorescent glow.

Yet now—he could see!

With a bull bellow, he slashed sideways, through tendrils. Up and down his sword edge went, and now the plant mass below was emitting more of those faint, shrill cries of pain.

It sought to protect itself, drawing back its pseudopods, seeking to cover its membranous mass with those feelers, as a man will try to cover his head against attack by lifting his arms. It let go of the barbarian; Kothar fell heavily to the stone floor.

But he was up and leaping, Frostfire swinging.

A dozen tentacles fell away before his attack, until the pulsing middle of the plant lay exposed. One good thrust into its living center might finish it.

Kothar panted harshly, swinging up his blade.

Then he halted, thinking. Of what good was it to slay this thing? It could not harm him, now he could see it.

"Can you speak, foul excrescence'?" he shouted.

The thing whimpered.

Kothar asked, "Is there a way out of here?"

A voice touched his mind. *When keeper comes, door opens.* The thing was silent. Then: *Not harm me, I help.*

Kothar nodded, went to sit in a dark corner of the chamber. By the eerie light of the plant, he saw a stone-walled room, in the middle of which lay the glowing organism. The sloping ramp down which he had tumbled was to one side. In a section of the stone wall, Kothar made out faint lines that suggested there might be a stone door hung on big hinges there.

It was through this door that the keeper would come. Kothar put his stare on it, and held it there.

After a time he asked, "How are you named? How did you come here to do Candara's bidding?"

Long time here. Always. Candara find me.

There was a pause. It took the plant a long time to marshal its knowledge and put that knowledge into its telepathic signals.

Candara build room. Give food. It grow.

A pause. Call it Thyllu. Thyllu eat all. Candara feed.

The plant thought no more at Kothar. They shared this chamber for a little while, then the man would be out and on his way. The Cumberian sat with his sword across his knees, waiting patiently as a wolf might wait for food along a trail. Many hours passed, and the stone door remained closed. Kothar supposed that the keeper believed the plant to have feasted well on the barbarian, the plant would not be hungry for a long time.

He himself was ravenous. It had been many hours since he had tasted food. He would eat when he had left the chamber of the plant. In the meantime he would fight his impatience and his hunger as he had fought the plant.

He dozed a little; it was easy, in the blackness.

When his eyes opened, the plant had stretched its remaining tendrils to the wall around the door and above it. It waited as patiently as did Kothar for the coming of the keeper.

Catlike, the Cumberian came to his feet and stepped close to the wall.

He did not stand here long. By some developed instinct, Thyllu must have sensed the coming of its keeper.

The door swung inward. A blazing torch was thrust in. At the same time, tendrils dropped to wrap about the arm holding the torch, and tugged.

A little man, shrilling obscenities, was pulled inward. Thyllu so maneuvered him that he could not see the barbarian.

Kothar slipped out into a narrow corridor.

He ran.

He was in the cellarways of the palace, he knew soon enough. His nostrils caught the scent of food from the basement kitchens, and he angled his run so that he came to an open doorway that gave into a wide room where meats were roasting and bread-stuffs were baking. Several young girls, with aprons twisted about their slim middles, were attending the ovens and the braziers.

Kothar did not hesitate. Food was before him, and he was like a starving animal. He raced in, snatched at a turning leg of beef and at two golden loaves of bread just off the baking slabs. A girl turned her head, catching sight of him. Her eyes opened and her jaw dropped.

Then her eyes rolled up in her head and she crumpled.

Kothar leaped over her on his way for the farther door. He did not know why the sight of him had inspired such terror. It was good that she had fainted. Unconscious, she could give no signal.

Two other girls saw him and fell to the floor.

Kothar raced on, up stairs and along empty corridors. Finally he came to a room with a single wooden door. This he entered, bolting the door behind him.

And then he froze.

A giant monster stood facing him, covered over with green stuff, which matted his hair and streaked his face and painted his mail shirt and kilt with ghastly flecks of green.

Kothar growled and raised Frostfire.

The giant imitated his action, and Kothar realized he was staring into a mirror. Laughter barked from his lips. "By Dwallka! No wonder those girls were frightened. That green ichor's turned me into some kind of man-beast!"

He sat down on a chair and, lifting the leg of beef to his strong teeth, began tearing at it. He ripped great chunks of meat from the bone, chewing with delight. The meat was savored to a nicety. Those girls were excellent cooks. The bread, too, was sweet to the taste and satisfying to the belly.

Kothar ate until there was only a bone remaining. This he tossed aside into a corner, rubbing his forearm across his lips. He would have given much for a beaker of ale, because thirst was a living thing in his throat, clamoring for satiation.

He shook himself, staring about him.

This room was part of the tower base, that had been fitted out with a table and a chair, probably for the use of the guards. A lone window, bisected by a single bar, was set high up in the stone wall. It was a narrow window, but even a man the size of the barbarian might squeeze through it, once the bar was removed.

Kothar pushed the table against the wall below the window, vaulted up on it. Carefully he examined the seating of the bar, found that the masonry was cracked and in disrepair. His hand brought out his dagger and he began prying with the point, dislodging bits of stonework.

Within minutes, he had freed the bolt holding the bar in place on the stone sill. A push of his hand swung the bar to one side. Hoisting himself up, Kothar wedged his shoulders into the opening and shoved outward.

His head thrust through the window, he stared down at a stake-filled moat, then upward at windows glinting golden with candlelight in the night darkness. Between his window and those higher in the tower were a series of crude carvings, placed there for ornament by some unknown mason centuries ago.

Kothar put out a hand, closed his fingers on the carving of a gargoyle. His iron fingers tightened. Slowly he slid his legs out the window and caught hold of a stone leopard's head. His arm muscles swelled as he lifted himself upward by sheer strength.

His toe fumbled for a hold. He loosed his right hand, reached higher for another carving. With toes and hands he worked his way up the face of the rounded tower until he was hanging below the first of the lighted windows, staring inside.

At first he did not understand what it was he saw. The room was dark, but lighted by strange red and blue and yellow shafts of light that moved this way and that, forming little patterns of purple and green that mingled with the others in a color dance, making the barbarian dizzy. Not until his eyes became accustomed to that pattern did he realize that he was also seeing portions of a nude female body that was bathing in the shifting rays.

Queen Candara was laving herself in those healing rays. She was turning, arms high, crooning deep in her throat, as her flesh gathered the medicinal powers of Xixthur deep within its tissues. The Cumberian grinned. Aye! Let her keep forever young, if she wanted. Let her delude herself and play the fool, not knowing that her fate rested in the big hand that fumbled for the dagger at his hip as Kothar shifted position.

One swift throwing of his knife would end the life of the queen. She could atone for her betrayal of him as the lifeblood oozed from her wound.

As he drew back his arm to make the throw, the metal scabbard holding Frostfire grated across a stone carving.

Candara opened her eyes, stared right at him.

Kothar cursed and tried to hurry his movements. Pinned as he was just beyond the window, with a sixty fool drop onto sharpened stakes in the moat below him, he was a dead man if the queen screamed and there were guards within sound of her voice.

"Aiiiieeee!"

Her wail woke echoes in the most distant corner of the castle. It made the door from her bedchamber into his alcove burst open with a crash as two men in mail shirts fought to get inside.

"By Dwallka!" Kothar swore, and hurled the dagger.

But Candara was bending, reaching for a wrapper, and the knife whisked past her head to thud into a wooden beam. At the same moment both the men-at-arms brought out their swords and lunged for the barbarian.

Kothar flung one glance below him at the stakes embedded in the moat bottom. Then his war boots were pressing hard on the stone sides of the round stone tower and he launched himself off the wall like an arrow from the bow.

He went outward and downward.

Somebody shouted for archers, behind him.

Below him the stakes were coming up fast to impale his body. The barbarian had sought to angle his fall so that he would land on the far edge of the moat, where the wooden stakes jutted outward instead of upward, to delay attackers seeking entry into the castle. He was going to miss those stakes and land on—No, by Dwallka!

He had timed his fall almost to perfection. His feet went down onto the rounded stakes that jutted away from the castle and he slid backward toward the pointed stakes. His hands scrabbled at slippery wood from which the bark had been peeled, seeking to stay his fall.

An arrow thunked into a stake, a foot away.

Then his fingers were tightening, his slide was being slowed and then stopped. A man without the sheer animal might of the blond barbarian would never have been able to brake that slide, but the Cumberian managed it—though his palms stung and bled where splinters had rammed into him from the pressure of his handgrip.

Ignoring the pain of his hands, he pulled himself up and over the points and dropped on the far side of the moat. Arrows were falling all around him now, but the archers could not see too well in the starlight, and within seconds the Cumberian was dodging behind a house, racing into a cobblestoned alley.

He ran for many minutes, until he was at the city wall.

For his steel thews it was a relatively simple thing to leap onto a sloping hovel roof, run to a slated house roof and from the peak of a chimney, jump upward until his hands caught the stone wall capping. He drew himself upward, hooked a leg on the wall top, and jumped down the other side.

Bells were clanging in the castle.

Like a wolf, Kothar loped off into the desert. Once out on those barren grounds or hidden in the misty regions of the Haunted Lands, no man from Kor would ever be able to find him.

Oh, he was safe enough, the barbarian knew. But it rankled inside him that he had failed so ignominiously to blood his dagger in the soft flesh of Queen Candara. Not only that, he had left Philisia to her mercies if the royal bitch learned the woman was in her city.

The Cumberian could imagine the tortures Candara and Zordanor would inflict on Tor Domnus's former mistress if they laid hands on her. And there was nothing that he could do about it.

Raw fury pulsed inside the barbarian as his war boots made soft sounds, padding along the pebbled pathway that would bring him deep into the heart of the Haunted Lands. His fingers opened and closed to make mighty fists with which he beat the air. Somehow—he must find a way to even his score!

CHAPTER SIX

He ran on through the thickening mists of the Haunted Lands like a coursing hound, knowing no fatigue, no tiredness in his rolling muscles, only the savage bite of defeat and the fierce need for vengeance. Candara had betrayed him! Candara had gone back on her royal word, she had gulled him instead of rewarding him!

He would make her pay!

By Dwallka, he would!

He was so lost in his thoughts and roiled emotions that he ran headlong into two soldiers in the boar's head uniforms of Prince Tor Domnus before he could halt his run. His weight bowled them backward, but not before they caught a glimpse of his hard brown face and shaggy blond hair.

Their howls were loud and piercing.

Kothar pulled Frostfire from the scabbard, but other men were joining their voices to those yells. "I've stumbled into the vanguard of an army— Tor Domnus's army," he rasped.

He whirled and ran, but now they were calling his name and arrows began flying blindly through the mists. Two hit his chainmail shirt and bounced off, a third scratched a red furrow across a bare forearm.

But Kothar was running for his life, and he soon outdistanced the shafts. He could still hear their voices calling to one another, and the deeper growl of a sergeant bellowing orders to spread out and link hands.

They meant to take him here in the white fog and carry him captive to Tor Domnus for punishment. To his surprise, Kothar found that Frostfire was naked in his hand; he had forgotten to sheathe it. His grin was cruel. Let them come, then. He was ready for them.

He ran on, listening to the calls going back and forth.

The prince himself was galloping forward, eager to be in on the capture. Kothar heard his voice crying out warnings to his soldiery that if they failed him, he would flay the skin from their bodies.

Two men came out of the mists to one side. Kothar gave them no chance to cry their warning. He leaped and his sword flashed wetly in the mists. Its edge sheared through chainmail and flesh and the man sagged. The second man lunged at him with his own blade, intending to take any reward Tor Domnus might give by wounding this man himself.

But the mercenary had never fought a man like the Cumberian, who was in front of him one moment and three feet away the next. Steel rang out as Kothar parried a vicious stab at his belly.

The clang of the steel echoed across the misty plain. It was like a clarion call to the men who marched with the prince of Urgal. Voices bayed in triumph, and there was the sound of running feet.

The barbarian sprang forward, Frostfire glinting. His first blow drove the man reeling backward as it caromed off his sword blade and hilt. His next sliced through chainmail into warm flesh. The man opened his mouth to call for help and it was then, as the first mewling sound came out, that Frostfire's point took him in the throat.

It was too late to run. The harm was done.

A dozen men were on top of him, blades ripping the air. Kothar parried and gave ground, but the odds were too many. He could not fight a dozen men at once, unless his back was against a rock. He turned and fled like a deer, his eyes hunting a boulder big enough to guard his spine.

An arrow dug into his thigh, but he ignored it.

More arrows were sliding through the mists. One hit his left ankle, piercing the skin but falling off. Kothar ran harder, knowing the exertion was causing his heart to beat the faster and his wounds to bleed even more, but knowing also that to remain and fight would mean capture and an agonizing death by torture.

He lost the twelve men behind him, but they were coming on, able to follow his progress by the drumming of his war boots on the rocky ground. The barbarian considered removing them but the sharp stones underfoot would cut his feet to ribbons.

Kothar came to a big rock and turned.

He set his bearskin cloak to the wet stone and waited, grimly determined to die here in these mists with a hundred foes already dead before him. There was no escape, he knew that; he must have some rest or bleed to death. Frostfire was ready in his hand. All he wanted now was enemies to slay.

And they were coming…oh, yes! He could hear their voices as they advanced slowly through the fog, calling to one another, keeping in touch.

Ah, but wait!

There was another sound he could hear.

It was faint and seemingly far away, but it grew louder, louder, and Kothar remembered that squelching sound he had heard on his way to Kor—and he called to mind the memory of the awesome beast he had seen through an opening in these same mists.

"By the gods," he breathed.

Squelch, squelch, squelch. Now over those sounds, as three-clawed massive feet were put down in soft mud and lifted out, he could hear the vast breathing of the unknown monster, which was like a gigantic forge bellows worked by a giant smith.

Just beyond the rocks were the marshes of Xanthia, an unexplored region of Yarth where, according to rumors, only strange beasts and monsters dwelled. Kothar could smell their dank stench as the wind shifted.

Kothar jammed his spine against the boulder and waited.

A mercenary came through the mists. He saw Kothar and slid to a halt on the wet rocks. He lifted his head and bellowed, "Here, over here! This way. I've cornered the barbarian against a big rock."

He ran forward, but stopped just out of sword-stroke distance. The Cumberian snarled in his throat. The man was so tantalizingly near! To leap away from the rock, to blood his blade in his body, to leap back! He might kill this lone man, but the slaying would not help him, all things considered.

The others were coming now, moving from the mists into the open space where he stood. Kothar drew a deep breath. They were forming a battle line, advancing on him, shields up and swords ready.

Tor Domnus himself was reining in his white warhorse, laughing to see the barbarian about to make his last stand. In his fine armor and with his glittering helmet, handsomely carved and with a horsetail as its crest, he made a martial figure.

"Disarm him only," the prince shouted. "I want him alive!"

Squelch! Squelch!

The sounds were fainter, as though the monster tiptoed. Kothar grinned mockingly at Tor Domnus on his fine white horse. Didn't the fool or these idiots who passed for soldiers hear those noises? Were they not curious as to what manner of thing could make them? In another moment—

The ground shook under his feet. The huge boulder rocked. The sound—the bellow of insensate fury which the monster was emitting through its gigantic jaws—was like a titanic thunderclap. Even Kothar froze motionless, and he had been expecting that frightful trumpeting.

The soldiers of Tor Domnus turned to statues. Their eyes were suddenly enormous, their mouths were open. Not a man moved against Kothar, not a man stirred by so much as a muscle twitch.

Only their eyes spoke for them, turned upward in the mists where a—something—towered high above the head of the barbarian. Kothar caught the stench of the beast now, it was very close, it was visible to the awed mercenaries to whom it must have seemed like a creature out of a nightmare. Clumps of weed and marshgrass were plastered to its greyish scales. It stank of rotted vegetation and of bits of decayed meat. Its breath was as the miasma of a poisoned pond.

Scales and claws grated on rock as the monster advanced.

Then a shadow touched Kothar and, glancing up, he beheld the long scaly neck and lower jaw of this behemoth out of Hell. Teeth glinted as the jaws opened.

A soldier screamed.

The vast head darted downward. Those jaws closed down on living flesh, on half a dozen men. The jaws closed and bones broke as flesh was ripped open and blood flowed out. Kothar shuddered. By the gods! He wished no fate as this on anyone, even on his enemies!

If he could have saved them, he might have leaped forward. But his barbarian soul was awed enough to hold his body motionless. In his race memory there was a hint of some such creature as this, and others like it whom his people had fought, long and long ago, and which should be dead yet still lived.

The monster gulped its meal and ate again.

The spell was broken, now. The men who still lived turned to flee, screeching out their terrors. They drove back into the mercenaries behind them, from whom the monster was hidden by the mists. These soldiers, thinking only that their companions had been terrified by a single man—Kothar—cursed their contempt and sought to pass the cowards and get at the barbarian with their swords.

The result was chaos.

A muddle of snarling, angry men, some of them terrified witless, fought to break free of one another. As a result, they were bunched together as the beast came forward, head downward and jaws agape, to gather in those men with a single bite.

A clatter of hoofs told when Tor Domnus fled for his life on the white warhorse. He alone was mounted, he alone could race away from the scaled thing that was eating his men. The hoofbeats receded into the mists, and faded away.

Kothar saw a giant three-clawed foot descending toward him as the monster stepped over the boulder. The only thing that saved him, he realized, was that big rock against which he had placed his back. The thing had not seen him, its attention had been caught and held by the line of men before him.

Kothar flung himself sideways.

The huge foot planted itself on pebbles, then lifted as the beast went on, drawn by the screaming, fleeing men who threw away shields and swords and ran to save themselves from such a death. A cry was halted in mid-sound. A man screamed and screamed—and was silent. The crunch of teeth on mail and human bones, the drip, drip, drip of blood from grinding jaws to the ground, were horrors against which he closed his ears.

He stumbled to his feet, tiny against the titanic bulk of the scaled monster. The tail alone must be more than forty feet long! It quivered and shook and when it lashed sideways, the barbarian was certain that the beast would kill him. But apparently the tail had shifted for the purpose of maintaining balance, for the thing did not turn on him but went on after the fleeing soldiers.

Kothar raced off into the mists. He had no goal, he just wanted to be away from Tor Domnus and his men and put the beast far behind him.

He paused in his running to snap the arrowshaft still protruding through his thigh and cast the parts aside. He made a crude tourniquet, fastening a length of material from his kilt and knotting it.

Now he walked until his muscles wearied.

He lay down to sleep on the moist stones, enduring the dampness and the cold like the half-savage he was, happy that he was still alive. Thoughts of vengeance on Queen Candara buoyed his spirits, though he saw no way of accomplishing that revenge. Alone and wounded, what could he do against the armed might of Kor?

When the mists grew pale, he knew it was dawn.

He walked on, hearing only his own footfalls in the uncanny silence of the fog. He did not know how long he strolled, but he came eventually to the end of the mists and walked boldly across the barren ground.

Toward noon, he saw the cross in the distance.

A man was tied to the cross by wrists and ankles. In front of him, half a dozen desert wolves were crouched, feral eyes fixed on the helpless thing that writhed there. Kothar strode forward. Whoever the man was, he was human. The wolves could wait for a different meal.

His savage shouts and the glint of Frostfire as he waved it drew the famished beasts toward him. They were used to seeing a man on foot, they viewed him as a meal. The cross that had been set up in the rocky ground and to which the man had been lashed was new and strange to them, and so they had waited, studying it until certain it was not a trap. Then they would have attacked.

Kothar slew three of the wolves and wounded the others until they turned and fled from his bloody blade. Then the barbarian turned and walked toward the man. To his surprise, he recognized Kylwyrren.

The magician smiled through his pain at sight of the Cumberian. His white-haired head inclined in a little bow. "Greetings, man of the north. We meet again."

A dagger slashed the ropes that held him prisoner to the crucifix. The old man sagged and would have fallen except that Kothar put his arm about him and eased him to the ground.

"I have no water," Kothar growled.

The magician shook his head. "There is no water behind the mists, in this hellhole. But perhaps in the camp that Tor Domnus abandoned there may be a canteen or two that some terrified soldier threw away." The old man chuckled. "Something must have frightened the prince very much. Was it you?"

Kothar spoke of the scaled thing that had come out of the marshes in time to save his life. "I do not know what it was. It was huge. It ate half his army, I think."

"I have heard tales of such beasts that dwell in the marshlands of Xanthia, though I have never seen them, not even in my crystal ball." His pale hand lifted and gestured. "Can you carry me, barbarian? To the abandoned camp? It may be that I can help you in your quest."

The Cumberian lifted the old man easily. As he stalked along, he asked, "What do you know of my quest?"

"I peered into the ball for Tor Domnus. I saw you fall into your trap in Candara's palace. I saw your attempt to kill her. I watched as you fled into the mists. Now you seek revenge."

"She owes me a reward. Let that reward be her life!"

"Kor is a very strong city. It has many men-at-arms inside its walls. Even such a warrior as yourself can never hope to walk into it and work your will of its queen."

Kothar confessed his puzzlement and his hopelessness as far as any chance of gaining his revenge on Candara was concerned. It was in his mind to take leave of the Haunted Lands and seek his fortune elsewhere.

"There is a way," murmured Kylwyrren, but he would say no more until he was in the abandoned camp.

Here he found a carafe of fine wine, abandoned by Tor Domnus who had thought of nothing but escape from the strange monster that had come up out of the marshes of Xanthia to eat his soldiers. There was food too, hastily thrown aside for swifter running, and weapons and rich brocades and even chests of jewels and coins.

Kylwyrren and the barbarian feasted until their bellies swelled, sitting on the X-chairs that had also belonged to Tor Domnus. The magician had gone to the ground where his tent still stood and peered inside, nodding his head in satisfaction when he beheld that his magical accoutrements were undisturbed.

"Tor Domnus had other things on his mind than taking my properties back with him to Urgal," he told Kothar. "Besides, he attributed all of his troubles to my failure as a mage. My magicks were not strong enough to ward off such evil as had befallen him in these barren lands, and so he crucified me, expecting that wild animals would slay and eat me, and he would be rid of me forever."

Kylwyrren sighed. "Could he have forgotten so soon that it was my magicks—the necromancy he appears to hold in such low esteem—that first brought Azthamur to Urgal and his service? That it was my enchantments that held the demon ensorcelled so that it must serve him as my prince willed? Well, I know ways to remove those necromancies! Ah, then will Tor Domnus rue the day he left me to die on that cross."

"Azthamur is dead," Kothar protested. "I slew him."

The magician cackled laughter. "You bested him in a fair battle, barbarian. No more. You slew his humanoid-fish shape, true. But the demon Azthamur you could no more slay than you can slay the mists you see low on the horizon, yonder.

"No, no. Azthamur lives, waiting to serve me. Though not in the fish-man body in which he appeared to you. He shall have his own shape now, as I send him after Tor Domnus. Here, give me a hand."

The barbarian loaned his great strength to the tasks imposed on him by Kylwyrren, for the mage had promised that, when his own vengeance was a thing accomplished, he would make certain that Kothar should have his. He carried heavy metal alembics and reliquaries from the tent and set up a little bronze altar on which Kylwyrren might offer incense and pour libations to the demoniac being that served his will.

He stood close beside the mage when he did these things, for the necromancer warned that sometimes these beings out of the nether worlds did not understand such things as friendship, and one or another of them might well eat him in a thoughtless moment or carry off his soul to whatever bottomless pit he made his world. The barbarian was restless and uneasy while Kylwyrren chanted and made his magicks, he would rather have been on a fast horse galloping through one of his northern forests, but he made do with this new friend because of what Kylwyrren had promised.

He handed Kylwyrren the golden rod with which the old man drew his pentagram, making it large enough so that Kothar might stand inside it with him.

"For Azthamur is a vengeful demon," Kylwyrren explained. "Seeing you, he will want to rip your soul from your body and carry it off to the hundred hells where he dwells in his demon shape. I would not want that to happen, nor would you."

Kothar moved his broad shoulders uneasily.

Though Kylwyrren assured him with a smile that it would do him no good against such as Azthamur, Kothar drew Frostfire and held it in his hand as the old man began his incantations to the demon of Urgal. A wind had come up during the night that blew little dustdevils around his feet and made him bury his chin deeper in the folds of the bearskin cloak that guarded his throat.

Then, as Kylwyrren chanted faster, the wind sank away and an utter stillness came upon the land. The sky darkened slowly, it grew overcast and grey, and underfoot the ground trembled. More and more that stretch of rock and sand quivered, until it ran like jelly in a bowl. Kothar was hard put to maintain his balance, though the magician himself seemed untroubled.

Kylwyrren exclaimed worriedly, "There is something wrong! Never before has Azthamur behaved in such fashion! Azthamur! Azthamur! I summon you up in the name of the thousand and one demons who are your brothers and your sisters! I call on you in the name of the arch-fiend Nabbadon himself!"

The ground quieted but the wind commenced to moan, ruffling the bearskin cloak that Kothar wore. The air hushed. Then a thunderclap came close to breaking eardrums as something black and polymorphous appeared inside a blaze of brilliant scarlet light.

No shape had Azthamur, that black blotch that hung between Yarth and sky, it was quivering sentience, alive, sinister, evil. Its very evil beat out at the mage and the barbarian in waves of nauseating fury.

"I am here, magician!"

The voice was mere whisper, filled with hate and the lust to slay. The blackness bellied as if troubled by a strong gale. Tiny red eyes opened in that blackness and glared hard at the Cumberian.

"Him I want, Kylwyrren! Him I must have before I do your bidding. Send him out of the sacred pentagram to me."

"Forget your feud with Kothar," shouted the mage. "I offer you a different victim—Tor Domnus, prince of Urgal."

"Aye. Him I mean to have also, in my abode. But first the barbarian."

"Not so. Tor Domnus is your victim and I adjure thee by the rites of evil, by the eleven incantations to Salara, by the—"

"Enough, enough! I hear your voice, old man."

"Then begone about your business."

"I shall yet come for him! Hear you Azthamur, enemy? I shall come, I shall come—when I have done with Tor Domnus!"

The blackness swirled, faster and faster, until it was no more. It disappeared so swiftly that Kothar grunted and blinked his eyes to the hot sunlight that poured down on him as a result.

Kylwyrren was grave, thoughtful as he gathered up his appedimenta. "I do not like this, Kothar. Azthamur has an unholy hate in his demoniac soul against you. He will not rest content until he has come for you, dragged your soul from your body and drawn it down to his lair in the hundred hells."

Kothar growled, "I fear no man or demon."

"You'll do well to worry about Azthamur. Never before has he been beaten. It irks his pride. His injured pride will not let him rest until it has been salved by the sight of your spirit writhing in some agony of his devisement."

The old man shook his head. "I fear for you. There is no enchantment that can keep you safe, no amulet to wear about your neck. I did not suspect Azthamur felt so strongly, or I might not have summoned him up. But once I did so…"

He broke off and walked across the ground toward his tent. Kothar rumbled anger in his throat, following him, arms laden with the altar. He was not afraid, he did not know what fear was, but he admitted to a sense of uneasiness, being honest enough to doubt that Frostfire could kill such a being as Azthamur.

When his gear was neatly placed within the tent, Kylwyrren turned to the big barbarian. "You helped me, Kothar. It is my turn to help you."

He bent and lifted a shovel and placed it in the hands of the Cumberian. "Stand you here beside me, on this bronze plaque containing the sigil of Nabbadon himself."

Kylwyrren began to chant and the outlines of the world around them shimmered, grew grey and hazy. When the mage was done, the shimmering disappeared and when he stared about him, Kothar saw that they were in the foothills of a nearby mountain range. He did not bother to ask the old man how he had accomplished such a miracle; it was enough for him that they were here.

The white-haired magician pointed at the ground. "Dig here, Kothar!"

And Kothar dug, until he had uncovered a marble slab three feet down. He growled, glancing up at Kylwyrren inquiringly. The mage smiled, nodding.

"Lift the slab, barbarian," he murmured.

Kothar bent, fitting his powerful fingers into the space between the slab and the stonework below. He grunted, tugging. The slab was heavy. Heavy! But great was his strength and as his back muscles bulged, the slab lifted, slowly and steadily, until the barbarian could set it on end and stare down at what was revealed beneath it.

"By Dwallka—a tomb!" he breathed.

Kylwyrren nodded. "Yes, a tomb. Here lies the greatest of the warriors of ancient Vandacia. His name was Aywold the Wise. He is covered now by a sheet that rots in the dampness of the ground. Remove it."

With his swordhand, Kothar yanked away the rotting stuff of a funeral shroud. His eyes stared down at the skeleton of what had been an immense man, clad in link mail from head to the boots on his feet. The link mail was rusted, as was the hilt of the sword in the decaying scabbard, and there were scraps of hair here and there on what had been a face, once on a time.

Kylwyrren made gestures with his hand, chanting.

The dead body and its accoutrements quivered, shimmering as the air had shimmered and the barbarian choked back a curse. The body below his feet was changing, taking shape. The rust spots were fading, the armor and the weapons were brightening. Flesh came to clothe the bones of the long-dead Aylwold and the hairs of his beard turned a reddish brown and fluffed out until—

Eyelids opened. Pale blue eyes stared up at the barbarian. This was no lich! This was a living man below his war boots.

"Who are you, man?" asked Aylwold.

"Kothar of Cumberia. And I think I have a need of you!"

"Sharp wits, barbarian!" cackled Kylwyrren. "Indeed you do have a need for Aylwold the Wise. I have brought him back from the Otherworld where his spirit dwells—to offer you both the gift of vengeance accomplished."

Kothar put a hand down. Aylwold clasped it, let the northman yank him upward until he stood uncertainly on his own feet. Aylwold grinned, staring down at himself.

"I live again, as a man. By my sword, I'm not sure whether I'm glad to be here or not. The Otherworld has its advantages, old one. Still, I heard you speak the name of Candara, whom I hate for what she did to me and my companions, and to satisfy the need for revenge in me, I will listen to your words."

Kylwyrren spoke swiftly as the Vandacian listened, nodding from time to time and shouting with admiration as the mage told of Kothar's fight with Azthamur and how he had taken Xixthur out of Urgal, and later how he had escaped the trap Candara set for him.

He swung on Kothar, a big man and wide in the chest, wearing old-fashioned armor but even more dangerous in appearance because of it. His long reddish-brown hair blew in the wind off the wooded slope behind him, and his hand curled lovingly about the braided hilt of his longsword.

"A good tale, man. I envy you your deeds. So Candara built her city, did she?" At Kothar's exclamation, he grinned. "Aye! 'Tis the same Candara, on my hilt. Long has the demon queen lived. Long, long! It's time she died, barbarian. Let us go together and slay her."

"Not so fast," howled the magician. "There are your companions to be raised from their graves. Would you deny them a taste of their own vengeance on the woman who poisoned them all?"

"Not I! It will be good to see the Ten, again."

"Stand you on the bronze plaque, Aylwold."

It was a tight fit for three men, especially since two of the men—Kothar and Aylwold—were big of chest and wide of shoulders. But they managed it and the air shimmered around them, seeming to press them closer together and the foothills went away and in their place—

There was an island, bordered by reeds and swept by a damp breeze that held the smells of salt water and tiny woodland flowers. The wind that rippled the surface of the marsh-waters was chill, raw. Kothar shook himself and glanced at the magician.

"A queer place to bury the dead," he groused.

"Centuries ago, the marshes had not come so far inland," Kylwyrren answered. "There was water close by, true, but this was all dry land, then."

"I mind this place," Aylwold growled, looking about him. "Over there—those stones half buried in the loam. They are blackened, you'll note. It was at a campfire ringed by those stones that Candara poisoned the Ten while I was off on a hunting trip." He sighed and stepped off the plaque, reaching for the shovel Kothar held. "We were of the Royal Guard, and I was their captain. King Calyxius had sent us with his sister Candara to make sure she stayed far away from the borders of his land.

"Candara had a thousand men and women with her, the riffraff of the world, the scum of Yarth who flocked to her evil banner. She wanted us dead, that none might return to Calyxius to inform him of her plans."

The shovel hit into the soft dirt. Weeds and dirt and flowers flew in huge chunks as the Wise One worked. He began to speak in rhythm with his tool.

"Me she slew as I entered her encampment, two days' march north of here, laden down with dead deer and boars for the feasting. An arrow out of the darkness, without warning. Like that!" He dug the shovel deep.

Kothar dropped into the hole Aylwold had made, bent to tug free a root. Below him a number of bodies lay entangled in their common grave. These were the Ten, great warriors all, Aylwold assured him. They were the Royal Guard of Calyxius and in Vandacia during those days when he had been alive—Aylwold informed the barbarian—only the mightiest warriors of Yarth could be taken into such a select company.

But—

"Ten men against Kor?" Kothar wondered, uncovering a mailed hand.

Aylwold barked laughter. "Ask Kylwyrren, barbarian."

The magician smiled. "Those ten are as ten thousand, Kothar. Be not alarmed. Join them in the brotherhood of fighting warriors, and go about your destiny in peace."

They rose from their grave, ten huge warriors in link mail as old-fashioned as that which Aylwold wore, skeleton figures in rusty armor as they lifted up in answer to the ringing words of the magician. But as they stepped onto the ground, out of the pit, they fleshed out and their armor grew bright and new.

One by one, they came forward to meet Kothar and greet their old leader. Fandlon and Ibanar, Kasthin and Morion, Petrollix, Aberthan, Nixol, Judkin and little Ilthur who had a wooden bow hanging from a shoulder.

They were hardbitten men, they had the look of warriors. There was confidence in their bearing and in the manner in which they swung their weapon-belts about so that their swords were closer to their hands. They looked at Kylwyrren in curiosity and listened gravely as Aylwold the Wise explained why their spirits had been called back from the Otherworld and their bodies made young and warlike once more.

"We are your men," Ibanar said to the barbarian.

Little Ilthur unslung his bow and tested its catgut string. "Long has it been since I pulled at The Slaughterer. Ah, it feels good to hold his length and fit an arrow to his string!"

His laughter rang out, loud and happy.

The magician said, "Come! Azthamur is about his business and there is no time to waste, if Kothar is to slay Candara. Gather you on the plaque— yes, yes! All of you, I said. The plaque can hold you all."

The bronze plaque grew as the mage made hand motions above it. Soon the Ten, with Aylwold and Kothar and Kylwyrren, were on its surface and the island under it was shimmering with haze and disappearing from their view.

There was a thump. The shimmering went away and before their startled eyes were the walls of Kor, the outlaw city. Above the wall-tops they could make out the leaded rooftops gleaming in the morning sun and see the flash of armor where a guard strolled back and forth along the wall walk.

Kothar stepped off the plaque, followed by the others who paused at the sight of this city that had been no more than a dream in the mind of Candara when she had murdered them. It was now an actuality more than a thousand years old. Kothar turned to Kylwyrren who was shaking the dust off his robes.

"My thanks, mage. But ten men against Kor?"

Kylwyrren chuckled. "Worry about Azthamur, not Kor and Candara, Kothar! You shall see the wisdom of my words before long. But now— farewell."

The magician and the plaque shimmered into invisibility.

Kothar grunted and turned his face toward Kor. There ahead of him was his enemy, that traitoress demon queen who had used him and then sought to slay him in an abominable manner.

Kothar began his walk toward Kor.

CHAPTER SEVEN

Metal clanked beside him as the Ten and their leader walked to his striding. To his left was Ilthur with his longbow in his hand, to his right was Aylwold, his sword in his right hand. None of them had shields, and the breezes that whipped dust from the plain across which they walked also rippled the hairs on their unhelmeted heads.

A horn blared somewhere behind the walls.

Men ran to close the great gate, for there was something grim and terrifying about the way in which Kothar and his warrior friends walked that alarmed the men and women inside the city named Kor. They had seen them materialize on the empty plain, they knew magic and necromancy were involved, and they were fearful.

The men in link mail did not hurry their strides. There was no haste in them, though Kothar himself seethed and sweated in a rash of impatience. At last he said hoarsely, "Those gates will be closed when we get there. We'll never get inside Kor then!"

Aylwold chuckled. "Be at ease, Kothar. We men of Vandacia have strange ways, now that we are dead. Strange, strange ways!"

Ilthur laughed softly, raising his bow. "I am almost within arrow range, Aylwold. Suppose I announce our intentions by feathering a shaft on yonder fat man leaning over the parapet?"

"Better to use your arrows on the men at the gate, Ilthur! Remember, we have no siege engines, and we cannot climb such a tall wall without ladders."

Ilthur drew back his bow, held the arrow poised for flight. There was a twang of catgut and the shaft flew with blinding speed—unreal speed, Kothar saw, since his keen eyes could not follow its flight through the air—until it thudded into the chest of the fat man at the parapet.

A wail went up from inside the city.

"No man can shoot like that!" the barbarian grunted.

Ilthur smiled faintly. "I am no man, barbarian—not anymore. I am a spirit living inside a body made by Kylwyrren's magic. There is a—difference."

They walked up, seeing the wall walks fill with archers bending bows, stringing them. Moments later they were standing in ranks, bows up, arrowpoints aimed at the oncoming twelve. At a shout from their captain, those bowstrings twanged and the air filled with arrows.

Kothar ducked; his sword turned two shafts.

Beside him, Ilthur never moved. Three shafts hit him—and bounced off! Aylwold on his other side chuckled with grim mirth.

"Aye, barbarian! Eleven we are in number, but as ten times ten thousand in effectiveness. Being dead men already, how can we be killed? And Kylwyrren has made our flesh like iron, that will turn any arrow, any sword edge. Now do you feel better about matters?"

They walked on, link mail chinking to every stride. Kothar told himself that he was mortal if the others were not, and that it behooved him to be careful in the fighting that was coming, lest he be slain before he could run steel into Queen Candara. Then he grinned. By Dwallka! He had never fought carefully in his life. He was not about to begin now.

Ahead of them was the gate, closed and bolted.

Aylwold snapped an order to the others and ran forward, passing Kothar. As they had done at other times—though carrying a bronze-headed ram between them—the ten sprang forward, following their leader. They ran swiftly, with awesome speed. They came closer to each other as they ran, so that they were shoulder to shoulder, bared heads lowered.

Kothar gasped, "Fools! You'll knock yourselves silly!"

They never heeded him but ran on, always more swiftly. Now they were within the shadow of the gate overhang, now they were hitting the great gates with their lowered heads, like men turned into rams. The gates splintered, crashing inward under that one great blow. Wood tore off iron hinges, chips of hard oak flew through the air.

Kothar was running too, waving Frostfire.

His throat thickened with the battle lust. By all the gods of war! These were comrades to fight beside! As the gates went down he could look into the city itself, where the cobbled square stood, and see men running to fight the invaders whose blades were out and whipping left and right.

Only Ilthur stood back a little, whipping arrows to his bow and firing them swiftly. His shafts always found their marks, digging into mail and flesh and dropping men in mid-stride.

Kothar was beside him, cutting down a man with a warhammer in the act of swinging it.

Ilthur laughed, "My gratitude, Kothar—but there's no need to protect me. No weapon can harm this body of mine. Go you on your way, and leave the taking of the city to us!"

Ahead of him, Aylwold was cutting down guardsmen and mercenaries with every thrust and cut of his great blade. Fandlon and Petrollix swung battle-axes side by side with Nixol and Judkin whose hands were wrapped about the long hilts of their swords as they slashed and slew. Aberthan and Ibanar, Kasthin and Morion fought with blades in their right hands, stabbing daggers in their left. And as they fought, they chanted a song that was as old as Vandacia itself.

We say, we warriors of the East, man and woman, child and beast,
For any who oppose our lords—must die before our bloody swords!

The chorus of that song rose upward, swelled and grew into a pulsing rhythm that seemed to drive fear into the ears of their enemies just as much as did their dripping blades. Chanting, moving forward with every step covered by the body of an enemy, Aylwold and his Ten advanced across the cobble-stoned city square.

Kothar did not wait for them. No man was he to let another do his task. And his task now was to find Queen Candara and slay her. Aye! Before the demon Azthamur came for him.

His teeth showed in a savage snarl as he hurled himself forward, Frost-fire cutting a path for him with point and edge. Men dropped before his blade, men shrank from the glare of his battle-brightened eyes. In moments he was through the thin line that opposed him, running swiftly down a street. He went past the Inn of the Queen's Navel with a single glance at its closed windows.

Philisia was somewhere inside that inn, but he had no time to spare for her. Candara was on his mind, and it was only her face he wanted to see at the moment.

There were no guards at the open gates of the palace wall. They had been summoned to the city gate to repel the attack of the madmen who had appeared out of thin air. He ran into the courtyard, glanced about him at the silent, still bulk of the palace.

"Candara!" he bellowed. "Demon-woman—I've come back for you!"

Lightly he ran up the narrow stair, bursting into the room with the heavy brocade draperies and the hooded hearth. The room was empty. Sweeping aside a hanging with a hand, he ran easily up the narrow stone stair revealed to his eyes. Candara had her bedchamber somewhere up above him, and it was there he would corner her and drive steel into her flesh.

He came onto a broad landing that he recognized as part of the round tower in which the demon queen had her bedchamber. This door before him, this wooden thing with painted signs upon its planked surface, was the door into her room. Kothar put a hand on it, pushed inward.

The door held. The barbarian shoved a shoulder against it, pushed. The door did not budge. Kothar grinned coldly and stood back. He swung Frostfire in a vicious sweep, saw the cold steel bite into the wood and bluish fire spring to life, which signified that there was magic in the wooden door which the bite of the magic sword was freeing.

Again and again he struck, until the door was a splintered thing barely hanging on its iron hinges. Then Kothar raised a war-booted foot, kicked hard.

The door went inward with a crash.

Queen Candara stood in the middle of her bedchamber, sandaled feet planted inside the red lines of a pentagram. Her cheeks were flushed, her eyes brilliant with hate and fear.

"Stay back, Kothar!" she shrilled. "Or you die!"

He laughed harshly and leaped, and the demon queen raised her arms and cried a single name.

"Azthamur!"

There was no reply to that lone scream, and now Candara shrank and would have run but Kothar was on her, sweeping her into an arm and carrying her across the room with him, slamming her back into a draperied wall.

"You die, woman," he whispered, and lifted Frostfire.

His eyes touched her face, saw the exquisite, dusky beauty of the long-lashed black eyes, the red mouth that was like a fruit and sweet to the taste of kisses. The demon queen wore a clinging garment of black samite, that showed the curving lines of her body, and revealed the length of a shapely leg where the skirt was slit for greater ease of movement.

Then his gaze slid to her soft warm throat.

There, where the pulsebeat showed beneath the blue-veined skin, he would slash with Frostfire's edge! Then Candara would perform no more of her wickednesses on Kothar the barbarian-swordsman!

She stirred a little in his grasp. Their ears could hear the howls and screams of her soldiers and her citizenry as the men from their ancient graves stalked through the city, slaying as they went. Her long lashes quivered as she stared into his hard eyes.

"No need to slay me, Kothar," she whispered. "There is no need of hate between us. Remain in Kor with me. Be my king, my prince!"

His left hand that gripped her upper arm shook her savagely. "There can never be anything between us, Candara. Once—before you sprang that trap on me—it's true I thought about being your consort. But no more!"

"Call off those ghouls you brought from their graves, or there won't be any city for either of us to rule. Listen to me, Kothar! I was a fool. I admit it freely. I did not appreciate what a man you are."

His sword came up. He turned it so its keen edge lay an inch from her soft, pulsing throat. Death glared back at her from the blue eyes into which she stared, and she shuddered, for the demon queen was afraid. Yet she spoke bravely enough, chin high in defiance of his steel.

"The gold and jewels of this part of Yarth can be yours! Together we will attack Urgal, make it our city!"

He chuckled, remembering Azthamur. No wonder the demon failed to answer the ringing call she sent him. He was too busy slaying and feasting in Urgal to bother about Queen Candara and the spell she must have been making, seconds before he broke in on her.

He growled, "As Azthamur failed to answer your call, so do I!"

He thrust the sword Frostfire forward.

Its edge never touched her flesh. There was an invisible barrier before her which even Frostfire could not penetrate. The muscles of his right arm swelled with his effort, but the blade never moved.

Candara smiled slowly. Kothar felt the tension ease from her flesh. He rasped, "What demon protects you now, woman? Or whose spell is it that keeps my steel from drinking your blood? Zordanor's?"

She shook her head slowly. "A greater mage than he, by far. Have you ever heard of Mindos Omthl, barbarian?"

Unconsciously, Kothar eased his clasp of her arm. She freed herself gently, as if not quite daring to test his rage again. Her left hand came up to massage her bruised flesh where already a black and blue mark marred its whiteness. Her black eyes blazed triumphantly at him.

"I went to Mindos Omthl, Kothar, threw myself on his mercy! He vowed to help me, and he has. You cannot work your will on me, man of the north. You're helpless!"

"Not quite, by Dwallka!"

He swung his fist at her middle, but it seemed he tried to hit the wind. Something caught his huge fist, held it motionless, inches from her belly. And the queen laughed softly.

"Try again, barbarian!"

She stood proudly, defiance in her every line. For a long moment they confronted one another, warrior and demon queen, until a lassitude came upon the big barbarian and the weight of his sword grew heavy in his hand so that he was forced to lower it.

"You shall come with me to the magician," she said softly. "With his help I shall conquer Urgal which is a greater city than Kor. Tor Domnus we shall put to death and I shall rule in his place."

"Tor Domnus is a dead man," he replied dully. "Azthamur went to him and ate him or whatever it is that demons do to men they hate. As he will try to do to me, I suspect—in time."

Her laughter was triumphant. "Foolish Kothar, who thought to defeat Candara! You are no more than a living dead man, now. Mindos Omthl has laid a spell on you, by which you must obey my whim."

It was true enough, Kothar thought glumly. There was a sluggishness in his flesh and a dizziness in his mind, so that he could scarcely think for himself. Somewhat clumsily he sheathed his blade and then looked at the demon queen.

A part of him understood that he was under a spell and fought against its hold. But it was a fight that he knew he could not win. An untutored barbarian from the northlands could never hope to defeat such a magician as Mindos Omthl! Yet he must make the attempt! Even as lethargic as he was, as helpless to fend for himself, he must find a way to conquer.

"The alcove, Kothar! Lift Xixthur, carry it for me."

He heard her words dully, as from far away. Where she bade him, he walked, entering the alcove, seeing his dagger still stuck into the wooden beam where he had thrown it at Candara. He bent and his big hands went about the metal bulk of Xixthur. He heaved upward, lifting the metal thing to his shoulder.

That which it had taken four men to carry here, he supported easily. He turned and stared at Candara. She went ahead of him to the door of her bedchamber and led the way down the staircase. But where she should have walked straight ahead, toward the gallery overlooking the courtyard, she turned aside.

Her hand fumbled at a stone carving. With a faint rumble, hidden machinery purred to life, and a stone section of the wall slipped back revealing a narrow tunnel. Into this the demon queen stepped with Kothar on her heels.

The stone rolled back into place, shutting off all light. Candara reached behind her, caught the barbarian's free hand.

"Follow where I walk. Take no step to left or right that I do not take, for there are hidden pitfalls here."

He followed as might a man in a dream.

They came at last to a small door which Candara opened. Stone steps ran upward to a trap door. This Candara lifted, and came out onto a stretch of pebbled ground some hundred yards beyond the staked moat of the castle.

She stood a moment as Kothar joined her, the wind whipping her black samite garment, staring at the walled city of Kor. There was a flush of anger in her dusky cheeks, defiance in the tilt of her chin as she listened to the sounds of slaying coming from behind those walls.

"Over a thousand years I ruled in Kor, barbarian," she whispered. "And now my reign is at an end." Her eyes slid sideways to touch him and the Cumberian marveled, even in his bemused state, at how much hate he could read in her glance.

"I owe my defeat to you!" she snarled. "But you shall pay. Oh, yes— you shall pay. Between us, Mindos Omthl and I shall conceive of a punishment to fit your deed. Be assured of that."

She turned and walked away and Kothar followed as might a dumb beast of burden. They walked for miles, until Kor seemed far away, and then the barbarian saw a misshapen thing standing at a small hovel, with three horses saddled and bridled for the riding. Zordanor came forward at sight of them, moving with his crablike gait.

"You did not slay him, highness?"

"Azthamur is in Urgal, taking vengeance on Tor Domnus whose whims he obeyed so long as the spells of Kylwyrren held him in thrall. Now Azthamur is free."

Zordanor shuddered and made in the air the sign of Huldor, who is a beneficent demon. He bobbed his head and peered around him as if expecting to see the lord of the hundred hells rise upward from the ground itself.

"It behooves us to ride for Mindos Omthl, highness. He alone possesses the power to protect from such as Azthamur."

She nodded and moved toward a white mare. The hunchbacked magician advanced to cup his hands for her sandaled foot so that she might the more easily mount into the high peaked saddle. Then he hobbled toward a blue roan and raised himself into the saddle.

"Mount you also, Kothar," smiled the woman cruelly. "I would not have you worn and exhausted when we come to the tower beside what used to be the Sunken Sea."

She touched her horse with a toe and moved out across the barren lands. Zordanor came after her, turning in his saddle to watch Kothar, balancing Xixthur on his shoulder, rise up into the saddle of a rawboned bay. The bay sidestepped under the weight of the barbarian and the metal thing, but the strong hand on the reins and the voice of its rider calmed its fears.

The little cortege wound through the Haunted Lands, traveling over rocky ground and through the misty lands, skirting the great marshes of Xanthia until the barbarian could see the tower where resided the magician Mindos Omthl, rising upward on the rim of a downward slope where once had rolled the waters of the Sunken Sea.

As he rode, the Cumberian had fought against the strange spell that held him, but fruitlessly, so that he seemed still to be in a dream, unable to move or even think for himself. He accepted what happened because a deadliness of spirit lay inside him, and he had not even the desire to fight back.

It was as they paced their horses slowly through the mists that they heard the faint shuffle of unearthly feet, as though some awesome beast or demon were creeping through the fog, hunting for its prey. Candara reined in, smothering an outcry. Zordanor huddled his mount beside hers.

Kothar alone seemed unaffected by that sound, so alien to their world. He sat his saddle gripping Xixthur by a mightily muscled arm, but he looked neither to left nor to right, not even when the demon queen stiffened and Zordanor crouched down inside his cloak at sight of the black, polymorphous thing they glimpsed where the mists roiled and parted.

In that clear space for an instant, they saw a living embodiment of unutterable evil. Zordanor spoke the word, "Azthamur!" But he spoke it silently and under his breath so as not to attract the unwelcome attentions of that demon which quested here and there for they knew not what.

No pentagram had Candara and Zordanor to protect them, and both queen and magician sensed that Azthamur would not be particular about what souls he feasted on. They sat their saddles in an agony of terror until the mists came together and hid the dark demon from their eyes.

Long they stood there, hardly daring to breathe.

Not until a full hour later, after Azthamur had gone on his way, did they dare to move. Zordanor leaned forward, whispered to his queen. And Candara nodded, pale of face and quivery of hand, as she lifted the reins and shook them so that her white mare might proceed along the way to Mindos Omthl.

Almost in silence, they continued on their journey.

And so they came at last into the shadow of the tower and heard the metallic voice of the brass figure boom a greeting at them. Candara slipped from her saddle, casting a triumphant glance at Kothar.

"Step down, barbarian," ordered the demon queen. "We are at the end of our journey."

The barbarian did as directed without feeling of any kind. He stood like a dumb beast with the metal thing on his shoulder until the doors of the tower opened and the brass man emerged. Up to Kothar he marched and took Xixthur away from him and walked back into the tower with him.

Queen Candara and Zordanor followed. At the sill, the demon queen turned and beckoned impatiently to the Cumberian. Kothar walked toward her, unable to do anything else.

Up a spiral staircase they went, until they came into the room where Mindos Omthl worked his thaumaturgies. The old magician stood tall and regal, his eyes blazing beneath bushy white brows, his thickly veined right hand tightening and loosening on his long robe. Gravely and with dignity he greeted Queen Candara and Zordanor, and with great curiosity, turned his stare upon Kothar.

"So then, this is the barbarian who has served me so well. I am sorry I was forced to place a spell upon him, but I could never have brought you here with Xixthur without it."

Candara dismissed the Cumberian with a wave of her hand. "He has performed the task you set him, mage. Let us dispose of him."

Mindos Omthl smiled at Candara. "Not yet, great queen. Not yet. I may have a need for this Kothar."

He turned toward the queen. "Turn on this metal machine of yours, if you please. I would bathe in its rays."

Candara advanced across the room, bent to touch the metal object with a linger. Instantly the lights sprang to life behind its lenses, shooting outward across the figure of the old man as he stood and let his robe slide to the tiled floor. Across his sunken chest and skinny thighs those beams of light played. To the dazed Kothar who stood watching all that took place with dull eyes and enthralled mind, Mindos Omthl seemed a gargoyle figure of a man, painted red and blue and yellow by those lights.

Long did Mindos Omthl bathe, and across his face was the shadow of a fatuous smile. When he was done, he reached for his robe and slid into it. Then he moved across the room and gesturing Queen Candara and Zordanor to him, stepped inside the red pentagram on the stonework floor.

"I shall summon up Abathon out of his dwelling place amid the ten hells of Kryth, now. Stand you within the holy lines with me." For an instant, the magician stared at Kothar, then made a sudden decision.

"Step you forward also, barbarian. Otherwise Abathon will think you surely to be a sacrifice for him."

Kothar did as he was ordered, silently.

In his quavery voice, Mindos Omthl began to chant, even as his gnarled old hands swung the golden censer and Candara pressed closer to his gaunt frame.

Within moments there was a rustle as of dried leather and once again the demon Abathon stood inside the tower room. Two red eyes stared at the magician, then turned to look at his companions.

"I have bathed in the rays of Xixthur, Abathon," shouted the old man, triumphantly. "That which we planned for me to do, I have done. I shall grow youthful and strong, and with this woman here, Candara of Kor, we shall rule this corner of Yarth that is known as the Haunted Lands."

A wicked chuckle broke the silence that followed. "Fool that you are, old one! Did I not warn you? I can give you your lost youth now—and I shall. But I also warn you—this youth will last but for an hour and may never again be duplicated!"

"You lie," shrieked Mindos Omthl.

The demon queen smiled sadly. "It is true what he says, great mage. I know the powers of Xixthur only too well. He can maintain youth if one possesses him. He can prevent you from aging—even at such an age as you now possess. But he cannot make you young and keep you young!"

Mindos Omthl staggered back a step. His hand, questing for support, touched the iron-hard muscular arm of Kothar. His eyes under their shaggy brows turned toward the young giant.

"Not to be young again…after all the years I spent in my quest of Baithorion's lost secret… I think my old heart will stop!"

Suddenly Mindos Omthl stiffened. "Wait! Abathon—listen to me! There is another incantation—that of a transference of souls! I mind Baithorion himself is said to have used it from time to time, to experience pleasures denied to his real body!"

"True. Baithorion possessed such a spell."

"I have it here, in the parchments my agent found for me in Anthom. I shall perform it, with your help!"

Abathon was silent for many moments. At last his red eyes blazed. "It is true. With my help and that of the spell of Baithorion, you may transfer your spirit into that of any body you choose—"

"And I choose this body," yelled Mindos Omthl, slapping the bemused Kothar on a shoulder. "And do not tell me this transition is temporary. I know better. It will endure. My spirit shall be in the barbarian body, his spirit locked in mine—for all Time!"

"Yes, if I slay your old body with the spirit of that barbarian inside it," the demon admitted.

"I order you to slay it, when his spirit is in it."

"I hear, mage. I shall obey."

Kothar raged and fought against this dread sentence, deep inside him. He was aware of what was happening, but his body did not belong to him any longer, it was under the spell of Mindos Omthl. His fingers would not lift to lock about the hilt of Frostfire, his legs would not carry him so much as a single step, so that he could flee from this ensorcelled tower. He was forced to stand like any dumb beast and hear his sentence pronounced, his eyes compelled to watch the ceremony that would put his spirit into the scrawny old body of the great magician.

Mindos Omthl reached for a parchment, unrolled it and began to read its words in sonorous tones.

Abathon rose upward, began a strange dance in his eerie manner, at the same time chanting words in a language no human tongue could pronounce. Candara cried out, shrank against Zordanor.

Kothar felt light, airy. He was being freed from the grip of flesh and blood, he saw the walls of the room recede and turn to bluish haze. He quivered there, between his powerful body and the space around it, helpless to do a thing.

He wanted to yank his sword and lay about it, to slay this magician and the demon queen and her own mage so that he would be safe, but he could not touch even his body, so ethereal had he become. He hovered above his motionless flesh and saw, to his left, that there was a glowing nimbus rising from the body of the old magician.

Now he was being swept forward across the room on his way to the body of Mindos Omthl, while the spirit of the mage went past him to inherit his own body.

The thundering words of the old magician appeared to rock the tower to its very base, and at the same time they drew him down inside the scrawny body that had belonged to the great mage. In moments, Kothar felt himself trapped within that ancient bag of bones.

The parchment scroll dropped to the floor.

The body of Kothar, with the spirit of Mindos Omthl inside it, drew itself up to its full height. A happy cry burst from the beardless lips.

"I am young again. Young! Stronger than ever I was when I was a youth. Gods of Yarth, I feel vibrant, quivering with strength. My thanks, Abathon—my eternal gratitude!"

"Pay the sworn price," cried the demon. "Send me your old body and the fresh young spirit inside it. There will be little blood in your still-living corpse—but what there is, I would have!"

Kothar felt hands placed on the bony body which he now inhabited, hands that shoved him forward to the rim of the pentagram and beyond it so that he stood unprotected against the red-eyed demon who paused to savor this moment of its triumph.

Kothar found he could now lift his skinny arms about which the sleeves of his cabbalistic robe flapped loosely. With them he tried to ward off the oncoming demon, knowing in his heart that even if he possessed the strength of his real body, it would not have been enough.

And then—all movement ceased.

At first Kothar thought the spell—which had been broken by the transference of his spirit into the body of the old magician—was upon him once again. But even the demon Abathon did not move, and as Kothar rolled the rheumy eyes of Mindos Omthl, he saw that the old man—yes, and the demon queen as well!—were just as motionless as he.

Something black oozed along the topmost step of the spiral staircase that led down into the lower floors of the tower. It ran slowly, slowly, and the old heart that now belonged to Kothar lurched with an awful terror.

This was Azthamur, coming for his spirit!

No longer did he adopt the guise of fish-man. Instead the demon was in its own natural casing, a black polymorphousness that might assume any shape it cared to take. Right now it was an oozing excrescence of evil, sliding up the stone stairs and across the room.

Horror etched Kothar, in whom was the spirit of Mindos Omthl, into a grotesquerie of utter despair. The spirit of Kothar laughed grimly. Well, he would die here this day, but he would drag these others down with him, the magician who had stolen his body, with the demon queen who had sought to betray him.

Flowing and slithering across the flooring, Azthamur advanced on Kothar. Backed into a corner was the lesser demon, Abathon, red eyes wide in awe as it beheld it's superior in the worlds of demonry. Abathon alone could move yet he, too, was under something of the evil spell that flowed from Azthamur like a mist across the swamps.

To the body of Kothar came Azthamur.

Black tendrils slipped upward, along those thickly thewed legs. More liquid blackness crept higher, about the thighs, encasing his lean middle, slipping upward across his chest.

The horror of the moment shook the soul of Mindos Omthl. "I am not the barbarian," he screamed thickly. "I am the magician, the magician!"

"Liar, liar," whispered Azthamur.

"The spirit you seek is in the body of—"

"Silence!" thundered the demon. "From henceforth you shall suffer in silence whatever agonies you shall endure in my lair, man of the north! Never again shall you speak!"

The body of Kothar was surrounded by utter blackness. A moment it stood so, and then it crumpled, as Azthamur flowed down and away from that limp flesh. For an instant the stupefied onlookers caught sight of the grey something that was the spirit of Mindos Omthl, writhing in pain, struggling for a freedom it would never attain.

The blackness flowed faster and faster. Seeing it leaving, the spirit of Kothar fought as silently and even more fiercely than had the spirit of the old magician, to escape his own prison. He needed desperately to be out of this scrawny body and back into his own. Perhaps the fact that his own body was untenanted, and that it acted as a natural magnet for his soul, helped his struggles.

In a moment he was free of the inert clay of the mage's body and back inside his own. He raised his head, feeling a numbness over all his body. His spirit flowed outward, into fingers' ends and toes, into every section of his heavily thewed frame.

Kothar staggered to his feet.

The demon Abathon was coming for him, from across the room. But slowly, as if afraid that Azthamur might discover the imposture of Mindos Omthl, and return. Kothar was standing now, scowling blackly as he watched his doom advance on him.

He said, "We have no quarrel, demon, now that Mindos Omthl is gone. Go your way in peace."

Abathon chuckled. "The magician promised me a feast of blood and spirit, barbarian. I do not mean to leave without it!"

Kothar swung about, his big hands reaching for Candara and Zordanor. His iron fingers tightened on soft flesh and hard bone. He whirled, flinging a screaming Candara from him, so that she slipped and stumbled straight at the demon with the red eyes. Shrieking, Zordanor left his feet and tumbled, rolling over and over until he came to a halt before the grim being.

"Take them in my place," Kothar rasped.

He yanked Frostfire into the light, to bolster his argument that the demon should take substitutes for his own flesh and blood. A moment the demon paused, eyeing that long blade. He sensed the magic in it, and wanted no part of it.

Abathon put a tendril on Zordanor, holding the man still. "There isn't much blood in this one," he complained. "Ah, but the other!"

Candara screamed and tried to flee but about her was a black loop, holding her still. With her long red nails she sought to scratch Abathon, but only sank her fingers' ends into wet black ooze.

"Kothar—save me!" she screeched. "Share my throne with me. Let me be your slave. Only save me!"

His hard laughter rose upward. "What? And step into a trap door again? Or have another such spell put on me as held me thrall to you while you brought me here? No, no, Candara. The farther you are from me, the safer I shall feel. And Abathon will take your spirit far—very far!"

He waited until the demon drew both man and woman into its embrace, until the demoniac blackness had encompassed them. There was only a faint mewling from Candara and from Zordanor, and then no sound at all. In moments, Abathon receded into his ten hells, and of the queen and her personal magician there was no sign.

Kothar growled and shook himself.

He stepped from the pentagram and moved across the tiled floor. There was a need in him to get out of these Haunted Lands where no man could trust an-other, and the demons seemed to be more malevolent than they had been in Commoral or Gwyn Caer. He would ride to Kor and find Philisia.

Then he would go north with the woman into Phalkar.

www.ingramcontent.com/pod-product-compliance
Lightning Source LLC
Chambersburg PA
CBHW031102260626
47172CB00001B/187